Nobody's Hero

Imogen felt as though she was a 'Nobody'.

Rob showed her that she was somebody.

He was her unexpected hero.

DEDICATION

To Ronald

A friend who pulled me out of the darkness.

For all the wild memories.

You helped me grow, to learn to trust,

and most importantly to love.

I will forever be in your debt.

To Dawn

We were both fortunate to be loved by this amazing man,

and to love him in return.

But you got the best part of him, his heart.

Treasure the memories.

.

This fictional story is based on
the life of an amazing man.

Ronald Osborne.

Just like the rest of the Wildflower Series,
it is a biographical fiction.
One thing that isn't fiction... His heart.

The two women who loved him most have made
this story what it is, and because of their love for
him, his character and emotions are accurate to
honour him.

To honour Ron,

20% of all sales will go to a local charity supporting children and young people to have opportunities and to grow up to be happy and healthy.

A charity he supported.

For more information on the chosen charity

Visit the website.

www.imogenkelsie-thewildflowerseries.co.uk/nobodys-hero

A friend

Ron saved me in every way a girl can be saved.

If ever there was a definition of what
a true friend is... It would have him as an example.

I was nobody, he showed me I was somebody.
He showed me love and taught me how to love.
I didn't always realise what I had
and at times I took his love for granted.

I will forever be thankful for having him in my life as I know
I wouldn't be here if I had not met him.

I will always love you my friend.

Donna x

A Husband

I will be forever grateful for having him in my life.

I can never fathom why God would give me someone so good
only to snatch them away again. I know you are safe with Him,
loved and warm, but I can't reach you there.

The extraordinary unconditional love which he showed me was
unbelievable.

I was his girl. His everything.
He was my man, and my everything.
My life was empty before I met him, he made me whole, my
other piece of me.
I didn't function without him.

I have never known such a wonderful caring man who was not
only loved by me, but also by my family and very dear friends.
The world lost angel the day I lost him, and I will honour him
always for the rest of my life.
Thank you, God, for letting me have him for over ten years.

Dawn x

I'm Nobody's Hero...

But for you I'd lay down my life.
As long as you are by my side everything will be alright.

I am nobody's hero but for you I'd tear down the stars from the sky.
You know I'm not afraid to fight. For you I'm not afraid to die.

Don't be afraid.

When all your faith has gone, I will pray for you
Just keep holding on, I will be there for you

I've seen the storm I've been through the rain
You've got to know that I feel your pain.

When you're on the edge, I will rescue you
When you need a friend, I'll be there for you.

If you would lean on me, dream on me, and just believe in me.

I'm nobody's hero.

~ Jon BonJovi ~

Welcome to
The Wildflower Series

Nobody's Hero is spin-off from the Wildflower Series.

The Wildflower Series is a biographical fiction series
following the life of Imogen-Kelsie.

Up until now the Wildflower Series has shown the world
through Imogen's eyes, showing the many secrets which Rob
kept.

Now it is time to see life through Rob's eyes,
to really get to know and understand 'Nobody's Hero'.

Nobody's Hero is in 2 parts.

This book - Part 1 - The Wildflower Years

We get to see his story through his eyes and also showing
Imogen's story from a different view. There is a lot of cross-over
with other books in the Wildflower Series.

I hope it helps to give you a greater picture of the characters.

In Part 2 - A Time for Love.

We follow Rob's life after Imogen.
Will he get the happy ever after he deserves?

The series is set in the United Kingdom.

Music features highly in the Series. So much so that the novel has a soundtrack of suggested songs relative to the story.

The suggested song list can be found on the website.

www.imogenkelsie-thewildflowerseries.co.uk/interactive

Rob's timeline can be viewed, for reference at

www.timetoast.com/timelines/2299638

Two days...Many years apart.

Both days changed the course of Rob's life.

The day he met Imogen....

... and the day he met Frankie.

Prologue

Looking back at the day Imogen met Rob....

It was the first day at college. Imogen was standing in the canteen staring at the map in her hands. She was lost, frantically trying to find her next class.

Panic was beginning to set in.

She looked up at the clock, her next lecture was due to start in 10 mins, her anxiety was beginning to take over failing to keep it under control.

"I can't do this!" She told herself as all the words which Jacob had planted in her began to repeat in her head, though they sounded as if they were real.

She closed her eyes, taking in a deep breath before exhaling slowly.

"Please God, help me" she whispered.

She turned, almost walking into a tall man. She looked up, drawn to his smile.

Suddenly she felt awkward as a blush seared through her cheeks, feeling like her face was on fire.

She turned her head to the side to avert his gaze, mumbling apologetically attempting to hide her rosy features, but the sudden rosiness of her cheeks gave her away.

He was towering over her as he leant in to show her where she needed to go. He turned, picking up his helmet and jacket which hung on the back of a chair.

"Oh, and that's the bridge, worth checking out" he said as he winked and smiled before walking away.

"Will he look back" she wondered as she watched him open the glass door leading outside.

He glanced back over his shoulder; Imogen pursed her lips trying not to smile. She had a boyfriend, she loved Jacob! She had to remind herself as her heart pounded in her chest. No matter how much she tried to fight it she felt drawn to finding out more about this nice handsome biker!

Maybe she could get a ride out of it? she thought! She'd always admired bikes, always wanting to give it a try.

That moment changed the path of Imogen's life... but did she ever realise how much it changed his?

We begin Rob's story back at that moment...

Chapter 1

Rob didn't know it, but that day was going to change the course of his life.

The sunlight shone through the window delivering a warmth and creating rays of brightness which cast upon the glossy stone floor, reflecting onto objects within the canteen. The morning had past uneventful, and it was as though he could hear his faithful Buzby crying out for him. September was the beginning of the new academic year, but it was also the end of summer, bringing with it the Autumn where good riding days would become scarcer. He wondered if he had time for a ride before his Art class, he looked at his watch, 20 minutes.

"Can't miss first day!" He grumbled under his breath.

Walking through the canteen he began reflecting on yet another year at college, the eternal student drifting through life. Another course as he continued to struggle to find his path. It seemed as though everyone knew what they wanted to do in life, except him. It felt as though everyone had their lives figured out. His brother's and his little Sister definitely did! The pressure to succeed was suffocating.

He wasn't like them. He felt as though his life was a ticking time bomb. Before his life was to end, he wanted to do something, to make a difference, to be remembered. Something which seemed impossible. There was nothing special or unique about him, life seemed hopeless.

He thought back over his life, back to the time his life changed forever...

His life changed one day, aged 8yrs old. He was a typical boy going to school, having fun with his friends, happy and enthusiastic. That day he kept feeling weak, drowsy, dull, his eyes began to swell slightly.

As an infant he would sometimes have swelling around his eyes. The puffiness came and went, never causing serious problems, so it wasn't seen as a cause for alarm.

That day was no different. His mother sent him to school, as always it was assumed it was due to allergies.

The next day, at school he started vomiting and his vision became blurry. He was sent home; his mother took him to the Doctor who hinted at how it was a stomach virus or food poisoning, or perhaps the beginning of the flu. It would pass… He was very wrong!

His symptoms improved slightly and over the coming weeks he kept trying to ignore his symptoms, hoping they'd just vanish like the wind, but they didn't.

A few weeks passed... Doctors' appointments, tests… A hospital appointment... He sat playing with the toys in the room as his mother and father sat talking to the doctor... The doctor was speaking words he didn't understand, but words he now knew well... nephrotic syndrome, dialysis, kidney transplant...

His kidneys were damaged.

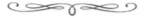

He sat by the window reflecting over what had transpired in the following years since that diagnosis. All he had wanted was a normal childhood, a normal life, but instead his life became one doctor's visit after another.

His life filled with hospital appointments, and hospital stays. As he grew up, he began to understand his future. Knowing that eventually his life would become, kidney failure, dialysis, and relying on receiving a kidney transplant. A ticking time bomb, though without seeing the time dial, bringing a cloud of uncertainty.

There was a depression that no one understood. Everyone was making plans for their lives. He wanted to live life to the full and experience every moment. He wanted to make a difference, to leave his footprint on the earth, to leave with a bang rather than fizzle out, unnoticed. He just had no idea how.

He stood up and began walking through the canteen, glancing around the room at the students. His eyes caught a glimpse of Imogen. He felt drawn to her. As if something was guiding him to her. He slowly walked in her direction continuing to observe her.

She was casual but smartly dressed. Tight black skinny jeans and a white blouse. A customised denim jacket which was faded and ripped but perfectly so, making it all the more obvious by the new perfect stitching in rusty coloured thread. Her long brown hair was pulled back into a ponytail. A neck scarf accentuated her neck.

She had a style which stood out among the crowds though her body language gave the opposite. As though she wanted to become invisible, to sink into the background.

There was something in the way she held herself, as if unsure of where her limbs should be in order to appear natural. Her face was pale. He could see her insecurities and her fear even though she was trying so hard to hide it. He watched her as she looked at the map in her hands.

Imogen was stuck in a trance like state, biting at her fingers as her anxiety began overtaking her, consuming her, making her emotionally paralyzed. As if all her thoughts were in a mental traffic jam.

He saw an innocence in her demeanour. Something about that innocence was drawing him to her but he could also sense in her a darkness threatening to consume her. A darkness he knew all too well. He couldn't take his eyes of her even if he wanted too. He didn't realise how close he was to her until she turned, almost walking into him.

She looked up. Their eyes met.

He watched as her face developed a rosy glow, a pink like a spring rose, the colour so cute against her pale skin. He was drawn to her innocent little smile, and those dimples...

In that moment he felt a connection to her in a way he'd never had before. It felt like he was looking in a mirror seeing his inner self being reflected back, the part of him which he managed to conceal so well. He was drawn to her smile and her shyness which showed deep emotion. Something beautiful, something real, but also someone lost.

Her blushing showed her soul, complimenting the innocence in her eyes which were like doorways, revealing the delicate sweetness within. A pure light within the darkness.

"I'm so sorry" she mumbled as she tried to look away to find a distraction.

He watched her trying to hide her blushing. Something which he found amusing, and it just made him want to know her more.

"Where are you looking for?" He asked, allowing her time to compose herself, fighting back the smile that he wanted to break out.

"Erm, English literature... Room 103..." She spoke in a sweet broken voice.

Pointing at the map, he showed her where to go, helping her to negotiate the maze of confusing corridors.

She looked up at him as a thankful smile crept across her face. They stared into each other's eyes for what felt like forever until the bell chimed.

She dropped her gaze.

He turned picking up his jacket and helmet. He paused for a moment before turning back towards her. His hand gently touched her shoulder.

"There's one more thing...." He declared.

She turned, looking up at him.

"....And that's the bridge..." he continued. Secretly hoping she would find her way there to meet him again...

He began walking away, leaving her standing there. He tried to fight the urge to look back. As he reached the glass conservatory style doorway he hesitated. Glancing back over his shoulder expecting that she would have gone. He smiled as their eyes met. Watching as she bit her bottom lip, dropping her gaze and picking up her bag, before turning and walking away quickly in the opposite direction, out of the canteen and into the corridor.

Rob opened the glass door stepping out onto the path outside and began walking up the side of the building to the art department wondering if he would see her again.

In class he couldn't concentrate, distracted by the weather and although he tried to deny it, her. The lecturer talked incoherently as the students were instructed to draw the fruit bowl which was positioned on the table. Staring out of the window he continued to think of her and that chance meeting.

Although she didn't look or act like the kids fresh out of high school, he could tell she was still a lot younger than him, but still he couldn't get her out of his mind. He wanted to befriend her, help her.

He wondered what had drawn him to her. He thought how it wasn't a sexual attraction. It was something which he couldn't explain which made him more determined to discover what it was and where it might lead.

He began trying to sketch her from memory. He wanted to find out her name, what else she studied, where she was from.

"She studies English Lit. So maybe she also studies English Language?" He thought.

He was studying English Language that year... He wondered if she would be in his English class. He wanted to be more to her than the stranger who gave her directions. He wanted to be a real person to her.

His thoughts were disturbed by the lecturer looking over his shoulder.

"Robert! That doesn't look like a fruit bowl to me!"

He crumpled the drawing up in his hand throwing it into the bin before making a start on drawing the fruit bowl.

The bell rang for lunch.

"I've got time for a quick ride before English" he spoke to himself as he looked out of the window contemplating how the weather was beginning to turn, clouds were filling the sky. He watched the branches of the trees which lined the verge begin to blow in the breeze, noticing that some of the leaves were beginning to show their first autumnal blush declaring that autumn was clearly setting in.

He walked outside through the fire escape, standing under the bridge where his bike was parked. As he unlocked his small bike, his faithful Buzby, his hand patted the bright blue fuel tank while dreaming of riding a bigger bike one day.

He'd always wanted to become a professional rider but to succeed in that he would have needed money, and more importantly family support, something which he never got. He always felt forgotten. If anyone else wanted anything, they got it. His sister got to go to one of the top private girls' schools, Dame Allen's, no expense spared on her education, him on the other hand, the local school was adequate enough...

He thought back over his school years. He was just one among hundreds at school, it all felt mundane. There wasn't anything unique, just average and so often overlooked. After all, what was one boy among so many others? He knew everyone and everybody knew him and that was that. Over the years he tried to stand out, sometimes acting the clown, something which he found gained friends, and as he moved through the years up to high school he realised that he was good-looking, with a ready dimpled smile which could quickly turn into a cheeky grin like a

Cheshire cat, a pair of deep searching eyes, a mop of messy hair, encompassed in the mysterious brown skin.

He had the kind of good looks that stands out at first and then fades into the background after a while, so he learned to play on his Spanish heritage as the Spanish were well known to be sexy and romantic, slowly he began feeding off the advances of his female classmates but, the façade was never permanent and the real genuine boy began to show, and eventually he began being seen only as good old reliable Rob, every girl's best friend. In short, he was an ordinary boy leading an ordinary life.

As he grew into adulthood nothing really changed. He was neither a best friend nor even a real friend to anyone. He was simply there, constant, reliable with a character that was smooth and warm and capable of easily familiarizing with the personality of his acquaintance. Never was he judgemental, not like his family. He was a constant 'friend'. No one hated him or disliked him but then on the flipside also no-one really loved him, always a second thought, and only thought of when he was useful. But even so he was always there beside anyone who needed him. He was never appreciated duly for what he was worth, or ever really thanked, and at times it wore him down, chipping away at his self-worth. It was almost like he was meant to just 'be'; something naturally there.

He climbed onto his bike, turning the key while fastening his helmet. He glanced up to the bridge wondering if she would be there.

"Just a quick ride, lighthouse and back…" he thought, contemplating visiting the bridge before his next class, just in case…

Down kicking the kickstart, the engine began to purr, he gave it a few good revs, putting into gear, before riding off onto the main road along the coast up to the lighthouse.

Arriving at the lighthouse. He climbed off his bike admiring the view. The coastline was brilliant in the mid-day sun, the lighthouse gleamed with its bold white against the clear blue sky. The weather was perfect. Clear blue skies, no wind, a cool but ambient temperature -in reality more like an absence of weather. The cliffs jagged and folded, shrinking into the distance.

The tide was out revealing the causeway to the lighthouse, people were walking along the causeway and scattered on the adjacent rocks. Many times, he would creep over before the causeway was consumed by the tide, a place to be alone. In those times he would sit for hours watching and listening to the foamy crests of waves crashing against the rocks, the only sound other than the cry of the gulls.

He bought a burger from the vendor and ate it while watching gentle waves crash against the shore. Marine biology... now that could be an interesting career move, he thought... He'd studied A level biology the year before when he had contemplated following his older brother into dentistry.

His oldest brother had opened his own surgery.

He could remember his mother frequently telling him how he'd be guaranteed a job. It wasn't what he wanted, as the year passed, he began to loathe the idea of dentistry, and he didn't want to work for his brother! Jumping back on his bike he headed back towards the college eager to see her again.

Chapter 2

It was a new academic year. New subjects but the same college again. He watched new students eager and keen with their whole lives ahead of them, but for him it felt like Groundhog Day. He walked quietly through the familiar corridors to his next class keeping his head down, and his gaze to the floor. Outwardly he was confident. The person everyone wanted to know, everyone wanted to talk to, but inwardly he was no-one, unimportant, and made to feel like an 'epic failure'.

He walked up the stairs in the Art department, before walking towards the glass doors of the bridge. The bridge was a strange corridor which joined the first floor of the arts department with the first floor of the English department. He always thought how the design was a bit crazy. If you were on the ground floor and wanted to get across to the other department you either had to climb the stairs and cross through the bridge, then walk back down the stairs on the other end, or exit the building by the fire exit and walk across the grass and gravel in the hope that someone would be at the other end to open the adjacent fire exit.

The bridge felt like a conservatory. In the spring and summer months it was like a sauna. The bridge wasn't just a corridor, it was much wider. Underneath the windows sat a black leather settee and a small table. A picnic style table with seats attached, like the ones found within the cafeteria also filled the space. A vending machine stood in the corner against the wall.

Before pushing the glass door, he hesitated.

"I'm just getting a drink... that's all, I'm not looking for her... If she's not there I'm pretty sure that I'll see her around again, it's not like it's a big campus or something!" He told himself.

He pushed the door stepping into the bridge.

She was sat on the black leather settee looking at her watch, her face again portraying that anxious fear which he saw earlier. She looked up and, in that moment he could see a calmness overcome her.

She smiled before standing up, walking towards him.

"Hi again" She greeted him, trying to mask her shaky breath.

After a short pause she continued.

"I'm Imogen"

He stretched out his palm which she reciprocated, shaking his hand. Her hand was cold and clammy.

"Oh, and I'm Robert, but you can call me Rob. Nice to properly meet you"

Letting go of her hand he turned and began walked towards the vending machine buying a bottle of Dr Pepper, before sitting down on one of the chairs around the picnic table.

Imogen sat opposite feeling nervous, not knowing what to say. There was a silence. Though not as awkward as it would have been had it been anyone else. For some reason he brought a calmness to her crazy.   She didn't manage well in social situations, always worrying that she would say something wrong, always second guessing herself. Most of the time she wore her headphones even if she wasn't listening to music, though most of the time she was... She used music as a way to distance herself from the world.

She stared into space as though lost in thought. Though her thoughts were blank. Normally her mind was filled with thoughts, with those thoughts twisting and turning, suffocating her with their whispers.

Rob sat watching, wondering what was going through that mind. He could tell just by looking at her that she was a nerd. He stared at her backpack, guessing that inside would be books, files organised with stickers and sticky notes, and a well-stocked pencil case. Usually he disliked nerds, particularly the way they acted superior and full of self-importance, but there was something different about this girl.

"Maybe some cosmic forces are at play" He thought to himself as he took a drink of his pop.

Wiping his mouth, he looked at her. She lifted her gaze and their eyes met.

"Did you find your class earlier?" he asked attentively.

"Erm, yep... thanks for that... I would never have found it without your help..."

"Good…. So, what ya listening too?" he asked trying to engage in conversation.

"Oh, you won't know them" she stated.

"A bit presumptuous?" he replied

"Erm…" she started, pausing, feeling guilty. Thinking, had she offended him? She felt like kicking herself, she was always putting her foot in it.

"Erm.. Capercaillie…. They're a Scottish folk-rock band."

"You're right! Don't know them... Isn't Capercaillie some weird bird?" he asked.

"Yep it is." She replied, biting her bottom lip, looking down.

"I have a good eye for birds…" he replied, a smirk creeping across his face, knowing that he wasn't referring to the feathered variety.

He'd used that line before and always got a reaction, but not this time.

"Could she really be that naïve?" he thought. A small smile began trying to creep in from the corner of his lips. He took a drink to disguise his amusement.

He watched her fidgeting and glancing up at the clock. To Imogen the ticking began to sound louder than it was.

"I've, er.. got to run" she said nervously as she stood up.

Hesitating for a moment she smiled, before hastily walking away.

He watched as she left through the double doors towards the English department. He smiled a cheeky mischievous smile as he finished his pop. He knew no matter what, he had to see her again, he had to get to know her. A few moments later the bell rang.

Rob left the bridge also heading through the doors into the English department. He sauntered slowly along to his English class as fresh-eyed students hurried past.

He stood outside of the class looking in. He was filled with a sigh of relief when he spotted her sat near the back alone, barely aware of her surroundings, or perhaps avoiding her surroundings.

He watched her from the doorway, watching as she glanced around. He watched her as she observed everyone in conversations. He watched as she again looked down, her eyes moving quickly over everything in front of her. He could see her anxiety, the same anxiety which he had, but was able to hide, to surpass. Hiding the many times that he felt like the world was slowly disappearing in front of him. Moments when he was left wondering...

"Maybe it's just me who is fading away".

The moments where he felt like he didn't matter anyway, the moments where he was left feeling empty, his lungs burning as if starved of oxygen. His heart hitting his chest so hard he thought it would explode, and the void.... That was the worst of those moments. The black hole in his head, the vacuum, the nothingness, the absurdness of his existence slowly swallowing all of his hopes and dreams.

Those times which kept him awake at five a.m. and made him wonder:

"Why am I living anyway?"

He wondered did she also feel that way? He watched as she organised her pen, pencil and notebook neatly before disturbing them. He watched smirking as she stared down, resisting the urge to re-organise them.

"Right class. Settle down... You should have received the reading list before today and had the chance to look over......."

He entered the class. The lecturers voice became an inaudible noise. He'd learned with his many years being a student to shut off.

He continued to watch Imogen as she frantically pulled a book from her bag and began flicking through the pages, finding the right section and beginning to scan across the pages. He could see her focus, a studious nature.

"Yep, Nerd" he laughed under his breath as he placed his helmet on the table next to her.

"Hey!" he spoke softly so not to startle her.

She looked up to see Rob's smiling face.

"Mind if I sit here?" he asked as he sat down, not giving her a chance to reply, pulling out a wad of folded paper from his pocket and began searching his pocket for a pen.

Imogen smiled trying not to laugh but her dimples giving her away.

He smiled, shrugging his shoulders. He could see her begin to relax. Reaching over he took one of her pens...

"You don't mind if I borrow this? I seem to have misplaced mine somewhere..."

She smiled, giving a little laugh and a smile which softened his heart.

"Maybe having a nerd to help me wouldn't be such a bad thing" he thought to himself as he tried to hide the grin.

As the minutes of the lesson passed the unfamiliar tension began to fade. Group work gave them the chance to talk.

To Imogen those group exercises usually filled her with dread, but this time was different, interlaced within the discussions were a few small conversations as they sat together. It was as though they were creating a new dynamic, Rob listened as she thrived, her thoughts tumbling out from her, filled with passion, and Imogen relaxed with a sigh of relief when Rob agreed to relay their thoughts to the class.

The lesson ended. Rob passed her the pen and their hands touched.

Quickly she pulled her hand away feeling guilty for wanting the moment to last longer.

They walked out of the class towards the fire escape door. His hand rested on the handle. He paused wondering what to say next.

"See you tomorrow?" he asked.

"I'll make sure I bring spare pens" she laughed as he stepped backwards pressing down on the door handle, almost falling backwards as the door began to open.

"Tomorrow" he replied bowing. Then with a forced casualness he pushed the door fully open. Extending his hand as though to urge her to go first.

She looked at him, not used to such gentlemanly behaviour.

He'd been brought up that way, to have manners. His mother had many times growing up hit him across the back of his head for not displaying 'proper' behaviour. Some saw his actions as out-dated, but to him, it was one of the few things he thought his mother had done right in bringing him up.

Imogen continued standing in the doorway, hesitating. Lost in one of those moments with an awkward silence which seemed to last forever. She smiled before dropping her head, walking past him, out onto the grass.

He stood watching as she walked past him. She walked a few steps before casually glancing back, almost stopping before walking away. Rob began walking in the other direction towards his parked bike.

He knew that something had begun that day, just no idea what. She gave him a reason to keep going, to want to return to college the next day, just to see where this connection would take them.

He returned to his home, to his room. His room was a small box room, the smallest in the house, as if a visual representation of where he fitted in the family dynamic.

It was cramped and cluttered. A dim, cave-like room, baby blue. The paint was beginning to peel, and areas were faded from the sunlight streaming through the window. A small window provided some light, the only benefit was if he leaned over, he could see the waves in the distance.

Under the window sat a small desk, and against the other wall an old pine wardrobe. A cheap pine framed bed was compacted into the room, against the wall, between the window and the door. The bed had needed to be cut shorter to fit into the room. He was unable to lie stretched out.

He was the tallest, too tall for such a small room, and it always felt like the four walls were closing in. Many times, he dreamed of escaping, discovering the world outside of those walls, shirking his responsibilities and experiencing life. He sat on his bed, his thoughts tumbling through his mind like they always did, feelings of regret, feelings of failure. He'd dreamt of becoming a pro-racer, travelling the world while riding fast bikes. But it was only a dream, a dream dismissed as childish by his mother. He'd read interviews of pro-racers and pro racing drivers and they all had one thing in common, a supportive family who made sacrifices to help them reach their dream, well that was never going to happen! He thought as his eyes found their way to the poster on his wall from the world superbikes.

He thought how at home he was always reminded of where he fitted in the grand scheme. He'd gotten used to his place in the family, where he ranked in the order of siblings. His oldest brother had left home, building his own business. He was the success story, the go-getter, the model child that their mother had so carefully crafted. The dentist with his own practice.

Sitting on his bed he took a mouthful of pop. In his head he could hear his mother's voice, telling everyone about how her son was practicing dentistry... All Rob could think of was if he was so good why was he only practicing...

He almost choked on his drink as he tried not to laugh at his own joke.

His other brother was at the local university in his second year. He returned home sporadically for a free feed and for his mother to do his washing.

So all that remained was himself and his younger sister. He was the second to last. Isabella was the last, but the girl his mother had always wanted. She was always the smart one, the beautiful one, the one who outshone them all, especially him. In gatherings she'd be the one everyone turned to admire, and though his mother would deny it, she was the favourite, and he was the least favourite. So, he always got less support, less consideration, always compared to his siblings, and always found lacking in some vital ingredient for success.

His mother was the task master, the one who wore the trousers. She organized the chores which Rob always seemed to get the brunt of. She was the decision-maker dictating everyone's general direction in life. His mother never worked; she would say bringing up all of them was a job in itself. She was old-fashioned, Rob presumed that was from the upbringing back in Spain. She moved over to England to marry his father, then began having children.

It wasn't that there was no love between his mother and father, there was, but it didn't feel like the type of love parents should have for each other, it was as if they lived together but there was little emotion. He never saw any intimacy between them, but maybe they kept that to behind closed doors? A mixture of middle-class values and a strict Spanish culture.

His father did nothing but work; work at his job to pay for the mortgage on their big house, working to pay tuition fees for Isabella's education, but also working outside of work hours, working at fixing up the house and doing whatever his wife demanded of him. He always looked tired. Once in a while he would smile or laugh and when he did the world brightened for those precious moments, but then he would sink back down into his whirl of fretting.

His father wanted him. At times it felt like his father was the only one in the family who loved him and didn't see him as a failure or a burden. Throughout his childhood he had taken to following his father around the house, learning what tools to use for what, how to fix a leak, make a wall frame, insert a new window, and in time in the garage learning how to fix a car, perform an oil change...

He returned his thoughts as he gazed out of the window, the clouds filling the sky making it darker than it should be, he could smell the food cooking.

"Robert! Come down for dinner and lay the table" His Mamma's voice echoed from downstairs.

It was Isabella's turn to lay the table, but he knew she would have an excuse to get out of it.

He walked into the dining room at the back of the house. A huge mahogany table took up most of the vast space. The far wall was filled with bookcases, against the other wall lay an old display cabinet, with glass windows, filled with trinkets. A large shelf across the middle was filled with dishes and cutlery, the lower draws were filled with tablecloths, different ones for different days and different occasions. Beside the large bay window stood a small bureau with a computer and an old pine comfy chair, where his father would sometimes sit watching the birds in the garden. The other wall was filled with photos, childhood memories, his brother's graduation, as usual he was the least represented.

He covered the mahogany table with one of the tablecloths and began laying the table. His mother began bringing dishes of food in from the small kitchen, she frowned as she noticed the tablecloth, obviously he'd chosen the wrong one again!

They all sat down, his mother gave thanks and said the grace before they began eating. The meal was filled with small talk, Isabella was asked what the first day of her new year was like, the last year of her GCSEs... As usual he was forgotten, he wasn't asked about his day, he never was...

When he had finished, he asked to be excused and returned to his room, to have an early night knowing the sooner he went to sleep the sooner tomorrow would come, and he would see her again.

Chapter 3

That following morning at college he searched for her with no success. The lunch bell rang. He looked out of the window, watching the clouds filling the sky, creating a darkness, giving the anticipation of rain.

"Oh well looks like I'm eating here today!" He sighed as his stomach grumbled.

He'd forgotten breakfast yet again.

He couldn't hide away on the bridge and eat from the vending machines, he needed something real to sustain him, to get him through an afternoon full of classes.

"At least next class is English so she should be there" he thought as he made his way to the canteen.

He glanced hesitantly through the glass door of the canteen observing newbies pushing and shoving like maniacs on a mission as if they were still in high school.

"Am I that hungry? Hungry enough to withstand the torture?" he asked himself.

His stomach answered with a loud grumble. He grasped the handle and pulled it towards him, the door resisted. Looking down he caught glimpse of the large black and white 'push' label and again released a sigh at his stupidity.

"Third year here, you think by now I'd know how to open the door!" He spoke to himself as he pushed the door entering the busy canteen.

He ordered a burger and plate of chips and walked towards the window, greeting, and acknowledging people as he made his way to a table. The rain began pouring down, he began following the raindrops falling down the windowpane.

He glanced back at the crowded canteen watching people, it had always been a fun pass-time, to try and analyse people, and their behaviours. At times creating a running commentary as though he was a wildlife reporter on a documentary. He spotted her. He began watching her navigate through the crowds alone, looking desperately for an empty table. He stood up and slowly walked towards her continuing to watch her, her anxiety was outwardly visible. He tapped her shoulder, she jumped.

"Hey, you look a little lost again" he spoke softly, smiling, a bright smile that made her day a thousand times better.

Being in his company brought a calmness. She smiled back at him,

"Hi again" she replied shyly.

Rob paused, looking back at his table.

"Would you like to come sit with me?" He asked casually.

"Yeah why not" she replied trying to play it cool.

Imogen sat down opposite him, watching as he shoved a handful of chips into his mouth, washing them down with a large gulp of pop before taking a large chunk of his burger. Imogen looked at the mountain of fries on his plate, her stomach began to rumble, instinctively her hand rested upon her stomach trying to muffle the sound. Pausing he watched her as she looked away, looking down, then rummaging through her bag for her purse.

He continued to watch her as she looked through her purse counting the loose change, before looking up at the menu.

He watched her sigh. She stood up,

"I'll just be a minute" she spoke quietly before walking over to the counter, picking up a cereal bar, and a bottle of pop, before returning to her seat.

She looked so thin, he'd guessed that she was a dancer by the slacks she was wearing that day, and the gym bag. He watched her bite into the cereal bar. He pushed his plate into the middle of the table.

"Chip?" he asked, she hesitated,

"Go on, it won't kill ya, I ordered too many, you're not going to leave me to eat them alone are ya"

Her stomach grumbled; she pursed her lips. She was hungry but was too proud to admit it.

"It's ok, I'm not that hungry" she murmured.

"Go on..." he continued holding a chip in front of her.

"Payment for me stealing your pens and your notes?" he continued.

She couldn't resist him, and she guessed he wasn't going to give in. Smiling she gave a silent agreement,

"Thankyou" she quietly replied picking up a chip.

"Help yourself..." He continued, pushing the plate further towards her.

She began eating some of the chips, trying not to eat too many, but enough to quench her hunger.

She looked out of the window trying to avoid his gaze.

The bell rang, the crowds began to funnel out through the doors.

"Are you coming Imogen asked, standing up, putting her bag over her shoulder.

"Eurgh, do I have too" He whined.

Imogen reached over grabbing his hand.

"Come on!" she replied pulling his hand, fluttering her eyelashes.

"Pretty please! I doubt I could tolerate that class without you!" she pretended to beg.

"OK, just cause it's you" he replied standing up.

"We're going to be late" Imogen replied, the worry evident in her tone.

He thought how he was going to make it his new mission in life to help her let her hair down, break a few rules, thinking how she had no idea what she'd let herself into. He looked at her, then at the window and sighed.

"No, we're not… come on" he replied as he took hold of her hand, leading her out through the conservatory door, onto the path outside.

She stood there for a moment looking at the gloomy clouds as the water droplets began to fall, cold and wet on her skin.

"Come on" he grinned like a Cheshire cat as he again took her hand.

"You're crazy!" she screamed as they ran in the rain. Chaotic and wild, running along the access road which ran alongside the college.

The water streamed through her long wavy hair, down her neck, soaking her clothes. The chilly wind cut through her like a knife, but she couldn't care. He was wild and was re-igniting something inside her, the wild child she once was. He watched her come alive, watching as her face lit up with one of those innocent smiles which were beginning to awaken something within him, something pure, bringing out his best side. They reached the bridge, stepping underneath to escape the rain. The rain ran down her face.

"What now? Clever clogs" Imogen asked sarcastically as they stood by the closed fire escape.

"Hmm! I don't know" he shrugged laughing.

She couldn't help but laugh at him, his care-free nature was infectious. She watched as he knocked on the window of the classroom, pulling a funny face at those inside, before pointing in the direction of the fire escape.

He turned back towards her, scooping her wet hair off her face and carefully placing it behind her ear, for a moment it felt as though time stopped. Imogen bit her lip, shivering, her eyes looking everywhere but at Rob. He moved closer, wrapping his leather jacket over her shoulders, her eyes caught a glimpse of his. Looking at those eyes that looked so deeply into her own, that pensive look melting into a smile. As Imogen stepped back the door swung open interrupting the beginning of a moment. Imogen bowed her head, stepping through the doorway.

Looking back, she smiled...

"Come on, or we'll be late"

Chapter 4

That first week passed quickly but that first weekend dragged, feeling longer than any other normal weekend. He couldn't wait for Monday to arrive. It hadn't helped that the weather was poor, the sky a constant grey with intermittent rain showers. Trapped in the house, unable to hit the open road.

The Sunday afternoon the clouds parted, allowing him the opportunity to escape. He thought how Autumn had definitely arrived, coming faster that year. He knew winter wouldn't be far behind which meant less opportunities to get out on his bike.

He hit the road, riding up the coast. Gazing straight ahead, only half-aware of a world outside of his helmet as his hand teased the throttle, savouring the almost soundless changing of the gears, anticipating the pattern of traffic lights, eager for the quiet country roads ahead which would allow him to open up the throttle. Soon the town was behind him, the road stretched ahead hugging the land. the road was clear taking on an almost meditative quality.

He cleared his mind of everything except the road ahead taking each turn in his easy stride. At 60 miles per hour the engine was working hard, he could feel the power beneath him. He longed for a bigger faster bike but would never part with Buzby. That bike had saw him through the past few years. From his CBT when he first began learning to ride through to passing his full licence. In those years he had gotten out of a few scrapes almost unscathed, He'd he had also spent many evenings working on it with his father, when his mother would allow. The garage and that bike had become sanctuaries. Any break from his mother was a nice break considering how authoritarian she was.

Rob pulled into a quiet bay near Berwick. Dismounting his bike, he sat upon the rocks watching the waves gently caress the sand. The autumn breeze carried fine drops, a mix of salty spray from the nearby waves and some a fine drizzle of rain, as though a promise of the rain to come. The air temperatures dropped as a chilled air moved through the secluded bay. In the clouds overhead streaks of light began breaking through creating a rainbow over the water. It was moments like that which reminded him that live was worth living. He let his eyes rest for a moment, feeling the ambiance.

The anticipated dusk came sooner than expected. The days were getting shorter earlier, the last of the sun's rays hidden behind the soft grey clouds. He climbed back on his bike looking at his watch, he knew he would be late for dinner again. He wasn't looking forward to his mother's stern words about 'family time'.

He sped the whole way home, cutting what would usually be a 2-hour trip down to 1hr 15mins. Arriving home, he parked his bike in the garage. He placed his helmet upon the table near the door and hung up his jacket before standing for a few seconds at the door, hesitating as he always did, as if to mentally prepare himself for what was on the other side. He could hear the distinct chatter. Taking a deep breath he opened the door entering the house through the kitchen, walking into the dining room.

His mother looked up glaring at him with a look that spoke volumes.

"What time do you call this Robert! You are late again" she scowled, unimpressed.

"Sorry mamma" Rob replied as he sat down and began serving himself.

Their previous conversation continued as if uninterrupted.

He sat quietly watching and observing. The meal ended and everyone left the room leaving Rob to tidy up. He sat for moment alone before taking the dishes into the kitchen. As he began washing the dishes his father entered, picking up a tee-towel and began helping, drying the dishes. His father looked at him long and hard, a look of concern,

Rob smiled as though to say "I'm fine"

Their conversations were never deep but at least his father attempted to make time for him.

"How's the bike going?" his dad asked inquisitively.

"Fine, belted up to Berwick, no problems. Need an oil change soon if ya fancy helping" Rob replied.

His father nodded in response.

"So, how is college going?" his father continued.

Rob paused holding a plate in his hand, thinking of what to reply, not knowing what to say. Wondering if he could say that some girl had turned his world upside down?

"Hmm" Rob shrugged passing his father the plate.

"You've seemed a bit distant lately…. But this week there's been something different about you…" his father continued trying to get more from him.

Rob washed the last dish, placing it on the draining board. The conversation was beginning to make him feel uncomfortable, feelings and emotions weren't part of normal conversations, with certain topics being frowned upon which created a distance.

"I'm fine Dad, honest…" he replied placing his hand on his arm, in a thankful gesture.

"And thanks for the help" he continued before walking out of the kitchen.

He returned to his room; the afternoon darkness was beginning to take over the early evening sky. His only comfort in that house was Levi, the family dog. Though he spent more time with Rob, usually lying on his bed watching, at times he was like a shadow. At times when he'd been ill in the past Levi wouldn't leave his side, his head resting upon him, as if to say I'm here to protect you.

He remembered back to the days when Levi would be sat at the gate waiting, in anticipation of him coming home from school.

Levi nudged at him with his nose, Rob looked down, looking deep into those big brown eyes.

"Who could resist those doggy eyes?" Rob asked rubbing him behind his ears.

Staring over at his desk his bible caught his eye. Everyone in the house had to have their bible! He'd once deliberately misplaced his, to find a replacement bought, and a stern telling off! He'd soon decided it was easier just to have it there, just as an ornament, though occasionally he felt drawn to flicking through the pages. His heart and mind were in turmoil when it came to faith. His faith was like the tide, and it ebbed away an awfully long time ago. At times it felt like he was sinking in the sea becoming lost and alone. His so-called faith had begun with his mother dragging the whole family to church, every Sunday.

He thought of his mother the epitome of the perfect Christian, yet all he saw was shallow conflicts, a hypocrite, the more she pushed him towards church the further he wanted to run.

Though in contrast to that year where it felt like the tide was coming in. He had found help, support, and friendship within a small social group at one of Whitley bay's churches. He'd never been to one of the services, just the small group attached to the church. The group was run by a musician called Matt, who he'd gotten to know the previous year, a friend of a friend. The more time he spent with Matt he realised he was a genuine guy, and he didn't know many of them, especially not genuine Christian guys! So, when Matt suggested going to the Christian men's group, he thought he'd give it a go, nothing to lose. It was also the type of church his mother disapproved of, modern with a rock band style worship group. In part that helped push him to them.

The group was made up of mostly males, around his age, some of them were fellow members of Matt's band. They talked, and occasionally those conversations led down the path of faith, but mainly the conversations were about life in general, just a group of guys putting the world to rights. He began to get more involved, asking questions, and attended a course run by the group. But still he was in turmoil, and that past month had stepped back.

Picking up the bible, he spoke out loud to himself,

"I don't know what I believe"

Flicking through the pages he let it fall open, scanning the page his eyes were drawn to a passage...

Seek the LORD and his strength; seek his presence continually!

"Coincidence" he laughed as he placed the open bible down on the desk and returned to his bed,

Turning on the radio, he sat trying to relax, trying to fight away the boredom. Sitting with nothing to stare at but the wall with chipped blue paint. As he peeled a little of the paint away, he thought how the paint was over 20 years old, painted blue as a nursery for him, which then became his room. Apparently, it wasn't worth wasting money to redecorate, yet his sisters' room had been redecorated many times with each new passing fad.

He closed his eyes listening to the music, his hands rhythmically tapping his hands upon his legs in time with the music, allowing his thoughts to drift without direction, though his thoughts kept returning to Imogen.

His phone vibrated on his desk. Turning over his phone, it was a text from Matt.

Hey mate, we've got a gig tonight at the Uni. Need some moral support. You want to come? Not seen you at group lately. How is the new course at college? I know you've not been feeling right for a while, join us, lighten the load, let your hair down, I'll buy your first drink, if that'll persuade you...

Glancing back at the bible on his desk he wondered whether to go. He'd distanced himself from the group those past few weeks, but he always loved Matt's music.

Matt had given him a CD of their music, which he listened to frequently, a mix of Christian type songs mixed with normal rock type songs. Some original songs, and some covers.

"That's not church music" his mum would say, which made him more determined to go to the men's group and their non-church gigs.

He thought how the gig was at the Uni so couldn't be too 'Christian'.

Matt regularly invited him to the church services, where his band also played, but he always refused, not ready to take that step. He thought how it couldn't be all bad with a band like Matt's, but he'd had to tolerate enough church without going voluntarily!

Holding his phone in his hand, he wondered whether to go or not. He decided going would be better than sitting alone in that small room all evening.

You only live once! He thought as his fingers typed his reply.

"Send me the details, I'll be there."

Chapter 5

Rob entered the student union walking down the stairs to the bar in the basement below. As he neared the bar he could hear the sound of a band warming up and sound checks co-existing with the sounds of glasses being stacked behind the bar, and fridges being stocked up ahead of the crowds which were hoped to fill the room. The expected crowd was mostly students from the university. Rob found his way through the warm bodies to order a drink. He sat at the bar ordering a bottle of Bud.

As the bar slowly began to fill he watched Matt continue to set up. Matt glanced over catching his eye. Rob waved his hand and nodded in a response. Putting down his guitar Matt jumped off the small stage and walked towards him. Ordering himself a drink he spoke to Rob.

"Hey, mate, glad you could come" Matt spoke placing his hand on his shoulder, leaning in for a feigned hug.

Matt signalled to the barman who instinctively reached into the fridge for a bottle. As the barman began to close the fridge Matt shouted over,

"Oh, and another of whatever this guy is having"

The barman placed the drinks on the bar in front of them.

"Well I did promise you a drink... Cheers" Matt exclaimed.

"Thanks... and Cheers" Rob replied, allowing their bottles to clink.

Rob continued with small talk...

"It looks like could be a good night, you've already got a bit of an audience"

"Yep..." Matt replied, nodding scanning the room.

"So, how's college?" Matt asked inquisitively

"It's not been too bad..." he ended mid-sentence as he spotted what looked like Imogen in the distance.

She looked at ease, as though she belonged there, though he was starting to see that no matter where she was, she 'fitted'. It was just obvious that she didn't believe that. His eyes were fixed on her. He watched as she flicked her hair over her shoulder. She wore a Celtic - styled high-boddist top and her heeled boots peering out from under her frayed ripped jeans. As she leant over to untangle the wires, he wondered why she was there, how she was there.

Matt's eyes followed Rob's.

"Hey. Eyes off mate" he spoke softly yet sternly.

Imogen looked over. He caught a glimpse of her smile as she spotted him. She walked over,

"Rob, this is Im...." Matt started, before being interrupted.

"I know" He replied holding out his hand.

"We're in the same English class... This is the friend I told you about Matt. The one who helped me on my first day" Imogen responded.

Matt almost choked on his drink "I'll be dammed" he laughed as he began to walk away, glancing back with a slight shake of his head in disbelief.

Matt paused, turning, still smirking, he shouted over,

"Imi, we're starting in 10, will need you ready in 20...... Rob! No buying her alcohol! And I'll be watching!" Matt spoke sternly before turning back and continued to walk towards the stage to continue setting up.

Imogen couldn't help but laugh.

"Well that's us told!" she uttered through her laughter; Rob caught her laughter as though it was infectious.

"So, how do you know Matt? And what are you doing here? Aren't you kinda a bit young to be here? He smirked.

Imogen scrunched up the right side of her face sighing before answering.

"Well... I'm here 'cause I'm doing a couple of songs with the band, I'm not being served alcohol, and when this place really opens up I've got to stay back stage if I'm not on stage, it sucks! and I know Matt 'cause he's kinda like my brother... His parents kinda took me on as a bit of a project..."

He looked at her, not knowing what to reply. Behind those slightly pursed lips was a smile just waiting to be tempted out.

"Well, If we're going for total honesty.... I'm glad you're here and can't wait to hear you sing." Rob responded.

Her dimples appeared, giving away the smile to follow.

"Want a drink?" Rob asked.

"Coke please." Imogen responded.

"A coke please mate" Rob called out to the barman.

The barman placed the drink in front of her, picking it up and taking a sip through the straw cloyingly she asked

"So... how do YOU know Matt?"

"I've been to a few of the men's group get togethers that he goes to" he answered.

"Aagh!" she replied with a curious glint in her eye, wanting to press him for more information.

As the band began playing, Imogen looked around hesitantly.

"I like this song" Rob spoke regaining her attention. She smiled, for a moment she began to relax.

"Yeah, me too" she replied.

The break in her temperament didn't last long. He watched her fiddle with her fingers, biting at her nails and her fingers, and nervously scanning the room. He wondered if she was looking for someone specific or just nervously surveying the audience.

"Hey, I may not have ever hear you sing, I don't even really know you yet, but I know you're going to be great" He spoke as his hand reassuringly brushed her arm.

"So how do you know that? Psychic?" she replied. His comment bringing a smile to her face.

"Nah, I just have faith... well faith in you anyways?" he smiled.

"Well, I suppose I should go get ready..." she spoke nervously.

"See ya later, or tomorrow at college? He asked.

"Yep, definitely" she replied almost confidently as she began to walk away through the crowds.

A while passed with Rob quietly enjoying the music. The band paused for a moment before Matt spoke into the mic.

"We're inviting someone up to join us for the next couple of songs, she sings with us regularly back in our church... We're going to be starting with a duet of a good old evanescence number, followed by a solo which I guarantee will knock your socks of, if ya wearin' any. So, let's welcome a fantastic singer. Our dear friend Imogen..."

The crowd erupted. Rob watched as Imogen nervously walked across the stage to the microphone. Adjusting the mic stand, her hands were visibly shaking. She scanned the room. He could read the disappointment on her face, someone was missing.

"A parent? Maybe?" he thought as he watched her.

Seeing her nerves portrayed so openly reminded him of that lost girl he met almost a week earlier. He wondered how she was the same girl standing there ready to sing in front of so many.

She looked forward, breathing in deeply. She looked over at him, catching his eye she smiled. She turned slightly giving Matt the nod to begin. As the band began playing, she closed her eyes as if absorbing herself in the music and began to sing.

"How can you see into my eyes like open doors...."

She had the voice of an angel yet could also sing with a power that he had not expected. Taking hold of the mic she removed it from the stand and continued to sing, fully immersed within the song. He watched her long hair flowing wild. He watched as she casually flicked it back over her shoulder as she continued singing.

As the song progressed it was easy to see she belonged up there. On that stage her body language displayed more confidence than he'd seen in her before. As though a different person had taken over her, no longer the nervous anxious girl, and it was as though she had discovered her good looks.

He smiled. In that moment he forgot all the chaos that was his life.

As the song finished the crowd erupted. As the applause died,

The band began playing a slower softer tune, Imogen, again scanned the room, before again catching Rob's gaze. She stood absorbed in the music. The room gradually fell silent. Imogen pursed her lips before beginning to speak over the instrumental. Her broken voice slightly revealed her nerves.

"I wrote this song… There are some songs you write 'cause you want others to hear them, but then there are other songs that you write 'cause you have to hear them… This is one of those songs. I wrote this song as I needed reminded of my own self-worth.." she paused scanning the room, her voice almost breaking as the words left her, she looked down, then back up taking a deep breath, she continued.

"…and I guess I need reminded of that quite often, but I hope that you like it, and maybe it'll help someone else too…" Her words trailed off as she glanced over to Matt, who stopped playing for a moment, allowing a silence before repeating the rift with a little more volume.

Rob watched as she closed her eyes, took a deep breath and began to sing again.

Although the words she as singing were an original, it was as though he was listening to a well-known song, the words spoke deep into his soul, he was falling in love with her voice.

Her song finished, she disappeared backstage, not seeing her again for the rest of the evening, obeying the rules. Rob stayed till near the end the night. As last orders rang, he looked at his almost empty bottle, wondering whether to buy another. He looked at his watch shrugging, deciding instead to leave and catch the last bus home.

Chapter 6

Monday lunchtime he made his way to the bridge waiting patiently, hoping to see her. They had English together straight after lunchbreak. Imogen arrived on the bridge; she had also hoped he would be there.

"Hey!" Imogen spoke wiping the sweat from her forehead, taking a drink from her water bottle.

Rob watched as she raised her foot up onto one of the chairs and leant forward to fasten the lace on one of her trainers. Her long hair was tied up, though a small section still found its way to falling in front of her face. Straightening up she tucked it behind her ear. She was wearing gym leggings with a pair of cut-off jeans shorts on top and a spandex gym top which revealed her intensely aerobicized midriff. Putting her water bottle on the table next to him she leant into her bag pulling out a t-shirt.

"Sorry!" she spoke apologetically as she pulled the t-shirt over her head.

"Dance class ran over; can't believe I've only got 10 minutes before English!"

She sighed as she untied her hair, shaking her head, allowing her hair to fall down over her face before flicking it over her shoulder and tucking it behind her ear.

"There, done" she said as she sat opposite.

"You were pretty awesome last night" Rob proclaimed.

She looked away for a moment, then bit her lower lip and then up at him, always feeling uncomfortable with compliments.

Rob reiterated.

"Really, you were awesome" His words were purposeful and distinct.

Imogen blushed, deciding to change the conversation, to steer it away from talking about herself. She kept looking at his helmet, wanting to ask for a ride, but not daring too.

"What got you into bikes?" she asked as she stole a chip, innocently fluttering her eyebrows giving a sweet puppy dog glance.

He paused,

"I loved riding bicycles from an early age, basically as soon as I could pedal without stabilisers. I would be riding my bike everywhere. I would literally ride it all day and into the night until late in the summer evenings. When I got old enough, I upgraded to a bike with an engine..."

He stopped, looking at her he asked, "Have you ever been on a bike?"

"Nope, not been on one, though I do like them, maybe one day" She replied, followed by a sigh, hoping he would read between the lines.

The bell rang signalling the end of lunch.

"Well here goes!" Rob announced as they headed to class.

Rob kept thinking of that conversation during English and knowing they had a free afternoon that next day he resolved to bringing a spare helmet and take her for a ride.

As they left the class, they again walked towards the fire exit, neither wanting to part but neither knowing what to say. He opened the fire door, almost repeating the actions of the previous week.

"After you" he spoke simulating an elegant bow.

"Such a gentlemen" she replied smiling.

"I've been called a lot of things before.... But that's not one of them" he replied jokingly.

"See ya tomorrow?" he asked inquisitively.

"Count on it" she replied as she walked away.

That evening he studied the weather forecast for the following day.

"Please don't rain" he thought out loud.

He thought of where he would take her. He imagined seeing the look on her face when he'd invite her for a ride. He thought how he'd only known her just over a week, though he didn't really know her, but he wanted too. Something drew him to her, there was something different, an innocence, but he could see the adventurous spirit buried deep. It was almost as though it was a challenge to release it, and he never backed down from a challenge!

The next day following her dance class he waited for her. He could see her exiting the building walking down the path towards him.

"Your chariot awaits, dear princess" he spoke with a cool assertiveness as he again threw an over-exaggerated bow, before handing her the spare helmet.

"Really!" she beamed with excitement.

He grinned like a Cheshire cat seeing the excitement in her eyes.

She placed it on her head. He stepped forward fastening the straps.

"All safe and secure... do you trust me?" he asked.

She nodded excitedly, yet a little scared. He climbed on and started the engine.

"Hop on and hold on tight. Relax and stay seated centrally, mirror me, I'll not do any crazy stuff... Well not this time! Tap me 3 times if you need to stop" he instructed.

Imogen climbed on, her hands resting on his waist.

"Right, let's go" He shouted over the roar of the engine. They pulled out of the car park down towards the coast.

They pulled up at the lighthouse.

"How was that?" He asked as he dismounted, helping her off, his hands around her waist.

Lifting her visor,

"That was awesome" She replied like an excited child.

"The day's still young if you want to go further?" he asked.

She nodded.

"Well, let's go" he spoke as he climbed back on the bike, revving the engine. She knocked down her visor and climbed back on.

"Ready!" he shouted.

"Yess!!!!" she shouted excitedly as he dropped the bike into gear and pulled off.

They hit the open road, although he'd ridden that route so many times, and it wasn't the first time he'd taken a pillion there was something more exhilarating about that ride.

Imogen clung on to him tightly, her senses on high alert. The air was rushing past them, filling her with smells of the gas, the trees, the ocean, and the exhaust. Visually everything was a blur. She'd imagined what it would be like to ride, but reality was so much more than her expectations.

They stopped at a lay-by just outside of Corbridge. Rob unfastened her helmet then taking her by the hand walked her up to the top of the hill.

"Welcome to my favourite place!" He announced, his arms open wide, turning taking in the stunning scenery, in all directions.

He sat down on the grass. He watched her taking in the view.

"I can see why it's your favourite place" she replied as she spun around, taking in the expanse of green divided by walls of mossy grey stone which stretched out before them.

"You know I buried my dead rabbit here" he spoke.

"Really?" she asked.

"Nah, but it sounds poetic" he replied laughing.

He continued to watch her, arms outstretched soaking in the environment. He had friends, everyone knew him, but no-one really knew him, he never let anyone in, but he was starting to see something different in this girl. Something was drawing him to her, wanting to know her better, thinking how there were parts of her nature that were like looking in a mirror, he'd just gotten better at hiding them.

Imogen sat down on the grass beside him, her demeanour becoming more relaxed, as she began soaking up the atmosphere. Rob opened his bag pulling out 2 bottles of coke and a couple of packets of crisps.

Imogen smiled as he handed her the bottle.

"Well, I know you like coke, but I didn't know what crisps you like so I brought a selection." He spoke as he scattered the crisps in front of them.

"So thoughtful, thank you" she replied, scanning through the packets.

"You know apparently you can tell a lot about a person by their choice of crisps" He smirked as she picked the packet of pickled onion flavour crisps.

"Yeah right!" she laughed.

They sat in the cool autumn breeze, sometimes talking, but sometimes in silence. Though the silence wasn't uncomfortable, it felt natural.

"Have you done the English homework?" Imogen pressed, pulling out her file from her bag.

"Nah, not yet… actually not even looked at it" He replied.

Imogen shook her head trying not to laugh.

"What am I going to do with you?! It's due in tomorrow" she spoke sternly, the natural teacher within her seeping through.

"Let's look at it now. Get it out of the way? Much nicer doing out here." She pressed.

"Eurgh…" he grunted.

"I take you on your first ride, I bring you to this beautiful place and how do you repay me? By trying to force me to do work! Maybe you should get a job as a prison warden, I hear they like delivering torture!" he paused before continuing with a sigh.

"OK, just for a little bit, then it's time for fun! All work and no play is not right"

"Deal!" she answered.

Rob scooted closer as Imogen opened her file. It wasn't long until they began laughing and kidding around while trying to read the piece they were studying.

"Right, that's enough work" Rob declared as Imogen was frantically writing notes. He flicked through his phone turning on his playlist.

"Dance with me?" He asked holding out his hand.

"You're crazy!" she replied looking around as he pulled her to her feet.

"Didn't know you could dance?" she quizzed.

"Man of many talents! Or had you not figured that out yet?" He replied cheekily.

"Just a bit of salsa, it's the Spanish in me" he replied as his arm encompassed her waist and pulled her close. She enjoyed the pressure of his warm hand on her back, as he began to lead.

"OK, just one… Let's see what you got…"

She had gotten used to dancing alone. It felt good to be dancing with someone. She thought how Jacob refused to dance, he didn't seem to take any interest in her dancing or singing. Her thoughts wandered... Jacob... Should she have said before now that she had a boyfriend?

"I'm allowed friends! Boys and girls can be friends..." She thought.

Her thoughts disappeared as she got lost in the moment. Dancing over the grass barefoot. She felt right in his arms, their steps flowing between them, swift and vibrant, full of energy.

Dancing together, he watched as her hair bounced with each move. He could see the laughter glitter in her eyes as he spun her and dipped her back. The song ended, she stood in his embrace. Taking a step back, she turned away slightly as the guilt crept back in.

"Not bad!" she stated casually as she fell back to the floor scooping her hair off her face.

They sat together; His hand reached for hers. Their fingers entwined in a loose grip. He let the events of the last 2 weeks envelop his thoughts. He thought how the more he got to know her the more he wanted to know, he'd never met anyone like her before.

They sat talking as the hours passed. Their conversations filled the air, littered with smiles which were the real communication, not the words. At first both were a little hesitant to open up, but it wasn't long till their conversation became the best conversation he'd ever had. He opened up to her in a way he never had before.

It was as though she gazed into his soul; her eyes seeing him in a way no one had ever done before, able to see him in ways that he could only dream of seeing in himself. She was a mystery. A dangerously beautiful mystery.

He talked about his health, his family, how he didn't feel where he fitted in this crazy world. She listened with an attentiveness which was a part of who she was, it wasn't feigned, she seemed to genuinely care.

The evidence of her listening was shown in what she said in her replies and questions, in her emotion as she listened and the emotion in the silences. If he was honest, it was her most attractive feature which he guessed was what naturally happens when two people meet and connect. He'd only just met her, but something urged him to trust her.

In return she began to open up to him, touching on her crazy life. her hopes and fears, beginning to touch on emotions and thoughts that she had never told anyone else, though still remaining a little guarded. She always believed no-one would like her if they knew all. He knew it would take a while to break through but wanted to break through that wall she'd built around her.

She changed the topic of conversation. But whatever they talked of never mattered, only that they were talking. He could have listened to her talk forever, talk about something, talk about nothing, it didn't matter as beneath the conversations something was growing, something different.

The sky began to darken, signalling it was time to head home though neither wanted to leave, it was as though they'd both found someone who understood and accepted each other in a way no one ever had before.

By the time it came to leave they knew more about one another than possibly many members of their own families.

They walked back down to the bike.

"So, where am I dropping you?"

"Erm, Cullercoats" she replied as she looked at her watch.

"You live in Cullercoats? So do I" he replied.

"Nah, I live in Wallsend, but my dad will be at the Bay Pub so will meet him for a drink first and go home with him" she replied.

"So, you're not going home to swat up?" he asked sarcastically.

"Must be your bad influence rubbing off on me" she replied playfully punching his shoulder.

"Jump on, your chariot awaits" he replied rubbing his shoulder pretending her pitiful attempt at hitting him had hurt.

They returned back to the coast as the sun began to set. Rob pulled up outside the Bay, the time to part arrived.

"Do it again sometime" she asked

"Hell, yeah" he replied

"See you tomorrow" he spoke kissing her hand.

"Yep, meet in the cafeteria at lunch?" she asked.

"Yeah, see ya then" he replied smiling.

He returned home, sitting on his bed he began to reflect, thinking about her, wondering what made him able to open up to her, what made her so different to everyone else in the world?

He thought how once she started talking, he couldn't stop her, not that he would ever want her to stop, she spoke with such innocence and kindness, and a real concern that was so quick that, it was natural, yet for some reason she doubted herself.

He thought if she could see herself through his eyes...

Chapter 7

"Hey!" Imogen said placing her hands on his shoulders as he sat staring out of the window in the cafeteria.

"Jesus! Give a guy a heart attack why don't ya" he replied jokingly.

"Well, I need a new pass-time." She joked in return.

"Did you get the notes written up last night?" she asked inquisitively.

"Yes! Though I think the teacher will have a heart attack... Me handing homework in on time" he looked at her before continuing...

"Are you always such a nerd?" he asked sarcastically.

Imogen again playfully punched him.

"Ouch!" he spoke rubbing his arm pretending it hurt more than it did.

"What is it with you beating me up?" he asked.

"I hardly touched you, you wimp!" she replied.

"Yeah, I know. Bet you couldn't punch your way out of a paper bag"

"Cheek" she replied.

"And I know you're a lot smarter than you let on, it's like you got a 'rep' to protect, do you think you're a Danny or something?"

"Danny?" he replied in a questioning tone,

"God! I can't believe I've made friends with someone who doesn't know the classics! ...... Grease!" she continued.

"Oh yeah, got ya... Though you do know grease 2 has bikes" he replied with a wink.

"But anyway, as I was saying before we got side-tracked, smart but a bit unorganised, but I can work on that"

"Well I guess in return I can work on your nerdy stuck-upness!" he replied.

"Cheek! ...... You don't mince your words do you?" she asked raising her eyebrows, though secretly enjoyed their roasting of each other.

His music was playing in the background, the cafeteria began to fill.

"Well maybe I'll start right here, right now" he declared. Imogen looked puzzled, wondering what he had up his sleeve...

Turning up the music, Rob stood up and outstretched his arm.

"Wanna dance? You're dressed for it!" he asked spinning around culminating in an over-exaggerated bow and pulling a face.

She looked around.

"People are watching!" she proclaimed.

"You dance, so I assume you dance on stage..." he replied.
"Yeah but... That's different" she answered.

Situations like that would usually send her spiralling possibly leading to a full-blown anxiety attack, but with him somehow, she was different, as though almost excited by the adrenaline. He did something to her, she couldn't understand it but she was beginning to realize that Rob brought something out in her. His energy was infectious.

"How's about you show me how it's meant to be done first?" Imogen joked.

Rob began flicking through his phone, footloose began to play. He placed the phone on the table and moved some chairs as the intro played.

As the song began Rob began dancing. He'd never had a dance class but had a natural essence. Everyone began watching. He didn't dance to show off but was used to the attention and he liked it. She scanned the cafeteria as everyone either joined in, sang along or clapped along with the music. She watched him, trying not to laugh she thought how different he was to anyone she'd met before; he had an infectious nature which infected everyone around him.

"Go Rob!" Imogen shouted being pulled into the excitement.

He pulled her to her feet.

"Come on, show us your moves, show us what ya made off..." he spoke loudly grabbing the attention of most of the cafeteria.

"Cheer if ya think Imogen should show us how its done" he egged on the crowd, and again pulling a silly face.

Imogen began to blush.

"God!" she said laughing.

Although she was a dancer, she would never have dared to dance in public unchoreographed, and not in a crowded cafeteria.

Normally that would have had her running away in fear, her worst nightmare. But being around him brought out something she'd lost a long time ago. She was enjoying them playing off each other, being with him was exhilarating, and daring.

"Fine! Anything to get you to stop making that face!"

Imogen began dancing, Rob took her hand and spun her. Pulling her inwards he placed his hand on her back. Instinctively her hand rested upon his shoulder. Their free hands joined. They stood for a moment before he used his hand to cause her to dip backwards quickly followed by a breath-taking spin. She felt free and exhilarated, dancing swift and vibrant, and full of energy. In that moment she forgot about the others in the canteen, it was like being back on that hill, dancing alone.

As the song progressed, she relaxed allowing a small smile to form on her lips. Together, they danced to the music, it felt as though their feet in perfect sync to the beating of her heart. She'd had to dance with boys before but never like that. She thought how as a dance partner he was perfect. She wished he was on her course.

He caught her eyes, blue as spring rain, deep and irresistible. He hadn't danced with anyone like that before and knew it was something he wanted to repeat. The song ended, he pulled her into an embrace. The canteen erupted with applause. She looked up deep into his eyes lost in that moment. She looked away, before looking down feeling embarrassed.

It was just a dance, she told herself. Though no matter how much she tried to convince herself, she couldn't escape the fact that there was something between them. Not in the way there was between her and Jacob, but something, something different.

The bell rang.

Rob stepped away still holding her hand, making an over exaggerated bow.

"Not bad for an amateur" she joked.

"Maybe you should join the dance class!" she continued while laughing,

"Come on... We'll be late for English." She spoke trying to return to a state of calmness.

"We could always skip it, hit the road." He replied, fluttering his eyebrows.

"After! You're a bad influence on me!" She joked as she took his hand and began running...

"I'll hold you to that" he replied.

Over the following two weeks, they began meeting up before each English class and the occasional planned run in on the bridge before and after classes. Those rides following English became frequent, and their conversations became much deeper.

Their rides became regular escapes. They correlated their timetables so that they knew where each other would be.

On the bike she began to learn how to mirror his movements, and their conversations delved to topics that neither had opened up about to anyone else.

Through their conversations, it wasn't long till he realised she had a boyfriend, he had a feeling, but one conversation confirmed it.

Wednesday afternoon, Imogen walked into the bridge.

"Hey" she greeted him her deep blue eyes sparkling.

"I wanted to ask what you're doing Saturday night?" Rob asked as she sat next to him on the settee, placing her feet on the table.

What followed was a silence...

"Erm, weekends I'm down at Durham with Jacob... My boyfriend... He's at Uni there, I can't not go, he won't like it" She looked down at her feet.

His first thought was that she had a boyfriend. The second thought was the way she stated he wouldn't like it if she didn't go, and the way her body language spoke he knew he didn't like this guy.

Stuck in a trance like state. He glanced around the bridge, anything to avoid eye contact, void of emotion.

He tried to convince himself that he hadn't seen her in that way. She was too young for him. There wasn't that physical attraction, the sparks flying. He'd chased girls before, been physically attracted, and the cheesy chat up lines came easy, using them to keep up the walls, keeping them at arm's length. He told himself that he never saw her that way.

He thought how that moment when he first saw her was somehow different, something had drawn him to her. He was drawn to her in a way he didn't understand. He tried to disguise his disappointment.

"Another night?" she asked breaking the silence, oblivious to his thoughts or disappointment.

Continuing she asked

"What did you have in mind? I bet drinking, dancing, getting wild?"

He smirked.

"You know me so well" he replied sarcastically with a slight disappointment that she was making assumptions like everyone else. He had thought that over those weeks she'd gotten to know the real guy behind the mask.

Imogen looked at him as though she could read his thoughts.

"I know you're a lot more than that, I was only joking..." she spoke softly placing her hand on his shoulder.

"You know... I'm going to a church thing tomorrow night, some magician will be swallowing razorblades and stuff" she spoke,

She looked at him with those eyes which over those weeks he was finding he couldn't refuse.

"Church aint really my thing... "he replied trying to avoid those eyes, she pursed her lips, her bottom lip protruding out.

"Come on... It's not going to kill ya, you went to Matt's small group... and it's in Jesmond so you can buy me a drink after?"

"Little miss goody two shoes breaking the law and drinking?" he replied as his tone returned to them playing off each other.

"Give and take... You give, I take..." she stated, before taking a pause then continuing.

"I'm not that innocent that I've never had a drink before, you've not met my dad yet!" she replied trying not to laugh.

He smiled, "OK, I'll go with ya and I'll keep an open mind"

Back home that evening he sat in reflection. He didn't know what it was that they had, but he knew that what they had was worth keeping hold of, and not throwing away.

He wanted to find out more about this boyfriend but didn't know how to broach the topic. He thought how over those past few weeks that occasionally the thought of seeing where their friendship could go had crossed his mind a few times.

But now, knowing she had a boyfriend, he knew he couldn't cross that line, he wasn't that guy. Though he'd crossed that line in his head. He wondered if he'd met her first would things have worked out differently. Would she have seen him differently?

The next day, Imogen waited for Rob following dance, her last lesson of the day. She stood underneath the bridge, next to where Buzby was parked.

She knew he'd be finishing soon, she stood staring at her watch, wondering if he would turn up.

Rob walked through the bridge, looking around, wondering if Imogen would walk through, he'd looked for her throughout the day. He stood looking at his watch.

Trudi walked through the bridge, pausing.

"God! You two are hopeless!" she laughed.

"Don't know what you mean" Rob replied looking past her to the glass door.

"You, and Imi…. You're here, staring at your watch... She's below next to ya bike doin' exactly the same" she laughed as she continued on through the bridge, turning, watching Rob as he grabbed his helmet and bolted through the door, past her, and down the stairs to the fire escape.

Before opening the fire door, he took a second to compose himself. He opened the door, seeing her standing by Buzby.

"Hey" He said as he came up behind her, placing his helmet on the seat of his bike.

"Hey, we still on for tonight" Imogen asked hoping he hadn't changed his mind overnight.

"Yeah, sure" he replied.

"OK then! Meet you at the Bay? We can get the metro together"

"I could pick you up. We could go on Buzby?"

Twisting her face, she looked at him.

"If ya wanting to go to the club after, then you can't take Buzby! Can't have you drinking and riding, had enough of that with me dad!" She replied.

He could see the pain in her eyes, there was still so much he didn't know, so much he wanted to know.

"Hey" he spoke softly and reassuringly as his hand rested upon her arm.

"Look at me" he continued softly, gently lifting her chin, their eyes met.

"I wouldn't do that, and definitely not with you on the back…. If we take Buzby I'll stick to the soft drinks, with you, pinky promise" he stated holding up his little finger.

She smiled, placing her hand on top of his and pushing it down.

"OK, We'll go on Buzby"

"I'll need your address if I'm picking you up, I'm starting to think you don't want me knowing where you live!" he continued sarcastically.

Imogen scribbled her address on a piece of paper in her notebook before tearing it out and placing it in his jeans pocket. She began to walk away, before stopping and turning, her finger resting upon her lip as though to indicate she was thinking.

"Actually..." she began, walking back towards him, pursing her lips.

"You could drop me home now... that way you can't use the excuse later about getting lost!" she continued.

Rob cleared his throat as an objection.

"As if I would do that..." he answered.

Imogen smiled, raising her eyebrows.

"I know you..." she replied taking his hand.

They arrived in her street, she climbed off the bike. Rob turned off the engine. Imogen unfastened her helmet, passing it back to him.

"I don't know why you're trying to give it to me... You'll be wearing it in a few hours, you may as well hold on to it, it's practically became yours anyway..."

Imogen laughed.

"OK then!" she replied.

"You wanna come in?" Imogen asked.

"Yeah OK" he replied pulling the bike onto the path, parking it near her front door.

As he entered the house, he was struck by how empty it was. Imogen walked to the fridge, opening it to get out a couple of cans of pop.

"Help yourself to anything, I've got pop, chocolate, crisps and pot noodles… I've not really done a proper shop this week…" she spoke as she handed him a can.

He thought how it was like an empty student's house, a little tidier but it didn't feel like a home. The dining room was large open planned with an adjoining kitchen, there was no dining table, just a small coffee table.

"Ha, is that you?" he asked, scanning the pictures on the wall. Imogen nodded, raising her eyebrows.

"My God! You look like such a boy in that one" he continued as he pointed to a picture of a young Imogen with very short hair"

"Forever the tomboy!" she exclaimed as she opened the living room door and walked through.

He followed her into the living room, noticing that both rooms had large pot plants that reached upward with broad and spreading leaves, bringing some colour and life to the large bare white rooms.

Imogen sat down on the settee, moving a scattered pile of notes off the settee onto the small bar table in the corner of the room to make space for him.

"That's a bit of an odd addition to a living room…" Rob enquired curious.

Imogen laughed.

"Yeah my dad does crazy things sometimes... one day we were in Salt Cove down the coast and he decided he liked the small table and stools, so he got me to distract the barman while he loaded them into the car.." Imogen recalled smiling, trying not to laugh.

"Tell me your joking!" Rob replied

"I wish I was!" she replied laughing.

"So... fancy any food? Pot noodle? Or I think there is bacon and eggs..." she asked changing the subject.

"Hey..." he answered reassuringly.

"You don't have to make a fuss over me" he continued with his hand on her arm.

"Let's just chill, for a while, then if ya wanna we can go out, grab some proper food before the church thing" he pressed.

He watched her expression change. A nervous uncomfortable look, as though wondering how to respond without revealing too much.

"Oh, and my shout..." he responded as though reading her mind.

Imogen smiled relaxing into the settee.

"OK! You're on!" She replied.

They sat for a while talking before Imogen went upstairs to get changed.

Returning downstairs, she asked.

"So where are you taking me?"

Chapter 8

They rode into town, eating at pizza hut down at The Gate, before heading along to the Church in the centre of Jesmond. From the outside it looked like a normal old church, but inside it looked more like Matt's church. The band were warming up, the guitar riffs filling the air.

Soon the room filled with teenagers and Uni students.

The speaker talked centre-stage; the band positioned right of centre. He spoke confidently,

"The word of God is sharper than a two-edged sword... so, only in Christ do we find a God who truly understands our failures…...."

At that point Rob wasn't really listening he was too busy looking around and watching in amazement as the speaker stopped talking and proceeded to swallow razorblades, one after another, then swallowed one end of a length of string, pulling the string out of his throat to reveal that the razor blades were threaded through the swallowed end of the string.

He watched as Imogen was in awe of how it was done, noticing her eyebrows lift, her eyes slightly scrunched, focussed, as though her mind was trying to unravel the mystery. The speaker's message was broken up by worship provided by the band. He thought how it wasn't as good as Matt's band and the singer had nothing on Imogen, but they were good.

During the worship, he watched her holding her hands up in the air as if to feel god's energy filling her from above. He continued to scan the room, watching, at times confused.

As the message continued it steered onto topics which struck a nerve, the speaker began talking about depression and anxiety. Rob became more focussed on the words being spoken, it felt like the speaker was talking directly to him, he watched attentively as the speaker spoke out.

"All of our lips have heard words of discouragement, many of you here will be, or have suffered from depression. All of our hearts have felt it. Every one of us has known, at one time or another, the slap of setback, the grief of loss, or the disheartening effects of stress. To be human is to feel that numbing, exhausting, de-motivating fog of depression. But I urge you... Cast all your anxiety on him because he cares for you…... And the God of all grace, who called you to his eternal glory in Christ, after you have suffered a little while, will himself restore you and make you strong, firm and steadfast."

The service was coming to an end. The razor-blade guy was leading the crowd of teenagers and students in a final worship song, as the music played, Rob looked around.

He was standing in the centre of the aisle, next to Imogen, but away from the crowd of teenagers. Youth leaders and teenagers were hugging and crying. Some had made life transforming decisions to give their life to Jesus.

The night had touched him, and even though he knew he would never forget that night, he wasn't ready to take that step that those other teens were taking, and in a way it felt false and staged, not genuine, and he still had so many doubts so many unanswered questions, and still at times it felt like a pantomime, a show, but behind the smoke and mirrors was there anything real?

He watched a girl walk up to the front, handing over a blade, he watched as she removed her jacket, and knelt down. He could see the scars on her arms, from cut after cut, etched deeply into the upper part of her arm some were old and faded, some bright red, which were obviously fresh. He looked at the crowds singing, focussed on the band, trying not to watch what was transpiring in front of them.

He looked at Imogen who was also drawn to the girl at the front. He watched her as she twirled her hair, biting her lip, looking down at her shoes, fussing with the sleeves of the sweater she was wearing. He looked at her face wondering what she was thinking. He'd noticed some scars on Imogen which she was very good at hiding. He'd wanted to bring it up in conversations many times, not knowing how to broach that topic in conversation. He had wanted to ask where they'd came from, willing to admit he'd had his moments too. To admit that he'd also fought his demons and at times he still was fighting. But the time never felt right. The music began to fade. Imogen tapped him on the shoulder.

"Wanna get out of here?" she asked, while continuing to be distracted by the girl at the front, who was being hugged by many different people.

"Yeah..." He replied picking up his jacket, putting his arm around her.

They exited the church, the sky was black, the only light came from the flickering streetlamp above, and the occasional car headlamp speeding past.

"Hey, let's get you home" he spoke, placing his arm around her.

"Can't we ride for a bit first?" she asked, still fidgeting, pulling at her sleeves, pulling them over her wrists, looking anywhere but directly at him, a little of her vulnerability showing through.

"Yep! Of course, anything for you princess..." he replied pulling her in tighter.

They rode around for an hour, down empty streets, Imogen holding on tightly, counting the streetlights, letting the vibrations and sound of the engine soothe her. The back of his bike was becoming a place that provided complete freedom. A chance to think, but also a chance to clear her mind, to take a break from over-thinking, over-analysing, but above all the only place she could be herself without needing anyone's permission.

Pulling up at the lighthouse they looked out over the causeway, the water slowly beginning to cover the path with each incoming wave. The lighthouse was lit up, illuminating the sky.

"You Ok now?" He asked.

"Yeah... I just needed a moment, you know.... Sometimes things can be a bit hard, but yeah, I'm OK now, I'm always OK when you're around." She answered.

She walked along slowly, her hand skimming the railing, as though to cause a distraction because she'd revealed too much.

"Come on... sit for a while..." he replied, reaching for her hand.

"And,... Yep things like what he spoke about does hit a bit hard, I know, I've been there, got the t-shirt... Did it for you?" he continued.

She reflected the conversation away from herself.

"You know you can talk to me about anything, and if you've got any questions on faith and stuff then ask me and I'll try to answer..."

"Well if that's true maybe you could answer my question, I don't want to hear the spiel, I want to understand you..." he urged.

No-one had ever really pushed her to open up, never digging deep to understand her, she'd always wished someone would care, would notice, but when faced with someone wanting to know, she couldn't help but freeze, to try and shut it down as it would mean having to become almost 'naked', and she wasn't sure if she was ready to open that box, to reveal all. She'd already told him more than she'd ever told anyone else, but was she ready to go all the way?

He just wished she would open up to him.

"Those scars... Do you cut yourself? Or have you in the past? I saw that the girl got to you..." he asked

"Lets walk a bit" she exclaimed deflecting the subject, taking his hand pulling him down towards the path looking over the railings, watching the waves crash below.

"What are you afraid of? We all have fears" she asked as she climbed over the railings, facing outwards, yet holding on but leaning forwards.

"At the minute... I'm afraid of losing my idiot best mate!" he answered holding onto her wrists.

She looked at him sighing.

"And here was me thinking you were a dare devil!" she replied as she climbed back over.

They stood in an uncomfortable pause.

"Best mate? I like that though how's 'bout partner in crime" she laughed as though she was drunk.

She took his hand and began running before letting go, spinning around, faster and faster, until she fell to the ground landing on the soft grass.

He sat down beside her, his hand resting on her shoulder.

"Hey..." he spoke softly as though to say everything is OK, you don't have to put on an act for me.

She turned looking at him.

"I'm sorry! I guess I can be a bit of an idiot sometimes." she whispered.

"Yeah but you're my idiot, so I guess it's OK" he replied.

She sat watching the waves, allowing them to calm her.

"Anyways, you never answered... What scares you?" she asked again.

Rob looked at her.

"OK, I'll play along and answer your question, but then you have to answer mine! Deal?" He asked holding his small finger out as though to do a pinky promise.

Imogen nodded.

"I don't think I'm scared of anything, though I guess what scares me is being forgotten. I'm afraid of dying. I'm afraid that when I die that time itself will forget me; that I'll live an unimportant life, I won't be remembered. I am afraid that despite all the good I do, I'll still be no-one." The words just fell from him, thoughts which he'd never spoken out loud before.

"I will always remember you! You have a purpose; you just can't see it in the darkness. We all leave our footprints on people's hearts; we don't always see the impact, and a wise writer once said we never die till the ripples we leave end or something along those lines... God has a purpose for you. What matters is that you hold strong a faith in love. God has faith in you. You don't have to be perfect and neither do I, we learn as we go, we learn together, catch each other, and keep walking" She spoke with such compassion, her words echoed in his mind.

They sat talking for almost an hour. He talked, she listened. No-one had listened to him in that way, everyone always wanted something from him. Her words showed a kindness, a concern which came naturally.

He continued to probe, continuing to ask her questions, to urge her to open up to him, and he knew he wasn't going to give up till she did.

"So... I answered your questions, I've talked about me, you listened... so please... talk to me... this isn't a one-way street" Rob urged.

"OK... Well I'll start by admitting yes, those scars, well you know, I don't have to spell it out..."

She paused, taking a deep breath before continuing, opening up about things she'd never spoken before. Opening up about her self-harm and touching on the years of abuse which she had endured. Once she started talking, she couldn't stop. Very few people had ever urged her to open up. Some had created feigned attempts, but she always shut them down and they never probed further, confirming that their 'concern' wasn't genuine. She'd mastered the "I'm fine" when asked how are you? Knowing it was just an empty platitude. But he had kept pushing and something in her made her feel that maybe she could trust him, he wasn't like anyone she'd ever met before.

"I know I'm broken; bet you're going to run a mile now" she uttered under her breath looking down.

"Never" he replied, a silence followed.

"I like fixing things, didn't you know…" he laughed nudging her.

"Time to get you home" he continued not knowing what else to say.

"Yeah, I suppose it is getting late" she replied wondering if she'd revealed too much, wondering whether his reply was an empty reassurance. The ride back home her thoughts were consumed by wondering if having heard some of her darkest parts he'd run a mile.

He pulled up outside her house, the kitchen light shone out onto the path.

"Thanks for the ride" she spoke as she climbed off the bike, wondering if it would be her last.

She paused for a moment before continuing.

"Sorry if I kinda freaked you out a bit before…" she stated looking down at her feet.

"Hope you enjoyed it…. The service that is…" she continued nervously swinging her arms.

Rob nodded. Not knowing what to say, wanting desperately to find the words to reassure her, to tell her everything was OK, but couldn't find the words.

"You know, you'd think by now we'd have each other's phone numbers" he declared cheekily.

"Yeah, we should" she laughed putting her hand out.

"Well pass me your phone" she continued.

Taking his phone, she typed in her number and dialled, her phone rang in her pocket. Cancelling the call, she handed his phone back to him.

"There, done!"

"Well…. I guess I'll see ya tomorrow in English? Or maybe on the bridge beforehand"

"Yep.. see ya tomorrow" she replied as she turned towards the path.

"Yep, see ya tomorrow Princess" he replied as she began walking towards her house, he watched as she opened the door, entering and closing the door behind her.

He wondered what had made him start to call her Princess. In the past whenever he'd used that term it was more as an insult, mainly to those who felt self-intitled, but she wasn't like that, in fact was the complete opposite, he thought how maybe he was saying it because she needed it, she needed to know how special she was, because it was obvious that was something she lacked, she had so much love to give, but got very little in return. He resolved in that moment to do everything in his power to try and make up the shortfall.

Kicking the kickstart, he started the engine, pulling out of the street and heading back to the coast. Before heading home, he stopped at the Sea Front, looking out over Cullercoats Bay reflecting on that night. He stood by his bike looking out over the sea in front of him, it had not long-gone midnight. The sky was clear, the night sky illuminated only by the glints of starlight and the radiance of the moon invading the darkness.

Memories of the night filled his mind; the magician swallowing razor blades one after another, speaking about Jesus, faith, and love, some things he'd heard before but had never really listened.

But those words kept repeating in his mind.

The word of God is sharper than a two edged sword... so, only in Christ do we find a God who truly understands our failures…..

His mind then returned to their conversations at the lighthouse. He could see her clearly in his mind smiling and laughing, remembering her on the railings with her arms outstretched her head leaning gently on the railing, before leaning back looking up at stars above, the moment scared him, but looking back made him smile being in her wildness. He remembered her taking his hand as they ran along the path, seeing the wind blow her hair. He thought of what she said to him, he thought how she was so complex, how one moment she was wild, the next a scared little child, while also at the same time being wise and full of love.

He thought how like she said that maybe they could 'catch each other.

He returned home, quietly opening the door so not to wake anyone, using the torch on his phone as he walked through the house up to his room. Closing his door, he turned on his light.

Looking in the mirror seeing his old eyes staring back. He smiled at himself, something was beginning to awaken in him realizing that peace could only be found once he had found himself. Once he knew who he was, accepting who he was, and who he wanted to be, and where he wanted to go.

Chapter 9

Three weeks past.

Rob walked into the bridge one lunchtime, watching. The bridge had begun to become a hub.

The bridge was filled with chatter, students laughing and giggling amongst themselves. Rob stood leaning against the window watching, watching Imogen.

She sat side by side to another student, listening...

Really listening. Her compassion stronger than any he had witnessed in anyone else before. He smiled thinking of her pale blue eyes, which could probe deep into a person's soul, the look that she gives which says, "I know something's not alright; and when you're ready, we can work it out together."

Imogen's hand gently rested upon the girl's shoulder, bringing to life the realization that she was not alone.

He had come to realize over those weeks that she was unlike anyone he had ever met. She was the kind of person who lived her life the way she believed people should, but in that genuine and non-judgmental way that was rare.

His family were supposed to be Christians, yet he thought how she had more 'Christ' in her little finger than they had collectively. Though he also saw the wild child continually searching for something deeper, a faith in action. He loved her wild nature which flourished around him, which gradually others were seeing as she began to come into her own.

Continuing to watch her interactions he thought how it was as though a love radiated from her bringing out the best aspects of those she met. To her, their flaws entirely invisible. She brought a calmness like no other like a calm sea.

Her conversations fleeted between care and sincerity combined with conversations which were beautifully chaotic, a kind of verbal dance that would make you laugh out loud, brightening even the darkest of days.

Mid conversation with Trudi, she glanced up at him and smiled. Those dimples brought that sense of playfulness out of her.

He thought how over those past few weeks the bridge had become full of friends, a hub in a way it never had been before. He thought how she always said it was because of him, but although maybe they initially came because of his persuasion, and his personality, in reality, they stayed because of how she made people feel, creating a safe place to belong.

Walking over to her he placed his hand on her shoulder. She leant back reassuringly, placing a hand on top of his without breaking eye contact or conversation.

In that moment he thought how he'd found a friend who saw him for who he really was, yet still came closer, loving him for who he was, he wanted to be the same in return though questioned if he could be enough.

She turned her head slightly while still engaging with Trudi. Their eyes met, she smiled that sweet innocent smile, the dimples deep pits which accentuated her cheekbones.

"We were wondering when you were going to join us, sauntering over there like billy no mates" She laughed as he sat down beside her.

"We were just discussing how we should go into Whitley at the weekend, but Imogen has to go to JACOB!.... Geesh, you really need to talk some sense into her Rob!" Trudi spoke with a sarcastic yet concerned tone.

"And I was telling Trudi how Thursday is a much better night to hit Whitley, student discount...... Triples for singles...If ya going to drink... and there's Karaoke!"

"So, is little miss goodie two shoes going to let her hair down and have a drink??" He replied, smiling and baiting for a reaction.

"I might...It's just I don't need alcohol to let my hair down, but if I did drink, I bet I could drink you under the table, it's in the genes" she replied cloyingly.

"In your dreams..." He replied looking deep into her eyes teasingly, almost daring.

She smiled raising her eyebrows and biting her lip staring at Rob, both caught in a moment.

"Ahem!!" Trudi interrupted breaking their moment.

"Some of us have classes on Friday! Not like you two slackers..." Trudi spoke.

"OK, compromise... We'll go out next Friday, I'm sure Jacob will be OK with me going down Saturday..." Imogen responded shaking on it.

Rob watched thinking how much this Jacob controlled her, he could see how during the week she was like a blooming flower, yet a Monday morning she would return to the girl who walked with her head down, questioning herself, hearing her say

"I can't do this!" or "I'm useless"

From the beginning he formed a dislike for her boyfriend Jacob, something didn't feel right. He tried to convince himself it wasn't because there was a hint of jealousy, but over time he found his original gut instinct to be true.

The bell rang. Rob stood up, and taking Imogen's hand he guided her to her feet, bowing his head... "My lady, can I escort thee to English class?"

Trudi shook her head in disbelief.

"Get a room guys!" Trudi laughed.

In quick reply Imogen looked around trying not to laugh,

"This is kinda a room, so we already got one"

She turned back to Rob.

"Yes, my dear sir, it would be an honour" She replied, performing a curtsy. They walked hand in hand out of the bridge and down to class laughing.

As class ended, he looked at her.

"So...... Thurs-Bay???? Tonight, is Thursday? You up for a night of karaoke, alcohol and dancing with this stud?!"

Cloyingly she looked around "What stud, where? She answered trying not to laugh...

"Yeah, OK why not...!" she continued as he took her hand and spun her around in an almost pirouette.

"I'll meet you at the Bay... We can grab a drink there before walking into Whitley?"

"OK.... 8?" He asked...

"Well, if you want me to meet you at 8... I guess you'll have to give me a ride home, you know it takes a girl hour's to get ready..." she answered, fluttering her eyebrows while gently biting down on her bottom lip.

"Any excuse to get on my bike!" he laughed...

"One day I'll teach you and you can ride your own bike, not that you could keep up" he continued.

"Hey!! You love it really!!" she replied playfully punching his arm.

"I know my place....I am your chauffer madam", He spoke jokingly, his hand placed upon his stomach, bowing as if addressing royalty.

"Anywhere you wish to go, I am at your command" he continued, returning upright.

Imogen couldn't help but laugh.

"Tell me about it... Stud" she spoke flirtingly almost trying to re-enact the scene from grease...

As she turned to walk out, he broke into song...

"I've got chills there multiplying.... And I'm losing control..."

They danced and sang the duet as they made their way through the corridor to Rob's bike, Imogen didn't care if anyone was watching. They fell through the fire doors to his parked bike. Neither could stop laughing.

Rob dropped her at her home before heading back to his house.

As he walked through the door his mother shouted.

"Roberto, is that you? I need you to go and get some shopping"

"Yes, mama..." He sighed,

He thought how it was always him who had to get the shopping, the others all had important lives. He thought how as soon as the list of chores gets posted his sister would bury herself in the textbooks, reeling off a myriad of excuses. She has to get her homework done right now or she'll fail..., and then by default all of the chores would land on him.
He sighed...

"I'm going out tonight mama"

"Hmm, out drinking again. When will you take some responsibility for your life?" she sighed in a disapproving tone.

"... and you will eat with the rest of us before going out!" She instructed as Rob took the shopping list.

"Yes, mama..." he replied as he left the house.

He returned with the shopping and put it away. He sat quietly through dinner. He couldn't sit still while his thoughts danced in infinite directions. They'd hung out so many times, many walks and bike rides, study sessions, the night at Jesmond, but this felt different. Or maybe he just wanted it to be different.

"So, who you going out with?" Isabella asked.

Rob remained quiet not wanting to engage.

"I've heard you've got a girlfriend... People talk you know..."

Laughing, she continued,

"She must be special if she can drag you to church! Rob's in love with a Church girl!" She exclaimed as she ate a forkful of food knowing her statement would get her mother's attention.

"She's not my girlfriend... We're just friends" he replied under his breath.

"Who is this girl Roberto?"

"Just a friend mama"

"Do we get to meet her?" his mother probed inquisitively, eager to know more.

Rob looked over at Isabella giving a cold stare, Isabella gave a patronising grin knowing what she had started.

"Leave the boy alone Rosa, I'm sure he'll bring her around when he's ready, won't you son" his father intervened.

The clocked ticked loudly and slowly as he watched the minutes pass.

"May I be excused mama? I have to get ready..." He asked.

He hoped that he could use Isabella's announcement to his advantage, meeting a girl changed things, his mother a little more lenient.

She nodded, he excused himself, taking his dishes into the kitchen.

Isabella followed.

"Well, don't I get a thank you?" she asked, as though her announcement was done as a favour.

Rob began to walk past her, failing to reply, hearing Isabella mumbling about how ungrateful he was.

"Oh, and since it's not like you've got a life you can sort out the bins for me...." She instructed in a patronising tone as she hurled the binbag at him.

"Thanks Bro!" she continued, not giving a chance to respond.

After carrying the binbag through the garage to the outside bin, he returned inside, pausing at the bottom of the stairs, his hand resting upon the banister shaking his head in disbelief at his sister's self-imposed entitlement.

He headed up to his room...

6 o'clock...

His focus was scattered, what to wear? He tried on 4 different shirts before deciding on one.

"It's not a date" he kept reminding himself though no matter how many times he told himself that, he was still filled with nervous anticipation, so excited, even giddy.

He walked down the stairs, grabbing his jacket.

"Right, I'm off! I have my keys..." He called out loudly as he opened the door. Leaving before his mother could interrogate him some more.

He looked back as he walked down the drive, watching his mother twitching at the curtains.

He walked down to Cullercoats Bay, looking out over the beach below. Under the moonlight the water was still, as though the tide was ready to turn. The heat of the day had been replaced by a cool breeze and Rob sauntered along the path with his hand skimming the metal railings. He entered the Bay scanning the bar looking for Imogen. It was her father's regular. He'd seen her father a few times briefly already when dropping her off or when picking her up but he had never officially met him. He was a strong Geordie man, down to earth, common, but Rob liked that, a refreshing change from his family.

"Ye' alreet kidda" he heard a voice behind him. Imogen's father stood with a pint in his hand.

"Erm, yes sir! Just looking for Imogen"

Imogen's father laughed,

"Enuf of the sir! Call me Smudger"

He looked back over his shoulder, to the barman.

"Oy! A pint for this young lad... what ye havin'?"

"Erm... a pint of lager please" Rob replied, a little nervous, as he continued to look around searching for Imogen.

Imogen's Father handed Rob a pint.

"Come on! She'll be back in a minute, gone to freshen herself up or summit, whatever girls do..."

Imogen returned from the toilets. Rob looked up, she looked like perfection. Her long hair falling down onto her shoulders, clipped at the side to keep the hair from falling onto her face. Her dress accentuating every curve. She sat down beside him, reaching over the table for her drink.

They finished their drinks. Rob stood up, not knowing what to say, what to do.

"Shall we get out of here?" Imogen asked.

Rob took his hands out of his pockets, suddenly unsure of where to put them. Nervousness wasn't usually his gig,

"What the hell's going on, get a grip" He told himself before replying.

"Yep, come on then" he continued as Imogen linked arms with him.

As they headed out through the door her father shouted,

"Have fun kids"

"We will" Imogen replied as the door began to close behind them.

They stepped out onto the pavement, pausing for a moment before continuing along the path walking along the coast into Whitley Bay, moving between the pools of streetlight, avoiding the cracks, as if they were children, almost dancing along the pavement which was still wet from the Autumn rain.

As they walked, he wondered whether she deliberately got him to meet her in the Bay for him to see her father.

"So, was that the official 'meet' the father test?"

It was as though Imogen could read his thoughts, something which was becoming more common the longer they spent together.

"Haha, well he does like you more than Jacob, but he knows we're just mates"

Rob's heart sank a little, he wanted to say if you'd met me first would you love me instead, but he didn't.

Maybe it's better this way he thought. He thought how, in a way he was glad she was 'taken' he had resolved to never get into anything serious with anyone, just fun, he couldn't put anyone through being with him, taking care of him, watching him die.. If she'd been single would he have chased her like a conquest, use her and throw her in the trash? He thought of all the girls he'd ghosted. Being around her made him question himself, his behaviours, his attitude to life, she was changing him, yet she didn't know it.

"Hey, what ya thinking about, you're all serious" Imogen spoke pulling a funny face, which snapped him out of his thoughts.

"Nothing, just thinking about stuff, thinking how lucky I am to have you as a mate, my wing-man!"

"Ahem!!! You're not running off with some chick and leaving me alone... Maybe another time when the gang is with us but tonight it's just us against the world"

"You want me all to yourself... ? I get it" he joked,

"Get over yourself... I just can't be in Whitley alone.... it's just not safe...." she replied, her tone dropping, showing a glimmer of her vulnerability.

Rob looked puzzled, there was still so much he didn't know. Her eyes revealed a beautiful but broken soul and her movements told of a need for nurture and protection. He didn't understand how one moment she could be wild and confident and the next moment like a scared child, but it was something he was seeing more and more.

"I said to meet in the Bay so I could travel down with Dad... I kind of don't like travelling alone much... I have this habit of getting attacked..." she answered his silent question.

"Don't be silly" he laughed.

But as he looked at her, he could see it in her eyes, he could see she was being serious. She spoke of the many physical attacks over the past few years, and the fear she felt whenever alone, needing to be on guard, panicking, the constant fear. He wondered how anyone could hurt such a beautiful soul. He knew right then that all she needed was love and security, something steady to hold onto.

He thought how perhaps in that rescuing of her he was also rescuing himself too.

"You'll always be safe with me" he spoke softly pulling her into a tight embrace.

"I know I am" she replied.

The moment was interrupted by the sound of her phone, a message. She glanced down at her phone, a message from Jacob.

She replied,

Out with friends

Omitting the fact, she was out with just one friend... Rob. Putting her phone back in her pocket she took hold of his hand.

"Come on! You promised me karaoke" she spoke cheekily.

They entered Banana Joe's. The club was packed with students, inflatable bananas were being thrown across the club as someone was singing on the karaoke.

"Want a go?" She asked.

"Why not" he replied.

"Well! Get the drinks in and I'll put us down for a few... Grease?? Meatloaf??" she exclaimed.

"Yeah, OK.... and I promised your dad I'd look after you, you aren't legal yet remember"

"Grrr, yeah whatever, you just don't want to be humiliated by a girl!" She laughed.

"Like you said, you don't need alcohol to have fun! There is plenty of time for me to corrupt that sweet little brain of yours" he replied, kissing her hand.

He returned with an archers and lemonade, and a bottle of bud.

"I got you one then we can both go onto soft drinks...."

"... maybe you'll be a bit of a positive influence on me... I guess all this alcohol isn't really doing my already Fucked up kidneys any good"

She sighed shaking her head. There was so much she wanted to say but decided to leave it for a time when they were alone.

"You? One drink? Yeah right whatever! I've heard the stories! And I've witnessed your pitiful attempts at hiding a hangover..." she laughed.

Her comment left him feeling a little dejected. Looking at him it was as though she could read his thoughts. She took his hand, staring deep into his eyes she smiled. Trying to change the path of the conversation she continued...

"Come on... Lets have fun!"

Imogen got up to sing. Rob watched in awe like he did that night at Matt's gig. Her voice filled the bar, a change from the out of key drunken songs. Swells of power rose up in her throat.

Her voice was haunting, like that first night. He wondered if there was an end to her hidden talents. She dragged him up for a duet... You're the one that I want, recreating the song from earlier that day.

The night was filled with karaoke performing renditions of meatloaf duets, and Rob telling jokes which were so stupid they were brilliant. She laughed more than she had ever laughed before.

They left Banana Joe's, heading to Deep to finish off the night dancing. The club was packed, the strobe lights masking so many of the crowd's movements. The music felt like a drug, intoxicating them. They danced till closing, leaving in the early hours of the morning. Bursting through the doors into the artificial glow of the streetlights which created beams of light which caught in her hair.

Staggering, adjusting to the cold fresh air, they walked down onto the beach, across the damp sand to the water's edge, dodging the gentle waves as they lapped up the sand.

The full moon shone down on them, a light drizzle mixed with the fret coming off the ocean gently showering them,

He looked at her and wondered whether it was just the alcohol making him notice her even more. Her skin was illuminated by the stars; she looked pale, like her heart would stop any moment, so thin that she could break. He watched as she walked along, dancing, wishing that he could reach out and brush his hand against her perfectly shaped cheekbones. He refrained from doing so, instead he continued to succumb to the endless torture of watching her without being able to touch. She was like a fallen angel; a mystery which he was slowly unlocking. A dangerously beautiful mystery. She had a kind of understated beauty, perhaps it was because she was so disarmingly unaware of her prettiness.

He didn't want to admit that he was believing that he could be falling for her...

Imogen shivered as the cold air hit her skin. Rob instinctively took off his jacket, draping it over her shoulders. Stepping back, he looked in awe.

"What?" Imogen asked as he stared at her

"Nothing... It just looks so much better on you..." he answered before evading her eyes, picking up a pebble from the sand and skimming it across the water's surface.

"You're so pretty you know" He blurted out, shocked by the realisation that he'd spoken those words out loud.

Her breath toppled out of her soft lips "But I'm not pretty," she replied, before continuing...

"You're blind mate, or drunk.. or both??... I'm not pretty, or good looking, I'm plain and ugly...."

"No," he interrupted, stepping closer

"You are pretty! Though not just pretty... but beautiful... Your eyes are filled with such beauty and compassion, deep and mysterious. You have hair like the wind, wild and free. You may think you don't fit everyone else's definition of pretty, because you are so much more. You have the look of adventure, a heart of gold, a spirit that soars, and to me that will always be my definition of pretty."

He pulled her in close, holding onto his jacket, wanting so much to kiss her, to kiss away the hurt and the lack of self-worth. He thought how if it took him his whole life, he wouldn't stop until she could see what he saw.

"You're so drunk! You softy!" She laughed, stepping away,

"I'm hungry! Kebab?" she asked though it wasn't really a question, taking his hand and running along the beach and back up onto the promenade.

They walked back up South Parade, all the bars were closed, only a few revellers remained on the street, sauntering up to the centre of town, like they were.

Rob stepped into the takeaway ordering a large kebab. They sat on the hard metal seats on the street, Rob opened up the kebab, handing Imogen a can of coke"

The tray was filled with overly thick slices of kebab meat soaked in grease, covered with lashings of chilli and garlic sauce, salad and pitta bread. He picked up the pitta bread breaking it in two.

"Tuck in then, we'll see who the softy is" he encouraged.

"You're forgetting I'm a real tough Geordie girl, you honestly think a bit of chilli is going to scare me" She laughed as she scooped up some kebab, placing it in the pitta bread and eating it.

Rob copied, taking a mouthful.

"Jesus! That's hot!" He exclaimed taking a drink.

"Point proved, softy! Another win to me!" she laughed licking the tip of her finger and touching the air as if to record a point won.

Finishing the kebab, they sat together.

"Come on... Let's get you into a taxi." Rob spoke breaking the silence, leading her over to the taxi rank, his hand outstretched.

"See you Monday, text me when you get home" he spoke as he placed her in a taxi giving instructions to the taxi driver.

As he said goodbye, he thought how it was going to be a long weekend without her, he was beginning to hate the weekends, knowing where she was.

As he walked home back along the coast, he thought of the conversations they'd had earlier that evening, and the many conversations before. He thought about her fears of being attacked, his shock hearing of the attacks she had endured over the years, the conversations they'd had before on their bike rides, with her admitting that she had gone through periods of self-harm, and the shame that followed. The abuse, wondering how she hadn't been hardened through all she had endured, still believing good existed.

He stood looking over the railings, watching the waves hit the rocks below. He thought back to the night at the lighthouse. He wondered did it stop with the self-harming or was there something deeper. Had she ever had suicidal thoughts?

He thought how many times he'd been there... He'd been to that dark place, not that anyone would know that. He knew of being in that place so dark you want to jump, to end it, to stop the pain, but when she was with him the pain stopped, the darkness lifted, there was light seeping through the cracks. Through her he had a reason to not think about it, a reason not to die. He'd found a purpose. He had to save her, and through saving her, maybe he could save himself too.

His phone vibrated in his pocket, looking at the phone was a message from Imogen.

Got home OK, night x
Oh, and pick me up Monday?

He smiled as he replied.

Night x and yep, see you Monday.

As he put his phone back in his pocket, he smiled, taking a deep breath, he continued home.

Quietly he entered the house trying hard not to make a noise, not wanting to disturb everyone. He entered his room, collapsed onto his bed, closed his eyes and fell asleep.

Chapter 10

Saturday

Rob walked through the party, drink in hand. He was in his element being a social butterfly. Always sociable, friendly with everyone, flitting from person to person, bouncing around a room full of people, the life and soul of any gathering.

He'd received a Facebook invite earlier that day to a house party. Some guy he was in a class with the year before. He was now at uni.

At first, he wasn't going to go but he needed to escape that house! It had rained all day so he couldn't escape on Buzby.

Over the roar of music, a distant, hazy chatter could be heard.

Rob heard a voice behind him

"Hey Rob, nice to see you" He turned, recognising the face in front of him but not being able to place the name.

"Hey guys, this is Rob, the one I was talking about... from college"

"Ah! The fun one with all the drinking games?" he heard someone reply.

"Yep" Rob replied lifting his drink.

He looked around, wondering was that all people saw, the laughter, being silly, the clown, the most exhilarating and the most damn fun? Well he did play that part to perfection! He thought to himself as he picked up another drink.

"Well I may as well live up to my reputation" he muttered under his breath, scanning the drinks available. Not enough variety for rainbow he thought to himself, Reverse bingo? With a bit of truth or dare? He thought.

"Hey mate!" he shouted over.

"Do you have some paper, a pen, and a photocopier?" he continued.

"Yep, one moment" the unknown guy replied.

"Hey Kye, grab us a drink!" He heard someone beckon over.

"Kye, that's it" Rob thought feeling thankful he didn't have to ask him what his name was!

Bringing the paper and pens, Kye spoke loudly

"I knew it was a good idea to invite you" Kye spoke as he grabbed a drink from the table and walked away.

Rob wrote out the numbers 1-100 on a sheet of paper.

Kye returned.

"Go photocopy that for me mate" Rob asked as he took another piece of paper and wrote the words.

Shot, Truth, Dare.

Kye returned with the photocopy, and Rob tore up the sheets into individual numbers, keeping the 2 sheets separate, folding each number like a raffle ticket.

Kye stood up on a chair,

"Right, everybody! I invited an old mate along who is great with drinking games and stuff, he's got a game for us so everyone listen up"

Everyone looked at Rob.

"Ok, so we're going to play a bit of reverse bingo with shot, truth or dare twist"

Everyone looked a little puzzled.

"So, everyone is going to get some numbers... I think about 5 each" he said passing one set of tickets to the Kye to hand out.

"I have the same numbers in this bowl... When I call out a number you tell me if you've got it, and I will issue you with a shot, truth or dare... The winner is the one with the last number..." He continued holding everyone's attention.

The game started, everyone got into the swing of it, Rob took swigs of a bottle of vodka throughout, watching everyone.

The game ended, everyone a little more drunk than when they'd started.

"Great game mate!" Kye spoke tapping him on the shoulder, before walking off,

"Let's get some music pumping!" he exclaimed

As the music began, Rob collapsed onto the settee still clinging to the bottle of vodka. Alone. He'd done his part; he was now redundant. His hands gripped the bottle, his eyes swivelling towards the back of his head. The nausea swirled unrestrained in his empty stomach. He tilted his head towards the edge of the couch taking another long swig of the clear substance, finishing the bottle, he allowed it to fall to the floor.

He drifted off. When he opened his eyes, he wasn't sure for how long he'd been out for. Everyone was still partying, though it looked as some had left. He lifted his head trying to sit upright, feeling light-headed. Clearing his throat, he tried standing up, just to fall back down on the settee. His mouth was sore from the amount of alcohol that he'd consumed. Finally standing he took a step forward in an unbalanced attempt to walk. He began staggering towards the door, before walking out, he looked around, no-one noticed, he'd served his purpose. He picked up another bottle from the table, a half empty bottle of flavoured vodka.

"One for the road, they won't notice, payment for services" he thought, lifting the bottle into the air as he walked out.

Closing the door behind him, he stumbled down the steps onto the street. He could still hear the music thumping as he walked away.

He drank as he walked down into the centre of town, his stomach began to heave, his head spinning like being on a carousel, slow at first but gaining momentum, falling to his knees. Bending over he continued to heave, his stomach expelling everything he'd ate and drunk for the past couple of hours till there was nothing left but yellow bile.

He wiped his mouth still tasting the sick in the back of his throat. The bottle had smashed on the floor in front of him, as he tried to sit up his hand caught a shard of broken glass cutting his palm.

As he began to sober up, he walked to the nearest taxi rank,

"Cullercoats mate" he spoke as he stepped into a taxi.

As the taxi drove out of town, and along the coast road, he sat with his head leaning back, drifting in and out of consciousness.

He entered the house, walking up the stairs to his bedroom, collapsing on the bed, feeling the comfort of the bed overtaking his state of drunkenness. He closed his eyes and drifted off.

He awoke in the morning to the sound of his mother shouting loudly. He lay face-down, still in his vomit stained clothes from the night before, and a blood stain on his white bedding from the gash on his hand. At first, he couldn't remember how it happened, the night before had become a blur.

His mother knocked on his door.

Once on his feet the room swayed almost causing him to lose balance. He reached out for the door, leaning against it, as the handle began to turn.

"Mamma, I'm not dressed, don't come in" he spoke quickly not wanting her to see him in that state.

"Are you coming to church this morning" she asked loudly through the door, though it sounded more like an order than a question.

"No, mamma. I'm not..."

Before she could scold him for not going, he continued

"I'm going to Matt's church this afternoon" The words poured out of his mouth.

"OK, though I would prefer if you would also join us as a family but if you must, at least you're going to church, if that's what you call it"

"Yes, mama" He replied breathing a sigh of relief.

When the family left, he carried his clothes and quilt cover downstairs into the utility room and put them in the washing machine.

His phone pinged with notification after notification, posts and pictures of the night before. His brain felt like it would explode within his skull, waves of nausea adding to his misery, and his dehydration too obvious to ignore. He took two paracetamol and washed them down with a pint of water.

By lunchtime his headache was beginning to subside.

"What time is this church?" his mother asked following Sunday dinner.

He couldn't remember, he had only mentioned Matt's church as a quick reaction, with no intention of actually going. He'd never been to a service at the church, only small group sessions.

"Erm, 5.30. He answered quickly hoping she wouldn't notice.

"Well, shouldn't you be getting ready soon? It's almost 4.30!"

He knew he wasn't going to get out of it. With Matt's band playing it couldn't be that bad, he thought.

"Yep, going to get ready now mama and I'm going on Buzby so will only take me 5 minutes" he answered.

Returning to his room he sent a text to Matt,

"Hey, mate. What time is church?"

His phone pinged quickly after with a reply.

"I almost fell off my chair when I got your message... It starts at 6, but we'll be in from 5ish practicing"

Rob laughed, putting his phone back on his desk. He rubbed his hand, the gash on his palm still causing some discomfort. No-one had noticed, or if they did, they never said anything.

5.30pm. He pulled up outside the church, he could hear the music from outside, the beat of the drums, Matt's guitar… and that voice he'd come to love, the voice of an angel. He stood outside listening as they practiced.

He entered the church as others began to walk past him. Inside it wasn't like a church, it was like a big concert room, filled with chairs, a stage at the front, where the band where practising. To the side was a simple glass pulpit. The only thing which indicated that it was a church was the cross which hung on the wall above the stage.

The worship band had stopped playing. Rob walked to the front, greeting Matt with a handshake.

He looked at Rob and over at Imogen.

"I kinda thought you'd be a bad influence on her but it seems I was wrong….. She's obviously being a good influence on you getting you to walk through these doors on a Sunday" he spoke almost jokingly, yet with a hint of seriousness.

"Hey, what you doin' here" Imogen asked interrupting.

Matt looked at the both of them and decided to make himself scarce.

"Well, I'm going to grab a drink and mingle before we start…. Rob… I'll catch up with you at the end" Matt spoke before walking away.

"Erm, I thought I'd come see what Matt's church was like, didn't know you'd be here... honest" he replied to her question putting his hands up.

"I believe you, I'm not here every Sunday, just every other Sunday with Jacob being in Durham..."

"Anyways, enjoy... and I'll catch you at the end? If you've got Buzby you could drop me home? You did say you were my chauffer" she laughed.

"Yep, of course" He replied. Happy to see her earlier than planned.

The service was not like any he'd been too before, though slightly resembling the youth service in Jesmond. The building was filled with music, everyone singing along, people with hands in the air worshipping.

He was used to standing, singing an old out of tune hymn before sitting listening to the minister talk endlessly in a monotone tone, broken up by a few more hymns. The same structure every week, the sermon philosophical with no real-world implementation. It always felt pointless, old, out of date.

The minister stood up to speak, a young man, wearing normal clothes. His words were short but tugged at him.

"You only have to open you mind and your heart to the power of His love. He is there, healing wounds if you let him in........ put all your trust in our father the creator, not in an empty religion; Our Lord is love, truth, blessed peace, forgiveness and joy. Love and fear cannot co-exist, and so choose Him; choose Love... Go out, taking his love with you, walk in his path, be his feet on the ground......"

At the end of the service he watched from the back as the band packed away. Everyone made an effort to speak to him, it was nice but a bit overwhelming and, in the end, he was getting tired of repeating himself when people asked what brought him to the church.

"I know, Matt and Imogen, and I've been to a few of Matt's small group sessions" he repeated over and over, almost like a broken record. By the end, it had almost became a rehearsed answer.

Imogen walked up, a thankful distraction. Grabbing a drink, she could see the relentless questioning was becoming too much.

"Hey, you wanting to get out of here? I'm whacked!" she smiled winking.

"Yeah sure" he replied.

She turned directing her conversation to those talking to Rob.

"I'm sorry to steal him away from you, I'm sure he'll be back" she spoke as she looked up at Rob smiling.

They stepped outside, the streetlights were beginning to turn on, he'd been there just over 2 hours, normally 40 minutes of church drove him insane and desperate to escape.

"Oh and I'm sure the reply is you're welcome!" Imogen winked.

Rob diverted the conversation.

"It's lucky I've kept the spare helmet on the bike" he smiled as he passed it to her.

"Though really we should get you your own helmet" he continued as he fastened his straps and turned the key in the bike.

He drove her home.

Climbing off the bike she unfastened her helmet and went to pass it to him.

"Keep a hold of it, I'm picking you up in the morning and am not going to need it in the meantime......"

"See ya tomorrow" he spoke before pulling down his visor, revving the engine, knocking it into gear, and riding away.

He watched her in his rear-view mirror standing, holding onto the helmet watching him ride away.

Arriving home, he parked Buzby in the garage, entering the house.

"What time do you call this?" his mother spoke sternly

"Church!? .... You have been lying to me!" she continued, her voice raising.

"No, mamma I haven't been lying! Church started at 6, I just got there for 5.30 to see the band beforehand.... It finished half an hour ago and then I dropped Imogen home"

His mother looked sternly unsure whether to believe him. He could see the look in her eyes, she never believed him, never gave him the benefit of doubt.

"Why would now be any different?" he thought to himself.

"I don't know why I bother! You never believe me! Can't do anything right!" He spoke angrily but also disheartened as he walked up the stairs.

Entering his room, he slammed the door behind him.

Sitting on his bed he thought of the service, and then thought of the night before. He liked who he was when he was with Imogen, he liked who she thought he was, he wasn't liking that person he was the night before.

Chapter 11

The weeks past.

Rob finally gave in to the relentless nagging by his mother to bring Imogen to their home. He'd broached the topic with her hoping she wouldn't want to go, that way he would have an excuse, but instead he found she wanted to go.

It was the beginning of November. Imogen walked up from the bay, a small bouquet of flowers in her hands. She could feel her heart beating so fast and so strong that she suddenly had the urge to throw up, nervous because she had no idea what to expect or what to say when she finally met his parents. She walked slowly through the streets away from the coast, heading inland, to his street. Standing on the corner she looked over.

"Here goes!" she told herself, as she took a deep breath and continued to his house, opening the old wooden gate, walking up the path till she was standing outside, she looked at her watch, she was early.

Her hand rested against the old knocker on the old green door, hesitant, contemplating whether to knock or wait.

The door opened causing her to catch her breath. She hadn't knocked, she wondered how he knew she was there, and whether he'd been watching for her to arrive. Rob stood there grinning like a Cheshire cat. She looked in from the open door observing the wide hallway. Imogen entered following behind Rob, scanning the walls in the hallway and up the stairs, walls filled with family photographs, photographs of children.

The smell of home-cooked food filled the air. The house felt welcoming. His mother appeared from the kitchen, wearing an apron, her smile so endearing as she walked towards her.

"Erm, these are for you..." Imogen spoke quietly, nervously, as she handed over the bouquet of flowers.

"Thank you..." his mother replied smiling. She looked at Rob.

Imogen extended her arm for a handshake to greet his mother which went unnoticed and ignored. Instead, she moved forwards giving a warm big hug and a kiss in both cheeks.

"Veo por qué te gusta esta chica, Roberto..." his mother spoke, winking at Rob causing him to blush.

Tugging at his arm Imogen asked, puzzled.

"What did she say?"

"Erm, she just said you are very nice..." he replied to her question being thankful that Imogen didn't understand Spanish.

Imogen followed Rob into the dining room. A huge mahogany table took up most of the room, covered with a white lace tablecloth, the table was becoming filled with food, as his mother carried dishes in from the kitchen. She sat down at the dining table still appreciating her surroundings. Light shone in from the conservatory doors, and in the centre of the table stood a lit candle filling the room with a sweet scent.

Imogen sat through the meal, quietly eating, watching the family around her. She had been a part of family dinners like this one at Sienna and David's house. She wondered if everyone else had family meals like this, and she was the exception. Rob watched her, sensing her nervousness as the family quizzed her. When the meal finished, Rob began clearing the table, Imogen sat, her hands fidgeting on her lap.

"Can I help?" She asked, pursing her lips, she followed him into the small kitchen.

"I am Cinderella.... Are you my princess charming, the one to rescue me?" he spoke softly, yet cloyingly with the back of his hand resting upon his forehead.

Imogen laughed, picking up the tea-towel she flicked him with it, biting her bottom lip. "You wash... I dry..."

After tidying up, they took Levi for a walk along the coast.

"So, you survived the family interrogation" Rob laughed.

"I enjoyed myself, really... I wish I had that" Imogen sighed.

"I guess I should stop complaining about my family..." Rob replied feeling guilty for all of his complaining over the past couple of months.

Imogen stopped for a moment, looking at him.

"No...."

He looked back at her, she put her hand on his.

"No one can tell you that you cannot be happy, others only see from the outside, you live your life day in day out. Some people think my set-up is great, and yeah it can be fun! How many teenagers can say they practically have their own house? But were they to step in my shoes the rose-tinted glasses would come off...."

"....Anyways, maybe with me around you'll become the golden boy! I get the feeling your mother likes me??"

Her humorous tone changed as her hand gripped his tighter, her other hand gently resting on his arm, looking up, deep into his eyes. She continued.

"...You know I'll always stand up for you... For the rest of my life I'll make sure you are seen for who you really are"

She turned, and in a moment was back to the sweet, mischievous wild girl.

"Are you going to walk me to the Bay?" she asked with a look of mischief.

He smiled nodding. As they walked down to the bay he wondered if she'd even realised how much those words meant to him, to actually have someone on his side, to have a friend.

"See ya tomorrow?" She spoke, leaning in for a hug.

"Yep, see ya tomorrow Princess" he replied walking away.

He entered the house removing Levi's lead, taking off his jacket, hanging it up on the coat stand near the front door. His mother peered out from the living room.

"I like this girl, you hold onto her, you treat her right, maybe I will get another daughter?"

"Mama I've told you she has a boyfriend!" he answered abruptly as he walked up the stairs.

Chapter 12

The first term of college was coming to an end, with only 2 weeks left until the Christmas holidays. Jacob had returned, his university finishing for Christmas which meant he rarely saw Imogen, except within college. He found it hard being second in her heart, but it was something he was willing to accept. Rob had begun to enjoy spending so much time with Imogen. The bike rides, their conversations, studying together, and family meals. The progress of their relationship had been natural and unforced. They simply wanted to be in one another's company.

He had begun going to church frequently, at first just to see her and Matt but soon found a place where he belonged, a place where he was accepted for who he was, not just for what he could give.

He felt blessed. He had never imagined that he would find a friend who could be so understanding, Imogen got him, she understood him in a way no-one else did... Around her his depression almost disappeared, only rearing its ugly head in times when he was alone, usually at night, the weekends were the worst.

During the week if he began to slip into the darkness, he could text her or ring her, but at a weekend he knew she would be with Jacob.

He watched from a distance as Jacob met her from college, she turned waving goodbye, Rob caught the look on his face and watched as he tightened his grip on her hand pulling her away.

Over those past months he had already decided he didn't like Jacob. Something didn't feel right, sensing a control, which when he met him, he realised his instincts had been true.

The way his grip tightened on Imogen's hand, the way he answered for her, but most of all the way her body language changed when she was with him, though he knew she was blinded to it. He thought how in her case love was definitely blind!

Rob quickly got the vibe that Jacob didn't like him either, he didn't like him being her friend, though he thought how it felt like he didn't just not like her having him as a friend but didn't like her having friends at all.

The college term finished; he knew it would be 2 long weeks till he would see her again, apart from church... Though he wondered if Jacob would be there.

He sat in his room Monday morning, the first week of the holidays, 2 days before Christmas day. He'd returned from home from shopping, he hated town at that time of year. He had weaved through the crowds, edging through the dense flow of people with his bags. Usually he hated the crowds, the queues, the overly attentive shopping assistants eager for a big Christmas sale, seasonal music playing in every store... Though that day was a little different, that whole Christmas season felt different, even the music didn't feel as irritating. He found himself humming along, interacting with store staff, and even sharing in with the season's greetings. He realised something was changing, something in him.

He sat wrapping presents. The usual socks, perfumes, and other boxed toiletries, gifts with no real thought, nothing personal, except for one gift, one he still had to wrap. He sat holding a box, a small jewellery box, opening it he stared at the small, simple Celtic cross. He knew Imogen hated shopping for herself, that selfless heart, and the apparent guilt he knew she felt whenever she dared to put herself first.

He thought back to a few weeks earlier. She had persuaded him to join her as she done her Christmas shopping, getting all her shopping in early, a thought-out list, everything personal.

He watched as she stopped glancing at a jewellery store, something had caught her eye. She held her money in her hand, before putting it back in her purse, and turning away.

"See something you like?" he asked as he looked over the display trying to work out what had caught her eye.

"Nah, not really, it's ok, and we're here for gifts, not me… come on we got loads more to get... you do know I only brought you along to carry my bags?" She replied jokingly, before glancing back over her shoulder.

"Yes, your majesty, I am your humble servant…" he joked placing his arms on her shoulders, pretending to massage them.

"Didn't your dad give you £50 to get yourself something?" He asked.

She stopped, pausing before replying...

"What do you think I'm using to buy all these presents?"

He went back to that store trying to work out what caught her eye. He spotted the small sterling silver Celtic cross.

Simple and delicate with a small blue stone in the centre. He paid for it without hesitation. He sat holding it in his hand hoping she would like it, hoping that he'd chosen correctly. He closed the box, wrapping it up, and placing it on his bedside table wondering how to give it to her.

Christmas eve, he could hear the family downstairs, he contemplated joining them. His phone pinged.

Happy Christmas Eve! Are you coming church tomorrow? Gotta give you your present. I'm going to Matt's for Christmas dinner after... Will make a change from being sat at home... alone! If I don't see you, I'll pop round after if that's Ok? Got a little something for the family.

He sat in contemplation. Hitting reply he hovered his finger over the buttons, wondering what to write.

Hey.. I'm gonna go to Church with the family, make an effort and all, but it'll be finished long before acorn is... I'll swing round after on Buzby?

His phone pinged...

OK. See ya tomorrow xx

Putting his phone down he smiled, then shrugged his shoulders,

"Best go make an effort!" he said to himself as he stood up.

He entered the living room as they were about to start a new game of monopoly.

"Any space for me?" Rob asked from the doorway.

His father looked up, beckoning him in. He looked at his father closely. A playful smile appeared on his face. The twinkle in his eyes shone brighter than any Christmas lights. That evening felt like being part of a real family rather than being the outsider, he wondered whether it would last or just a passing phase.

Christmas morning, the same as every Christmas morning which came before. His mother took a break from the kitchen preparing the Christmas dinner once everyone was downstairs.

They all sat, opening one present at a time so everyone could "appreciate" each other's gifts. After the obligatory "oohs" and "aahs," holding up their presents for family review, before moving onto the next person.

He looked at everyone around him, Isabela's beaming smile, Levi rummaging through the discarded wrapping paper, his tail not wagging side to side but going around and round like a helicopter blade. He was thankful for having a family, to be able to celebrate Christmas together, all the things he used to take for granted. His family wasn't perfect, but at least he had one.

After the presents, they got ready for church. Rob hovered around the door.

"Mamma, I'm taking my bike cause I'm heading straight to Imogen's church straight after…." He paused waiting for a reaction

He continued "I'll be straight back after the service finishes…"

He waited, holding his breath for a reaction, one that didn't come.

"OK" his mother responded.

He held the door open as everyone exited the house, he stood for a moment, confused as to what had just happened.

He locked up, pulled Buzby out of the garage, watching as the family made their way up the road to church. He pulled up at the church, parking Buzby securely in the church carpark, before walking around the side of the building to the entrance, in time to meet his family, entering the church together.

The church always felt dingy and uninspiring, and the congregation brought to mind an old people's home and a hospital outpatients department in equal measures. He sat on the cold pews, thinking how they could have put the heating on in advance, it was so cold you could see your breath. The service finished, he gave the required pleasantries, before quickly walking out of the church and running around to the car park, to Buzby, to head along to Whitley bay. He looked at his watch, knowing that the service would have started 10 minutes earlier...

He muttered to himself as he jumped on his bike, tearing out of the carpark along the Broadway. The roads were eerily quiet. He arrived outside the church.

"Well, should have only missed 15 minutes he told himself as he unfastened his helmet, hearing the sound of the worship group through the open doors.

As he walked through the doors the warmth hit him, a stark contrast to his family's church. he started bobbing his head to the rhythm of the drums.

Following the service, he mingled with members of the congregation before searching for Imogen. He spotted her tidying away the wires. She flicked her long brown hair to one side in an unconscious act, something he'd watch her do so many times though this time something caught his eyes.

Dangling from her small perfect lobes were long gold earrings which although looked exquisite, and accentuated the length of her neck, they looked out of place, he could see them pulling down on her lobes.

He'd never seen her wear long earrings, whenever she'd worn any before they were small, usually silver, and not something you would be drawn too. He thought how they must have cost more than he got in a month! He watched her tug at them uncomfortably. He thought how they must have been from Jacob, thinking how instead of getting something she would like, he got her something which screams, look at me, look at how great a boyfriend I am…

He realised they had held his gaze too long, and with his mind drifting he hadn't noticed her walking towards him, and as if able to read his mind. She answered.

"Christmas present off Jacob… They're nice, but not really me" she laughed as she rubbed her aching lobes.

"Nah, definitely not you… But I hope this is!" he replied reaching out with the small present.

He watched as she opened it, her face lit up, biting her bottom lip she tried to hide the grin which was trying to escape.

"I love it!" she beamed hugging him.

He took the necklace and placed it round her neck, gently scooping her hair out of the way before fastening the clasp. She turned, he watched it fall delicately in the centre of her neck.

"So where is posh boy anyways?" he asked breaking the moment.

"It's Christmas day, so he is with the family, and I'm banned 'cause well, I'm not the right fit for them, I guess… Though I did go to midnight mass with them"

"You... at midnight mass? That would have been a sight" he laughed thinking of the time he dragged her to church with his family.

"Yep…...You gotta do what you gotta do…." She replied pretending to yawn.

"So, are you going to give me a lift to Matt's? You know, I could go in the car with them, but I prefer to ride in style" she winked, smiling her cheeky smile while biting her bottom lip.

"When have I ever refused you?" he asked in reply

She scrunched her face, biting her bottom lip with her finger resting upon it, as if to demonstrate that she was thinking.

"Hmm, don't think so..." she laughed as she nudged him playfully in the shoulder.

"But I think you need to take those hideous things out of your ears before putting your helmet on... don't want them getting caught and ripping your ears up..." He instructed.

"Yeah, good idea... They are really starting to annoy me" she laughed as she began unfastening the clip and removing them from her ears, before placing them in her pocket, and following Rob out to the bike.

"Oh, yeah, forgot... drop me at yours. I've got a little something for the family, and a dog toy for Levi... I'll then walk around to Matt's" She interrupted while fastening her straps.

"Trying to score brownie points?" he replied sarcastically.

"And well what about me?" he continued.

She feigned a look of shock as she punched him in the shoulder raising her eyebrows.

"Ow! Pack it with the abuse" he spoke rubbing his arm pretending to be hurt, though she couldn't punch her way out of a paper bag.

"I've got your present right here, but if you're going to keep misbehaving, I'll not give you it!" she replied jokingly.

"Yes miss… Sorry miss" he replied while trying to keep a straight face.

They arrived outside his house. Rob pushed Buzby up the drive, and into the garage. Imogen followed. As they stood alone in the garage Imogen looked up at him with those puppy dog eyes that he could never resist.

"Hey, before we go in… Here's your present" Imogen spoke softly as she removed a small box from her rucksack, passing it too him.

She held her breath as he took hold of it, their hands touching for a moment. She breathed out before taking a deep breath in, wondering if he would like it and whether it was an appropriate present for a 'friend'.

He opened it to find a silver St Christopher.

"To keep you safe whenever you're on the road, 'cause God needs all the help he can get when it comes to you…" she laughed.

He looked down at her, taking her hand, their eyes met. The moment was broken as Levi came bombing through the door from the kitchen running between them, almost knocking Imogen off her feet.

"Yes! Levi!" she spoke as she knelt down to his level, taking out a wrapped present from her bag, pressing on it to make it squeak before passing it to him.

With the wrapped toy in his mouth he continued to make it squeak, incessantly, as he ran back through the house. "Thanks for that!" Rob commented, shaking his head.

"Your welcome!" she replied sarcastically, following Levi through the kitchen and into the house.

Chapter 13

A few days later, Sunday. Rob arrived at church; his face dropped as he spotted Jacob. He walked up to Imogen leaning in for a hug, looking at Jacob out of the corner of his eye.

He felt a feeling of triumph as Jacob looked on feeling jealous and intimidated... Rob turned away with a slight grin on his face.

To him she wasn't someone to be owned or a piece of property to be won.

Was Jacob jealous of their friendship?? He thought. As he took his seat, he thought why should he be jealous? Jacob had her, and well there was nothing romantic between them.

He knew it would be unlikely that he'd see her before they returned to college.

The days up until new year's was a blur, filled with boredom. New Year's Eve instead of going out to some crazy party he decided to ride down to the quayside to watch the fireworks. As the fireworks lit up the sky, he took time to reflect on that year which he was stepping out of. He took a moment to acknowledge how far he'd come in that year. The year he met Imogen and for some unknown reason that changed him. Thinking how he had begun focusing on the relationships that really mattered, surrounding himself with people who would be there when he needed someone.

Making real friendships rather than being used as cheap entertainment. He could see his efforts to make this world a better place, to dwell on the positives, rather than sinking in the depths of the darkness which regularly consumed him. As the clock chimed in the new year he was soaked in the atmosphere, taking in a deep and relaxing breath, as the quayside erupted in cheers and the words Happy New Year resounded down the river.

The New Year had come, another year alive, and beginning a new year, excited about what it would bring. He returned home to bed, sober, starting the year on a high.

He was awoken by Levi, nuzzling at his face... He looked over at his clock 9am. Rubbing his tired eyes with the insides of his palms, he pulled himself out of bed remembering how he'd agreed to a bike ride with Charlie, though not a bike ride on Buzby, but a ride on his old pushbike, he'd agreed as part of a New Year's resolution to get fit.

He'd been friends with Charlie for many years, not really friends, more of an ally, someone a little older, supposedly wiser, someone to put the world to rights with.

In the garage he gave his pushbike the once over, oiling the cogs, gears and chain, and checking the breaks.
He looked at his phone.

We still on for a ride or are you bottling it?

He sent a quick reply

Yes, am still up for it, see you outside the bay in 20!

He packed his bag, shouted through to the house that he was off, but got no reply. He opened the garage door, sunlight beamed through, his eyes adjusting to the light. The sunshine was brilliant but deceptive, unable to penetrate the coldness of winter.

Reaching the Bay, he waited patiently for Charlie to arrive, looking around unsure which direction he would be coming from.

After a few moments he saw him cycling towards him, stopping in front of him, reaching out his hand as though for a high handshake. Charlie smiled like a long-lost brother. Rob reciprocated reaching out his hand taking hold of his with the perfect squeeze and eye contact, before leaning in for a casual manly hug.

"So, up the coast then down the beehive, and back?"

Charlie asked straightening his back, his hands gripping the handlebars, ready to move.

"... Or is that too far for someone out of shape?" he continued laughing.

"Shut ya face and ride!" Rob replied as his foot hit the pedal, pushing down to gain momentum.

They cycled along the coast covering the miles pedalling, his legs remaining in motion, admiring the view, taking in the beauty around him. It was just like being on Buzby, but slower, and he was having to work harder, but whenever he climbed on two wheels and hit the road, he was always keen for more...

It wasn't long till they hit the beehive, and they cruised down the twisting road which curved through the fields on either side, the road dipping and swaying, constantly changing, which created long stretches broken up by tight corners and chicanes,

"We stopping for a pint at the beehive?" Rob shouted over his shoulder to Charlie who was falling behind.

"I think you need a break old man" he continued, slowing the pace as the beehive pub came into view.

"Cheeky! And any excuse for a drink!" Charlie replied overtaking, before shouting back

"Loser buys the pints!"

"You're on!" Rob shouted taking the bet, pushing down on the pedal, pedalling faster, slipping through the gears as the road slanted uphill. Reaching the beehive a few seconds short of Charlie.

"Well, I guess I'm buying them, old man!" he exclaimed.

Sitting on the old rustic picnic table outside of the quaint little countryside pub, they sat drinking there much deserved pints.

"Cheers!" Charlie spoke lifting his glass to toast the new year.

Rob lifted his glass, reciprocating, the clink of the glasses mixing with the sound of the wind rustling through the trees. They sat talking, passing time.

As always, they bounced remarks back and forth like a kid's rubber ball, alcohol always intensified the roasting. They were never sure if they got wittier the more they drank, or if it was just the effect of the alcohol making everything seem so much funnier.

"Can you get done for drink riding in charge of a pushbike?" Rob asked returning from the bar with another 2 pints.

"Well, if anyone can it'd be you!" Charlie replied as memories filled his mind.

Memories of Rob riding away from the firestation pub after quite a few drinks, the bike swerving in all directions. Rob would never dared to get on Buzby after a drink, but a pushbike was different, a whole different ballgame!

Charlie steered the conversation away, though still laughing.

"Anyways.. I'm surprised you managed to make time for me since you're always off with that new girl of yours" Charlie commented as he took a sip of his pint before wiping away the foam from his lip.

"Shes not my girl she has a boyfriend who she loves, although I have no idea why! I'll always be second in her heart, but with a girl like her second is alright by me!"

Charlie almost choked on his drink, trying to clear his throat while trying not to laugh he replied.

"God! Have you had a personality transplant, abducted by aliens, or something!"

Rob sighed looking down at his pint.

"It's not like that, she's not some conquest, she is so much more. I don't know if I do like her in that way, maybe it's just everyone's opinions clouding what is real. The assumption that a girl and a boy can't be platonic, then there's my mama's expectations thrown in... But what I do know is she's more like me than anyone I know, and just when I think I know her, she throws a curveball and I learn something new which makes me in awe all over again. But, she's not some entitled princess..." His words trailed off.

"Sorry... I'm just kidding with ya mate... It's really good to see you doing well."

Finishing their pints, they went on again; following the road inland until they reached the hill path. It scrambled steeply up, and they plodded slowly one behind the other.

The late morning sky was adorned with wisps of drifting white cloud. He stopped for a moment admiring the view, the brilliant greens banished every dark thought, though those thoughts were becoming fewer and farther between. Rob's stomach rumbled as he realised, he'd skipped breakfast.

"Fancy stopping for a bite somewhere. I'm starved" Rob announced as Charlie caught up with him.

"Love to mate but I've got to get back, I'll be splitting off at Monks' but we have to do this again soon." Charlie replied, holding out his hand, to which Rob instinctively reciprocated, shaking on it.

They continued back down the old trail and onto the road into Monkseaton where Charlie split, leaving Rob to continue on, heading back home.

He entered the house through the garage, into the kitchen, shouting through that he was home, but the house was eerily empty. He shrugged his shoulders as though to indicate that he didn't care. Picking up the frying pan he tossed it in his hand as though flicking pancakes.

"Bacon sandwich it is!" he declared to himself.

As he walked through the corridor towards the stairs, he spotted a folded note by the telephone. Placing his plate on the small table he opened the note which detailed how they'd gone out for a walk, and possibly lunch, before detailing a list of chores for him to do.

"Well I wasn't here, so guess its not all their fault" he spoke to himself as he sauntered up the stairs to his room.

Sitting in his room, his happiness and optimism ebbed away, very quickly changing back to what had been his default. Feeling empty, deprived of any comfort, feeling worthless and disposable, wretched and cold.

"Guess I'm still a work in progress, or maybe I just need a change of scenery!" he spoke out loud as though having a conversation with himself.

"New Year. New resolutions" he continued as he through Levi's ball against the wall and catching it as it bounced back.

He thought about who he was.

He'd always been a giver, eager to please. Even as a child he hardly ever cried, seeking to make others happy. He returned to thinking about old friendships, and also family, those who so often sought him out in times of trouble, and he gave all he had, even to his own detriment. Yet whenever it was his time to need someone, when his time to suffer came, his world was suddenly empty, everyone turned away, everyone switched off,

"Well, all but one" he answered.

A few days into the new year he returned to college, and back to normality. The following months continued, with him and Imogen growing closer, and the bridge continuing to be a hive of friendships, all which centred around them either individually or as a pair.

Moments of emptiness still came like an ambush, yet in the company of a true friend a real smile can return, a real laugh, a real warmth.

Chapter 14

It wasn't long until the days began to lighten, spring was on the horizon, but after a mild Christmas and New Year, the weather turned, becoming colder, bringing snow, sleet and ice which put paid to their rides, both having withdrawal symptoms.

Easter was approaching, the half term only a few days away. It was late that year, the beginning of May.

They sat in English wearing matching tie-dyed t-shirts made the night before in an arts session which Rob had dragged her too. The sun was streaming down through the window, the sky clear. The perfect weather for a ride.

Imogen sat with her books open trying to study, the lesson being used as a time of self-study as their first-year exams were on the horizon. Rob was sitting next to her, as usual. Although he sat with his books open, instead of reading the book he was casually glancing through a bike magazine, making occasional responses aimed to distract Imogen. She tried but was failing to not look.

"Will you stop it?" she whispered so not to peak the attention of the teacher sat at the front.

"Our exams are coming soon!" she continued nudging him.

"Hey, don't interrupt me, I'm studying" he joked as Imogen stole the magazine from his hands, placing it under the desk, pretending to cough as the teacher looked up from her book, looking in their direction.

"I didn't know bikes were on the curriculum" she muttered under her breath as she gave a side glance trying desperately to hide the smile which was being teased out.

Imogen looked back down again trying to read the open textbook, twiddling her pen in her hand. She glanced over to him, as he also looked over in her direction, pulling a funny face. She turned her glance away again looking at the book in front of her,

She couldn't resist looking back up.

"God! I've read the same sentence 15 times!" she tried not to laugh.

"You're such a bad influence!" she continued smiling, knowing that although at times he drove her crazy, and disturbed her study, she had never had a friend like him, or really had a friend at all.

As the lesson was nearly over, and the bell would be ringing soon, Rob slipped a folded note across the table. Imogen opened the note, the words....

You, Me, Buzby, open road......??????

Nodding, and unable to contain the smile which crept across her face, she began watching the clock, the minutes ticked by slowly. Waiting. The anticipation building.

As the bell sounded, Imogen threw her books in her bag. Taking her hand, he ran out of the classroom and down the corridor, like an excited child. Out of the side door, the bridge overhead.

Buzby stood waiting. Rob passed her the spare helmet which had practically become hers. He fastened his leather jacket. Climbed on, turned the key and just sat for a moment, listening to the purr of the engine.

"Hop on my lady your stallion awaits!" He spoke with a cheeky grin and a glint in his eye.

She'd heard those words so many times before, but they never got old. He fastened his helmet as Imogen climbed on behind, wrapping her arms around him. They headed out of town, hitting the country roads,

"Do you really trust me?" He asked over his shoulder as they sat at traffic lights.

"You know I do!" she shouted in reply.

"Hold on! You've been on her plenty of times before but today I'm gonna really show you what this old girl can do! And... Remember, mirror me!" he shouted as he opened the throttle wide.

The road stretched onward, hugging the land, Rob took each turn in his easy stride,

"Whooo!" Imogen screamed as they reached speeds she'd never been at before.

Over their many rides she had begun to learn to mirror his movements, but this ride took it to a whole new level. Leaning into the corners so that they were almost parallel with the surface, almost defying gravity, bringing a high which she had never felt before. Riding with him was like a drug, always wanting more. A few miles outside of Corbridge Rob pulled into the layby, the spot where they had stopped so many times before.

"That was awesome!" she squealed hugging him like an excited child who had overdosed on sugar.

She collapsed onto the grass, pretending to make 'snow angels', staring at the clouds, slowly travelling across the sky, in blissful contentment. Feeling calm, relaxed and sleepy, coming down from the high, soothed by the gentle warm wind was discreetly singing a silent lullaby.

He couldn't help but feel amused thinking how one moment she was so innocent and child-like, yet in many ways she was more mature than most her age, portraying a wisdom which many spend their lifetimes searching for.

She turned her head to her right, looking at Rob who had laid down next to her, also staring at the clouds. He turned his gaze towards her.

"Why are you with Jacob?" Rob asked

Imogen failed to answer.

"You and me, we make a good team, don't we? I can't give you a long life together, we probably wouldn't grow old together, but it can be fun while it lasts"

Avoiding the real question, as she couldn't answer it truthfully, she answered.

"Shut up you fool! You'll be around forever! You'll be Godfather to my kids, and I'll be killing you for leading them astray, like you do me"

"I can really see Jacob allowing me to be godfather..." Rob laughed as he pushed Imogen down the hill, rolling down after her.

She sat up, pursing her lips.

"Hey, its Spring Harvest back end of next week... There's still spaces if ya fancy joining me? You, me, tent? Am sure we can get up to some crazy antics!?" she declared, hoping he would join her.

He scrunched his face shrugging his shoulders.

"Come on! There'll be archery and all other bunch of crazy activities…. I need my partner in crime…. And our band are playing on the last night… I thought you were my groupie?" She continued almost begging, though it didn't take much to twist his arm.

He thought how a year ago he'd rather slit his wrists than go to some Christian holiday, but he was up for anything if Imogen was in.

"I knew you'd agree… I think you'd probably do anything I ask… I like having a servant, my knight upon a silver stead" she replied winking.

"If you say so…" he laughed as they headed back towards the bike.

Climbing on to Buzby, Rob turned slightly towards Imogen as she stood fastening her helmet

"You know servants and knights get paid, slaves don't, so if I'm your servant dear Princess how do you plan on paying me for my quality services?"

"Hmm.. I guess we'll have to negotiate that one I think!" she replied as she climbed onto the bike wrapping her arms around his waist.

Monday, the first day of the Easter break. Rob sat on the pavement painting the fence, at his mother's request.

He spotted Imogen walking up the path, he smiled, though his smile soon faded as she came closer. Her red eyes giving away the tears which had fallen.

"I had to come here, I had nowhere else…. I can't be alone but can't go anywhere else, need somewhere to hang…. The nurse said I needed to be with someone just in case…." Her words tailed off.

Rob looked on with concern, trying to guess what she meant as she wasn't making any sense. Imogen explained that she been to Drs for the morning after pill.

"I already feel like I'm literally going to throw up, but I don't know if that's just because it was one of the symptoms I was told I'd have, don't know if it's all in my mind or not, whatever.. I deserve to feel rotten…" she sobbed.

"I feel so stupid!" she continued.

"Why didn't Jacob go with you?" He asked, though he was in part glad she'd came to him.

"He had some family thing, told me to go deal with it." Imogen sobbed in his arms.

He had thought that nothing that guy could do would shock him, but he was constantly being proved wrong. Rob held her in his arms.

"Sometimes I want to kill that guy, I'd happily do time for you… and don't go trying to defend the waste of space" he spoke holding her.

"You should have rang me, you know I would have been there in a heartbeat!" he continued reassuringly.

"I know you would" Imogen smiled

Look it's a lovely day, I'll go get a blanket and make you a hot cup of tea and we'll put the music on and we can just lie in the garden for a little while, then when you're feeling a bit better we can finish the fence, together.. Deal?" he suggested.

He walked into the house, went to the kitchen to put on the kettle then ran upstairs grabbing a blanket. He lay it on the grass,

"Right! Drink!" he commented as Imogen lay on the blanket soaking up the sun's rays, with Levi jumping at her, pawing with his fore paws for attention, his wet tongue licking furiously upon her face, before burying his head in her armpit.

As he stood in the kitchen waiting for the kettle to boil, he heard his mother shouting from behind him.

"Roberto, why are you not painting the fence like you promised, slacking off as usual!"

"No mama. I'm just taking a short break, it will get done...Imi is here, she's not feeling well, I'm making her a drink and going to sit with her a while then will get fence finished."

"Imogen... Is she ok...? My sweet girl... You go look after her, I'll bring out drinks, ask her if she wants any food".

Rob sighed at the sudden change in his mother's tone, knowing that nothing had really changed, he still was never good enough, it just wasn't always on the surface now, especially when Imogen was around. Maybe, just an act, a deflection to hide who she really was, to give the impression she was the perfect mother, but then, any break from his mother's normal behaviour was a nice break considering how domineering she was.

"Oh, and I'm going away over Easter weekend... I'm going to Spring Harvest with Church for a few days, leaving Wednesday...

We'll be back Sunday night." He instructed as he carried the drinks outside.

Imogen's phone vibrated. She looked at the message.

Have you dealt with it!?

As a tear began to fall, she replied

Yes

She placed her phone on silent, placing it face down on the grass, and lay back, trying not to look at her phone.

He watched her fidget on the blanket, knowing she could never sit still for long, like him she was always on the go, living life fast, at times it was like looking in a mirror. Finishing her drink, she sat upright folding her arms.

"Right!" she declared.

"I've had enough of sitting here... Didn't you say we had a fence to paint?" she asked as she picked up the paintbrush.

"That's my paintbrush miss!" he joked, fighting her for it as she placed it behind her back, running around the garden.

"I'll go get you one" he replied as she ignored him and walked over to the fence, beginning to paint.

He returned sitting next to her, without a second thought he brought his paintbrush up to her face, applying a spot of paint to her nose, causing her for a moment to look mad, holding her brush up, ready in retaliation, before pursing her lips trying not to smile though her dimples deceiving her.

"I'm not going to stoop to your level of childishness" she spoke trying to be sensible.

"That'll be a first!" he replied laughing.

In reply to his comment her brush made contact with his cheek, she couldn't hold in her laughter any longer. He smiled back in return, that cheeky grin which declared his mission was complete, that even if for a while she was happy, and had forgotten about the events of that day.

As the late morning turned to afternoon, they took a short walk along the front, as Imogen was overcome by cramps. He held her in his arms, still trying to hold down his rage. They returned to his house sitting on the sofa, Imogen sat next to him before placing her head on his lap. He pulled the blanket over her, gently stroking through her hair as though to soothe her.

Time passed. Imogen looked up. The clock on the wall, indicated it was 4pm, yet she lay down at 2pm. She sat up confused, her memory of the time was no more than ten minutes, twenty at the most. With a long exhale came the tell-tale signs that her brain was still waking from a nap, the remnants of a dream still lingering, grasping to remain.

"Hey sorry, I've been crap company" she apologised continuing to wipe her eyes.

"Yeah I know I'm so boring I drove you to sleep" he answered, before smiling.

"You know I don't mind" he winked.

She looked at her phone, filled with notifications of missed calls and messages. She shrugged, placing her phone back down deciding not to answer.

"Thanks for everything" she responded full of gratitude, as he pulled her in for a hug.

"So what we going to do now? The day is still young" He asked, leaning back.

"Wave dodging? Bike ride? Or another movie? Though this time I won't fall asleep, unless you choose something cheesy!" she replied.

"Me, cheesy? As if!" he responded as Imogen raised her eyebrows, nodding.

She stayed till early evening before Rob took her home.

Chapter 15

Rob sat in his room, a warm Wednesday afternoon in May. The warm spring sunlight streaming through his window. The phone rang, the ringtone revealing that it was Imogen calling...

"Hey Hey, what ya doin' " Rob answered.

"Hey, just dropped my bags of at Church... The bus is leaving in an hour-ish.. Wondering where you're at?! We're gonna have SO much fun!"

Rob laughed, "Yeah... God help them! Am just getting ready to leave, meet you at the church soon."

"OK, see ya soon, just don't be late! I think I'm going to head into town to get some sweets and pop and stuff for the bus journey"

"Grab some for me, I'll see you in 20!" Rob replied before hanging up, fastening his bag, heading downstairs.

"See you in a few days Mamma" he shouted as he walked out of the house, not bothering to wait for a response.
He crossed the street to catch the bus into Whitley.

Imogen walked into town to pick up some supplies for the long journey. She began walking back down to church, happy in her own world. The sound of someone walking behind her made her feel nervous. She quickened her step, resisting looking back. She could hear laughing. She turned to look.

As she turned a fist struck her face, the world around her began spinning as she lost her balance, falling to the floor catching the back of her head on the brick wall alongside her. She closed her eyes tightly, afraid to look, hoping that was it, that they'd continue walking. She raised her hand to shield her face. She curled her fingers into the palm of her hands, not even feeling them dig in.

A foot made contact with her stomach as she crouched into the foetal position. Panic began to override every sensation of pain, too exhausted to move, only able to breathe. Her shoulders shook in fear as they took it in turns to kick her.

For a few moments it stopped, she removed her hands, opening her eyes to look around, all she saw was the sole of a trainer making contact with her face.

Soon they'd had enough and walked on laughing. Opening her eyes, slowly and cautiously she looked around, noticing they were no longer there. She didn't see their faces, maybe she knew them from school, she thought, though with her history she knew they could have just been random youths, looking for a bit of fun. She'd begun to lose count of the number of times she was attacked. She couldn't understand why. She began to think that maybe she had a label on her that she couldn't see.

A label that said, "attack me, beat me, bully me, make my life hell".

She pulled herself to a sitting position, shuffling till her back was against the wall, she waited, unable to move, in shock as her mind replayed the attack, and the pain began to become more evident as the adrenaline began to wear off. She remained seated, looking up and down the street making sure they'd gone, people continued to walk past oblivious to her, she was invisible. She reached for her phone dialling the first person who came to her mind, the one person who was always there.

Rob answered.

"I'm at church before you ask, or what have you forgotten?" he laughed.

"You know I left Buzby at home" he continued. Imogen didn't reply. All he could hear was her crying, sobbing down the phone, unable to piece the words together.

"I've been attacked..." she spluttered finally able to form words. She slowly climbed to her feet, noticing a blood stain left on the wall which she was using to steady herself.

"Where?" he asked, shocked and concerned.

"I'm walking back now, I'm just up the street, I'll be back soon, I just need to hear your voice, keep talking to me..." She continued as she slowly walked up the street.

His voice gave her the strength to keep going, as she staggered along the street, almost falling through the church door. Rob tried not to stare at her face, but he kept finding his eyes diverting to it. Drawn to her red-rimmed eyes, and cut lip, watching her bottom lip tremble. She fell into his open arms.

"Sshh.. It's Ok. I'm here..." He spoke softly, reassuringly trying to contain his anger.

He held her tightly, not wanting to let go. His hand rested on the back of her head, as she rested her head against his chest. Part of him wanted to run out the doors, find the thugs and return the favour, but as she clung to him, he knew he was needed there.

After a few moments in his arms she stepped back.

"I've just gotta go to the bathroom..." She spoke, still shaking.

"OK, I'll go make you a hot cup of tea..." he replied filled with concern, glancing down at his hand, seeing the blood from her head upon his palm. He wondered how anyone could hurt her.

Imogen stood staring at her reflection in the mirror in the toilets, frozen to the spot, her hands tightly gripping the sink, the tears began to fall.

"Hey"

She could hear Rob through the partially opened door. She turned to look in his direction...

"Hey" he repeated softly, slowly entering the toilets.

"It's alright," he whispered. Pulling her in for an embrace,

"You can cry." He continued, which was all the permission she needed.

"Sometimes I just wish they'd finish the job and just kill me!" she let slip out, though wishing she could take back those words.

"Hey... Well I for one am glad they didn't...." he answered continuing to hold her tightly, wishing he could take all her pain away.

A few minutes passed, she stepped back, wiping her eyes.

Smiling she laughed,

"You do know you're in the female toilets"

"Really? I didn't know!" He answered sarcastically, laughing and shaking his head,

"Come on! Your drink will be getting cold" he said taking her hand, leading her back out into the church hall.

The church leaders wanted to call the police, wanting her to go to hospital to be checked over, which meant leaving her behind.

"The police had never been any use before" she stated to their disbelief.

She refused to go to hospital or home, begging, insisting there would be more people to watch over her at harvest than back at home. Luckily with one of the leaders being a doctor, they agreed.

They climbed on the bus for the long journey ahead.

They arrived at spring harvest; it was a good week tarnished by the attack. The days were filled with seminars and worship, fun activities, sports, games interlaced with free time. The weather was hot, more like summer than spring.

The Saturday, they spent the day down by the lake.

Imogen sat on the jetty, leaning back, feeling the hot noon sunrays on her body. The lake was as flat as a mirror, without a ripple in the silver-blue water as if time itself had been frozen.

She removed her t-shirt revealing a crop top and shorts. Rob stared at her, the bruises were beginning to show, purple marks deepening over the week, noticeable against her pale skin.

Imogen dangled her feet over the edge, kicking lazily at the cool water which sent ripples, creating widening circles until they disappeared, toying with the idea of swimming. It would be something to do, a break from the sweltering heat, thoughts swam in her head.

Her head felt hot, the heat sinking into her black hair. She turned to her side and dangled her arm down to catch the water with her fingertips.

"You're looking a bit hot there!" Rob called over, laughing.

"So do you!" she joked in reply, scooping some water in her hand she splashed it in his direction.

"Oh, so this is how we're playing is it?" he replied playfully, reaching for a bucket and filling it with water, before throwing it over her.

"That'll cool you down" he laughed

"Oh really?" she replied standing up, grabbing hold of his shirt, she stepped back, stepping off the edge of the jetty, pulling him in with her. The cool water moved over their skin as they swam.

"Are you cold?" she asked as she watched him begin to shiver.

"Me, cold? Never!" he exclaimed.

She was a surfer so was used of the colder water of the North Sea. He had always shuddered at the thought of giving it a try whenever she suggested he join her.

"Come on!" she continued taking his hand and swimming back to shore. Climbing up on the jetty, she picked up her t-shirt, using it to dry her hair.

"What about me?" Rob asked.

Imogen looked at him shaking her head,

"You've almost got no hair, come on... race you back, I'm planning on whooping your ass at archery this afternoon" she said as she grabbed his arm pulling him along.

As they walked back to camp, Matt was getting out of his car, unloading his guitar.

"Do you two ever just act normal?" he shouted over, looking at the two of them resembling drowned rats.

"Never!" she shouted excitedly.

"Life would be so boring!" she continued laughing, dragging Rob up to the main camp site to dry off.

The afternoon was spent at the archery range on site.

"I'm gonna whip your ass!" He spoke as he took aim, taking his shot, straight and on target.

He smirked observing where his arrow had landed, taking a moment, acting casual he positioned his second arrow, then a third, each as perfect as the last.

"Beat that!" he smirked, almost daring her,

Imogen pulled back on the bow, before letting go, watching the arrow fly through the air, missing the target by a couple of inches, Rob laughed. Imogen pulled a stern face, with renewed determination. Playing off each other, daring each other and winning had become a crazy pastime for them. Imogen took aim, filled with concentration, hitting the target with each shot.

"Not bad..." he nodded as he removed the arrows from the target, handing them back to her.

"But I still win!" He exclaimed dancing, displaying the cheeky grin which always melted her heart.

"You won this round!" she exclaimed, wondering what she could challenge him with next.

That evening after dinner Imogen walked into the main tent, their church band were providing the worship that evening.

"You've missed a good few days Matt" she spoke as she began sorting the leads, Matt looked over.

"I can imagine...." He replied.

Imogen could sense something in his tone.

"If you've got something to say, say it!" she replied.

He hesitated for a moment.

"You know... You've got a boyfriend. Not that you act like you have... You know I really like Rob and all but..."

Imogen shook her head, rolling her eyes,

"Me and Rob are just mates... He gets me.... Girls and boys can be just friends without there being something in it!"

"OK" He replied

"And if only you knew!" she muttered under her breath, that past week still feeling raw, but Jacob was nothing but perfect in his family's eyes.

It was through them that she first met him. Sienna and David were good friends with Jacob's parents. From that first meeting his parents had looked down on her with disdain, as though she was a piece of dirt, the project kid that their friends had taken on. Although Matt's parents at times treated her as part of the family there was always a degree of separation. Photos of Jacob featured on their wall, yet she never found herself gaining that position. She knew Jacob would always be perfect in their eyes and maybe she'd always be the messed up broken girl that needed to be hidden away.

"What? Did you say something?" Matt asked, breaking her thoughts.

"Me? No!" she replied.

"Let's get this stuff set up" She continued, coldly. Dwelling on the fact he hadn't commented on her injuries, or where she had got them from, it felt as though the only one who cared was Rob.

His words though pulled at her a little. Was she walking a tightrope, dangerously balancing between friends and so much more? She had texted and spoken to Jacob on the phone, but his attitude was so nonchalant that it hurt.

That evening Rob watched as Imogen stepped up to the microphone to sing, the voice of an angel, he never tired of listening to her. He watched her, her black eye still visible, under her make-up. The attack continued to haunt him. He thought about the hidden scars, the internal scars that such an attack would leave. He remembered the conversations they'd had before, conversations about assaults before, but he'd never really understood.

Following the worship, he looked at her, it was as if she could read his mind, she knew the questions going through his head. He'd been going to the church with her for months, he had always been in awe of her faith. No matter what happened, nothing ever shook it. He couldn't understand. His scars, his past and his pain was still there, and putting faith in some God didn't wipe all that away, he was still living with the ghosts, but he was beginning to see some hope, some light at the end of the tunnel, just it wasn't enough yet, and wondered would it ever be.

She nodded,

"I'm still sad, I'm still scared; I don't know if that will ever change, I don't know if all these bad things, these attacks, everything, whether any of it will change, but it won't rock my faith, I know that in every storm there is always an eye. Always a safe place in the midst of destruction. Jesus will always be my eye when storms of sorrow come; and I know that never once will he leave me on my own, and...."

She punched him playfully in the arm,

"... and, I'll also always have you there with me riding the storm and in the eye."

As Imogen's passionate words faded, he took her hand.
"Yep... I'll always be there, whatever you need..."

She twisted her face...

"Hmmm, well I do remember you promising to teach me to ride! And I'm now 17, so am legal....." she stated, mischievously hinting.

"When we get back home... I promise..." he replied.

"Pinkie promise?" she asked holding up her little finger, his little finger joined hers.

"Deal" he said smiling.

He thought how she seemed to manage to keep up the pretence, even in front of him, but he could see the tears she tried to hide,

and could hear her crying at night when she thought he was asleep.

The weekend, ended far too quickly, the Sunday afternoon they climbed onboard the bus heading back home.

Chapter 16

They pulled up in the carpark behind the Park hotel at dusk.

"You ready to learn to ride?" He asked.

"Though, you better go easy on Buzby.. she has feelings you know…"

She climbed on Buzby gripping the handlebars, Rob leaned over, behind her, resting his hands on top of hers.

"Pull in the left lever all the way and then push the left gear pedal down until it clicks"

"Ok done that!" She replied nervously…

"Then open the throttle a little bit and slowly ease out the clutch lever." He continued, slowly moving his hands away.

Listening to the sound of the engine she slowly released the clutch, the bike shot forward, then silence as she stalled the bike, placing her feet on the ground, wobbling, trying to stop herself falling.

"Oops!" she giggled.

"Ok, let's try again but this time give it more throttle" he replied patiently.

"You'll get this" he spoke reassuringly

She thought how he always had faith in her, when no-one else ever did.

"Right". She declared as she started the engine, pulling in the clutch with her shaking hand.

She opened the throttle a bit wider and released the clutch a bit too quick. The bike shot forwards, the surprise of this and the acceleration caused her throttle hand to twist even more and with panic and no real knowledge of how to stop the bike she spanned the length of the car park.

"I'm doing it!" she screamed excitedly, though quickly followed by shouting,

"You never told me how to stop!" she continued as she crashed into the hedge!

Rob laughed picking her up, then picking up Buzby.

"Sorry buzby.." he said as he patted the engine.
Imogen shook her head, laughing...

"You and that bike!"

They sat on the hill looking over the long sands.

"You know I got a letter today... with a cheque in it..." Imogen spoke sadly.

"Compensation... for all that stuff that happened in London when I was younger. It doesn't feel right"

Rob held her hand as she poured out her thoughts, did she want it? It felt like dirty money, a pay-off. She talked of how no amount of money could undo it all.

"It won't undo anything..." Rob replied attentively.

"...but that doesn't mean you shouldn't use it... Do something with it, something for you, be selfish for once, and do something fun! You gotta live for now..."

Passing her a drink he continued...

"You know...... Just a wild suggestion... But maybe you could use the money to get some proper lessons, I doubt Buzby could cope with another ride by you..."

He nudged her on the shoulder

"Ow!" she replied

"...And maybe buy your own bike so Buzby can have a bit of company?"

"You're crazy!!!" she replied

"...But I like it!" she continued with a wild glint in her eye.

The following day the sun was shining like a summer's day. They walked along the front towards Tynemouth, eating ice cream. As they turned the corner the Priory came into sight. As he looked ahead at the Priory, he thought about the words she blurted out back at church before leaving for Spring harvest.

"Have you ever thought about suicide?" Rob asked breaking the silence,

Imogen paused, looking out to sea. They had spoken about so much over the past few months but was she ready to open that box, to reveal her darkest moments?

"Yes.." she replied as she sat on the grass, Rob sat beside her.

"I guess my first suicidal thoughts were when I was probably seven. Back in London. The night after…. You know… well I was sat there, afraid to enter the flat, thinking what if next time I'm not so lucky, maybe next time nothing will stop it from happening... I can remember it very clearly, I think the way I voiced that was, I wish I'd have never been born then thinking if I died right now it would solve everything…. Then I came back up North… I can't remember if I thought that way again, though I probably did, but not seriously"

She hesitated, thinking, her mind replaying memories. As she looked out at the sea, she thought of the time she stood on the bridge looking over ready to jump, to end it all...

She continued… "I guess, it wasn't until a few years later, I think 13 ish….Some girls were holding my head over the platform at Wallsend, with a metro coming… in that moment I wanted the train to hit me…. I wanted so badly for it to be over, for that to be the end, and when it wasn't, I felt disappointment so the next day I climbed over the bridge, the one at burn bank... but I couldn't do it…... I wanted to die but couldn't take that step. I wasn't really a Christian then, but it felt like God was telling me I had so much to do, I had a purpose, do you get what I mean?" she asked, fleetingly looking up but then evading his gaze...

He nodded, listening, not wanting to speak. Not knowing what to say in response.

She continued "I guess since then it has reared its ugly head occasionally, I guess the thought is always there…. I find myself sometimes, like when I have been attacked thinking let this be it… I guess I'm not afraid of dying just afraid of who I'll leave behind... Though no-one really needs me"

He stood up taking her hand, holding her, softly kissing her forehead.

"I need you. You don't realise how much of an impact you've had on my life; you changed my world, I need you," he paused taking her hand.

"Come on" he continued leading her along the coast till they were stood overlooking the priory.

"I never changed you" she replied.

"Do you trust me?" Rob asked, holding out his hand. Imogen nodded, placing her hand in his.

"I want to show you somewhere" he spoke as he led her around the back of the priory, lifting her over the barriers, and up the side of the cliffs, leading her to a ledge. The ledge was man-made, concrete but it looked like it just grew right out of the ground, like a rocky outcrop, rustic and rough.

It was wide enough to sit back against the cliff with their feet outstretched. They sat watching the waves crash below.

"I come here a lot, though when I used to come here, I'd spend my time thinking of just jumping, falling into those waves below... Then I met you, and you gave me purpose, you showed me who I really was, and the darkness isn't as dark anymore"

She silently nodded, as though she understood. The tears began to fall.

"Hey, it's Ok" he spoke reassuringly wiping away the tears from her cheek.

"I'm a mess..." she replied trying to look away.

"I think we're both a mess" he replied nudging her, his reassuring smile comforting her.

"I get it, the darkness..." She spoke.

"It can creep up on you, I don't know, I guess in those moments I cry, but then sometimes I just cry, I can't control my tears. God, I've cried over some stupid things, but then sometimes, there is no tears, just emptiness. You know sometimes when you should cry, like at a funeral, but nothing comes, you know some people think I'm a nutcase. But, I think sometimes in the darkness, I'm afraid to cry, afraid to let it out 'cause the darkness can take over, I get scared in case I don't make it out again...."

Wiping her eyes, she looked up feeling a little embarrassed and vulnerable.

"I think I cry too much. Like, when I cry, I know who I really am. It's my strength and my weakness. Sometimes though I wish I could turn my tears off.... I guess, my emotions swirl like ocean currents..." She continued.

"You know... I actually got down on my knees and actually tried praying the other day" He spoke steering the conversation away.

"Really!? You actually prayed? My God, miracles do happen" she giggled squeezing his arm playfully.

"It's a bit high up here" Imogen spoke.

"....Good job I'm not afraid of heights...... but then I'm not really afraid of anything..." she continued.

He thought back to their conversation at the lighthouse, so many months earlier, she'd asked what his fears were, he'd asked the same in return, but as usual she deflected, not really answering the question that he had asked her.

He was never afraid to say what needed to be said, even if the truth was sharp.

"I think you're afraid to chase your dreams!" He answered.

"You're afraid of failure, of not being perfect I see you... you know I do... I see that you think that no matter how hard you try; you just can't do anything right. You can write thousands of words on a page, yet feel they're not good enough, nowhere near adequate. I see you create the most amazing choreography, or sing the most amazing song, then turn and say they weren't good enough, saying how 'this needs to change' and 'that needs editing' and 'this isn't good enough'" He stated.

His words hit a nerve which she wasn't comfortable addressing.

"I'm afraid? Maybe you're right but what about you??" she asked taking a pause, waiting for a reply which didn't come.

"You're afraid to think of the future.... Tell me.... What do you want to do with your life? What's your dream?" she continued.

He placed his hands behind his head

"I don't know nothing...not had one before... It's simply better not to want anything... it just doesnt matter."

"It does matter, and we all have dreams.... Come on what about when you were a kid, think back to when you were younger, what did you want? All kids want something..." she replied.

"As a kid.... I wanted to be a racing driver...... but that was never going to happen, there's no point having dreams when you're living on borrowed time."

"We all live on borrowed time, we never know when our time is up, I could die tomorrow, but I hope that when I die I will know I've lived my best life, and enjoyed the ride.."

"But you know exactly what you want....." he answered.

Imogen sighed.

"What do you want! What do you want now?" she continued probing...

"Ok.. There're things I want now that I never thought I wanted. And maybe I catch myself thinking maybe I could have them..." He replied, though Imogen was unaware of what he was meaning in part was her...

"Well chase those dreams... you know I heard it said if your dreams don't scare you, they ain't big enough"

"Bullshit!!! You talk to me about living your best life and following your dreams, yet you don't take your own advice!"

Placing his hand on her shoulder he spoke softly.

"Look, I'm sorry... really... but isn't it time you started fighting for what you want?"

"You know...I have never met anyone like you, or seen anyone dance the way you do, you sing with the voice of an angel, don't shut it away.... I've seen you shy away, and turn down gigs, it's always Jacob says, or Jacob wants.... The only time you sing in public now is church! Where is the girl who got up in front of a crowd of uni students back at Matt's gig??"

The tears again began to fall as his words struck a chord.

"Look, do something for me... Picture your life, next year, three years, hell, even twenty years! Where do you see yourself? What does it look like? If it's being a nobody, married to that jerk, being under the thumb then fine!" He spoke sternly, pausing before softening his tone.

"Look! Just whatever you do, don't just take the easy way out" "What easy way! No matter what I want to do, someone will disagree, or get hurt" she replied looking down, trying to hide the tears.

"Stop thinking about what everyone else wants! What that jerk wants, what your parents want... For once in your life just think about you!" he paused taking a breath, taking hold of her hand, lifting her chin, wiping away the tears.

"It's not that simple..." she answered choking on her tears.

"It is that simple" he continued.

"You asked me what I want, now I'm asking you...What do YOU want." He spoke softly.

She looked at him, she couldn't answer what she wanted, she had never let herself ask that question before.

"You know...sometimes I think about the things I never had, never had a normal childhood, but when I'm up there singing on that stage it's like nothing I've ever felt before, I can feel the love, but I don't do it for me, they're not there for me, they're there for God...

"...but, ok, yep, that night, at Matt's gig it felt different... They were watching me, it was me.... Yep, I realised I wanted more of that, but I'm not good enough....." Her words tailed off.

"You are good enough and everyone will love you, you know why I know?? I know because I love you, and I have pretty awesome taste" He laughed. Pausing for a moment he continued...

"You know… You're the best friend I've ever had…. I can talk to you about anything and you always understand… I've thought a lot about what you've said to me over the past few months, you do know you have changed me, I was lost till I met you, but I don't feel like that anymore, well most of the time"

"Ditto…. It's not all one sided…" She replied wanting to say so much more.

He stood up, holding out an outstretched arm,

"Come on! I think we've had enough of putting the world to rights, let's go have some fun!? Karaoke?"

"You're on!" she smiled as she took his hand and he guided her to her feet.

"Though after, we really need to get some studying done… We do have exams!" she stated.

Chapter 17

The summer was arriving; Imogen booked her CBT for after their end of year exams.

The day very quickly arrived. Imogen stood in the kitchen, waiting impatiently. Rob was picking her up to take her to the test centre in Newcastle.

Hearing the rev of that engine which she had come to love, she waved through the window. Grabbing her jacket, the bag, re-checking she had everything, especially her provisional license.

She walked out of the house closing the door behind her and walked up the path towards Rob and Buzby. She unfastened the leather bag which housed the spare helmet. As she unzipped the zip, her eyes lit up, the crisp white against the blue, it wasn't the usual helmet she had come accustomed to wearing. As she continued to unzip the helmet came into full view. Her eyes drawn to a flower, and underneath her name written elegantly.

"What's this?" she asked trying to contain her excitement.

Rob knocked the side stand down, climbed off, and stood facing her.

"It's about time you got your own helmet... See it as a late birthday present" he replied as he placed it on her head, fastening the straps, his hand accidently touching her neck.

"Come on" he continued climbing back on Buzby.

"We can't have you being late" he said as he kicked up the side stand, turned on the engine, pushing down on the kickstart, and dropping it into gear.

"You on? Ready?" he asked over his shoulder, as Imogen wrapped her arms around him.

"Yep, and yep" she replied.

They arrived at the test centre, the sound of revving engines filled the air, along with the sweet smell of petrol, oil and burned rubber.

"I'll go for a ride, I promise I'll stay away from the test route... you'll be fine..." he spoke scooping her chin.

"You've got this!" he continued.

He was the only one who ever spoke those words, and whenever he said them, she believed.

She sat her motorbike CBT test and passed.

She stood waiting for Rob in the test centre car park. The sun was shining brightly in the sky. While waiting she wondered how she had managed to pass when she had lost the instructor more than once!

"I passed!" She beamed.

He threw his arms around her before swinging her around, her feet momentarily leaving the ground. They stopped, standing in the moment, frozen in time.

"Of course, you did my young padawan"

"Like my new bike??" she asked, her teeth gently biting her bottom lip as she tried to control her beaming smile.

She had found the perfect bike. The riding school were selling one of their student bikes, and it reminded her of Buzby, but instead of blue, this bike was a stunning red.

"It's mine, or will be next week" She continued

"So, Buzby is also getting a companion? But she'll miss having you sitting in pillion" Rob replied with a wink.

"Aww, poor Buzby!" She replied sarcastically as she sat on his bike. Patting the engine gently, she whispered, while looking slyly at Rob.

"You're not getting rid of me; we've got many more rides together..."

"A bike needs a name." Rob commented.

Pondering, her finger resting on her lip, before announcing

"Kitt2"

Rob climbed on Buzby, Imogen wrapped her arms tightly around his waist.

"Let's go! We've got a fair to go to and some celebrating to be doing!! End of exams, and a licence to ride!" he shouted as he revved the engine.

They had planned to meet up with the gang down at the fair at the links. The vast array of rides could be heard across the bay, filling the air, becoming louder as they neared the links, each piece of music from the vast array of rides blended together to form one song, intertwined with exhilarated screams. The music was lively and fast, with the bass vibrating through their bodies. They lay on the grass sharing a bag of chips from the local chippy.

The sun was shining, the music was thumping, and he was surrounded by friends. He looked over at Imogen who appeared anxious. Her phone kept pinging, she would look at it then turn it back over, as if wondering whether to reply. He knew it was Jacob repeatedly texting her, like an incoming tide.

She stared at her phone. The messages began with subtle messages, followed by gentle persuasion which slowly became messages which were intended to make her feel overwhelmed with guilt.

"If that's Jacob, ignore him or tell him to go DO ONE! Or maybe I'll tell him for you" Rob spoke concerned, reaching for her phone.

She moved it further behind her back, knowing he meant every word.

"I told him we were all hanging out, but he won't quit, he wants me to go meet him… Maybe I should…" her sentence tailed of as she went to stand up.

Rob took hold of her arm. She looked at him, then away at the exit. Rob could feel the tension, and the guilt with every message.

"Today is your day girl! You're not going anywhere!" he said.

His tone softened; knowing she'd had enough people telling her what to do. That wasn't him.

"Pwease, pretty pwease… stay….." She looked at Rob pulling a goofy face,

Trudi returned from the rollercoaster,

"I thought you were the wild ones yet your sitting here like an old married couple" she joked jumping on Rob's back, pulling him backwards.

Rob and Imogen remained in silence, looking at each other. Trudi looked up confused.

"What did I miss?" she asked catching the moment between them.

"Imogen was about to go running to Jacob…. I was trying to persuade her that she should stay here with us" he answered.

Rob continued pulling a face behind Trudi's back

"God!" Imogen replied laughing.

Fine! Anything to get you to stop making that face!" she spoke trying to remain serious as Trudi took hold of her other arm dragging her towards the waltzer.

Dusk began to draw in. They all got wittier and crazier as the evening wore on. As the daylight faded, the fairground lights became more prominent, creating a myriad of dazzling colours luminating against the clear black sky.

Imogen felt drunk, though completely sober from daring each other to go on rides, each one more exhilarating than the last.

"God, I think I'm going to vomit! No more, I need a break" her voice staggered as she tried to hold her breath between her words, falling down onto the grass.

"Lightweight! I win again!" Rob declared,

"Ugh! Why is everything a competition between you two?" Trudi asked as she picked up her coat to head off.

"See you two children later" she continued laughing.

"Yes mummy! We'll be good!!" Imogen answered trying not to laugh.

Slowly everyone else also left, till it was only Rob and Imogen lying on the cold grass, watching as each ride closed, the links becoming darker, the stars gradually becoming more prominent.

"I think maybe we need to leave, before we get locked in" Imogen spoke looking to her right as the last ride switched off its lights.

"I'm not ready to go home yet..." He replied taking her hand, not ready to return home to the Spanish inquisition.

So many times, she had spoken those words, and every time he was there for her, she knew it would be wrong to deny him the same opportunity. She looked at him, torn.

"Fancy a trip up to the lighthouse? We may get to see the Northern lights?" he added enticing her to stay longer.

"OK" she agreed taking his hand. They arrived at the lighthouse crossing the causeway to lie on the grass below the lighthouse.

She couldn't deny it, no matter how hard she tried she found that over that year he had taken a place in her heart. Though she struggled to define what he was to her. A 'friend' couldn't encompass all of what he was, a "mate' sounded so cold.   He was more than just a friend. Maybe a friendship like theirs couldn't be quantified or defined??

There was a truth in his eyes. He spoke honestly as he always did, he never held back.   Sometimes bluntly honest like back on the ledge, he never told her what she wanted to hear, but always what she needed. Never pandering to her, instead giving it to her with pure honesty and integrity.

"You know being with Jacob isn't good for you, I see what it is doing to you…. It's like watching you tread water fighting not to drown taking all your strength to stop from losing yourself"

Imogen looked at him refusing to believe his words though deep down knew he was at least in part right.

"I love him… He loves me, I know he does… You don't see the full picture, what it's like when we're together…. We love each other, You only see a snapshot looking for the cracks but every relationship has its ups and downs and needs work and you have to make sacrifices…" her words trailed off

"It's how he makes you feel about yourself that is the problem. No-one who loves you should make you feel like that… I see it. I see how he makes you doubt yourself having you believe that you're not good enough, and controlling more and more of your life and decisions…"

"He's a realist and I'm a dreamer… Some things have to change, and I need to get my head out of the clouds" She answered.

"He's not a realist, and even if that was the case when you love someone, you're supposed to be their biggest fan no matter how crazy their dreams are… And yours aren't crazy! I see your potential. I'll always be your number 1 fan… And you should never change for anyone" he took a pause, looking at her.

Her head was down avoiding his gaze. Cupping her chin, he lifted her head before tucking her hair behind her ear. He looked deep into her eyes before continuing…

"Look... Your relationship is toxic; you will be more and more damaged by staying in it. It's important to make sacrifices in a relationship but your happiness, self-esteem and self-respect should never be sacrificed. If a relationship is built on love, it nurtures, restores, replenishes, and revives. It doesn't diminish. It isn't cruel and it doesn't ever violate a warm, open heart like yours. Jacob is suffocating those precious parts of you; you deserve to thrive, and you deserve to be happy. Fighting to hold on to it you will ruin you."

His words struck a chord, planting the first real seed of doubt. She was beginning to see something wasn't right, but just couldn't end it, she couldn't let go. For some crazy reason she loved Jacob and believed what Jacob gave in return was love.

Rob knew she had to come to that realisation for herself, he just had to watch and wait, as he knew he would be the one to pick up the pieces.

The following week they arrived at the test centre to pick up Imogen's new bike. Imogen paid for the bike, her hand stroking the bright red engine. Impatiently wanting to hit the road for Buzby and Kitt2' s first ride together.

As she cradled her new bike Rob produced a wrapped present.

"For you and your first bike" he smiled trying to contain his laughter as she unwrapped it. He'd had a sign custom-made for the back of her bike.

Could you be any more up my ass?
BTW my brakes are awesome? Want me to show you???

"What are you insinuating?" she quizzed.

Always a bit of competition between them, winding each other up, it was like a fun game of chess, which she enjoyed playing. He attached it to the back of her bike.

"So…." She spoke softly in a playful tone.

"Are we going home or taking a ride?????" she asked with her puppy dog eyes

"Fish & chips up at Seahouses???" he suggested with a pause.

"Though I don't know if you can keep up! Maybe too big a ride for a beginner…" he continued with a smug look upon his face, teasing a reaction.

She hit him playfully. "I won't be a beginner for long, soon I'll be whooping your ass!" She replied cloyingly as she climbed aboard her new bike.

"Seahouses it is then" he replied, his smile beginning to creep across his face.

"I'll go slow, don't want to lose you" he smirked.

"Oh, I almost forgot…" She grinned producing streamers which she then attached to the handlebars.

"Only you could do that! Now it is a chick bike" he laughed.

Rob climbed onto Buzby, revving the throttle. He pulled out with Imogen following closely behind. They rode out of the town passed the town moor, out towards the coast.

Passing through quiet country lanes which meandered from village to village with breaks of fast sweeping roads where the open countryside and clear sightlines allowed for quick and progressive riding enough to raise your pulse.

At those points Rob pulled away, with Imogen cautiously holding back. Rides like those were why she loved riding pillion, but she had also discovered she loved being in control of her own bike but would leave the speed to him.

Arriving in Seahouses they parked their bikes down on the harbour. The smell of kippers filled the air from the smokehouse above. They bought fish and chips and sat on the pier looking out over the sea to the Farnes. The water was glimmering in the midday sun. Above the gulls swooping down, circling and crying overhead.

"That was a good first ride, didn't have to slow down too much" he laughed, placing a drop of tomato ketchup on her nose.

She wiped it off laughing

"What are you like" she said.

"So, does Jacob know about kitt2?" Rob asked inquisitively.

Imogen dropped her head.

"I take that as a no" he replied in response.

"I maybe sounding like a broken record, but you shouldn't hide who you are Imi"

She knew he was right. It was becoming harder and harder to hide who she was becoming, and she no longer wanted to hide.

She sat pondering as she ate her chips, watching the waves lap against the harbour wall, the boats bobbing up and down. She thought how when she met Jacob, she was a different girl, she'd never been on a bike, her dreams were hidden deep behind closed doors, she was quiet, dutiful, the people pleaser desperate to be loved and wanted, and would change just to get that acceptance. She thought how earlier in that first year together, before starting college her world evolved around him, and how he wanted her to be. When she was away from him she felt like she couldn't live without him, she couldn't make decisions without his approval, but college, and Rob had opened up so many doors, daring her to dream, and the more time she spent with Rob and her friends she found herself becoming the girl she was destined to become, the girl she wanted to be.

She was beginning to like her new life. Though that life, those dreams, and everything which was making her who she now was, was hidden from Jacob, but eventually it became hard to keep up the pretence. She continued in contemplation, thinking how it felt like she was living 2 lives, the one with Jacob, being the dutiful girlfriend, learning to not speak, in fear of being ridiculed, he made all the decisions.

She thought back to the conversation at the lighthouse when Rob told her she allowed him to have too much control and looking back she was slowly realising that it was true though she'd never noticed. It had built up gradually beginning with offhand comments planting doubt till the comments became more of a request, then an instruction. She was beginning to realise that too often she allowed him to have a say in what she was wearing or was allowed to wear. Thinking how more recently the contempt was visible if she dared to go against him, daring to wear something that he or his family deemed inappropriate.

She thought back to a previous weekend. Jacob had returned to Newcastle for a friend's birthday party. She arrived at his parent's house in a dress, a dress which was deemed to be too short.

"You look like a slut!" he muttered under his breath as his hand tightly squeezed her arm before demanding that she was to go home and change into something more appropriate, then meet him there.

She pictured the hideous dress he made her wear to her sister's wedding which made her look old and dated.

She thought about how whenever she began to show her true self, to 'speak out of turn' his grip on her hand tightened. She thought how he would regularly imply that her opinion wasn't right causing her to doubt herself.

Rob broke the silence, disturbing her thoughts.

"So, have you decided what you are going to do when you finish your exams next year??" He asked.

"Jacob wants me to move to Durham to be with him" she replied quietly, her head down.

"We've had this conversation so many times I'm starting to feel like a broken record!" He stated.

"I asked what YOU want not that useless excuse!"

She sighed, pursing her lips together. She hadn't really spoke her wishes out loud before, they'd danced around them, but she'd never spoke the words.

"I want to study English and dance" she replied, pausing for a brief moment

"But it isn't possible" she continued.

"Why not?" He asked.

"There's 100's of reasons not to apply... It's too expensive, it's not practical, my parents wouldn't agree, well they wouldn't care

but wouldn't support me, so again, too expensive…… and… The biggest reason…."

She paused...

"I'm not good enough, I'll never be good enough…" her sentence tapered off as a tear began to form in her eye.

Rob knelt down in front of her, taking her hands in his.

"You ARE good enough!"

"I've told you a thousand times before, if not more… Has Jacob ever said you weren't good enough?" he asked, though knowing the answer.

"Not in so many words…." She replied, remembering many conversations undermining her confidence, subtle, but enough for her to understand what he meant.

So, who do you believe? Me, and everyone who has seen you dance, who've heard you sing…

"But it's not just him, it's everyone, and when everyone is saying the same then it must be true, and I'm not as good as you think, I'm an OK dancer, maybe even average, but that's never going to be enough… and I'm stupid for even trying, setting myself up to fail, as always, story of my life."

Her words tapered off, as she looked down.

His hand cupped her chin, lifting her head till their eyes met.

"I don't buy into that, and you know I'm never wrong… You will prove him wrong, and everyone else. I'll help you. Anything you need. We don't have to tell anyone…."

She smiled, nodding.

"So, let's go home and research some Uni's" he said pulling her to her feet.

"Well, wherever I go has to be not too far, have good surfing, some good bike riding routes, but also a good course... so I think maybe we've got our work cut out for us!"

He nodded, though the being close wasn't top of his list of priorities, he knew he'd miss her being far away, but he was willing to make that sacrifice, if it meant distancing her from Jacob.

They returned to Rob's house. Sat in the dining room, he turned on the family computer in the corner. They sat for hours looking through different courses, different universities. One stood out, a university with a motorbike track within walking distance, meandering coastal roads, and of course great surf!

"Right!" Rob announced.

"You're applying there!" he spoke giving her a high five.

When she left, she seemed so happy, as though on top of the world, though it never lasted long. He knew he had a long way to go before she would take that step.

With the First-year exams over. Summer had arrived. But with the summer it had brought the return of Jacob, something he knew would rock their perfect world, and most likely undo all the good he'd done.

The following day he texted her asking if she wanted to go for a ride that afternoon. She replied refusing, making an excuse that she wasn't feeling well. He rang, but the phone call rang off, going to voicemail. He knew she was avoiding talking to him, something wasn't right, and knew Jacob had to be involved somehow. He thought how maybe she had told him of her plan to apply to university and he'd got into her mind, planting doubt. Over the next few days, he didn't hear from her. He remained persistent, not willing to give up on his best friend, though at times was becoming frustrated, being second hurt more than he was ever willing to admit. He wondered if he would ever be first in anyone's heart, but was something he doubted, something he felt he didn't deserve.

A week past. The sun was shining, the day sweltering in the summer heat.

He sent her a text.

Hey, Buzby is missing Kitt2... Perfect day for a ride if ya can pull yourself away from posh boy

A few moments passed, his phone rang,

He answered. "Hey stranger!"

"Hey.." She replied.

"Look, I'm heading down Longsands for a surf in 10... If ya fancy meeting me... In about an hour, we could go for a ride?" She continued.

"Sounds good, I might take Levi down the beach and come watch... Never seen you surf" he replied smiling.

It was good to hear her voice, he knew it wasn't the time to probe on what had happened that previous week, but he knew he would find out, when she was ready.

As he ended the call, he looked down, Levi was sat upright, looking at him, with his ball resting in his mouth before dropping it at his feet. He didn't have to mention the word 'walk', it was as though Levi instinctively knew what Rob was thinking.

He looked at Levi.

"Yes, I'll take you for a walk" he spoke as he picked up the soggy ball.

They walked along the coast, down onto Longsands, Levi loved the sea-air, the feeling of shifting sands below his paws. As soon as Levi stepped onto the sand he rolled over, covering himself, though the golden sand blended in with his golden fur, the only give away was his sand encrusted nose.

He looked up at Rob with those big brown eyes and his golden tail swishing like he just got all his birthday wishes at once,

"I know what you want!" Rob spoke out loud picking up a sandy piece of kelp, bending his fingers around it, feeling the cool dampness, before throwing it down the beach, for him to bring it back releasing it at his feet, sitting, waiting patiently for Rob to throw it again.

Something which was then repeated not once, but over and over as he walked along the sand to the south end of the beach. Seagulls circled overhead; their songs carried by the cool coastal breeze. The waves crashed upon the golden sand, surfers filled the water, waiting, trying to catch the perfect wave.

He sat down watching, spotting Imogen in the surf. Watching her ride the waves with the same elegance which she showed in her dance.

He watched as she left the water, with Levi running into the surf to greet her, she placed the surfboard in the sand, with Levi jumping up at her inundating her with sloppy doggy kisses. "Let me ditch the board, and get out of this wetsuit... I don't know about you, but I'm starved! Fancy some fish and chips before we head off?" she asked as she dried her wet sand encrusted hair.

They ate, before Rob walked back home, Imogen rode along the front meeting him outside his house. Rob let Levi into the house and pulled Buzby out of the garage. They went for a long ride up the coast.

Chapter 18

The early summer was filled with days when they could just get up and 'be'. The first two weeks, Jacob was away on a family holiday. The days were filled with bike rides, rides on Buzby and kitt2, but some returning to Imogen riding pillion to get her speed fix, their bodies moving in synchrony, with it also bringing a growing synchrony of their minds. That summer was hotter than normal. Scorching hot days, which were more fitting to the Mediterranean than England.

Most afternoons were spent on the beach, Rob lying on the warm sand while Imogen surfed, improving with every wave, rising with the waves, riding freely upon their crest, feeling waves of serenity as steady as the ocean.

Days walking barefoot, with the hot pavement which meant dancing along a little faster. Days spent working on a church community art programme, creating a sweat, clearing overgrown gardens, and days dreaming up graffiti designs and vibrant mosaics, days with paint fights and water fights. A time when bikes, surf, music, art and dance flowed into one another and they were as inseparable as any true friends should be.

But over those two weeks he could sense something still wasn't right. whatever had transpired a few weeks earlier continued to have an effect on her.

Jacob returned, and their days together became sporadic, their meetings were few and far between. They sat on the beach, one of those rare afternoons that she could tear herself away from Jacob, or more likely he had plans that didn't include her.

He tried asking what had happened, but she repeatedly shrugged it off, nothing, nothing happened, nothing had changed, but he could tell something wasn't right. He continued to probe; she knew he wouldn't give up.

Imogen answered, at first repeating 'nothing', then indicating there was something, not wanting to go there. Rob kept trying to guess.

"You're not pregnant?" he asked.

"Nope!" she replied.

"Look, Jacob just didn't like me getting a bike, but I'm dealing with it, honest!" she continued, oversimplifying what had really transpired.

She was beginning to ask herself if rape was the right word to describe what had transpired. Though whatever it was that had happened there was no way Rob could know.

He could see through her, she knew she had to give more, but hoping he'd accept her reply.

"I can't tell you now cause I don't even really know myself, but when I'm ready, if I'll ever be ready... I'll tell you, just give me time" she asked.

He nodded in agreement, knowing he'd just had to wait; wait till she was ready. Whatever it was, it worried him, there was rarely anything she didn't tell him.

The back end of the summer holidays was Rob's yearly family holiday. Two weeks spent on a family holiday, away in Gran Canaria visiting family, like they did for so many years before. In those weeks away his mother always seemed a lot more chilled and he didn't feel like such a disappointment or failure.

They returned just over a week before the new academic year. Soon the weather began to turn colder, the summer holidays coming to an end.

The first day of the new academic year Rob waited on the bridge for Imogen before English. As she walked through the glass doors, he noticed how her demeanour had changed, her head bowed down, as though he'd gone back in time to that previous September, to the girl he saw in the cafeteria.

"Hey!" he called over to her.

She lifted her head looking directly at him. His eyes were drawn to her face, wearing make-up, which was unlike her. Looking closer he could see why. The make-up was being used to try and hide a bruised face. Looking closer he could see bruises which were beginning to fade, purple fading into yellow blotches turning her face yellow, as though she was jaundiced. She removed her jacket, wincing as she sat down on the old settee. On her arms were purple welts that unlike the bruise on her face, had deepened over the past week. He could see she was in pain, though trying to hide the intensity, he wondered if she could possibly have cracked ribs, he wondered how she intended to dance like that, but most of all was desperate to know what had happened and why she hadn't confided in him before college.

He wondered, could Jacob have done that?

"What happened?" he asked concerned as he placed a reassuring hand upon her shoulder.

She spoke of being attacked on the metro while out with Jacob the previous week.

She told him how a gang of youths boarded the metro, and how instinctively she knew there was going to be trouble. She told how her intuition was confirmed as she was startled by the sound of breaking glass as a bottle crashed near their feet. One of the gang had hurled a glass bottle down the carriage. She spoke of how the panic grew stronger, but how she thought that maybe this time being with Jacob, it would soon pass. Thinking how they only had to wait till the next station to leave the metro.

She told him how the gang walked up the carriage sitting across from them, they began making comments about Jacob, him becoming the target due to his upper-class manor, and with also being black he stood out.

She recalled how they slumped over, hovering above them as they sat, one of the gang began leaning on the bar which reached up from their seat to the ceiling of the carriage, banging on the Perspex behind her.

She told how she took Jacob's arm pulling at him, to stop him reacting, but he shook her off, and stood up, being overshadowed by the youth standing in front of him. She told how she watched as one of the gang pushed Jacob with his fist ready, as if waiting for Jacob to react giving provocation.

She recounted how she somehow found the strength to stand between Jacob and the gang leader. Rob listened in shock and disbelief as she continued to tell him what happened next.

Jacob fell back into his seat. Imogen continued to stand, in between, daring to fighting back, something, as though daring him to hit her, hoping to call his bluff. She'd never stood up for herself before but had hoped it would work. Her actions didn't go unnoticed by the rest of the gang, which caused the gang member to punch her in the face for daring to challenge him. The metro approached Tynemouth, instinctively she ran for the door, pulling Jacob with her.

She told him how the doors began to close, filling her with relief, relief which was short-lived. As one of the gang members stopped the closing door with his foot, causing it to re-open, following them onto the platform intent on teaching her a lesson.

Through her tears she recounted how on the platform they continued to attack her, each taking their turn. She told how she looked up at the driver watching from his cabin as one of the gang smashed her head against the carriage repeatedly.

"What about Jacob?" Rob asked concerned.

He'd never really liked the guy but would never have wished anything to happen to him, not really.

"I don't know..." she replied.

She knew that if she told Rob the rest of the story, she would not be able to control him.

"What do you mean by you don't know?" He asked knowing she was hiding something; he could read her like an open book.

Reluctantly, she told him how she tried to scan the platform for him as she was being attacked but she couldn't see him. It wasn't long until she heard the welcome sound of sirens and the gang dispersed. She told how she tried to look around struggling to open her eyes as she lay there, the paralyzing hurt spreading through her body. She recalled how it was a few minutes until she saw a hand reaching down for her, through her blurred vision she saw that it was Jacob, unhurt. He leant down beside her. His hand touched her right cheek leaning in closer, the pain from his touch was unbearable.

She told him how she found out that he had ran away, with the excuse of going to find help. She told him how they went to the police station but as with every other attack they didn't care, and through her tears told how his parents blamed her for putting their son in harm's way, looking at her as though she was a piece of trash.

Rob struggled to hold his emotions in check, Jacob had taken things to an all-time low. Imogen could almost read his mind.

"Hey, its OK... it was probably better that I took the beating, they would literally have killed Jacob... I'm used to it, I know how to protect myself." she spoke trying to make excuses for Jacob's behaviour, though she was struggling herself to believe the words which she had expressed.

"I'd like to give him a demonstration!" Rob replied sternly but looking into her eyes his anger calmed knowing what she needed in that moment was comfort from a friend rather than retribution.

After English, Rob asked if she needed a lift home, she tried to avoid answering, making excuses about needing to go to the library, not wanting him to know that Jacob was meeting her from college as it was his last day, before returning to university.

Rob sat on his bike knowing she was holding something from him. He circled the college campus, stopping across from the main entrance which also led out from the library. Watching as she walked down the steps, towards an unharmed Jacob, who looked like he didn't have a care in the world. He watched as Jacob took Imogen's hand. Rob's fist instinctively clenched as he quickly dismounted from his bike, removing his helmet and crossed the road.

"Hey!" he shouted as he walked towards them.

Jacob turned shaking his head. He continued to walk pulling Imogen with him.

"Hey!" Rob repeated as he began to catch up with them.

"You're such a pathetic waste of space... do you know that?" he asked as he grabbed hold of Jacobs shoulder.

Rob was seething as he glanced at Imogen before returning his gaze at Jacob, wondering how he could run and hide and let Imogen take the beating.

"How could you leave her to take a beating for you? You! Pathetic wimp!" he continued as Imogen stood between them, her hand upon Robs chest, holding him back.

In that moment it was hard for her to differentiate whether she was worried about Jacob getting hurt, or Rob getting into trouble.

"Just stop it! Don't you think I've been through enough without you two fighting!" She paused, the pain still evident in her voice.

"Rob... What the hell...... And Jacob... Funny how you're willing to fight for me now..." Imogen stood frozen but also torn.

Jacob took hold of her hand, leading her away, she began to follow, turning back, seeing Rob standing there watching her walk away.

"I'm sorry" She mouthed. As Jacob continued to pull her.

Shaking his head, he put on his helmet, revving up his bike, then in a moment he was gone, taking a fast ride up the coast to let off steam, but the emotions made him ride erratically, almost making a rookie mistake, luckily managing to pull Buzby back into line, avoiding crashing into the verge. He returned home, to his room, shaken and still angry.

His eyes were drawn to the framed photo of the two of them upon his desk. He felt an overwhelming sense of betrayal, the lack of willingness to fight not only for herself, but to stand by him while he tried to fight for her. Feeling full of rage, he picked up the picture throwing it against the wall. He stood for a moment breathing heavily, before beginning to steady his breath. He picked up the picture, the glass had cracked. His hand traced along the crack, looking at that smiling face, he was barely able to look at her picture without welling up.

He couldn't stay angry at her for long, and it wasn't her who his anger was aimed at, she just became collateral damage in that moment. All he wanted was to protect her, the way she deserved to be protected. He knew he would fight for her, until his heart was black and blue. He wasn't ready to give up on her, not yet, even if it hurt, even if she continued to put that loser first. He knew he would eventually help to cut her free.

He thought how 12 months earlier he didn't really care about anyone, or anything, not feeling anything. He picked up the phone, typing out a message before deleting it, trying to find the words to explain his feelings, he typed multiple versions of the same text, deleting each one, until he decided to ring her instead.

He rang her, calmed by hearing her voice.

"I'm sorry.." she choked as she spoke, breaking the silence.

"I don't know why you continue to defend him, any real man would have defended his lady..." he asked.

"So, what century are we in?" She asked in return, trying to lighten the conversation.

"Look, Like I said earlier…. I'm used to being attacked, it's almost became a pass time... Jacob has never had anything before, they would have pulverised him." she continued.

"Much deserved if you ask me... I'd happily give him a demonstration, ease him in gently..." he replied, pausing, trying to hold his emotions in check.

"Rob! Stop it! It's hard enough without you picking fights, why do you think I went with him! Cause I knew you'd be like this!" she answered.

"You went with him to protect him not that he deserves it." He replied.

"Well yeah but also to protect you... Do you honestly think I want my best mate done for assault and end up with a criminal record?" she answered.

Imogen changed the conversation and the attack was not brought up again, though that following week every time he saw her and saw the marks still evident he was reminded of it, also watching her wince in pain as she tried to continue as though nothing had happened, refusing to take time to heal, not wanting to fall behind.

Rob watched her one afternoon back at his house, he watched her as she stood in the kitchen drying the dishes, looking lost, frozen, staring into space.

It was like a horror movie, re-playing in her mind as if somehow her brain was unwilling to let the images go and, in its attempt, to analyse them it made her see it all over again.

She stared out of the window at the white clouds and longed to be amongst them, soaring and carefree, but above all pain free. She didn't know whether that attack hurt more than the others, or if it was just because it was fresher. From past experience she knew the more she tried to suppress it the more it would play again, but she couldn't help it. In moments she was again back on that platform.

"Hey" Rob whispered pulling her in close, his hand rhythmically stroking her hair as though to soothe her.

"It's OK" he continued before falling silent, knowing that words weren't what she needed in that moment, holding her till she felt OK.

He asked her to take time off from dancing, but in response she told him she couldn't let them win and couldn't let Jacob win. She couldn't jeopardise the future they had talked about.

With Jacob back at Uni, the gang settled back into their routine, but soon Christmas again arrived.

Chapter 19

The Christmas almost mirrored the one the year before, though he could see Imogen distancing herself from Jacob a little more.

Rob watched patiently waiting though as time passed, he wanted her to leave him not so she could be with him, but so that she could be her own person, free of the toxic and controlling relationship.

Imogen could see that her relationship with Jacob was becoming more strained, but that only made her more determined to fight for it, though sometimes she found herself questioning her actions. Too many times she had complained and even laughed at her father for the number of times he took her mother back, even after all she did, but looking at herself she could see the apple never falls far from the tree. She thought how if she hadn't have slept with him, taking that step that she had always refused to cross then maybe she would have walked away a long time ago, but sex was sacred. His parents distain for her had also growing deeper which meant she wasn't permitted to join them at midnight mass.

New Year's Eve arrived. Like the previous year she was again going to spend it at Durham with Jacob going to another fancy ball at the University.

Imogen sent him a picture of her in her dress. She stared at the picture before sending, feeling like mutton dressed as lamb. She knew she didn't fit in. Her smile camouflaged her feelings. As she sent the picture, she wished she was spending the New Year with her friends.

As Rob looked at the photo in his room, he thought how she looked like a Princess, and thought how he could never give her that life.

He sent a reply..

You look stunning..

Imogen read his reply over and over wishing she could see what he saw.

As he was about to leave his room his phone vibrated in his pocket.

Thank you xxx Have fun, give my love to the gang. Wish I was with you x

As he read her message, he wished she was there too but thought her comment was just pleasantries doubting that she would prefer a night on the town to an evening with fancy champagne and fancy food. He thought how Newcastle had always been the party central, but the stops were always pulled out on a big night like New Year's Eve, and he was determined to make it a good one. He headed for the metro to meet the rest of the gang in town for a night on the tiles, hitting the clubs. They spent the night working their way through the Bigg market before heading down to the quayside eventually finding their way into Baja. Inside it was like dancing in the Northern Lights; the club filled with dry-ice smoke which swirled in an array of blues, acid greens, hot pinks and gold. The music played over the dance floor.

Wiping the sweat from his brow he stepped back off the dancefloor, walking to the bar with his mind in a frenzy, his world spinning faster than normal. His legs were beginning to give way as he took hold of the bar, leaning against the barstool to steady himself.

"Double Vodka" He shouted to the barman, over the loud music, He stared at his phone, wondering whether to text. He placed his phone back in his pocket as the barman passed him his shot. He downed it in one, followed by another.

The group piled out onto the quayside awaiting the fireworks display. Under the influence of alcohol, everything felt like fun. Conversations which under usual circumstances would be dull, became thrilling as a result of muddled words, loss of filter and a burning desire to be brutally honest.

"Text her! Tell her you love her! You can always blame it on the drink!" Vicki shouted, jumping upon his back for a piggyback ride.

He shook his head, not daring to answer, a small voice quietly nagging in the back of his mind, reminding him that tomorrow his actions would have repercussions. Instead of giving a verbal response he used distraction, running fast. Vicki began screaming, exhilarated.

As the minutes began to countdown, music filled the air, festive beats lifted the spirits, the large crowd wanting to move, jump and sing. Everyone was anxiously waiting to ring in the New Year. It was a time to celebrate being alive.

Another year was ending, but another was also beginning. The gang continued to party for another hour before they all began to go their separate ways.

"Fancy jumping in with me?" Vicki asked as she flagged down a taxi.

"Nah, I'm fine. Need some fresh air first" he replied.

He stood watching the taxi pull away before walking back up to town. As he walked, he scanned his phone seeing a message.

Happy new Year!

He hadn't heard it or felt its vibrations. It had been sent at 12.08am. He replied the same message wondering what sort of night she'd had.

He returned home, intoxicated, happy, happy to be alive.

A few days later...Saturday afternoon his phone rang. An unknown number. He picked up the phone, it was Imogen ringing from a public phone in Durham.

"Please ring me back" she sobbed down the phone.

"Of course.." He replied confused and worried.

The call cut out. Quickly he redialled. She allowed two rings before she answered.

"Hey" she spoke through the tears.

"What's up?" Rob asked.

"Do you think you can ride Buzby in the snow, down to Durham?? Or if not meet me at central station..." She asked.

"Yeah sure, I can ride down. It's not icy, and most of the roads are clear.... What's wrong?"

Imogen fell silent, he could hear her choked breaths.

"Jacob's parents turned up.... We'd been out in the snow making snow angels.... I was in his room, in only my underwear, with my clothes drying on the radiator... They got the door guy to let them into his room... When they saw me, they threw me out, and threw my wet clothes at me... I had to put them on in the corridor, I'm cold, wet, luckily I had fifty pence in my pocket to ring you......"

Rob could feel the anger building up inside him, wondering how Jacob could stand by and allow his parents to do that.

"Shit!!" she spoke breaking his thoughts.

"My phone, wallet... Everything is in his room, I can't just stand here... I don't know what to do...."

"Look, I'll ride down, and be around for you when you're ready, in the meantime, does he have friends that you know well, any female friends? Can you knock on any of his friends? Someone who you can stay with till you can get your stuff?"

"Erm, yep... I guess I can try Caroline....."

"OK, I'll head down, it'll take me about half hour-ish.... Ring me when you're sorted"

"OK.... Thank you... I knew I could rely on you" she answered still trying to speak through the tears.

As soon as the call ended Rob headed down to the garage.

"Well Buzby, we've got a bit of a rescue mission" He announced as his hand skimmed across the fuel tank.

The snow which had fallen, had almost completely melted, with some remnants of slush the only evidence of the snowfall. As he rode South, fine water droplets hit his visor as he continued riding onwards. The skies were overhung with a blanket of grey, so much so that he could barely tell the difference between the sky and clouds. The nearer to Durham he got, the sky became clearer with blinding sunshine and the snow became thicker, taking all of his concentration.

Imogen found her way to Caroline's room, she knocked on her door, thankfully she answered. Imogen fell to the floor, breaking down, it was like every atom of her was screaming out, traumatized. Imogen went into the bathroom removing her damp clothes, Caroline passed her a bathrobe, and a warm cup of tea.

"Why is he being such a jerk?" Caroline quizzed, finding it difficult to think that her friend could do what Imogen had described.

Imogen knew that Jacob wouldn't be happy that she'd involved one of his friends, tainting his reputation, but she thought what other choice did she have.

Caroline sent a text to Jacob letting him know Imogen was with her. Telling him Imogen needed her belongings.

A reply quickly came.

Tell her to stay with you, they'll be gone soon, thanks

The reply seemed so short and cold, devoid of emotion.

She stayed in Caroline's room until she got the 'all clear' that his parents had gone. Imogen returned to Jacob's room, picking up her belongings, packing everything into her bag. Jacob was filled with excuses, before giving a feigned attempt at an apology.

"What could I do, they're my parents" he uttered reaching for her hand.

"Just like always!" She thought as she stood looking at him, she shook her head, not wanting to speak, not wanting to say something she would regret.

"I'm going. See you later..." she spoke coldly but calmly as she walked out, texting Rob.

Got my stuff walking down to the student union.

She dropped a pin to the location. Walking quickly, desperate to get away. Arriving at the student union, she spotted the welcoming site of Rob and Buzby. She fell into his arms.

"Why? Why do his parents hate me so much?" She asked.

"Shit!" she exclaimed.

"We need to get home! I need to go to Sienna and David's. They need to hear this from me, I can't have THEM doing it" she stated shaking, the fear of them finding out about what happened and also finding out that her and Jacob were in a sexual relationship.

She thought how they would spin it, that the girl they took in and subjected their son too had led him astray, that they would reiterate that she was trash or words to that effect. She knew they would never believe her side, especially if she didn't get there first.

"What will Matt say?" she asked .

"What if I get chucked out of the band?" she continued; the panic clear in her voice.

Her questions fell from her as her mind played a myriad of scenarios.

"Hey! Calm it…" Rob spoke as his hands rested tightly on her arms, returning her thoughts to the present.

He stared at her, allowing her time to calm down.

"Look! We can spend some time here, chilling... And when you're ready we'll head home, I'll drop you at mine, you can go round, then come back to mine after if needed. And if they love you, they'll understand, and it takes two to tango! And do you really think Matt will chuck you out of the band for that?"

She looked at him, taking a deep breath, nodding. He wrapped his arm around her as they began to walk down to the river. They walked around the base of the town, along the river's edge.

"I guess I'll just never be daughter in law material" she stated as they walked, her thoughts just tumbling from her.

"What do you mean of course you are! They're just stuck up and blind, my mum loves you, Sienna loves you..."

"Yes, but that's different..." she answered.

She continued

"I'm your best mate not your girlfriend, and Sienna would have a fit if say me and Matt, or me and Lucas got together.... I'm ok as surrogate daughter, the project kid, type thing but anything else.... Well...... I'm too damaged..."

He could see the hurt which she always tried to bury deep down, the belief that she would never be good enough.

"My mum loves you, and trust me, she never stops talking about how we should be a couple... God. If I was ever to say we were... She'd probably throw a huge party and start planning our wedding!" He joked, though partly serious.

He continued...

"You do realise, the only reason she's nice to me now is because of you?? Like I know she's always loved me, in her own way but I've always been the bad egg, black sheep, whatever you want to call it..."

She looked up at him.

"We're a right pair aren't we, 2 black sheep, this world is pretty twisted." She answered as her hand skimmed an old oak tree,

Snow still rested upon the benches as though to create a cushion. She stood looking out over the river. The sun shone brightly, as bright as a summer's day, shining without the added warmth that a summer sun would bring. The kind of magical sunshine that brought a smile no matter what had surpassed. The remaining snow reflected the sky. Though the snow was beautiful it was cold and sharp. Crisp, white, pristine,

Imogen let her eyes rest for a moment, as though connecting with the nature around her, before running up to some old ruins buried in the trees.

"Don't move" he stated, taking his phone out of his pocket.

"What on earth are you doing now?" she asked.

"Art assignment, light is perfect, you're perfect..." his words tailed off as he took her photograph.

Rob could see the event earlier was still affecting her. Feeling his heart breaking for her he put away his phone.

"Snowball fight?" Rob yelled.

In that instant Imogen knew he would have a whole stack ready to pelt her with.

"Hey, unfair advantage here I think, cheat!" Imogen replied as she frantically formed a snowball in her hands as a snowball hit her shoulder,

"You're on, you're so gonna lose!" she taunted from behind a tree.

"Wanna bet?" Rob shouted as snowballs flew through the sky in his direction, shattering creating the illusion of falling snow.

"Game on, sucker! You're going down!" he continued, sneaking up behind her, snowball in hand, throwing it at her back, for it to burst open on impact, showering crystalline fragments over her, and falling down her neck, and down to her back.

"Right, No more playing nice!. You're so gonna lose now, Rob!"

He watched the excited glint in her eye, he knew she could never resist a challenge, and he knew if only for a short while his job was done.

It was short-lived, the fight ended, and her thoughts were again taken over.

"Well, we can't stay here forever. I guess it's time to face the music."

They returned home, Imogen walked around to Sienna and David's, she stayed for most of the evening, she texted him on the way home.

In those following months he could gradually see an awakening in her, as though all of the separate incidents which individually she managed to give excuses for, became like snowflakes compacted to create a something which was bigger, and too obvious to brush under the carpet, but he knew it would still be a while till she would be able to break free.

Chapter 20

The term flew by. Soon March had arrived. He sat on the bridge alone thinking how soon it would be Easter, then final exams, and then it would all be over. Then restart again?

Imogen walked into the bridge beaming, unable to hold back her excitement.

"Guess what!" she exclaimed as she sat opposite breaking his thoughts.

He looked up, but she never gave him a chance to respond.

"I've got an audition for Scarborough, next week!" she continued though as the words spilled out her doubts spilled in.

"Wait! I can't do this! How on earth am I to get a dance perfected by then, how do I get there? I can't let anyone know"

His hand rested on hers.

"You've got this! Go on Kitt2, we'll do a dummy run at the weekend, always fancied a ride to Scarborough, we can check out the Uni and racetrack, and no-one else needs to know."

The weekend she made an excuse not to go to Durham, something which she was beginning to do more and more, using the last few months of college and impending exams as an excuse.

Saturday morning, she met him outside his.

"Ready?" he asked as he scanned the map on his phone to plan a route avoiding the motorway.

"Right! Got a route. Along the coast, a bit longer but more scenic, and since your still on L plates, it avoids the motorway, though we will have to venture on the A19 for a bit, but I'm sure you'll ace it"

As Rob pulled out of his street, she took a deep breath before knocking down into gear and following behind.

The ride was scenic, crossing the north York moors then climbing down past bays and inlets, the route filled with tight bends and open stretches. They pulled into Scarborough.

"Not a bad ride!" she exclaimed removing her helmet overlooking the harbour.

They sat eating fish and chips as they watched the waves hit the shore, scanning the bay, imagining what it would be like to live there, daring to dream.

Finishing their fish and chips they manoeuvred up off the bay onto Filey Road, up to the University then on up to Oliver's Mount to the racing track. The track was nestled into a hill which overlooked Scarborough's South Bay. As they rode up the small access roads to the top Imogen thought how picturesque it was. A hidden gem. Reaching the top Rob continued taking them on a lap around the track before pulling up at the small café near the war memorial.

"You know this has to be the best track in the world! Look at that view!" She exclaimed as they looked over Scarborough below.

"You're easily pleased... You've not been to Manx yet... Though, OK... It is pretty cool and quite an awesome track layout" he replied placing his arm around her.

He looked at her. He'd never seen her so happy and it felt as though she belonged there.

"You know Scarborough is pretty cool, I like it... But you know what it is missing?" he asked as his chin rested upon her head.

"What?" Imogen asked oblivious.

"It's missing you! Scarborough is OK... but with you here it'll be like heaven on earth"

Imogen nestled her head into his chest before glancing up pursing her lips trying not to smile, trying not to laugh.

"You getting all soppy!" she replied as her eyes again scanned the view below dreaming of being able to see that view everyday.

"Why don't you come with me? They do a great Marine biology course; you can play with your sea cucumbers! I don't know if I could do it without you" her words trailed off as reality sank in, college couldn't go on forever, and all good things always come to an end.

Although she was desperate to escape Newcastle, the memories, the fear, the familiar was always better than taking that step, the risk into the unknown.

"You know I can't go. I would in heartbeat if there was any way....

You know I have to stay in Newcastle. Everyone else has gone, Isabella will be off on some adventure as soon as her exams are over, I've got to stay" his words trailed off.

It wasn't spoken, but was regularly implied, it was his job, his responsibility to stay behind, to help his mother, his father's health was slowly failing. He wanted nothing more than to also escape, to be free, to live in a place like where they were standing. But it wasn't meant to be.

She wanted to beg, but she knew he was too loyal that he would self-sacrifice himself for others.

"Show me what you've got" he asked, changing the subject.

She looked around to make sure no-one was watching, she turned on her music on her phone and as the music began, she began to dance with passion. As he watched her dancing with sharp precision and accurate grace moving with purposeful clarity with absolute control, he knew they would accept her in a heartbeat, he'd lose her.

"Why don't you come with me again next week? Moral support and all that..." she asked turning off the music.

"I've got a hospital appointment that day, and I'll only get in your way, you need to learn to walk on those two feet of yours" he answered.

Not wanting to again feel the gut-wrenching feelings which were consuming him. He couldn't let her know how much he'd miss her, how much he needed her and had come to rely on her, he knew that if she knew, she would self-sacrifice herself to stay, knowing she would without hesitation because he could see himself in her. That beaming smile said it all, this was her chance, her dream, he just wished he could go with her, that he could give more, that he could be more to her, to share the journey they started together wondering if they could keep the promises they made with the ever-changing world. All he had was to be able to hold on to the memories.

They returned home, he walked through the door to his mother shouting, he'd forgotten to put the washing on again, he hadn't got everything on the shopping list.... She never said the words but reading between the lines she was implying he was a failure.

It seemed unfair that no matter how much he strived to be the man she expected him to be, he was never good enough. It was as though she kept taunting him with his failures, not caring or rather oblivious to what he was sacrificing.

The day of the audition arrived. Imogen set off alone following the route from the weekend. As she arrived in Scarborough stepping onto the shore she hoped the soothing onshore breeze would bring a calm to her crazy, to quell the doubts, to stop her feeling as though she was suffocating. The nausea swirled unrestrained in her empty stomach... Her heart felt as if though her blood had become tar as it struggled to keep a steady beat. She arrived up at the university, parking in the car park watching students walk past.

"I don't know if I can do this!"

She texted him as she stood outside of the university daring herself to walk up the steps...

Rob was sat in his room staring at the clock when his phone pinged. He read her message wishing he had gone with her, but he knew she had to step out alone.

"Knock-em dead, you've got this!"

His reply came as Imogen sat in the corridor. The clock in the hall ticked loudly as she sat waiting, moments of anxiety carefully measured into those tiny fragments of time.
She glanced at her phone, reading the message from Rob. His message calming her inner storm, helping her find her inner confidence, ready to dance like the rest of her life depended on it.

Putting her phone back in her bag she looked around at the other dancers waiting.

The door opened, a girl walked out, the door closed. She knew she was next.

She walked into the audition room; the door closed behind her.

She stood in the dimly lit studio, standing on the polished wooden floor, looking at her reflection in the mirrors which surrounded her. Her fears suffocated her.

A table stood in the middle of the room, four judges were sitting watching, shuffling papers. A stern-faced woman waved her forwards. It reminded her of the film, flash dance.

In that moment she knew how Alex felt when she walked into the audition, the quietness, the only sound the rustling of papers and her feet as she walked across the wooden floor.

The woman on the end of the table spoke with a commanding presence.

"Tell me, Imogen, what are you going to do for us today?"

Quietly, with her voice shaking, she replied,

"I'm dancing to flash dance. My own choreography"

Her hand shook as she handed over the CD with her music. The stern-faced woman handed the CD to the gentleman sitting beside her. She straightened her glasses looking down at the papers in front of her, before glancing back up at Imogen. Imogen walked to a spot on the floor, kneeling on the floor her head down, focussed waiting for the music to begin.

She closed her eyes, imagining they weren't there, imagining Rob was there instead, a calmness filled her as the music began to play; It was like liquid adrenaline being injected into her blood stream.

She realised in that moment she wanted this as badly as she wanted to breathe. She had been keeping up a pretence that she didn't mind either way, if she failed she could brush it off as not meant to be, not in God's plan etc..

Slowly she began to move as the instrumental faded and the words of the first verse began to play.

First when there's nothing....

Slowly the music and the words took over and she was taken to that place deep within her.

They didn't know of the horrors she had endured, the reason this song was chosen, how it echoed her life. She moved slowly and gracefully, her body interpreting the music, bringing the song alive, allowing her body to accentuate every word, telling the story, her story.

The music began to build,

You can dance right through your life

Dancing with sharp precision and accurate grace moving with purposeful clarity and absolute control. She danced as if it were the only way her body truly knew how to speak. She jumped with perfect poise and perfect landings, each movement flowing into the next. Her movements flowed with a dazzling grace, she could feel her soul become one with the music and she unleashed her emotions into her dance feeling every word.

The song ended. She looked down at her shoes for a few moments before finding solace by staring out of the window, then across to the judges, the stern-faced woman waved her out.

She walked out of the college and kept walking till she reached the cliff edge. She thought about the song and thought how unlike in the film Flash dance there was no man with roses waiting for her, she was alone. Fairy tales weren't real, well, not for her. She began doubting herself.

She fell to her knees feeling as though she had failed, wondering why she put herself through it, the doubts flooded her mind, the constant tirade of thoughts, 'you'll never be good enough'. The words of her old head teacher echoed in her mind...

"Nothing will EVER become of that GIRL!"

She sat on the cliff top crying feeling like she had failed, afraid to return home. She sent a text to Rob.

Audition over, heading home soon.

He was still sat in his room, still watching the clock, wondering where she was, had she finished, did it go well?

He read her message, nodding his head he looked at Levi who was staring up at him, as though he'd also been waiting for that message.

"She's finished and on way back buddy" he spoke rubbing behind Levi's ears.

"Come on let's go for a walk" he continued.

The hours past, with no further messages, he began to worry, dusk which was falling slowly bringing a darkness, he thought of the roads she would be travelling weren't well lit at night.

He was unaware she had returned to Newcastle, and had headed straight to church, not ready to face anyone, not even him. As she sat praying, begging, her phone pinged.

"Hey, you should be home by now slow coach! Where are you?"

She looked at her phone, and up at the cross. She knew no matter what, he was one person who always cared, was always there.

She whispered a thank you to God. A thank you for sending him into her life, before getting up, picking up her helmet and dialling his number as she walked out closing the door behind her.

He answered, she pursed her lips smiling as his welcome voice steadied her.

"Hey Sorry, I needed a few moments at church to sort out my head... I'm on my way" she said as she climbed on Kitt2.

Chapter 21

Imogen's audition wasn't discussed again, knowing she'd find out in time, instead she had to concentrate on their final exams, her final college performance, and making the most of the remainder of the academic year, with the future after college being filled with so much unknown.

Soon April arrived... Imogen walked onto the bridge; everyone fell silent. She looked around perplexed. Had they all been talking about her? She thought as she sat down.

"So... we were just talking about music..." Rob announced almost reading her mind, knowing the thoughts and scenarios which would be filling her mind.

"I was just tellin' the girls about the weird band you like..." he continued bating her into a reaction while tossing a crisp into the air, catching it in his mouth.

"They aint weird, and I know you've also taken a like to them, admit it... Though I could tell the girls your secret taste in music...." She replied, as Rob jumped up covering her mouth as though to stop her.

"Shhhh" he whispered.

"What's it worth?" she replied looking at him playfully and almost seductively, before laughing and stepping away, sitting down on the settee.

"This old thing needs replaced" she stated changing the conversation.

"Do you think they'll ever replace it, like when we've gone, or will we come back one day for a reunion and it'll still be here?" she continued.

"Nah, they'll never replace it, it's part of the fittings like Rob here... it'll be here forever!" Trudi replied.

Imogen glanced over at Rob, she knew it was a joke, playful banter, but she knew it would have cut deep. She smiled at him. Thinking of so many replies. She gazed into those eyes, as though communicating without words, I've got you...

"Anyway, Capercaillie aren't weird! They're Scottish, and well I don't know about you but I'm definitely part Scottish! Don't you know your history..." she laughed.

"I was born North of Hadrian's Wall, and once upon a time that wall was the border of England and Scotland, so I'm Scottish.

"You're nuts!" Vicki laughed shaking her head.

Imogen turned on her playlist,

"How on earth do you know what they're saying?" Trudi exclaimed

"You don't need to know the words, and sometimes the English translation is in the cover, and I'm learning Gaelic.

Rob interrupted with a quick-witted reply...

"What do we want?... More Gaelic speakers!........When do we want them?

........Anois!"

She laughed as the bell rang, knowing he would have thought of that joke a long time ago, waiting for the perfect time. Imogen left heading towards the dance department. As the gang stood up Rob asked.

"So.. Are you in?"

The girls nodded in agreement, handing over money to Rob, before walking out.

A week later Imogen turned 18. He called her up at midnight and wished her a Happy Birthday. She smiled, nobody had ever taken the time before, her birthday almost always forgotten.

She arrived at college; the bridge adorned with decorations.

"Happy birthday!" they erupted almost simultaneously.

Rob tossed a balloon in the air in the direction of Imogen. She caught it in her hands, bewildered that they would go to so much effort. Rob stepped in close, concealing the pin in his hand.

The balloon burst, halting every conversation and thought.

Falling from the balloon was an endless stream of confetti, and an envelope. She wondered how he managed to get the envelope in the balloon. As she opened the small envelope, she stood frozen, every muscle of her body just froze. He saw the shock register on her face before she could hide it. Her shock quickly morphed into excitement as a grin crept across her face, erupting into smile that continued to grow like a flower opening. Building from deep inside to light her eyes and spread into every part of her, a smile of complete happiness. He'd seen her smile so many times but that one outshone them all.

A small smile played on his lips as he watched. Inside the envelope were two tickets to see Capercaillie the following week.

"Who are you taking?" Trudi quizzed,

Imogen didn't need to think about it, there was only one person who could fill that spot. Imogen thought how it was the perfect birthday in every sense and couldn't wait for the following week, no other gift could surpass what was given.

"It's from all of us… but you can guess whose idea it was, and who contributed the most" Trudi whispered nudging her.

"Oh, and yeah we're coming to that bash thing tomorrow!" she continued, grabbing a slice of cake before walking towards the door to head to class.

"Tomorrow?" Imogen asked, shrugging her shoulders staring at Rob.

"Oops!" Trudie replied again shrugging her shoulders.

"Your dads organised a little gathering at the club" Rob replied picking up his jacket and helmet.

"It was meant to be a surprise..." he continued looking directly at Trudi.

Imogen knew her father wouldn't have come up with the idea alone or be able to organise anything, well apart from a piss up in a brewery she thought causing her to purse her lips to hide the giggle which wanted to escape.

"Come on, we can leave this all for later, we've got to get to class" Rob continued taking hold of her hand and began walking towards the door.

Imogen began to follow, stopping at the door allowing their hands to part. She looked back at the confetti on the floor, the decorations across the windows, and the food on the table.

"You coming or what?" Rob shouted from the staircase.

"Yep" she nodded before following him.

The following evening, he walked down to the club opposite the bay. Sauntering under the moonlight he looked out over at the bay, the water lay still. The heat of the day had been replaced by a cool breeze. Rob sauntered along, his jacket draping from his arm, and in his hand a clown's wig. He looked up at the club knowing it would already be packed with Imogen, and the rest of his friends, it felt good to say that word – friends. He was eager to get there, late due to having to undertake some last-minute chores. He moved between the pools of streetlight; his feet almost silent upon the path which was still wet from the spring rain falling earlier that afternoon. A pair of headlights came bouncing round the bend as he prepared to step out onto the road, startling him and blinding him temporarily before passing and disappearing.

"Can't die yet! Got to take a girl to her first concert!" he spoke to himself as he crossed the road, hearing the music drift out from the open door.

Thinking of how inside would be soft lighting, good music, good friends, and jokes which were so stupid they would be brilliant.

As he entered his smile dropped. Jacob was there. He took a moment in the doorway before deciding he wasn't going to allow anything to spoil Imogen's evening, he could tolerate the guy for just one night.

He went to the bar grabbing a drink to give him the ability to get through the night. Ordering 2 single whiskey's, he downed one, leaving the glass on the bar, and holding the other in his hand he walked through the room towards Jacob.

Pulling him aside, he spoke.

"I don't like you, you don't like me, but for one night she comes first!" he declared holding out his hand even though it was one of the hardest things he had ever had to do.

Jacob hesitated, but reciprocated shaking Rob's hand. Rob turned away wincing and recoiling before taking deep breath. He placed the wig on his head. As he straightened the wig he smiled as though putting on a mask. He turned walking towards Imogen.

"Happy birthday my lady.." he spoke though his cheeky grin.

"What on earth are you wearing!?" Imogen asked as she turned spotting him, trying not to laugh.

"Well you know me….born to stand out! and hey the whiskey here is pretty darn good too!" He declared downing the second glass, taking her hand guiding her onto the dancefloor.

The night past with the guilty pleasure of watching Jacob spending most of it watching from the side-lines as Imogen mingled with guests, being the perfect host. The party was filled with friends as well as fellow dance and theatre students, along with a few of her father's friends to help bulk out the large concert room. Playing the bigger person also made him feel like he'd won before feeling guilty, feeling like his thoughts had betrayed him.

The week passed quickly with the excitement building. Saturday night arrived   Rob stood in his room, trying on endless shirts and t-shirts.

"That'll have to do!" he told himself staring into the mirror on his wardrobe door.

He walked downstairs, straightening his collar.

"Roberto, a date with Imogen??.." his mother asked as he looked at himself in the mirror by the coat-stand.

"No, mama. I've told you she is just a friend; she has a boyfriend... "

"No, no, no.. I've seen how she looks at you, how you look at her, a boy and a girl don't get as close as you two have, how many shirts have you tried on for just a friend? She must end it with that other boy, it's not right.."

"Mama!" he spoke sternly.

"You're such a handsome boy. Go have fun." His mother had never made such a fuss, and she'd never referred to him as being handsome, well not since he'd been a young boy. It felt strange being given positive praise but was something he'd always wanted.

He pulled up outside Imogen's house. His eyes caught her as she walked up the path.

"Wow!" he muttered under his breath.

She stopped in front of him, the nail of her thumb in her mouth she looked up at him, biting down harder. She removed her finger, biting her bottom lip, her dimples slowly creeping upon her face.

She smiled

"You've been complaining that I'm always in jeans, so..."

He too smiled.

"Not really bike wear, but you do look pretty damn good" he replied stretching his palm out to her, which she took without hesitation.

"It's a good job I'm not wearing a long dress then isn't it" she joked climbing on the back of Buzby.

They sat in the theatre, the lights dimming. The moment she had been waiting for. Her adrenaline filling her every vein. The time had finally come to see and hear her first live concert.

As the music began playing, she began thinking how a song can touch you, the melody lingering behind. The music filled the air without effort. Her voice, haunting, the music, filled with grace.

They danced in the aisle as the concert got into full swing.

When the concert finished Rob dragged her through the auditorium, and backstage to meet the band. She had spent many times imagining what she would say to them, but as it became a reality, her words failed her, stood speechless as she received a signed jumper.

He watched her outside, still dancing, her hands stretched out, reaching for the stars above.

They rode home, she loved those night rides on the back of Buzby, she didn't want the night to end.

He walked her to her front door...

They stood holding hands, she looked at him with a thankful heart. It felt as though time had stood still, caught in the moment.

A moment which never saw itself to fruition as her father arrived home, their hands parted, as he walked between them.

"Ye allreet Kidda?" He asked Rob as he passed.

"Aye, Bri we had a great time" Rob replied.

"Pick you up Monday morning for class" Rob asked stepping back.

"I'll be waiting" she replied casually, watching him walk back to his bike.

Chapter 22

The following months were filled with study sessions broken up by rides to clear the mind and re-focus. As the exams approached the nerves were beginning to become too much, Imogen's anxiety sky-rocketed out of control. It hadn't helped that she had finally told Jacob, and her father, and her family that she was planning on going to Scarborough, if she got accepted. Making it all feel too real.

They sat studying in her house a few days before their first exam.

Jacob's reply echoed in her mind

"Don't get your hopes up"

Rob could sense she wasn't coping; she was ready to break.

"Come on!" he stated his hand outstretched.

"Let's get outta here, a quick ride is just what the Dr ordered" he continued, as she looked up, hesitating before closing her file, placing it on the floor beside her and taking his hand.

"Well if a Dr has issued a ride, then how can I refuse... Though I'd like to meet this Dr who prescribes bike rides!" she cloyingly responded.

They rode out to the lighthouse, looking out over at the northern lights. The lights danced across the dark sky, each tint slowly fading into another.

"I can't do it!" she screamed as they stood on the beach.

She began to hyperventilate.

She choked down the rising bile and unconsciously clenched her fist, feeling the pain of her nails digging into her palm.

"Hey! Yes you can" he replied stepping forward his hands resting on her shoulders.

"Come on!" he urged as he guided her along the beach and across the causeway. They stood on the grass underneath the lighthouse.

"You can do it, you will do it, cause it's your destiny, or God's plan or however you want to put it... and I'm here, I'll always be here"

"Just breathe" he told her pulling her in close, before guiding her to the ground. She lay with her head in his lap as he gently brushed her hair with his hand, soothing and calming her.

He'd watched her anxiety sky-rocket so many times fuelled with self-doubt and in those moments he'd watch as she would nip at her skin, the self-harm never completely disappearing. At times he felt like a broken record wishing she could see what he saw, but he knew that record would play on repeat until the day she finally became who she was meant to be.

Imogen fell asleep in his arms.

Sitting there looking over at the horizon he pondered on his nerves. He was good at masquerading his feelings passing them off with his nonchalant behaviour. He was also nervous for the exams, though more nervous of the results as proof of yet another failure to add to the growing list, though in part he thought with it being more A levels maybe his mother wouldn't be as interested. He thought how the last A levels he got a B in science, getting home happy just to be scolded because he didn't get the A that his eldest brother had, and how his other results destroyed the chance to get onto dentistry course at the local University, to follow in his brother's golden footsteps.

He'd shattered his mother's dreams of a family business.

He thought about his other brother studying international hospitality. He as allowed to chase his dreams, it just always seemed as though everyone else could except him.

Time passed as he watched the changing sky and the tide turning.

"Hey Imi… Time for us to get going or we'll get stranded over here" he whispered stroking her hair.

"Would that really be so bad?" she yawned.

Wouldn't it be nice to own that house…? To be able to be closed off from the rest of the world for at least half of the day!" she continued as she sat up.

"Ok, let's get back to the real world" she sighed taking his hand.

The exams soon came, soon came their last exam, their last day. The last day signalling the beginning of the end, or so he believed.

They entered the college together, walking through the college to the exam halls. Everyone was nervous and emotional as they stood in the crowds waiting to be allowed into the halls. Imogen looked around noticing the vast array of feelings displayed.

"Good luck! You've got this" Rob whispered kissing her cheek, before letting go of her hand.

"That was for luck" he winked as he took his seat, Imogen took the seat in front of him, turning to pass him a pen knowing he would have forgotten.

Smiling as the pen passed between them. She turned back facing forward, taking a deep breath, looking at the clock on the wall.

The Exam started, Imogen turned the page, reading through the questions before starting to write. Rob scanned the room, observing everyone and everything.

Turning the page, he began writing as the time slowly fell away.

After the exam, they all congregated on the bridge, for one last time, creating memories, writing on shirts.

Rob looked back over those 2 years. When he began, he thought they would be like the previous two years, how wrong he was! He was struck with the realization of how precious those years had been. How those two years, the friends he'd found, Imogen, and those days which they spent in college together had all changed the course of his life and changed him.

The summer came and went, filled with memories to carry forever.

Results day finally arrived. Rob stood in his room getting ready to head into college. He picked up his phone, his fingers hovering over the buttons. He began typing, knowing she would be even more nervous than him.

Results Day! Aargh!!!! It's OK for Brainiac's like you! What time you going to college, we're having a party later, you coming??

His phone pinged a quick reply,

Going at 10am, meeting Jacob outside college. Party?? Maybe 😊

He sauntered into college, collecting his results with Trudi.

He had hoped they could all open them together, he opened the envelope, he'd passed, but he knew his mother would still find fault, it was also Isabella's first year A level results, and he knew that her results would always overshadow his.

"So, what's the plan for next year?" Trudi asked.

Rob shrugged; he hadn't really thought that far ahead.

"I think I might try doing a course on classroom assistant/ teaching assistant... something like that..." he replied

"Just checking you are coming later?" he continued.

"Yep, of course!" Trudi answered walking out of college running to her parents who were waiting.

"See ya in 2 hours!" she shouted back, before showing her exam results, getting obligatory hugs from her proud parents.

He entered the house, no-one noticed or commented. He returned to his room desperate to know how Imogen did. He picked up a small box which sat on his table, staring at it he picked up his phone.

He sent a text

We're meeting south end of long sands in an hour, want picked up?? I'll be upset if you don't come

The time past slowly as he wondered what she was doing, and whether she would join them. He continued to stare at his phone, she'd seen his message. He knew she would pass but as the minutes passed scenarios began to fill his mind.

15 minutes had passed since she had seen the message.

He stood up determined to find her. He paced the floor in his small room hesitantly before grabbing his jacket which was draped over his chair. As he was about to walk out of his room Imogen sent him a message, asking him to come pick her up.

He pulled up outside. She grabbed her jacket and helmet, walking out to meet him. The smile on her face told him all he needed to know.

"Hello, my lady, your carriage awaits" he smiled gesturing, giving her a mocking extravagant bow with his helmet.

Imogen performed a curtsey in reply. Rob climbed back onto Buzby before Imogen swung her leg over the pillion seat. The engine roared as he revved the engine, pulling out of the cul-de-sac onto the main road, heading down to the coast.

He parked his bike outside of his house.

"Well? Are you going to tell me or do I have to tickle it out of you?" he asked as they walked arm in arm down to the beach.

"I got a letter this morning... before getting results, I got in!" She beamed.

He could see how much it filled her with excitement, he hugged her, though wondered if she would remember to ask him about his results.

"So what did that loser say?" he asked.

She stopped for a moment, hesitating, before telling him how she arrived at college, Jacob was standing outside the college with a big blue thumper rabbit.

She told him she had never seen such a big rabbit! And how for a moment she thought he'd accepted her choice and more importantly believed in her. She spoke of how she took the rabbit, but as they began walking up the steps, she realised the truth, his true thoughts revealed. Recalling the words which fell from him.

"I know you'll be disappointed, but you tried and that's all that matters."

She told Rob how she realised in that moment Jacob had no faith in her. Telling him how she reached her hand into her pocket for the confirmation letter.

How she stood for a few moments in shock and disbelief, before speaking.

"You may not have faith in me, but they can see my potential…… ……I've been accepted………" *She couldn't finish her sentence as she choked on the tears.*

She told how she stepped back, walking in alone to collect her results, recalling the car journey home, the uncomfortable atmosphere.

Rob listened, filled with a stream of emotions. Contempt for Jacob, pride and happiness for Imogen, but also disappointment. The one person who he thought would be interested in his results, be happy for him hadn't even asked how he did, but then he began to feel guilty for such selfish thoughts as though telling himself he wasn't important.

Imogen continued walking taking hold of Rob's hand, not wanting to dwell on the events of that morning any longer, deciding that the evening was going to be about celebration, and friendship.

Imogen stopped on the access road seeing the bonfire below.

She turned,

"Oh my God.. I'm so sorry, I'm such a selfish cow! How did you do?" she asked realising she'd been so obsessed with her results and Jacob that she had forgotten to ask about his results.

"It's OK, you're forgiven… and yep I passed… Couldn't have done it without your help though…" he replied.

"Sure, you would have!" she exclaimed.

"… and I certainly wouldn't have, or even gotten the place if it wasn't for you" she continued, thinking over the many memories, the many times he gave her the confidence to try, to believe.

They approached where the gang had set up a small bonfire, they spent the late afternoon drinking, singing, and dancing. The fire burned slowly as the evening progressed.

As the sun faded the atmosphere became more sombre. The sun began setting in the late summer sky as if mirroring the end of that chapter in their lives. The remaining light drained away, the day was turning to dusk; the only light was the orange glow from the bonfire and the streetlights on the streets above.

Trudi opened a bottle of cheap Champagne, the pop of the cork, caught Imogen off guard. Laughing she began passing round plastic wine glasses, before filling each glass. Imogen wrapped her fingers around the glass, as Trudi made a toast to the future.

"To the next part in our journeys' let us never forget what we've had here and now"

They raised their glasses. Imogen raised the glass to take a sip. She looked up at Rob.

He smiled.

"And here's to us, a friendship that can never be broken"
Their glasses clinked together,

"To us!" She replied.

It was a perfect evening. Imogen was happy that she decided to join them instead of spending the evening with Jacob.
That night they all vowed to stay in touch.

Imogen watched the sea, becoming lost in thought, lost in the rhythmic percussion of waves upon the sand. Her eyes steady to the horizon. The night was rolling in. The group slowly began to disperse until there was only Imogen and Rob remaining.

The sky was clear. The twilight beckoned the stars. They sat alone by the small fire watching the waves crashing against the shore, huddled together under a blanket as the music continued to play.

Her gaze slid to the side. As they sat huddled together she began to shiver. He pulled her against his chest.

He leant into his bag, pulling out the small box which he'd been holding earlier that day. The day before he bought her a small gift, to celebrate her results, he knew she would have passed, he never doubted her for a moment, but it was also a gift which he hoped would remind her of him, so that she would never forget.

He handed her the small box, tied with a neat ribbon. Imogen opened the box excitedly. Inside was a blue velvet ring box. She carefully opened the box, inside sat a beautifully delicate silver ring.

"It's a…." Rob started to speak

"Claddagh ring" Imogen replied finishing his sentence.

She gazed up at those warm eyes.

"The two hands represent friendship; a heart symbolizes love and the crown on top is for loyalty. You wear it on your right hand, when single it is worn with the heart facing outwards, when taken it is worn with the heart pointed inwards." He stated placing it carefully onto her finger, the heart facing inwards, their fingers locked together.

"I knew you would do it…. I'm so proud of you my little Imi, you deserve to get out of here, to make a new life… Hopefully this ring will remind you that wherever you go, I will always be with you…."

The sentence died.

He leant forward slightly; her pulse raced. A small lock of her hair tumbled in front of her face, resting on her cheek. With one swift slide of his thumb, it was brushed out of the way.

Imogen looked deep into his eyes as he began to draw in closer. Her eyes closed her head tilted upwards in anticipation. Was he going to kiss her?

Rob looked at her, hesitating, not willing to take that step, to taint their friendship. She was still with Jacob, and he thought how he could never give her what she needed, what she deserved.

She could feel her heartbeat so hard she feared he would hear it...

Did she want this? Nothing could stop the moment from continuing out to fruition.

She felt his lips on her cheek, so soft and with the smallest hint of coolness. A small grin crept onto her face; her cheeks painted themselves rose red. He pulled away silently, their eyes locked. After a few seconds he broke away and smiled,

"I just had to do that, even if it is only once."

"You do know you're never going to lose me, right?" Imogen asked, breaking the silence, nudging him.

"We can write to each other every day, so we are always in each other's lives, and if I'm not a good enough reason to visit, I'm sure the Bike track will tempt you..." she continued.
She looked up at those eyes, concealing the sadness.

Pulling him to his feet they walked along the sand.

"...and maybe I can get you out there, on the board..." pulling him towards the water, dodging the incoming waves.

"Not in this country you're not! Far too cold!" He replied as he picked her up swinging her around, spinning her in delicate circles, the pressure of his warm hand on her back. The cold waves lapped at their feet. Laughing they fell onto the sand, staring at the stars above.

"Aim for the moon…...."

In the pause Imogen interrupted.

"…....and if you miss, you'll still be among the stars…" Imogen smiled.

They returned to the bonfire watching the glowing embers die, becoming cold ashes. They poured one final drink into their plastic wine glasses, linking arms, and taking a sip from each other's cup they spoke the words, a solemn promise.

"So, let us drink from the same cup of life yet remain our true selves, an anchor for each other - two souls joined forever"

They stayed there till morning, waking to see the night become day, as the stars blended into the blue.

Chapter 23

September arrived. He watched as everyone was excitedly preparing for their new lives, while he felt stuck in repeat. He couldn't face the college again, alone. Facing the bridge without her, without the gang, without the real friendships he had found, but were now slipping away.

He decided it was time for a fresh start, a year away from studying, thinking ahead to the next year looking at different colleges, thinking of enrolling on a teaching assistants' course, hoping to find purpose.

He could hear the sound of his mother's voice like nails on a chalkboard. His mother found fault in his plan, he was fulfilling her expectations, being lazy, useless, lacking drive, in essence nothing. He knew no matter what he did it would be wrong. Isabella spoke of her plans to take a gap year following her A levels, but that apparently was different.

In the last few weeks before Imogen left it was as though they were trying to collect memories and reliving memories, neither really knowing where there friendship was going, making promises which they both intended to honour but both wondered whether they were just caught up in the naivety of youth.

The third week in September crept upon him, bringing with it the autumn, the summer leaving, but also the time for Imogen to leave.

Rob sat contemplating surviving without Imogen, knowing she would be on her way to begin her new life. He'd watched her grow, he helped her dream and believe, had been there every step of the way, but deep down there was still a sadness. He wished he was going with her but knew he could never leave, he was never allowed to leave, the rest were allowed to leave, pursue their dreams but he couldn't. As he looked out of the window a tear fell from his eye.

His phone pinged,

Hey, heading off now. I'm gonna swing past the bay, meet me at our spot in 15*?*

Wiping a tear from his eye, he quickly replied.

We don't need soppy goodbyes; I'll be with you so much you'll be sick of me! But if you want a race part way, I'm in!

It was the time. The time he knew was coming but dreaded. Having to say goodbye to the only person that he genuinely cared for, and someone who he believed cared for him. He rode down to the bay, stopping for a moment before continuing along to the priory to wait. He wondered how he was supposed to just go on without feeling like he'd lost a part of himself. As he stood he watched the waves recalling the many moments they had shared, remembering all the times they would just talk and laugh. Normal things that normal people would do. He recalled many of the many discussions, moments laughing and crying, both unafraid to reveal the unspoken, time when nothing remained hidden.

He thought how he'd forgotten how to live, she was the one who showed him the way, and when it felt like the world was falling apart around him, she made him feel as though it wasn't so bad. When he felt like nothing could ever make him feel better, she somehow managed to put a smile upon his face.

He wished he could go back. Back to when they first met to do it all over again, savouring every moment, knowing he wouldn't change a single thing. As he saw kitt2 come around the corner of the headland he wiped his eyes, composing himself, not wanting Imogen to see.

She pulled up, he was sat on his bike, waiting, visor up looking out over the shore.

There was kindness in his smile, a gentleness. He had become part of her soul. As she looked at him, she thought how he brought out the best aspects of those he met. She knew she wouldn't be taking that step had it not been for him, without him her life would have been so different, to him her flaws entirely invisible. He was her calm sea. Yet, most of all, he was her friend.

She wasn't going to allow this to be their end.

"Come on then! Let's get outta here" he smiled as he revved his accelerator.

They rode down the A19 then onto the winding country roads, just like they did that first time. As she rode behind him, she switched her attention to the changing scenery, she thought to herself how lucky she was to have someone who chose to care for her, and for once realising how hard it was to say goodbye.

Her mind wondered, thinking how every end is also a new beginning. She hoped that this new beginning would be the dawn of something special.

They stopped at the border for Whitby. Parked with their bikes side by side. Taking off their helmets, they looked over the harbour.

"Go on girl you can take it from here, your future awaits!" He spoke through his cheeky grin.

"I've got a little something for you.." she choked, handing him a CD.

"See ya soon" She smiled, trying to conceal a tear.

He leant over kissing her on the cheek, before turning and pulling off back in the direction they had just came from.

She remained seated looking over the harbour, and watching him disappear in her rear-view mirror. She breathed in deeply, before putting on her helmet to continue the final stage of her journey alone.

He returned home to his room; the realisation hit. He sat alone unable to help but feel isolated, returning to that nobody. His chest ached as though his heart was shattering inside him causing him to feel empty, like a black hole.

He placed the CD in his laptop, as the song began, he read the note inside.

I wrote this song for you, I recorded it with Matt in his studio. I'll never forget the moments you laughed with me, cried with me, helped me.

I don't regret any of those memories. Thank you for everything. I hope this way I will always be with you.

Her haunting lyrics swam through him, a song about unconditional love, the force that can lift us up even from the darkest of places.

I know….
The pain is all around you.
So linger in silence to be heard by nobody but us…..
….For the time you wait is time you waste…
It's time to listen to find your rhythm….

Chapter 24

The following day he sat in his room holding a notepad and pen. They had made a promise to write to each other, a promise he was determined to keep. He wondered, though would she?

He thought how perhaps she was already making friends, he hoped she was making friends. He began writing a letter which would be the first of many.

Hello!

I hope you have settled in nicely? Have you been surfing yet?

Have you remembered to unpack, organise your books and buy a fresh full colour range of felt tips?

Are you looking after your anaemia by drinking iron supplemented Tia Maria?...

Don't forget to tuck yourself in properly come bedtime....

His thoughts filled the page, mixed with jokes and scribbles, hoping to bring a smile.

I think I've made too many 'old' jokes, maybe because I'm old? Too many years at college with you I think...

When he'd finished, he placed the letter in an envelope, running out of the house to catch the last post.

A few days later he entered the house, a letter lay on the small table near the front door, he recognised the writing instantly.

Running up the stairs to his room he opened the letter.

Hey Rob,
I'm so alone in this small room, I want so badly to go and meet my neighbours but I'm afraid. Where are you when I need you? I wish you were here with me? Like when I started college, the day we met, I was so scared, afraid, the crowded cafeteria. Standing in the cafeteria, out of my depth, I looked up and you were there...

As he read the words, he couldn't help but worry, wishing he was there. He picked up the phone, hearing her voice. He listened as she talked for what felt like hours.

Those first couple of weeks dragged, though stayed in touch via text and the occasional long facetime, deciding it would be much cheaper than ringing, and seeing her face, it was as though she was still with him.

Each evening he began writing his thoughts and randomness, what he'd done that day, at times what he wrote never made sense, but he knew that didn't matter, it was keeping the connection. He looked forward to the letters from her thinking there was something magical about receiving a written letter. Most of her letters were like his, filled with random nonsensical chatter, with a few revealing so much more.

It was a weekend, early in October. She had told him how Jacob had promised to visit that weekend, there was a party planned in the student union.

My dearest Rob, I need you right now.......

He never came.. I'm sat here in my room ready, I know you will say go without him, and I want to, but I can't, I'm too afraid, I wish you were here.....

Her words spoke of her fears, how her anxiety was suffocating her how alone she felt, her words smudged by tear drops which had fallen onto the paper.

Her words stopped abruptly... he turned over the page.

I fell asleep, it's now 1am. Everyone is returning from the party, looks like they all had a great time. Goodnight my friend x

He read her letter, the anger and hatred began to boil, how did this jerk not realise what he had? He began writing but every time his anger was apparent, he scrunched the paper throwing it in the bin, pacing his room he tried to calm himself. Again, he took a piece of paper and began writing...

I wouldn't suggest doing your own thing all the time, did you really have to miss That party??

You're strong but I think your dependence on others to make you whole is a hinderance to your destiny. True your destiny means you're going to get there anyway but you'll realise so much more so much sooner without so much pain and insecurity.

God knows where you're going, you may not think you're worthy but if you aren't then who is? You have a beautiful soul

Buzby awaits Kitt2's company on the open road! Maybe I could come down for the weekend, stop over, we can hit the roads (weather permitting) during the day, and I'll get you out there, partying, they won't know what's hit them!

By the way I probably made my sleeping quirks sound quirkier than what they really are. Did I remember to tell you that I always put cheesy wotsits up my nostrils before going to bed, I wonder...

2 days later, knowing the letter would have arrived, he picked up his phone and dialled her number.

"Hey! So, what wild party are we going to at the weekend?"

She tried unconvincingly to explain how she was meant to be going to Durham that weekend.

"He stood you up! You deserve so much better!" He replied. His voice filled with concern, and love, trying to hold back his frustration.

She paused for a moment, he waited wondering who she would choose. After a long pause, she took a deep breath, finally she replied.

"You're on! Let's do this! They've got some crazy stock exchange game on at the bar on Friday night."

He rode down that Friday, dragging her to the bar. He'd always loved a good drinking game. He'd curbed his drinking and wild nights those past two years, but he decided it was time for him to rub off on her. It was her time, and it was a rite of passage, he knew she needed it, to come alive, for people to see who she was behind the mask, just like she did back at college on that bridge.

He rallied a group together, to beat the bank, he was in his element! She came alive around him, she always did. He was like the Sun. He had people orbiting around him. In one way or another all the people that met him were drawn to him.

She had been at the university for a few weeks, and apart from short conversations with others in her classes she barely spoke to anyone, that night she began to make connections, and began to make friends, because of him.

The Saturday they spent together, long rides up the coast, long conversations in which she could wrap herself up in his words. They spent hours at the fayre on the seafront. The old big wheel was rusty with red, peeling sun-baked paint, but adorned with a kaleidoscope of lights, music filled the air, the traditional fairground soundtracks. He tried to drive her crazy by singing the song Scarborough fair, as though on repeat.

They trawled the seafront going in every amusement, as though they were tourists. As he stood in front of a claw machine filled with soft toys, he placed a coin in the slot and stated,

"I'm gonna win you one" .

"You do know they're all a con?" she asked watching him concentrating.

"Shhh" he urged as he positioned the claw above an Eeyore. The claw fell down grabbing the soft toy, lifting it towards the shoot, the soft toy dropping short of the hole.

"See, told ya!" she declared smugly, as he placed another coin in the slot, aiming again for the Eeyore.

This time as the soft toy fell out of the claw it landed balancing on the side of the shoot.

"One more go, and it'll be yours!" he declared, as he again positioned the claw above the soft toy, this time it fell into the shoot.

"Jammy Git!" she laughed as he handed her the Eeyore.

"Now you won't be alone... Eeyore will look after you when I'm not here" he said as he handed it to her.

She took hold of the soft toy, his hands still resting on it.

"EEYORE! You look after her for me buddy" he said looking at the soft toy then returning his focus to her.

She looked up at him. Thankful to have him in her life, thinking of all the simple little gestures over the years. She thought how he was and remained the person who could pick her up when she was down, make her laugh, he made her question everything, and constantly changed her for the better, just by being there.

Sunday morning, they rode up to the mount. They sat on the grass verge overlooking the start/finish line and the paddock.

"I bet this place really comes alive on race days... we gotta come... Promise..." Imogen stated giving a sigh knowing whatever she asked she always ended up getting.

"I bet I could get round the track faster than you" She uttered, knowing she could never beat him but wanted to fuel their competitiveness.

"Go on then.. Let's see what you got..." Rob laughed.

"Ok. Watch me!" Imogen answered stamping her foot down as though to emphasise her point. She climbed on Kitt 2. She stared ahead as she sat, engine purring.

"You ready?" Rob shouted as he sauntered down to the start line.

"Yep!"

"Well...On your marks.... Get set...."

Imogen knocked the bike into gear waiting.

"Go!" Rob shouted.

Imogen pulled away from the starting line gaining speed as she reached Mere Hairpin. She had only ridden around the track a few times since moving to Scarborough but when she did, she would negotiate that bend slowly taking extra care. It wasn't like other bends, the 180 turn led straight onto a steep incline up the side of the hill.

"Here goes nothing, can't be that hard" She uttered under her breath as she began entering the bend, slowing just enough to get round though skimming close to the grass verge using as much of the track as possible. A smile crept across her face feeling cocky,

"Easy peasy" She whispered as she exited the bend changing gear. With her concentration dipping she over accelerated causing her to instinctively press on her foot brake pedal causing her front tyre to lift from the surface, causing the bike to perform a wheelie. The steep incline made her feel ss though she was going to fall back. Her hands gripped tighter as she used the force of her body to push down. The front wheel bounced as it hit the road. She swerved desperate to gain control. She began to wobble, losing control she fell from the bike.

Rob ran up the verge panicking. Imogen sat on the ground her knee staring at her leg bent staring at her leg.

"You OK?" Rob asked as he kneeled beside her.

"I've ripped my new leathers!" Imogen stated, trying to disguise her embarrassment.

"Better the leathers than your leg. Come on..." He beckoned offering his hand. She extended her hand taking hold of his allowing him to pull her to her feet.

"RIGHT!" Rob exclaimed as he picked up kitt2.

"I'm sure he'll live." He stated turning the bike and pushing it back to down the hill. Imogen hobbled behind.

"I think you should leave the racing to me"

"Though that wheelie was pretty awesome." He continued trying not to laugh.

Rob placed Kitt2 on his side stand next to Buzby.

"Come on... Let's get back to the dorm and check on that leg and get some food into you." He said wrapping his arm around her.

She hobbled as she walked towards kitt2, though her ego was more bruised than her leg.

Sunday afternoon came far too quick. They stood by Buzby, parked outside of the halls. Rob climbed on, ready to leave.

Before he left, she complained about how many brain cells she'd lost through him that weekend. The stock exchange and the karaoke on the Saturday night down in one of the bars on the seafront.

Sitting on his bike, holding onto her hand he casually replied.

"Maybe that means you might become normal, instead of the super nerdy swat you are!"

A smile tried to escape as he tried to hold in his laughter, he enjoyed winding her up. Deep down Imogen wouldn't have it any other way! He leant down kissing her softly on the cheek.

She thought how even in his humour he was building her up, as if trying to undo the damage from the torrent of people putting her down.

She thought how in contrast to Jacob, poles apart, he would use every opportunity to tear her down.

"Now, go make some friends! And write me, telling me all about it!" he declared before pulling down his visor, and riding away.

She stood there watching him turn the corner, disappearing from site. She wished he could stay permanently. She needed Rob at university! How could she make friends without him?

She was a different girl, a more confident, fun girl when he was around. Without him she returned to the quiet, shy, unconfident scared little girl. Afraid of her own shadow.

Night Sweetness (and Eeyore!) x

He posted the letter the next morning.

She received it a few days later, sitting in her room she read his words.

"Yes I've eaten" She replied out loud.

"OK cleverclogs, Geesh!!" she answered as she continued to read. He knew her far too well; nothing could get past him. Putting the letter in her pocket she walked over to the canteen.

She smiled as she passed students she recognised from the weekend, in return there were a few smiles, a few gestures, but it all felt forced. Though in contrast it was still an improvement to the week before Rob came down. Back when she walked through campus staring at the ground, feeling as though nobody noticed her, looking up taking a glance at her reflection in the window to make sure she was still there; that she hadn't turned invisible, because that was how she felt.

Entering the canteen, she ordered her food before sitting at one of the empty tables. She ate alone, pulling out the letter and her note pad.

Hi
Ok. Yes! You got me, I lied, but as requested
I'm at the canteen... Alone... Eating just as

you requested! Oh, and I'm eating what is
supposed to be meatballs????

She continued reading his letter. Laughing and smiling as is humour touched her,

She read his words "You're the sweetest girl…."

It wasn't true, he was the selfless one, she sometimes thought how selfish she was, how nearly all of the time it was all about her, and he was always there, with the right words, or just a hug, he always knew how to make her smile no matter how sad she felt.

She continued to read… Church? She wondered how she could tell him she hadn't been. She tried one week but found them too stuck-up, too judgemental, she couldn't handle it, and it was becoming a conceited effort to attend. She'd began to tell herself she didn't need a building, cause that's not what church really is, it's not a building. So instead of church she began finding a quiet place for solitude, reflection and prayer. Although she missed the community and fellowship it wasn't there in Scarborough. There wasn't a church she felt accepted her, a place where she belonged. She constantly felt judged and looked down on. She wasn't sure whether that was true or her mind creating narratives, but she wasn't going to put herself through it. She wasn't going to put up with people like Jacob's parents anymore.

She had sat in her room one evening watching Netflix. Drawn to a movie, a horror, stigmata. The final words stuck with her.

Jesus said… the Kingdom of God is inside you, and all around you, not in mansions of wood and stone. Split a piece of wood… and I am there, lift a stone… and you will find me.

She began using that as an excuse rather than admit she didn't fit in.

She continued to write…

I have been making an effort to talk to some people on my course, baby steps... and I'm not that special, if anyone is, you are! I don't think I tell you often enough how much I love you.. Ok I bet you're pretending to be sick ! I'll stop being a soppy chick... Church? I'll tell you all about it when I next see you... When is that??

Folding the paper, she placed it in her pocket, returning to her room and sat on her bed. She picked up Eeyore, pulling him close she whispered.

"It's just us now"

Two weeks past. Rob sat in his room reading the most recent letter to arrive asking when he was next coming down. It had rained for weeks. Her letters, although there was some humour, he could see she was still struggling. It was killing him inside knowing that he was there so far away unable to help.

He picked up a book of writing paper which he bought whilst out in town, thinking that if they were going to do this writing thing, then he should do it properly. He began to write.

Hey do, How's you. Thinking of you! Notice... Real writing paper!

I'm sitting on my bed in my undies listening to our mixtape. Mom and Pops have gone to London, so I've got the house to myself – well except for Isabella, Levi, the fish, caterpillar.... If you can call that alone????

He sat with the top of his pen in his mouth, thinking of something to write, something to bring a smile to her face, something to make her laugh and forget about the world for just a few moments.

He smirked as he began to write...

It's a pity you aren't here as I would have invited you round. We could have played Cowboys and Indians. I've been told I make a convincing Chief, especially when I'm war painted and sat on Levi (he's stronger than he looks) and if you're in a domestic mood (yes I'm laughing..) you could put on an apron and commence cleaning, washing, ironing.. and cook.. er lets scrap that last one, I've tasted your cooking!

But you could bring me a bottle of brown every half hour whilst I watch re-runs of Baywatch.... The dialogue is captivating!

Sexism I here you say... Well the following day I'd do the same for you, though I'd have to pass on the apron! You're really missing out, well it's time for me to get walking the dog-come-warhorse.

He pulled on his trousers and a t-shirt from his wardrobe. Levi sat watching, waiting. Putting on his lead they left the house. The streetlights were beginning to turn on, they walked inward towards the quarry. He sat near the lake with his sketch pad watching the light retreat from the water, watching as the sun sank lower toward the greying silhouettes of the woodland trees, which became more profound. Levi lay at his feet watching with those dark liquid eyes, eyes filled with love, a pure soul which he was blessed to have. He returned home, hanging up his coat he spotted one of Isabella's lipsticks on the table. He looked around, checking that she was no-where near. He picked up the lipstick placing it in his pocket and returned to his room.

Right I'm back....

Bike ride at the weekend.. sure!

Nice weather? Nah doubt it!

Well, I'm going to phone you now and hopefully see you at the weekend.

Hugs and kisses and a big smooch..

Rob x

He took Isabella's lipstick out of his pocket and applied it to his lips before kissing the paper. Wiping off the lipstick he picked up his pen.

P.S. I don't wear lipstick! Well not normally, this was exceptional circumstances!

Placing the letter in the envelope, and sealing it, he placed it on the desk ready to post that next morning. He sat on his bed and picked up his phone, dialling her number, waiting till he heard her voice.

"Hey you" he said smiling.

Chapter 26

Christmas soon arrived, with it brought Imogen. For a few short weeks it was like how it used to be, though another year where she spent New Year's at a posh 'do' at Durham.

They had talked so many times that past term about Jacob that he knew they were hanging on by a string. He'd never once visited Scarborough still refusing to accept her decision. He knew they couldn't survive another term like that. Secretly he couldn't wait, though he was no longer hanging on to the thoughts of them becoming anything more than friends.

A cold dark day in January Rob agreed to going out into town with a few mates. Standing in the club he watched the endless flirting and game playing. He stood back, leaning against the bar as they flirted effortlessly and shamelessly with a group of young girls. Rob wondered if they were old enough to be there. He rolled his eyes, and in his head, he created running commentary as though he was narrating a series on animal behaviour.

He glanced down at his phone flicking through old messages, disturbed by a girl's laughter he glanced up, a girl caught his eye. The disco lights momentarily landed on her, catching her blonde hair. When she turned her head it moved with her, and shorter strands hung forwards to hide her eyes. Her face was caked with make-up as though to hide the baby features underneath.

She caught glimpse of him looking at her. He averted her gaze looking back down at his phone.

Jesse walked over to the bar, ordering a drink, while waiting he rested his hand on Rob's shoulder.

"Come on Mate! Live a little! Don't ya think it's about time you got back in the game?" Jesse exclaimed.

Picking up his drink off the bar he continued.

"Y'no... If ya were a lass I'd be thinkin' you joined a nunnery or something"

He caught Robs gaze at the blonde girl standing alone.

"Go on give her a go..." he continued winking.

Rob walked up to her, engaging in conversation, offering to buy her a drink, she nodded following him to the bar. She sat holding her bottle sipping on the straw. A blonde curl fell in front of her face.

"So have you got a girlfriend?" She shouted over the music.

Downing a shot, he hesitated for a moment before replying.

"Nope, but if I had one, I'd know what she would look like, do you wanna see?"

"Go on then" she replied as he turned on the camera on his phone, turning the camera inwards he turned the phone to face her.

She giggled like an excited teen, he smirked knowing he'd not lost it. Thinking how he'd not pulled a chat up line like that for years.

"I love this song.. Wanna dance?" he asked.

"Yeah! Why not" she replied trying to play it cool.

The lads erupted in applause. He left with her number, unsure whether he would ring her, or chalk it up to one crazy night of fun. Though he knew it would most likely be the latter.
He returned home in the early hours, drunk. He picked up his writing pad and began writing, continuing from the letter he had started earlier that day.

I've met a girl called Rosie. She's blonde, beautiful, young....... Will it last? Maybe not, Conversation isn't too good, but hey that's what I've got you for! What can I say? I'm a chick magnet... I went to try on a hat for the winter, but they didn't have my size, my heads too big because of your letters!

Am I offensive, probably
Am I sexy? Definitely
Am I sexier than everyone, oh yeah!

Waking up in the morning he re-read over what he had written, laughing. He sealed the letter ready to send. Placing it on his desk he picked up his phone flicking through his contacts, landing on the name... Rosie.

Hi, its Rob from last night, wanna go for a coffee or something?

A few moments later his phone pinged with a reply.

I don't drink Coffee, but you could buy me a cocktail?

He laughed,

"Well may as well live a little" he told himself. They arranged to meet down at Tynemouth later that afternoon. Meeting up with her he was struck by how different she looked in the daylight.

Her blonde hair was poker-straight and pulled back into a low ponytail. She wore little make-up. Her eyes were not the watery blue he remembered but were more of a turquoise green. Her face was adorned with caramel coloured freckles which lay over her nose and upper cheeks. He discovered she was 18, a student who had moved up from somewhere down south.

He thought on his way home how she had told him where she was from but he couldn't remember, he wasn't really sure if he'd forgotten because he wasn't interested or whether it was just his head still fragile from the night before.

A couple of days later a letter arrived...

Blonde? Really?!
Thought brunette's were more your thing...
and I'd just found you the perfect brunette,
down here... no not me, I'm not perfect... her
names Clarissa... I took your advice and
made a friend; got a feeling we're going to be
glued at the hip. Stop thinking what you're
thinking!!! I know how dirty your mind can
be! When are you coming down??

Reading her words, he was struck by her nonchalant attitude towards him dating making him more determined to get out there and try dating. He didn't know how long it took her to write those words, or how many times she had to rewrite, not wanting him to know how much it tore at her heart, though she knew she had no right to feel that way. She had to make it seem as though she didn't care, throwing in a bit of humour to cover her true feelings. How as she wrote, she looked at Eeyore who had taken pride of place on her bed, the large thumper rabbit on the floor in the corner, used more as a reminder every time she felt as though she was failing or not feeling good enough. Thinking how much her and Jacob were drifting apart, wondering if she was in part to blame, because deep down Rob had stolen part of her heart, not in a passionate way, but deeper. She wondered had she been emotionally cheating on Jacob, and maybe that was worse.

He laughed at her insinuations into his thoughts.

He picked up the phone, her name pinned to the top of his contacts. He waited, hearing the ringing tone, the phone going to voicemail message, leave a message after the beep...

He hesitated for a moment before saying...

"Hey girl! If I'm correct, and I almost always am... It's you with the dirty mind, remember I've read your secret writings, were you not thinking of your fantasies?" He laughed before continuing

"And I'll be down at the weekend if that's ok."

That weekend he visited meeting Clarissa for the first time. They spent the Saturday down the promenade spending hours in the amusements with him laughing at the girls trying to beat each other on the dance machine, laughing watching Imogen falling flat on her backside, giggling like a school kid.

"More alcohol and Karaoke!" Imogen declared as she found her way back to her feet.

"Hell yeah!" Clarissa responded.

As they walked down towards the Packet Rob whispered to Imogen.

"She's not bad... if things go south with Rosie, do you think I stand a chance?" he asked cloyingly.

"Maybe.." Imogen winked before linking arms with Clarissa.

"We make quite a good pair, don't we Clarissa, and I think we can show the boys a thing or two" Imogen playfully declared looking back at him with her cheeky smile.

He watched as Imogen whispered to Clarissa with both laughing.

"Yeah.. two for the price of one" Clarissa replied.

Rob caught up with them, stepping in between them placing his hands around their shoulders.

"I'm hoping you're referring to drinks, and not trying to corrupt my innocent mind"

"Innocent" Imogen spoke through a feigned coughed raising her eyebrows laughing.

Rob looked at her from the corner of his eye with a smirk creeping across his face.

"If not drinks, can I assume you've been corrupted by her too?" he asked Clarissa turning his back slightly on Imogen.

"So... have you been privileged to read her saucy stuff?" he continued.

"Wait what?" Clarissa asked intrigued.

Imogen pulled at his back, giving him a playful hit in the side.

"Shut it, traitor" she asserted.

"Sorry, I thought she was inner circle…." He laughed.

Glancing over at Clarissa he whispered,

"I'll tell ya more later.." he winked.

"You're a dead man walking!" Imogen declared jumping on his back.

"Gidde-up horsey…. we've got karaoke!!!" she shouted, with her hand pointing forward, deflecting the conversation.

The afternoon passed turning into early evening. They sat collapsed on the old leather settee. As Clarissa walked to the bar Imogen whispered,

"Go get her, I think she likes you"

"Pack it!" he replied nudging her.

"Yep! We're in the Packet.." she laughed.

He laughed as he looked in her direction.

"Hmm" he shrugged.

"What have I missed?" Clarissa asked as she placed the drinks down on the table.

"Nothing!" Imogen and Rob replied in almost perfect timing, trying not to laugh.

The following day they began walking down towards the spa along the old cliff trail.

"So… Church?" Rob asked as they walked.

She scrunched her face scowling.

"Hey! Don't shoot the messenger…" he continued holding his hands up.

"The Acorn gang keep asking, and I'm running out of excuses…. And you don't sing anymore…" he continued.

"What do you mean? Have you forgotten yesterday…? Ka-ra-oke!!" she replied with an emphasis on the word karaoke.

"That doesn't count! It's not the same, You should be up there sharing that voice with the world…"

Imogen sighed.

"Look, the churches here are either boring and old-fashioned or stuck-up prudes, I don't fit, and you know I can't sing without back-up, having the band helped me, I can't do it alone… so till I find somewhere I fit then we'll always have karaoke!" she continued.

"Wave-dodging?" she asked pulling him towards the sea wall path deflecting the conversation.

He returned home later that afternoon wishing he'd stayed longer. His good mood seemed to vanish as soon as he walked through the front door.

"Back to reality" he uttered under his breath. The weekends at Scarborough were a glimpse into the life he could have been living.

A few weeks later, he broke up with Rosie. He contemplated on why it didn't work, maybe because of Imogen, maybe because he couldn't get Clarissa out of his mind... though he knew that was just a feeble excuse because he could never commit, his life was not like any others, he knew his time was short. His standards were high, if he was ever to go there, and to really invest time in someone, it had to be someone special.
He began writing to Imogen

Me and Rosie broke up, a friendship lost, something that will never happen to us, we have something very special, unconditional love. So, I'm single again... maybe destined to live alone, free, and die young? It's your fault... you thinking few women are good enough for me; hence no girlfriend, thanks a lot!

I'm being silly, I need you. You are a true friend – you always cheer me up!

Thinking... maybe you could work your match-making magic??????

I'm feeling better now, after writing to you, you've calmed me down like you always do, hey that rhymed! You'll make a poet out of me yet!

The next few months were filled with visits as the weather improved, going down almost every weekend. Imogen and

Clarissa had become almost inseparable, like twins but he was never made to feel like a third wheel, and like on the bridge, gradually more friends were joining the group. They began spending their days at the arcades and at the fair, with late afternoons consumed by karaoke which continued on into the evening.

He playfully flirted with Clarissa, and as always, he continued to outrageously flirt with Imogen safe in the boundaries of their friendship.

Like the bridge he belonged, everyone accepted him even though he wasn't at the uni, he became a regular face, the life of the party and the glue that held the group together.

He sat in his room, a warm Thursday in late March, knowing Easter was just around the corner dreaming of the next visit, he began reminiscing over the past few weekends, remembering the gang hitting the bars that past weekend, too many triples for singles resulting in him and Imogen trying to stop everyone from snogging each other.

He stood laughing as Imogen tried so hard to separate Clarissa and Simon, having failed to separate Nikita and Claire a few moments earlier.

"Aren't you gonna help!?" Imogen shouting over as he stood watching.

He stood with his hands up, as though to say not my problem, before sighing and walking over to help, to have Clarissa turn and kiss him.

He sat laughing,

"Alcohol is the cause of many a disaster"

Having the memories and the assurance of more were keeping him sane, no matter what was happening or going wrong back home, he always had Scarborough...

Chapter 27

Easter arrived.

Imogen stood in his living room, waiting for him to return home. She had arrived unexpected, unplanned.

"He won't be long" His mother called through from the kitchen, the kettle boiling.

She walked towards the wall, looking up at the framed photo of Rob as a child.   She could see the weary reflection of her face in the thin sheen of glass that covered it. She looked past her own dreary eyes and stared upon his face.

Her hand touched the glass, looking deeply at that soft face, that smile. That young boy had grown into the best person she had ever met. He had become her number one supporter. Her angel, her answered prayer, her hero. As the tears fell, she thought how he wasn't simply a good friend; he had become part of her soul. Whenever life had become a storm, he was the one who rescued her. His love was right there in everything he did. Preventing her from drowning. Bringing love when she needed it.

He was a man with an endless supply of emotional warmth and support. A prince among men. His heart shone through. He was a man who loved deeply and was filled with compassion and kindness.

Rob entered, about to head up the stairs to his room.

"Roberto! Your Imogen is in the living room" his mother called from the kitchen.

He walked slowly towards the living room door, looking in, seeing her standing there, almost in a trance. Her trousers were damp and had remnants of dry sand upon them, her face looked weary and lost, her eyes swelled red.

"Hey!" he spoke softly, breaking her trance.

She turned falling into his arms. She told him how she had just come from meeting Jacob on the beach, and how he'd ended it with her. His mother brought in a teapot, some cups, and cake.

Imogen sat on the settee, weary about getting it dirty, and wondering what his mother was thinking seeing her like that.

Jacob's words replayed in her mind as she sipped her tea.

"Imogen, I never sought to hurt you. I can no longer keep lying to myself. We are too different; we have grown apart" His words were still so eloquent but fake.

His words cut deep like a sharp knife; her heart had begun breaking in front of him.

She thought how in reality she couldn't help but agree. There was no love remaining, not really. It was as if all that love, 3 years of love became pain, the pain became fear, he'd somehow managed to almost control her for far too long. She thought how really, she should have been relieved that she was free, and she thought maybe soon she would be, but in that moment, she needed to grieve. His guilt-stricken face flashed in front of her. She knew there was something Jacob was hiding.

Imogen sat silent, staring into space, Rob sat beside her, his hand resting on her lap, waiting patiently. He looked over at his mother. It was as though his mother finally picked up on the silent queues that they needed to be alone. She stood up, leaving the room, closing the door behind her. He placed his arm around her, holding her, comforting her. Wrapping her in his love with his kind words. The calm silence as he let her cry portraying a wonderful compassion, an awareness of her vulnerability. Knowing it was not the right time to tell her she deserved better.

She cried until no more tears came.

"Come on! I think you need a nice long fast ride" he whispered kissing her forehead.

In those following weeks she began relying on him more than ever. Their days began and ended with each other's phone calls. He filled her emotional void. At times she wondered if she was using Rob as an emotional crutch.

Her letters at times became darker, he could see she was slipping away, he was beginning to notice on his visits she was retreating into herself, drinking for the wrong reasons, no longer for fun and socialising but instead using it as an escape, something which he knew all too well and a path which he didn't want to see her go down, knowing how hard it was to pull yourself back from the brink.

He sat reading her most recent letter. It detailed how Jacob had been trying to get in touch and had journeyed down to Scarborough with the promise that it would be different, Jacob had convinced her they belonged together, how she had given in to him, allowing him to have sex with her, then leaving, re-opening the wound which had slowly been healing. She told him how ashamed she felt as she admitted she'd let him do this twice, two separate weekends, each leaving her feeling like a fool, saying how ashamed, dirty, and how used she felt.

In the letter she begged him to come down that weekend, suggesting hitting the clubs and getting smashed.

Rob picked up the phone ringing her. He knew she had been trying so hard to pick herself back up and had been doing well till up until then. They spoke on the phone as Imogen broke down in tears.

She told him that no matter how many times she tried to say no, he wouldn't stop, utilizing phrases like,

"You know you want too.."

"It's your fault you're so hot that I can't resist you"

"You're supposed to love me or was that a lie"

Even when she managed to still stay resolute, he would ignore her, touching her, groping her, knowing what to do to get her to give in,

"See I know what you like..."

Rob could hear the shame in her voice blaming herself, hating herself for not being stronger.

"I'm not strong enough" she stated.

"I had no control; I couldn't stop it" she continued.

"Hey, it's OK, you are strong, you're one of the strongest people I know, you're just a little vulnerable and broken right now, but I'm here, we all make mistakes, he used you.... And yep I'll be down Friday, but why not do something fun? A little different, not including alcohol. I think you've had enough for a while and that's saying something coming from me!"

They continued talking for over an hour, moments of small-talk and humour interlaced with his steadfast love. He wanted to see her, hold her, and make everything OK. The conversation kept reverting back to Jacob. In the conversation Rob stated how what he did could be classed as assault, even rape. In the conversation she broke down opening up about when she got Kitt2, and the reason for those few days when she distanced herself, telling him what had transpired between her and Jacob. She spoke of how she now was beginning to believe Jacob had raped her, not only raped her but assaulted her by taking her by force by anal penetration to teach her a lesson. She spoke of how until now she'd never viewed that as rape either but maybe it was, though still she was partly to blame for not fighting harder. She spoke of how didn't think of it as rape as she didn't know you could be raped by someone you're sexually active with, and how she couldn't have confided in him back then as afraid of what he would have done to Jacob. She confided in him, speaking of how what he did those weekends, and what he did that day she got kitt2 were unleashing other memories she had tried so hard to bury, things that only he knew. He knew her pain, her hurt penetrated deeper than just Jacob, he just opened the box unleashing a lifetime of damage.

Putting down the phone he picked up his pen.

I said you're strong earlier coz not everyone can open themselves up the way you do. You've bounced back, many times, granted you've had brill mates, but hey you deserve no less!

Please let me now deal with Jacob in the only way he should be? You've kept me restrained for far too long.... I could... Ahem, maybe writing what I would do is not wise, it could be used in evidence against me in a court of law... OK I'm watching too many police dramas, but I could be like the world champion fencer...

The 3rd place fencer stood waiting; a fly was released. He cut the fly in half; the crowd cheered. The 2nd place fencer stepped up, a fly was released, and he cut it into quarters. The crowd erupted.

The 1st place fencer stepped up, there was a moment of anticipation for the world's greatest... also Spanish... the fly was released... his blade came down in a mighty arc, but the fly continued on its way. The crowd was aghast thinking he had missed. The swordsman continued to smile.
Someone yelled "you missed!"

You weren't watching he replied... Yes, the fly lives, but he will never be a father.

He went down to visit her that weekend, and most of the weekends which followed, she was growing stronger, determined not to give in to Jacob, and for a couple of weeks it was working.

One weekend he was unable to go, his mother had been complaining about the amount of time he was spending away insisting on a 'family weekend' which included helping her at a church function on the Saturday afternoon, watching as she played the perfect Christian, perfect mother. A role she played so well.

That Sunday lunchtime, leaving church he received a phone call from Clarissa concerned about Imogen. She had allowed Jacob back again, and after he left, she had gotten drunk, and was still drinking.

He jumped on his bike heading down to Scarborough, finding her sitting on the clifftop, an almost empty bottle of vodka in her hand.

"Hi!" she exclaimed throwing her hands around him.

"Tell me what happened, you know I'll never judge you..." Rob whispered thinking she'd gave in again; Clarissa had been sketchy over the details.

Clarissa had told him how when Imogen had let Jacob back in. She had decided to go out, not wanting to be in the same flat with him, not wanting to watch Imogen throw away her dignity again. She told how she walked out, returning a few hours later finding Imogen in a state, refusing to talk, knowing she was out of her depth she contacted the only person who could help her.

He stood in front of her, his hand gently reaching for her wrist. Imogen looked down at her feet not wanting him to see that ugly side of her, to prevent him seeing the depths she had fallen too.

"I tried... I told him not to come, but still he came, it's all my fault... I let him in... I tried to say no, I said no, but he didn't care so he got his way, you know I should have relented like I've always done...."

He could see the pain in her eyes and in her voice. In a split moment, her demeanour changed as though trying to distract herself from the reality.

"Come on , dance with me like we used to" she asked, though it wasn't really a request, stepping away spinning she lost her balance, falling, being caught in his arms.

They'd danced many times and flirted in the safety of their friendship, but he thought how this time was different. She wasn't herself, she seemed out of control.

Steadying herself she leant forward, her hands around him slipping onto his rear, and leaning in to kiss him. He let go, she fell to her knees.

"Don't you want me?" she asked as she began to sob, opening the bottle drinking the remaining of the vodka.

Rob stepped away. He wasn't going to be used as a rebound and wasn't going to be another person abusing her at her lowest point.

"Of course, you don't, you're too good for me, we all know I'm nothing but a fucking cheap slut!" she shouted.

"No decent guy is ever going to want damaged goods" she sobbed.

Rob looked at her, reflecting on how she was losing herself. The girl he loved so deeply was fading away. Allowing Jacob and all those who had abused her in the past to change her. To become someone she had spent her life fighting against becoming. He'd always looked up to how she could have endured all that she had yet not allow those people, those circumstances to change her. It wasn't just her actions that hit him but also her words. She never swore. Not real swear words, not words like that... She never criticized or held others to account, but she held herself to her own standard, something which he admired. But now Jacob had stolen his Imogen changing her into someone else, becoming unrecognisable. He refused to let him win, resolving that he had to get his angel back no matter what the cost. The girl he knew and loved was still in there somewhere...

In that moment he decided it was time for some tough love.

"What happened to the girl I met years ago? Once your life was all about God, now it's all about you! I don't recognise you anymore! No one can save you except yourself and you sure as hell won't find the solution in the bottom of that bottle, trust me I've been there!"

He walked away leaving her, it broke his heart but, in that moment, he felt it was the best thing to do. He returned to the flat.

"Watch her for me" he asked Clarissa as he climbed on Buzby.

He smiled a feigned smile before riding away, returning home.

Chapter 28

Two days later, a letter arrived, Imogen apologising begging forgiveness, her words struck him, and he began to worry about her state of mind, wondering whether he did the right thing.

He was drawn to her words...

Sorry,
I'd be devastated if I've lost your friendship,
you're the only good and right thing in my
life, and I've not always been as good a
friend in return. If I was to lose you my life
wouldn't be worth living, though there really
is nothing left to live for..

He began to write, trying to lift the mood a little, hoping his humour would break through the darkness.

When you wrote you'd be devastated if you lost my friendship, well you won't. Unless I die unintentionally... But if I do die, don't cry at my funeral or I'll be so upset that I'll never speak to you again, and this death thing can happen at any time, you taught me that...

For instance, me eating one of your kormas could be used as the ultimate definition of trust between friends.

With sincerest affections
Rob x

He took the letter putting it in his pocket to post before going for a ride to clear his mind. He placed the letter in the post-box. He stood next to the post-box looking out at the sea wondering where to ride. He felt the urge to head to Scarborough, her words kept repeating in his mind, something didn't feel right. He stood almost arguing with himself.

His phone rang.

Looking at the phone he saw the picture of Imogen, he smiled as he answered but soon the smile faded as he could hear the sound of desperation in her voice.

"I can't do it anymore, I just wanted to hear your voice, to say sorry, and to say goodbye." She choked through her tears.

He tried to calm her, discovering she was sat on the cliff top thinking of jumping. As she was talking to him, she was stood on the edge looking over at the rocks below. He tried to talk her away from the edge.

"Remember when you said you'd never jumped before because you didn't want to hurt those left behind, well I'm here, I need you, you can't leave me here alone"

He paused as she told him how she had taken a step back and was now sat on the cliff top.

"Wait for me, I'm on my way" he said. She hung up. He jumped on his bike, starting the engine. Before leaving he instantly sent a text.

Don't kill ya self! Coz then I won't have anyone to annoy! And then I would be sad! Go get a coffee at the Spa, see you there soon!

He made his way to Scarborough focussed on rescuing her, to save her. He travelled at speed, determined to get to her in time.

He arrived at Scarborough unsure whether she would be at the spa or still on the cliff, or worse, though he didn't want to think about that scenario. He parked at the spa, walking through to the veranda café. He spotted her sitting alone at a table in the far corner overlooking the bay. He walked towards her stopping next to her, his hand rested on her shoulder, she turned looking up to see Rob standing above her, she stood throwing her arms around him.

"I'm sorry!" she sobbed.

He wrapped his arm around her pulling her close, gently rubbing her arm. She sobbed into his chest unceasingly, her hands clutching at his jacket. He held her in silence, rocking her slowly as her tears soaked his chest.

"It's OK, I'm here now" He whispered. Never judging.

She looked up, blinking, her lashes heavy with tears, looking into those deep brown eyes, the colour of hot chocolate on a cold winter night.

Eyes that wrap around you like a blanket; engulfing you in their warmth, making you feel at home, feeling safe.

She stood safe in his arms as the rain began to fall heavy.

"Come on" he spoke as he placed a soft kiss upon her head before spinning her round.

Picking up her bag they ran, hand in hand along the side of the Spa and down the old concrete steps to the cove. The waters splashed against them. Imogen and Rob stood watching the water, dodging the waves.

"I thought I'd lost you" she spoke as she stood on the ledge, taking her hand he guided her back to the wooden seats against the wall. They sat watching the rain fall down and the waves crashing, forming a wall of water.

"You'll never lose me. I'm always here, and you should know by now that I will be brutally honest cause that's my job, I'm not afraid to pull you up, hurt your feelings if needed, or tell you when I think you're going down the wrong path, or tell you when you're just being a stupid pain in the ass, which is about 96% of the time, before you then go on to your next stupid ass thing, so I'm going to say you're a stupid ass 99% of the time, but I can still work with that. Crazy loves crazy, and I've always loved a challenge! But seriously… You know I'm always honest but aint that what you love about me? And you do the same for me, we're both broken, and I know your life aint easy, I know it's never been easy, but you've got to work at it every day, and not give up, you taught me that"

He pulled her in close wishing he could take away all of her pain.

Imogen looked up feeling lighter, feeling a glimmer of hope, for the first time in months feeling like everything could be OK. The sun began to break through the clouds creating a rainbow effect on the wall of water and a rainbow arcing over the bay. Grabbing her arm Rob declared,

"Quick, let's go find the pot of gold at the end of the rainbow" whilst leading her back up to the spa and down onto the beach running along the water's edge.

"You're crazy!" she screamed laughing and smiling for the first time in a long time, she watched him with awe thinking how Rob was always the glimmer of sunlight bursting out from behind the dark clouds making everything feel Ok. Reminding her life was always worth fighting for.

He returned home that evening, not wanting to leave but he knew he had too. He told her he would return that weekend. He knew she needed him, she was at her most vulnerable and although he'd talked her down there was always that niggling doubt that she would think about it again, and how maybe that time she wouldn't reach out and he wouldn't be able to stop her.

"If you need me, ring me!" he stated fastening his helmet to leave.

Imogen nodded.

"Pinky promise?" he asked holding out his little finger, she smiled allowing her little finger to link his.

He returned home. Sitting in his room he thought how even though at times she was hard work she was worth it, and how being there for her distracted himself from his own problems, she gave him purpose, and it felt good to be wanted and needed, to have someone rely on him, rather than be indispensable.

The Saturday morning, he woke up early to the sun streaming through his window.

He sat on Buzby, fastening his helmet and turning the key. He looked around, looking up at his house, the curtains still drawn, everyone still asleep. He pulled his phone from his pocket sending a message.

This is your early morning wake up call! The sun is shining... Well it is here.... Get up! I expect breakfast when I arrive, and then we're hitting the road, or mount, or shore?? Not decided yet...

He rode down arriving at her flat, following breakfast they head out on Buzby and Kitt2.

They rode down to the spa, the waves crashed against the sea wall running along the south shore.

They stood watching.

"Come on!" Rob exclaimed dragging her towards the paths along the wall.

They stood on the wall watching as the waves crashed violently against the base of the wall, watching as waves built up speed and height from far out in the ocean until the peaks rose high above the salty body of water and crashed over.

"We've not done any real wave dodging in ages, and I need to add something else to my list of whipping your ass at!" he exclaimed.

They stood side by side, watching, waiting, jumping back just as the wave hit, the winner being the one to stay the longest without getting hit by the oncoming wave.

After a while, Rob looked around, that look of mischief where a crazy idea was forming, Imogen watched excitedly curious to what their next wild activity would entail.

"What?" Imogen asked as he looked around, twisted his face, then grabbed her hand.

He dragged her back to the bikes. Jumping on Buzby, he declared.

"Hop on!"

Imogen shrugged her shoulders, then climbed on, Rob rode along the path towards the lower wall, water covered the path.

Rob stopped, watching the water.

"Hop off, I've just gotta try something" Rob instructed.

Imogen jumped off puzzled.

"Watch this!" he exclaimed as he revved the engine and rode onto the path, aquaplaning along the wall.

Imogen stood watching in awe as he managed to dodge the waves and control his bike with such intensity and watching as the spray was thrown up by the wheels, as though surfing on a bike. Combining her two favourite activities. As he pulled to a stop in a coordinated skid his back wheel spun creating a wave of spray which covered her.

He lifted his visor, looking at her.

"What??" he asked innocently.

She shook her head as she stood, wet, though couldn't stay mad.

"You're wild!" She screamed.

"Thought you knew that... . Isn't that why you love me? Hop on! You know you want too..." he spoke almost daring her.

She hesitated for a moment.

"I thought you were the wild one, oh well I guess I can add it to the list of things that I've beat your ass at! I'm notching this up on list of wins here."

She laughed shaking her head.

"I maybe wild, but you take wild to a whole new level, you are the master, I am just your apprentice" she exclaimed before jumping on the pillion seat, holding on tightly as they rode through the waves.

As they rode through the waves, she began thinking over their past, their wild adventures, reminding her of the good in her life, a reason to live. She thought how he always listened; he was always there to catch her. She thought how he didn't always do what she thought she wanted, what she thought would help, but instead always gave her what she needed, whether that be tough love and honesty through to wild distractions, and competition.

He knew her better than she knew herself, and she was determined to live up to his expectations, to be the girl he knew she was capable of being.

They returned to the car park, both wet. Imogen climbed on Kitt.

"Back home to get dried?" she asked.

"Yeah, then we can hit the mount for a race, and then the town for some pool, and plenty of drinks, gonna whip your ass at those two, and while we're on it, how about go-karting tomorrow?"

Imogen bit her bottom lip,
"You're on!, and I'm not going down easily" she replied as she revved her engine pulling away, causing an impromptu race back to the flat.

The remaining weekend consisted of fun, races, competitions, and evenings spent in the bars drinking, nights spent by a bonfire on the beach, and mornings watching the sunrise over the horizon.

Rob returned home, hating having to leave. Sitting alone a few days later, reliving the memories of yet another wild weekend, a successful weekend of beating her at every challenge set.

He sat writing.

Thanks for letting me whip your ass at go-karting, pool, cycling, well everything cause I'm perfect!

He sat remembering conversations from the weekend, Imogen discussing the possibility of getting a tattoo of a seahorse and where... He laughed as he continued to write.

Don't get a tattoo on your thigh because that would draw attention away from your best asset, yep, your posterior, you bum, bottom, culo... I think she gets the message......

He paused remembering the nights out, he thought how they joked about getting married when Imogen was rich and famous. He had joked about becoming her servant, bodyguard and general dogsbody, to which Imogen had replied,

"You may as well marry me and get my money that way, less work, though I'd still expect you to be my slave" she joked winking almost seductively.

He continued to write...

When you get a job that pays you lots of money after university you can arrange a date for us to marry, joking!!......though I noticed you were getting more than a few advances by men on Friday night even if you didn't realise, and also
the pillion seat on my bike is missing your backside!

That is 2 times in a row with me mentioning your bum!

What's going on??

He thought back to the previous Friday night in planet. He struggled with finding the right balance of allowing her to move on without her falling victim to more damage. He was never really a big fan of casual hook-ups and one night stands but he knew they had their place, but with her and her past and her experiences of 'intimacy' he knew those would tip her further over the edge.

He thought how he'd gotten into a habit of watching her from the corner of his eye and stepping in with the distraction of a dance if he thought things were going too far. They'd taken salsa classes together and he enjoyed dancing with her and overtime the more they danced and almost played off each other he improved, which he found came in handy on pulling the women!

The night club was packed, the dancefloor full of bodies moving as the music played over the dance floor. He stood at the bar aimlessly flirting, while watching Imogen dancing, watching men getting closer to her. She continued to dance oblivious as though lost in her own world.

He took a slow walk over to the DJ.

"Can you whack on a bit of Shakira mate" he asked as he continued to watch men almost groping her.

"Hey, let us show these lot how it's done" Rob spoke stepping in between Imogen and an older man.

As the music began to play, he spun her. He watched as her hair spun out and bounced more with each move and beat.

Holding her, he moved in a smooth motion taking control leading her as she began to follow. Sliding across the dancefloor as others moved creating space... She slid her right foot forward chasing his retreating foot with hers, like a fox on the hunt. With a seductive glint in her eye she fought for control leading him till he spun her, dipping her forward looking deep into her eyes. His fingers tightened on her ribs as his left foot came forward again, disturbing her foot and chasing it back. They stopped, toe to toe as he pulled her hips in close to his before she spun out. Her hands moved slowly from her hips, up her body accentuating her every curve before taking his hand, allowing him to spin her back in. They stood for a moment inches apart before he pushed her away, catching hold of her with his hand till they were holding with outstretched arms being pulled taut before reeling her back in and spinning her out and away.

Eventually the music came to an end. Rob gave a bow to those around them on the dancefloor, many had almost stopped dancing to watch.

"Whoop whoop!" he could hear Clarissa and Simon shout over from the bar.

"I taught that girl everything she knows." He shouted putting as much pride and sarcasm in his voice as he could.

His arm wrapped around her before kissing the top of her head with a smile.

"Now I think after that performance... you need to buy the drinks!" he stated leading her towards the bar.

Chapter 29

The first year ended, the summer arrived. Scarborough came alive with motorbike racing, and bike shows. Clarissa returned home. Imogen decided to stay in Scarborough, in halls not wanting to return home completely. She spent the summer fleeting between Newcastle and Scarborough, though back home it was harder to avoid Jacob, and even harder to avoid the questions.

He watched her back at acorn feeling like an imposter.

Being back home in Newcastle, she had a few slips back into Jacob's arms. Not because she wanted him but because as usual, she couldn't say no, returning to her default setting. He was always stronger than her, and every time he left, she felt dirty and used, saying she wouldn't let it happen again.

Rob had many conversations with Imogen trying to make sense of her own behaviour, and Jacob's behaviour. Rob knew he was deliberately using her like a slab of meat, but still Imogen had moments when she didn't want to believe. She wondered whether Jacob was intentionally using her or whether he was actually torn, and conflicted. Listening to her he thought how no matter what she always still tried to see some 'good' in everyone. Rob knew that others frequently saw that too, especially Jacob who had turned it into an artform, knowing what to say and do to break her.

As the weeks past she knew he had no intention of mending things, and that he was just using her. It broke Rob's heart watching her go through it. He tried to distract her. The Barry Sheene racing weekend was one of those attempts. He bought tickets for the weekend and delighted in giving them to her, seeing her face light up. That weekend he watched her being too distracted by the vast array of bikes and the hours of racing, with a mischievous glint in her eye as she watched the sidecar racing.

"Do you think we can ever give that a go?" she asked playfully. Rob laughed knowing she would in a heartbeat.

Between races they scoured the tents and sneaking across to the paddock, with her eagerly searching and hoping to see John McGuiness.

"You're such a girly girl!" Rob joked.

"Nah, girly girl's like boy bands and all that, real girls like a bit of rough, a bit of speed! Don't ya know I want a cool rider to knock me of my feet?"

"Ahem! You've got me.."

"Emphasis on cool" she replied laughing with a hint of cheekiness and her flirtatious nature shining through.

Trying to use humour to deflect him from the truth. Not wanting to admit that gradually over those weeks she was beginning to see that in every way he was what she wanted but had never seen it before, and now was afraid to admit it. He deserved someone who wasn't messed up, someone perfect, someone not her.

"Go make yourself useful and get the drinks!" Imogen exclaimed distracting herself from her thoughts.

As Rob queued at the bar tent Imogen continued to admire the bikes and browsed through the programme scanning the teams entering.

"Hey! There's a Geordie team…. I think we should throw our weight behind them." Imogen exclaimed as she ran over to Rob.

"Aren't you now a Yorkshire lass?" Rob replied.

"Nah! Come on man.... I may live in Scarborough, but I'll always be a Geordie Lass! It's in my blood... Broon Ale runs through these veins" she laughed.

"So what's this team you're going to lose your voice cheering for?" Rob asked looking over her shoulder at the programme.

"Grrr! I've lost it now.. BDS or something..."

Rob laughed.

"Hey! What you laughing at?" Imogen asked.

"I'm just wondering if that sweet corrupted brain is sneaking back...." He winked.

"God! You're such an ass!" she replied.

"Look! There! See!!" she stated, pointing

"OK. You got me!"

"And they're def. going to beat any team you're fancying... Their bike is red... and we all know red bikes are fastest" Imogen stated as she took her drink from him and began walking ahead.

"That is such a chick thing to say!" He stated as he caught up with her.

"Nah, it's scientifically proven!" she exclaimed.

"Put your money where your mouth is!" Rob joked.

"You're on!" She stated reaching her hand out to shake on it.

Come on next race starts in 10!" she continued grabbing his hand.

He watched the mischievous glint in her eye as they walked back to their bikes.

"Told ya! Geordie and red, perfect combo… Now for me to think about what you owe me" she laughed, biting her bottom lip she placed her finger on her lips.

He could only imagine the crazy thoughts which were tumbling through her head. Letting go of his hand she danced as she walked with casual looks over her shoulder portraying the seductive yet innocent demeanour which he loved.

"So do I tell your dad that?   Geordie and red? You could be disowned for becoming a Makem!" Rob laughed catching up with her, his hands gripping her waist, lifting her from the ground before spinning her around.

"Oh, Shit Yeah.. but I'm talking bikes not footy!" She laughed.

"Anyways... Food... Where you taking me... Loser!" she smiled as she climbed on Kitt2.

Soon the weekend ended, and days like those were rare, days where she wasn't consumed by her thoughts, and days where Jacob wasn't plaguing her with messages, or her memories returning filling her with guilt. Though the worst were those days where Jacob got under her skin, using her for his own sexual gratification then throwing her like trash.

He watched every time seeing her eyes stained with mascara from the fallen tears and seeing the shame evident on her face. He tried his best to reassure her but was finding it increasingly hard to not get worked up, filled with anger, and rage at Jacob but also disappointment that she wasn't strong enough, that she kept putting herself through the pain, seeing each time break her even more. He wished she could see and accept her true worth.

Many times, he stood in silence just holding her knowing that sometimes words aren't the right words to say.

Her question soon became answered.

It became apparent early in the summer that Jacob had a new girlfriend, and that they had been together since before they broke up.

She questioned him about it, and he shrugged his shoulders not even attempting to deny it. With her knowing the truth his comments and excuses of how he still loved her fell away and became replaced with

"She can't give me what you do so you're just going to have to suck it up and be a good girl and give me what she can't whenever I want it, and you don't want to make it harder on yourself by trying to say no cause you know I get it one way or another..."

Rob saw how that became the final straw that broke the camel's back, reinforcing her belief that she was nothing but a cheap slut to be used and disposed of.

A few days later Rob spotted fresh cuts upon her arms. He pulled her in close, not needing to ask.

She'd promised in the past to find other outlets, things which had been working, but he realised that those past months and Jacobs behaviour had her spiralling to the point she couldn't resist any longer, and that realisation, that blunt statement from Jacob had caused her to want to punish herself. The sobbing began almost instantly as though a dam was finally able to be broken.

Rob could hear it in her voice as she vented, in almost incoherent ramblings declaring that she'd just returned to what she always was, and what she always was meant to be, a whore, and how she felt like a prostitute...

"But at least prostitutes get paid!" she sobbed in his arms as he held her.

She asked why? Why she continued to allow it to happen.

"How could I have allowed it to continue, how could I be so stupid... I deserve it..." she sobbed into his arms.

Rob continued to hold her, not speaking, allowing her to just speak all the thoughts she'd held inside out, always listening, never judging, well not judging Imogen but definitely judging Jacob, till he began to doubt whether if they came face to face, he could restrain himself.

"Hey, it's not your fault, you're not the one at fault..." he continued to remind her every time her thoughts slipped back into blaming herself, slowly becoming stronger determined to never allow herself to fall victim again.

He encouraged her to stay in Scarborough, not coming back up, and that instead he would go to her, telling her how getting away in Scarborough also helped him. That summer he spent more time in Scarborough than back home. They spent most of the summer in Scarborough upon Oliver's Mount or riding along the coastline, and long summer days spent on the south shore. A summer which was filled with many crazy adventures.

Late august came the return of Clarissa. That year they were moving in together, into a flat upon South Cliff. Imogen moved out of halls and moved into the flat with Clarissa, both ready to begin their 2nd year. Moving in with Clarissa, having someone there also helped her to fight back, to find her dignity and draw a line under Jacob for good.

There were a few weeks remaining of summer, weeks where memories were made, weeks spending longer in Scarborough than back home, finding himself feeling 'Homesick' for Scarborough every time he did have to leave.

They all spent many evenings sitting talking in the flat drinking and binge watching old TV box sets, while also discussing ways to get revenge, crazy 'planning sessions' sat with a bottle of wine where crazy ideas were thrown into the air, with it almost feeling like a turning point. His Imogen was back, back to the girl he knew before Jacob tried to break her.

Those weeks before the new academic year were also unlike any other, as though trying to chalk up as many memories as possible to see him through the winter months.

He returned home the Sunday afternoon ready for the new term ahead, Sitting back in that room made him feel homesick, for a place which to him was now home, a place which wasn't his actual home but wished it was. He sat quietly thinking back over those past weeks, before becoming overwhelmed with regrets. How that could have also been his life, if he'd gone with her instead of remaining in Newcastle.

He picked up his pen...

Hi gorgeous!
I hope your alreet lass!
I'm missing you already, or is that the sun, sea, sand, Scarborough and Simon? (couldn't think of anything else beginning with S) but No it's you!
I can still hear Simon's laughter in my head, I think it's contagious!

But seriously I am missing you, yeah you, why not? You're lush, sexy, and have fantastically (is that a word?) blue eyes and you cheer me up with laughter and love every time I receive one of your letters. I think I'm realising more than ever that you are my 'special friend'.

Again, borrowing his sister's lipstick he put it on his lips to place a lipstick kiss on the paper...

As he looked in the mirror, he thought,

"If Imogen could see me now"

He laughed as he kissed the paper then under the lipstick kiss wrote the words....

I need a kiss kiss kiss when the sun don't shine because the weather is glum, I can still hear the sound of bikes running through my brain, dreaming of being out on that open road, a beautiful blonde on the back, my secret fantasy revealed... though if I was being real I suppose you'd be in the picture too, why has writing that just made me laugh?

Tuesday Morning.

The first day of the new academic year, Rob breathed in deeply preparing himself for the new year, the new start, back to college yet again...

That new academic year was meant to be a new 'fresh start'.

Beginning a course at Newcastle college studying teaching assistant and youth work. He was starting to feel as though everything was on track, or at least trying to make himself believe.

Isabella had left. Gone to work and travel abroad, beginning with a stint working as a waitress in Ibiza, or so she had told her mother, though he knew what Ibiza was good for.

Walking through the college grounds, induction day, he could still hear his mother's voice in his head sounding so proud as she talked to women from the church the night before at a church function which he was dragged along too..

"I can't believe, my precious girl….."

What followed was the usual conversation of how proud she was, that she was out there building a life, then rolling off the achievements of his brothers. She never said she was disappointed in him, but he could hear it in her tone.

"Oh Rob's back at college again…"

That was true he thought this time he was going to change the path of his future, to prove her wrong, to not end up a failed college student who couldn't get a job.

He laughed with other students who would also be on his course, some looked so young, fresh from school. He continued to laugh and smile, though in the back of his mind his thoughts played like an endless loop, asking how he'd gotten to this point in his life, trying to convince himself it was another chance to fix his life, to find the 'direction' he apparently missed.

Thursday arrived.

He finished his breakfast early heading for the college. First day of lectures, first day of what he hoped would be the last new start, though was lacking the motivation to do this all over again.

"Two days till the weekend" he muttered under his breath as he walked into the last class of the day, sitting down at one of many old desks which filled the classroom...

Scarborough was growing on him, till it felt like he was only living for the weekend, going through the motions.

He sat at a desk; his arms folded reflecting on how it had been a year since he was last sat at one of those desks.

"Rob?" the lecturer looked him up and down whilst also scanning the paper in her hand.

"Glad to see you finally decided to join us in the real-world rather than the dream-world"

"Great start!" he thought to himself.

The lesson dragged on. He imagined Imogen was again sat beside him, but she wasn't.

As he left the class, looking up at the dark clouds which were beginning to fill the sky, he began to doubt things could ever change.

He headed home allowing the day to slip by, returning to his room he allowed the darkness to take over as he tried to close his eyes in the hope that sleep would make the day pass quicker, bringing the Saturday sooner. His phone rang, half asleep he answered.

"Roberto... did you remember to pick up the shopping, oh and your fathers' prescription..." He listened realising it had slipped his mind. He paused not wanting to reveal he'd forgotten, he looked at the clock 5.30pm, it was too late to lie and rush out.

"Sorry mama" he answered hoping that she would understand, but her usual disappointment could be heard in her voice.

"Roberto! I cannot beli-" he stopped listening as he had heard that speech a thousand times before. He threw his phone across the room, before closing his eyes for a moment, drifting off.

He awoke from his bed, but it wasn't his bed, it wasn't his room. He opened the curtains to the view of Scarborough's North Shore, his phone rang, answering he could hear his mother's voice asking him how he was doing, her voice portraying a real interest and concern rather than the feigned interest he could usually hear in her voice.

Did time reset? Like some updated future, like everything being better, maybe being how they were meant to have been, no longer being a failure to his mother.

He stood up walking over to the mirror on his wardrobe, staring at his reflection as he continued to listen to his mother talking.

"So, as I was saying, everyone is asking after you, you know we're so proud of you..."

He began to feel uneasy, as he rubbed his eyes as he scanned the room, his phone dropped to the floor. It was still his room, he thought as he tried to understand his surroundings, everything began to blur as he closed his eyes wincing. Opening his eyes, he was still stood in front of his wardrobe. His eyes shifted to the floor where his phone lay, his mother's picture still on the screen, her voice still audible.

He picked up his phone.

"I can't believe you forgot again!"

He looked over at his bed, realising that nothing had changed, it had all been some kind of dream, nothing was different, he was still the epic failure, still a disappointment, her words and tone reminding him of how he'd let everyone down yet again.

"Sorry Mama, look I'll ring 111, and will see if I can go pick up from ASDA or something, I'll get them, I promise" he uttered though he knew his promises meant nothing to her, even though to him they did.

Ending the call, he lay back on his pillow for a few moments, blankly staring at the ceiling as tears began to swell in his eyes. He thought how many times he'd told her she could get prescriptions delivered, but she always dismissed him, as though that was only suggested to make life easier for him, rather than trying to make it so his father never ran out of medication.

"Right" He said sitting up dialling 111, before heading out on Buzby.

He headed to ASDA picking up the prescription which was so urgently needed before flicking through his phone to find the shopping list saved that morning. Not wanting to have to sit and eat with his parent's, he stopped on the coast to buy chips. He sat watching the bay.

He pulled his phone out of his pocket to ring Imogen, knowing hearing her voice would help, even if just to provide a distraction from his life, to tell him of the exploits down in Scarborough so he could close his eyes and imagine he was there with them, not missing out on anything.

"Hey! We were just talking about you..." Imogen spoke cloyingly as she answered.

They talked for what felt like ages, so long that the blue sky became darker, becoming almost black, the streetlights turning on. She brought that distraction that was needed, though still providing some reassurance, reminiscing over their first day,

"Never change!" she instructed.

"You're perfect as you are, and you'll ace it without trying. Why mess with perfection? ..... Though if you're determined to become a nerd, I give lessons... Though you do know how long it took me to perfect this level of nerdiness?" she continued, sounding happy and upbeat.

Hearing her sound so happy and confident and back to normal brought a smile to his face.

"So, what's been happening you're end? Is the plan going ahead?" He asked diverting the conversation away from him.

"Yeah, it's on! He should be here tomorrow, I think about lunchtime, and we have everything planned to perfection..." she answered through bated laughter.

They had previously discussed letting Jacob come one final time, to let him think he had broken her down again, but they had a plan.

She laughed as they recalled all of the things that they had talked about doing in earlier 'planning sessions' before updating him on the final plan of action decided upon by her and Clarissa that week.

She promised she would not give in, not fall for his charms and broken promises again, that she would see the plan through to fruition.

"I'll ring ya in the morning so we can go over the final details" Rob promised.

He returned home, putting the shopping away, leaving the prescription on the table by the door. He could hear the TV through the crack in the open living room door.

"Rob is that you?" his father's voice carried from the living room.

"Yeah, shopping's been put away, you're meds are on the table, night!" he replied loudly as he began walking up the stairs to his room.

The next morning, Friday morning, he arrived at college early, grabbing a coffee from the cafeteria he sat on the grass overlooking the carpark to ring Imogen.

"Right, so are we still on? ….. Got everything? ….. Remember to take evidence to send to his bimbo" Rob instructed as Imogen talked through the plan one final time.

"Right well he should be here in a couple of hours…" she exclaimed, her voice becoming broken, her nerves evident.

"You've got this! Have fun! Revenge is a dish best served cold" he continued, as she began to doubt herself.

Rob's words gave her a little Dutch courage to go through with her plan.

"You gotta ring me when it's done, I've got a lecture for about an hour but will be free after lunch, speak soon" he replied before hanging up.

She rang him back after lunch.

"It's done!" she laughed down the phone.

"I'm sending you a photo!" she continued.

He looked at his phone as they continued on-call, seeing a photo of her taken by Clarissa. A photo of her holding Jacob's phone, underneath were Jacob's clothes, and boxers strategically placed to get the best picture.

"So tell me all the juicy details" he asked.

They laughed as she recalled how she washed his spaghetti in dirty dish water and watched him eat it, and how she managed to throw him out of the flat naked. Telling of how he stood outside the flat, begging. His clothes, phone, and wallet, all inside while he stood shivering and exposed in the corridor. Saying how It felt like justice for that time in Durham.

She told Rob how she couldn't resist taking a photo with his phone of her with his boxers, sending it to his new girlfriend making sure she knew what he had been up to. Taking delight in pressing send!

Rob laughed as she continued to tell of how after a while, she passed him his clothes and all of his belongings before closing the door.

She told him how she continued sitting up against the door, listening as he attempted to get dressed, still begging, apologising.

"I'm still sat here, in front of the door" she continued.

"Well done! Just please don't give in, don't let him back, don't give him another moment of your life" he spoke with such love and kindness.

She smiled, a single tear fell from her eye, the last tear she vowed she would ever cry over Jacob.

"I'll be down tomorrow, go have a bottle of wine with Clarissa. Love ya"

"Nah, I'll have the wine on ice for when you get here" she replied.

That following day he woke up early returning to Scarborough arriving in time for a celebratory bottle of wine,

"We got posh plonk to celebrate" Clarissa announced as she tried to release the cork, causing him to almost jump as the cork flew past him hitting the window.

"Oops!" Clarissa laughed while also shrugging her shoulders.

"Let the celebrations begin…. So what other craziness do we have planned?" Rob asked as he took a large swig of his glass grimacing, pulling a face.

"Whatever the plan we need some decent drink!" he exclaimed.

Chapter 30

Rob returned from Scarborough the Sunday evening ready for the new week.

The weeks past with occasional trips down, wishing he could make it there every weekend, or even stay there permanently.

Every time he left, he found it harder to leave, the place had found a way into his soul. He found a place where he belonged. It wasn't just that Imogen was there, it was so much more, as he managed to embed himself into friendships.

Back home he found himself sinking back into the depths of depression which he medicated with alcohol though finding it only provided a temporary fix and soon he was again faced with his reality. The more he heard of the antics back in Scarborough they became bittersweet, at times they felt like a dagger as he began to resent his life. More and more resenting that year earlier, not taking the step and joining her in Scarborough.

Her letters were filled with fun and happiness. He was happy that she was having fun, she deserved it, but he still couldn't help feeling envious, then feeling guilty. He sat reading her most recent letter, writing about the trouble her and Clarissa were getting up to.

Talking about parties, in particular the party two nights earlier, a fancy-dress party. He had almost choked on his drink when she told him she was going as a cat in leather with a whip, insinuating that he could join them, with an almost seductive tone. She wrote about how much she missed him and wished he was there, a feeling which he echoed. Her letter ended on a serious note asking how he was. Could he be honest?

He'd spent so long being strong for Imogen, that it felt like now he could just let go, and maybe open up to her. He argued with himself, deciding to mask his true feelings, He was happy for her that she was finally free, and finally being the person she was destined to be, so he didn't want her to know how he was feeling.

He sat at his desk and began to write, wiping a tear from his eye.

After the last time I came down to see you I was in a sulk for a while but after 3 days I was back to my usual self.

He wished that was true. He paused before continuing to write revealing a little honesty.

So, I suppose I'll admit that I miss you, and still do.... From time to time that is!

How did the party go, did you go as the 'tuff' sexy lass from the matrix? Or did you go as a cat?

Pity I couldn't make it down, the thought of you chasing me wearing a latex catsuit and carrying a whip was very appealing. I hope you and Clarissa are enjoying yourselves and treating yourself to at least two bottles of wine a day. Here is my theory...

Alcohol kills brain cells, the weakest less efficient ones are killed first therefore the fit and healthy ones survive and replicate to produce more therefore actually increasing your intelligence and memory, and since your smart to begin with I'll make a genius out of you in no time!

He posted the letter the next morning on the way to college trying to keep going, hoping that eventually life would begin to work out.

Back home he was noticing that there was something not quite right with Levi, he was afraid that he was going to lose the only real friend he had at home, the only good thing. As he lay with Levi's head nuzzled into his chest, he thought of all the times he'd sat alone, holding back the tears, and he would be there with an abundance of sloppy kisses and cuddles.

He had made an appointment for the vet the next day, but didn't want that day to come, knowing that the most likely outcome was that he wouldn't be returning home with him. Something which came true.

Levi was put to sleep. He returned home, it felt like no-one else cared. He was supposed to be the family dog, but the 'family' didn't seem bothered. He sat in his room as his world began to crumble. He was struggling with college, and a hospital check-up a few days earlier reminded him of something he'd put to the back of his mind.

He sat and done what had become a normal, writing a letter...

Hey girl,

I lied. I'm not fine. Levi got put to sleep, arthritis, he has been struggling to walk lately. Why do we put dogs out of their misery, yet we have to suffer? I went to the hospital the other day... I should have told you, but I didn't want to put a dampener on your happiness. You know if I was a dog they'd have put me down by now...

I need your help now. I feel so alone without you. I feel so abandoned. Help me? I'm walking around, no-one knows me, the real me, having to disguise my true thoughts and fears.

He didn't want to write the thoughts which filled his mind, thoughts like how maybe it would be better if he was put down, if he ended it. His thoughts were becoming darker finding it harder to fight back the urge to just die. He knew revealing that would make him a hypocrite after the many times he'd talked her back from the edge. Not wanting to admit she was the only real string holding him in this crazy world.

I feel more connected to you than anyone I've ever met. I've been pushing back against the pain for so long, medicating with your friendship. Say I can come see you; we'll just be together. I need you; I need your company.

You know, sweet angel, I've always appreciated your spark your love, you're a survivor. I like that, you're gonna be just fine. Me? The jury's out on that one.

Pausing, and wiping his eyes, he couldn't help but change the tone. Always after opening up he would pull back with a joke, a way of guarding himself, injecting some humour, to mask his true feelings, something which was becoming a habit whenever he felt he was revealing too much...

Hey. Will you donate me a kidney when I need one? I know your answer... They sell them in tins in ASDA!

Those following days he didn't want to get up, not wanting to move at all. Giving the excuse that he was ill, that he'd caught some bug or something, knowing his mother would be a little more lenient. He thought how his mother never believed in 'mental health', instead it was just an excuse people used to shirk responsibilities or justify behaviours. He couldn't explain how he felt overtaken by a never-ending dark void that consumed everything, till he was left feeling nothing.

Imogen had received his letter and could read between the lines; she could feel his pain. She felt guilt and dejected that she'd not noticed, feeling selfish, then feeling more guilty that in thinking about how selfish she'd been she was again thinking of herself rather than him, wondering if she could ever live up to his level of selflessness, doubting if she could be to him what he'd always been to her.

They'd always had a connection that was almost as though they could read each other's minds, and feel each other's feelings, yet she had been too busy getting drunk, having fun, and enjoying life that she let it slip.

To the outside world, nothing showed in his face, nothing betraying his fear, it was a mask of defiance and surety. He never let anyone in, anyone get too close, though for some unknown reason Imogen had always been the exception. She wondered why he had chosen her, what made her so special? She doubted she was up to the job; she could never be half of the friend that he was.

She replied to his letter, inviting him down for the weekend. Wanting desperately to be the emotional support he deeply needed, to be his anchor, like he was for her.

Come stay with us this weekend. I can't bear to see you alone when you feel so down. I see your love too, the love you could give were it not for the fear, the pain. It's still there, and one day you will be set free, free to live the life you deserve. I'm not perfect, but I love you, and it's because of you I know what love means.

Give me a chance to find my feet, to stop my own head from spinning and I'll prove it. There is so much of your life that is a hell for your soul, and you stay there from strength rather than weakness. So let me join you in that pain, walk with you, feel the same torture I know you bare. And one day I'll find just the right way to bring you home, my love.

She posted the letter, but as she walked, she felt that wasn't enough, she wasn't doing enough! When she needed him, when she was on the edge, he was there in a heartbeat.

She dialled his number.

Rob lay in his bed, in that strange time between sleeping and waking, almost like a coma, just going through the motions.

His phone rang. She could hear in his voice the brokenness.

"Come down" She asked though the words felt more like an instruction than a request.

"Come stay with me, let me help you..." she continued.

He tried to find excuses, but in the end, there was no real excuse.

He decided he didn't care what his mother would say, for once he needed to do what he needed. He packed his bag, leaving a note on the table beside the front door, before leaving, jumping on Buzby, heading south through the grey clouds, the skies becoming brighter as he reached Scarborough, it almost felt as though it mirrored his soul.

He knocked at their front door, the door opened, he fell into her open arms. They headed up the stairs, Imogen guided him straight into her room closing the door behind her.

Standing in her room she reached out her hand taking hold of his. Their hands interlinked. She moved in close looking deep into those eyes. She could see him clearly, she was able to see him, everything he managed to hide from everyone else. She knew that like her he never felt as if he could measure up to expectations, never good enough, also burdened with the fear that he was running out of time. She would have levelled armies to save him if she ever had to.

He was like a leaf in the wind, and like that leaf, giving the appearance of being alive though in reality he was just dying slowly. Beneath the mask of the clown, and his extroverted exterior removed, the real Rob was revealed. The man who didn't know who he really was, and where he belonged.

He thought he was empty. The stupid thing was he wasn't empty at all. He was kind in a very honest sort of way and gentle in his nature.

She had always believed that it takes a courageous spirit to live well, to know how to walk the right path and to do it just because it's the right thing to do, and whenever she looked at him that was what she saw, she just wished that he could see himself through her eyes, if he could see the hero she knew him to be.

Nobody's Hero.

She was a nobody before him, he made her into somebody, he let her lean on him, and dream through him, and she bled on him. She knew he wasn't afraid to fight for her. He'd been through the storms; and they'd been through the rain together.

She knew that he had felt her pain and when she was on the edge, he was there to rescue her.

"When you need a friend, I'll be there for you" his words echoed in her mind. She hoped she could at least try and repay him.

She saw him, just like he saw her. She was that listening ear, the one who would wrap him in her love just with her soft face and kind words.

Standing in front of him in the silence, words weren't needed. Though there was so much she wanted to say.

She wanted to let him know she could see him, that she could see pain in those eyes. She could see the sadness hidden deep within his core, a slight open door to his soul, where only she could see.

"Rob, I can't heal you, but I can help you to heal yourself. I'm always here, a quiet place to reflect. In the stillness, you can let the tornado that is your pain slow down, perhaps stop."

She moved in closer, pulling him in, gently rubbing his arm. She took hold of his other hand. The heaviness in his stomach began to subside as her body pressed against his. Her touch made the room somehow warmer, within its wall's life seemed a little less bleak. He was appreciative of the simple gestures given to him. They stood together; words unspoken.

"You know. No matter how many levels of hell you descend down, I will follow, and I'll bring you back, like you do for me" She spoke breaking the silence.

"Come on... Let's go get some food, then maybe you might feel OK to face the others" she continued guiding him out of the room and out of the flat.

Chapter 31

He returned home a few days later to her letter. Reading it he thought how he wasn't fully OK, he didn't think he would ever really be, but he was somewhere that he could OK with. Knowing Scarborough, and Imogen would be there to help bring him back whenever his world became too dark.

He thought back over the fun they had, and how they seemed to be growing closer, though he never thought that possible. He began to try and work out what they were, what they had. He had resigned himself to the fact they would only be friends, in many ways was like the sister he always wanted, and he had become comfortable with that, being her 'family'. Comfortable with being able to be close and outrageously flirt in the safety of a friendship and thinking that even if she was 'there' and not still wrapped up in the fall-out from a toxic relationship, he knew he wasn't. He wasn't 'there' with her, though also doubted whether he would ever be ready to have a real relationship with anyone.

He made his way to church, knowing it would help bring him solace, though it never fully helped, instead was just like sticking a plaster on an open wound, hiding it away but it was still there.

Sitting looking out over the bay, resisting going home he continued thinking back over those few days, he sniffed his armpit, smirking as he remembered Imogen buying him some lynx body spray, saying it would help him attract the blonde chick he always claimed he wanted to meet.

He remembered back at the flat chasing her trying to spray her with his deodorant, Imogen grabbing his arms holding them down. She was wearing that same face she had when she had him beaten at whatever challenge they'd set. He remembered that smile which began to creep across her face as her left hand let go of his momentarily in order to scoop the ice out of her glass before dropping it down his back. She'd always fight dirty - all in the name of "fun" of course.

He pulled out his notepad and pen which was now always with him, and began thinking of what he could write, wanting to return to the fun letters they shared, and in the hope of not only bringing a smile to her face but also to lighten his day.

His pen hit the paper and the words poured from him.

Hey, you know that lynx spray really does work! On the way home I stopped off at the corner shop and when I went to pay the guy said it was OK and winked. Then coming out of the shop a traffic warden was about to write a ticket for Buzby, but one sniff of my armpit and he instead invited me home for tea... His wife was also a traffic warden... did you know that they carry handcuffs????

One glimpse of them and I fled. I think I should stick to Hi Karate aftershave from now on! Before leaving I gave them your details and told them of your latex catsuit and whip.....

Are you still there?? Or on your way up here with a dagger in your hand and a gin filled glint in your eye!

He laughed as he placed the letter in the envelope posting it in the nearby letterbox before heading into the bay.

As he walked through the doors, he heard a familiar voice of Imogen's father.

"Ye alrite kidda? Fancy a pint?" he asked.

Smiling Rob replied. "Aye, why not!"

Brian shouted over to the barman,

"Two pints when you're ready" before placing his arm upon Robs shoulder guiding him over to his usual corner.

"And while you're here you can tell me what mischief my daughter has been getting up to!"

He spent a few hours with her father and his mates, watching the racing and talking. The evening rolled in, and he knew he should be heading home.

As he was about to leave her father spoke to him.

"Ye na you're al-ways welcome here anytime, there'll al-ways be a pint for ya"

Rob nodded knowing it was true.

He returned to college determined to keep trying, knowing that the new year would bring work placements which gave him a purpose. He thought how it is said that everything you want is always on the other side of a hill which needs grit and determination to climb. You need to hang in there when it starts to get hard. The weeks passed as he threw himself into his work, with the occasional visit to Scarborough when the weather allowed.

November arrived, bringing with it, the half-term. The morning of 8th November, Rob sat in his room studying, his thoughts distracted by his phone ringing.

Her instant thought had been to ring Rob, and as always, he answered.

"Hey sweetness, what up?" he asked in his gentle loving voice.

He could hear the heartbreak in her voice...

She told him of a party event she saw on Facebook, an event that mutual friends were attending. A surprise engagement party.

She told him how when she looked closer, she realised the engagement party was for Jacob and Sara. She flicked through the event spotting a photo. Both of them posing. She told him how it was the girl he had cheated on her with, the girl who he was cheating on with her. They were engaged!

As he listened, he wondered why she kept giving oxygen to that waste of space.

She apologised, not knowing why it got to her, he was gone, she didn't want him or love him, repeating how if she was honest, she loathed him for everything he had put her through... But still for some unknown reason it still got to her.

His voice calmed her, knowing exactly what to say.   He asked if she would like him to sabotage their party. He had a variety of ideas – all messy, all imaginative, noisy and colourful which brought a smile to her face, making her laugh.

"So, what have you got planned for the rest of the weekend?" he asked deflecting the conversation away from Jacob.

"There's a firework display at the castle this evening so maybe sitting on the cliff, a few bottles and then maybe heading into town to hit the clubs" she replied nonchalantly.

"There's always space for you..." she continued.

"I've got loads of study to do" he replied.

"God what has happened to us, it's almost like we've swapped personalities!" she replied sarcastically.

"Yeah and while we're on that, are you still avoiding church?"

"Give a girl a break" she laughed, as they continued talking, neither wanting to end the conversation.

He put down the phone. He stood in his room looking out of his window, the sun was shining, it was a perfect day for a ride... He walked downstairs, putting on his jacket, leaving the house, and jumped on his bike. His mind was focused on Imogen as he rode and like being on auto pilot, he found himself heading to Scarborough.

He pulled up outside her flat.

Taking his phone out of his pocket he rang Imogen, looking up at her flat, smirking...

Imogen answered

"Hi Rob" she answered while giggling

"Hi Rob!" He could hear Clarissa shout echoing Imogen.

"It's only been an hour ish since we last spoke, are you really missing me that much?" Imogen continued while still giggling.

Looking up at their flat he wondered what mischief the girls were getting up to.

He laughed while trying to reply, "You know I always miss you…" he paused before continuing.

"Imi, what are you having for lunch, have you eaten yet? Cause I'm hungry" he asked casually.

The question didn't feel odd to Imogen, Rob regularly rang reminding her to eat knowing of her relationship with food which at times was balancing on a knife edge.

"I'm making some pasta" She replied

"Burning it more like!" He could hear Clarissa shouting in the background, mixed with the sound of laughter.

"Is there enough for me?" Rob questioned.

Imogen paused, a little puzzled.

"I guess so, but then with how much you eat maybe not!" she replied.

"Well I'll have to go hungry then…" there was a pause, before finishing

"….I'm outside."

The phone went silent. A few moments later the door opened, and Imogen fell into his arms.

They walked back upstairs to the flat, Rob instantly joking with Clarissa about Imogen's terrible cooking skills.

After a catch up, and eating the pasta, Rob sat with his hands behind his head, looking at Imogen, nodding his head, pretending to be deep in thought. As though simulating being a therapist and Imogen his patient sitting on the couch opposite.

"You know what you need?" he said as he leant back.

"Tell me Dr, what does your patient need?" Imogen replied,

"..Apart from a brain transplant that is!" Clarissa interrupted.

"You need a fast ride, so that rules out kitt2..." he continued directed at Imogen but giving a cheeky wink at Clarissa.

"Hey!" Imogen interrupted, throwing her cushion in his direction.

"I can ride fast"

"Yeah like a racing snail" he joked.

Pretending to cough as though to clear his throat he continued...

"As I was saying you need a fast ride on the back of Buzby to clear that mind."

Imogen looked at him.

"You're on!" Imogen replied standing up reaching out her hand.

Imogen and Rob went for a ride on his bike. Sometimes it was all Imogen needed, just to get on the back of Buzby.

She held on tight as he accelerated off, her hands wrapped around his waist, her head resting against his back as they raced down the long winding country roads. They pulled up at a quiet spot sitting amongst the purple heather. They sat talking, he held her hand in his, their fingers intertwined. His hand reassuringly brushed her face.

Their conversation steered onto relationships.

"What about us?" She asked him.

"We're best mates" he replied. The words shattered her already broken heart.

He looked away, his thoughts racing, anticipating where the conversation was heading.

"But I love you" she mumbled, looking away.

He thought how once, a long time ago he yearned to hear those words but over those years those feelings had gone, and now he looked at her more as a sister, more like his twin.

He had always been second in her life, and he wasn't about to ruin what they had, to become a rebound. He thought how the last time Jacob really got to her, her default reaction was to try and fall into his arms. Thinking if she had ever truly had feelings for him in that way they would have been revealed long before, and not as a reaction.

"No, you loved Jacob. Your just afraid to be alone and are searching for anyone to fill that void. I know you... Remember, sometimes I know you better than you know yourself"

He stood up, taking a few steps before stopping, looking out over the fields. Imogen stood up walking towards him.

"No, you're wrong... Just give me something and I'll wait for you, just give me that little bit of hope and I'll prove what I feel is real..." she replied.

"There is just the 2 of us here, now... Why won't you look at me? Why won't you tell me what you see, what you see about us? What am I to you? We're more than just mates, you can't tell me it's all one way... " she continued as her hand reached out resting upon his shoulder urging him to turn and face her.

She looked at him in a way she never had before. As a tear began to fall, soft wisps of her hair fell from behind her ear and caressed the skin of her neck, jaw, cheeks and around her deep eyes as though to hide her expression. It had started to drizzle, a light winter shower, as if to camouflage the tears about to fall.

He looked tenderly at her. He paused briefly. Taking her hand in his, he softly kissed it.

"You've never looked at me that way before" he spoke softly tempted to fall into those arms.

He paused, breaking away, not wanting to go there just in case he was seeing what his heart wanted to see. His heart and mind were fighting against each other.

He looked at her asking himself what he saw, the passion and attraction wasn't there, if it had never been there it fizzled away a long time ago, he saw a girl he loved deeply, but not in the way she wanted.

He continued...

"Now you are just searching for a rebound. You crave love, you always have. You can't just be, you can't just love yourself, it's like your self-worth is wrapped up in others..."

"…...We're too comfortable together, we've became like twins, we rely on each other, maybe too much. So, I guess we are more than just mates, and I believe in a kind of way we're soul mates just not in that physical true love way. I believe God brought us together to help us save each other, but tell me, do you honestly believe you love me in that way?"

He paused for a moment. She took hold of his hand and nodded, but before she could form an answer he continued.

"Because I don't believe you do! What you feel is not real. You don't love me, not in that way, you never have. Your trying to cling on to someone, anyone, too afraid to stand alone."

He paused continuing to feel conflicted. In a way he believed the words he was speaking, he thought how maybe a few times in their relationship he'd thought of what it would be like to take that step, but even in those moments there was nothing physical, the spark that she romanticised was never there. And if he were honest, he didn't love her in that way, but then he'd never loved anyone before, and he did love her just not in the way she deserved.

He'd listened to her many times talking of romance; it would make her eyes light up. Looking into those eyes he knew that in her own way she loved him, but he couldn't let her settle. He looked at her, her stunning deep blue eyes held a truth that his face could not hide.

"Look, even if I loved you, and believed you loved me, I can't give you what you deserve, you deserve someone who will love you completely. I will never really be able to love anyone that way, I can't leave someone behind, my time is borrowed. You will find someone, you will fall in love, with someone who can give you the world, your prince is out there waiting, and I'll make sure he's deserving of you"

He wrapped his arm around Imogen brushing her hair, softly, gently kissing her forehead holding her close.

She remained in his arms silent, her mind a whirlwind of thoughts and emotions. Wondering if it had been the wrong time to broach the topic, especially after getting distressed that morning about Jacob. She thought how no wonder he didn't believe her when she couldn't remove Jacob from her mind, to close that door, no matter how much she tried. She also reflected on his thoughts about love, and their love. He was right that she'd never had that physical attraction, but she'd had that with Jacob but didn't have real love, and she was beginning to think that if she had to choose she wanted what she and Rob had over physical attraction.

Two out of three aint bad right? She thought, though sometimes when she looked at him those past few months a spark was growing. She thought how some fires start from a spark where others grow from embers. She thought how some fall at first sight but was beginning to think it was a fairy-tale, she'd fallen at first sight before but was slowly beginning to believe that compatibility and security were more valuable than passion and lust. She had found herself having moments where she found herself feeling attracted to him like never before. He watched her grow from a girl into a woman and she knew she wouldn't be who she was without him. He planted a seed and now it felt as though it was beginning to grow, to break through the hard ground. What was there journey for, if not forever?

She felt as though she was arguing with herself, concluding that maybe he was right, and her feelings weren't real. She was clinging on to him like a safety net. She felt like she couldn't trust herself or her own instincts as they'd deceived her so many times in the past.

She smiled, deciding he was right, deciding to trust in him.

Rob broke the silence.

"You deserve to find that love that you always dream about to have the romance, the attraction, and maybe all of that kinky stuff that only I know about," he said laughing trying to lighten the mood.

Imogen hit him playfully.

"Hey, I'm only being honest! I know deep down you're not all that sweet and innocent!" he continued

He laughed, stepping back, lifting her chin.

"But hey you know I love you, I'll always love you, We'll always be together in some way, and our deal still stands... if ya still single when your 40, having failed to find prince charming, and by some miracle I'm still here, I'll marry you, a marriage of convenience...... We can grow old together, wild grey-haired bikers tearing up the countryside...deal???

The sky was turning grey as storm clouds threatened to erupt.

"Come on!" he said taking her hand.

Chapter 32

They returned to the flat as the rain began to fall heavy. As though the world was crying her tears. Clarissa broke open a bottle of wine unaware. She poured a glass for herself and Imogen. Holding a third glass she asked.

"Are you staying? Or is this a flying visit?

Looking out of the window, then looking back at Imogen he answered.

"Only if we're hitting the town, karaoke??" He replied.

Clarissa poured the third glass handing it to him

"Do you really have to ask?" Clarissa replied.

Both Imogen and Rob were trying to put the events of earlier that afternoon out of their minds, instead feeling blessed to just be together the way they always had been, able to just sit around a wine bottle or two and laugh together.

The empty bottle clinked against the side of the recycling bin as Clarissa opened a second bottle topping up the glasses, the rain had begun to slow. Imogen watched the raindrops slowly fall down the windowpane, watching a break in the grey clouds, the sun breaking through. As she drank the wine began to go to her head. Usually she could handle her drink, she'd drunk others under the table, including a lecturer egged on by Rob, and had many nights out with Rob and friends from the Uni, but that afternoon it felt like the first time she had drunk, her stomach ached like it had many times before, something which she tried to hide putting it down to IBS. She'd been to see her GP about it many times over the years and that was always the diagnosis, so she just accepted it. That day and the day before the pain had come in waves causing her to self-medicate with painkillers, hiding it, not wanting anyone to know, but that day had taken more than was allowed doses. Almost instinctively Rob placed his hand on her shoulder pulling her in for a hug.

"You OK?" he asked.

"Yep fine" she replied nodding determined to push through.

She continued to sit drinking, her thoughts swimming in her head, the alcohol making her already warped emotions worse.

Going to the bathroom she couldn't resist taking more tablets desperate for the pain to go, her head also began to thump as her mind raced in overdrive. Part of her also took them as a way to punish herself for her behaviour, she stared at the pink razor on the sink wanting to give in to temptation. Her hand hovered above before taking a step back, leaving the bathroom.

Returning to the living room she sat on the arm of the chair her mind continuing to replay thoughts and feelings.

She thought how she would wait an eternity to be with him, she would sink into serenity, just content to be close to him. Rob was the one that made her heart strong. His smile alone brought her peace and made everything OK. He was a part of her soul turning her into someone she could never have achieved on her own. She thought how before they met, she was nothing, she felt like nothing, empty, yet through him somehow, she was so much more than she ever was before. But only now she was realising when it was now too late.

Just as quickly she snapped out of it.

"He's your best mate, God he's practically your brother, everything he said was right" she told herself.

"Yep I'm just a hopeless lost cause, the champion of disasters and self-sabotage" she answered herself, before looking up thinking how stupid it was to have a conversation with yourself.

She watched Clarissa with her phone in her hand.

"Well this is our last bottle, but Simon has a couple. He's down at Claire's. Do ya fancy going there on the way down?" she asked though it wasn't really a question more of a statement.

She walked over to Imogen pulling her to her feet,

"Come on lets quickly get ready, we can't hit the town like this!" she declared as they walked out of the living room.

"Rob, you can finish the last of the bottle while we get ready!" she shouted back down the corridor.

Rob looked out of the window also replaying that day. Resolute that he'd done the right thing but worrying over her fragile state of mind. He slowly nursed his glass while waiting for them to return.

Clarissa had pulled Imogen into her room before rummaging through her wardrobe.

"And we need something to make the guys fall at your feet, or one particular guy" she laughed.

"Nah that ship has sailed" Imogen sighed.

Clarissa looked at her, puzzled.

"I'll tell you later, let's just have tonight" she declared, before picking up a dress.

"This?" she asked determined to deflect the topic of conversation.

"Yep!" Clarissa replied.

They got ready in quick time, neither were the type of girls to spend hours getting ready, but still looked stunning. They walked back into the living room.

"Wow! You two are looking pretty awesome tonight." Rob stated taking hold of Clarissa's hand, before offering his other hand to Imogen.

"Well, are we off?" he asked.

"Yep!" Clarissa replied.

They walked down the road jumping over puddles, arriving at Claire's flat, the music could be heard from the street. They walked up the stairs to the flat, the door was open as students flowed between flats. They met Simon in the doorway.

"You alrite mate?" Rob asked Simon, while leaning in for a hug.

Simon shared the flat with Clarissa and Imogen though spent most of his time at Claire's flat, the hive of action, the whole block filled with students, almost a replica of halls the year before. Their flat was different, their landlord lived on the bottom floor and regularly held inspections and didn't tolerate noise. Something they had learned over the past couple of months!

"Come on in and get a drink!" Simon beckoned walking back into the flat towards the kitchen.

Simon was very camp! A fellow dancer in the same class as Imogen. He was either Bisexual, or just hadn't discovered if he was gay or not. He would flirt with anyone, male or female, always welcoming. Like a chameleon. He could easily fit in as one of the girls, yet the next moment be one of the lads.

They stayed a while continuing to drink, Imogen managed to disappear into the crowd to the bathroom making herself sick in a hope to sober herself up, also worried about the amount of paracetamol and codeine she had taken that day, but also finding another way to punish herself. She thought how no-one knows the thoughts that go through her head, at times becoming afraid of the thoughts which consumed her. That day had been the first time in a long time she felt like grabbing a sharp object and cutting herself, she'd resisted back at the flat but it was getting harder to fight he urge.

She scanned the bathroom with no avail. She stood at the sink, wiping her mouth and taking a sip of water from the tap, before looking at her reflection in the mirror.

"God help me, let me be OK" she whispered a silent prayer though didn't believe he was listening, it had been so long since she'd spoken to him, at times doubting if he was there at all.

She walked back out finding Clarissa and Rob playfully flirting like they had done so many times, but this time was different, this time it cut like a knife.

"Get over it! He was never yours!" she told herself as she took a deep breath,

"Well I guess I'd rather he be with someone I know so I don't lose him completely" she muttered under her breath before composing herself and walking over to join them.

"Hey! Here she is! We were wondering where you'd disappeared too" Rob shouted over the music handing her a glass.

"Did you find some stud and take him to one of the rooms?" Clarissa asked laughing.

Imogen laughed, though inside her mind began to twist her friend's words and create hidden meanings.

"They all think you're a slut, a dirty slut and well they're not wrong, are they?" her voice played in her head, an endless stream of toxic thoughts.

"Nah, needed a quick toilet break" she replied downing her drink.

"So, are we heading down to the packet?" Imogen asked.

"Yeah!" Rob replied.

"Hey Simon, we're off down the packet, you coming?" Rob asked as he placed his glass on the table.

"I'll join you in a bit" he replied winking looking over in the direction of a group of students.

"OK, catch ya later! And good luck!" Rob laughed.

They finished their drinks before walking down to the seafront heading along to the packet for some karaoke.

As they walked down, Clarissa walked ahead, as though sensing that Rob needed to sort her out like he had so many times before.

"Hey look at me... I know you; I know the kind of thoughts that will be dancing around that head of yours. Stop it. You're loved, you're perfect, and I'll always want you and need you in my life, not always the way you think you want, but you're not really seeing straight lately so look to me, believe in me, believe in us. Now come on, let's go have some fun!" he spoke softly pulling her in for a hug.

"You'll be fine, I know it, like I've said before its written in your destiny" he continued before taking her hand, pulling her forward to catch up with Clarissa.

"We all good now?" Clarissa asked as they caught up to her.

"Yep, just needed to give my girl a pep talk, now come on!" he beckoned winking, Imogen smiled.

Getting the drinks in they sat in their usual spot, searching through the list of karaoke songs, compiling a list for the night, before handing it to the DJ. They sat talking until Rob's name was called.

Rob got up for a rendition of Bat out of hell, and as always, the bar erupted.

Pointing at her as he sang

"Gonna be dancing through the night with you…."

As the song ended, he walked over to Imogen.

"Live the life you dream girl" Rob whispered as he pulled her up to her feet.

"Now I maybe messing with your order of songs mate, but I think the bar needs a bit of this duo" he smiled as he beckoned over to the DJ.

The DJ nodded, perks of being regulars.

He led her to the stage for their infamous rendition of dead ringer for love. As they sang, Simon, and a few other of their circle arrived.

"Whoop Whoop!" she heard Simon and a few other's echo; their drunken states obvious.

Her hand went to her heart and her head rose as she belted out the final notes filled with the haunting feeling of knowing that her voice was hiding the pain.

The physical pain but also the haunting pain which continued deep down, the pain of feeling like their friendship was like a pane of glass she had cracked, the cracks slowly growing, imagining those cracks causing it to shatter completely, making it unable to fix, eternally broken.

Eventually those thoughts buried themselves back down to the deep corner of her mind, as she distracted herself with the present, determined to make the most of the moment.

As the evening began to draw in the group then headed up into town to the local club.

They danced into the night, everyone dancing like they'd forgotten how to stand still. They danced till closing. As the last orders rang, they collapsed into the leather sofa in the corner of the club.

"I'll grab the last round!" Clarissa shouted drunkenly over the music.

Imogen slumped, her head resting upon Rob's chest. A few moments passed; Clarissa passed along shot glasses brimming with sourz

"I got triples..." she exclaimed,

"I don't know if you should be having another one," Imogen laughed.

"Or you! It's been a long time since I've seen you a bit tipsy" He replied laughing taking a glass and downing it.

"Toast to us? Besties forever!!" Clarissa declared, downing the shot glass.

"Tomorrow they'll be hell to pay!" Imogen laughed as she downed her glass while watching Clarissa.

"Another!" Clarissa declared as she turned stumbling back towards the bar,

"I think we need to get her home!" Rob stated.

They guided her away from the bar and towards the exit, with her tumbling down the steps onto the cobbled street.

The cold air hit her. After a few paces she doubled over, Imogen stood holding her hair back as her vomit splashed on the stones.

Rob helped her to her feet, Imogen retrieved a bottle of water from a passing street pastor.

"No thanks. We've got this?" She replied as they asked if they could help.

They helped Clarissa take a few sips of water before walking arm in arm steadying her, heading back over suicide bridge, heading back home up to South Cliff.   They returned to the flat trying to be quiet.

They dropped Clarissa onto her bed, laughing.

They collapsed onto Imogen's bed. They lay together talking. She nuzzled into his chest; her eyes closed. Softly he began singing the words of that's what friends are for, stroking her hair. Her eyes closed as she listened to his calming voice.

And if I should ever go away.
Close your eyes and try to feel the way we do today
Keep smiling,
Knowing you can always count on me,
Cause That's what friends are for
For good times and bad times
I'll be on your side Cause
That's what friends are for…….

His voice was smooth and clear and quiet. Soothing. It was like the promise of tomorrow. It was beautiful, and she wished that he would never stop. She fell asleep in his arms.

Rob woke up early as the sun crept through the gaps in the curtains, he leant over gently kissing her forehead before quietly exiting her room.

Making a drink he wrote her a note. As he drank his hot coffee he looked around, reflecting on so many memories made in that room. He gazed out of the window watching the sun break through the clouds.

Leaving it on the kitchen table, he quietly left the flat heading back up home.

Arriving back in Newcastle he stopped at the coast wondering if she was awake yet, thinking over the previous day, wondering if he'd done the right thing. He'd told her to learn to stand on her own two feet and in a way, he had to do the same. He thought about what he put on the note.

Before going down to Scarborough, he had learned the family had decided on an impromptu holiday to visit family back in Gran Canaria, some relative was ill, he hadn't really taken much notice, apart from to refuse to go. But he found himself writing that he was going. Maybe the breakaway would be good, and maybe would be good to have some family time, even if he always felt like an outsider. He thought how maybe if he made an effort, he wouldn't feel that way, wondering if in part his behaviour, and keeping everyone at arm's length willed his beliefs into reality.

He knew his mother was always hard on him but he never doubted that she still loved him, maybe not in the same way, or equal to that of his siblings, but he thought can you ever love anyone the same? Maybe his illness made her create that barrier as a defence for when that time would come. Everyone deals with things differently he thought as he thought how he had dealt with the death sentence which hung over him like an elephant in the room.

He thought how Isabella was also going to be meeting up with them. He hated to admit it, but he had in a way missed her, the house too quiet without her, he'd even missed their fights and missed her getting one up on him.

He returned home.

His mother looked at him sternly.

"You never said you were staying out!" she spoke sternly.

"Sorry Mama, I was down Scarborough with Imogen and got caught in the rain so stayed over, I should have rang... Oh, and I've changed my mind, I will come with you, if there is still space that is."

"Of course, there is space, there's always space for you" she replied sincerely.

Chapter 33

Rob walked barefoot along the warm sand of the shore, a blank postcard in his hand. The cool water lapped against his feet, fizzing and bubbling like brine. The sun was beating upon his back.

He thought how the break had been good, and the weather and scenery helped, but his thoughts returned to Imogen. Wondering how she was doing. He'd been enjoying himself so much, feeling included, part of the family, feeling like he belonged, till it dawned on him that he hadn't really thought of her much during that holiday, or at least not as much as he usually did. He had to admit that before that holiday she had rarely left his mind since he first met her.

Nothing stays the same, everything needs to evolve to stay alive, and their relationship wasn't an exception.

He sat upon the shore, taking his pen out from his pocket and began to write.

Hi Imogen

It's my last day here and I'm kind of sad to be leaving coz I've had such a good time!

Yo estoy pensando que nuestra casa en Scarborough es major???

Me and the Bro have been to Tenerife a few times to see El Tiede mountain, the highest part of Spain, I got an awesome pic of me for you!

I managed to sneak out to a few clubs on a couple of nights and shocked everyone with my 'dancing', though I almost fell into a swimming pool at one club... yes I know! Swimming pool in a night club? I bet you're probably saying you want to go. Maybe we should suggest it to Baja? The rest of the time I have been on my best behaviour, I can see you laughing!! But honestly, I've been generally seeing the family, and admiring the scenery and local wildlife... especially the birds heh!!
There's some (HEH!)
Great looking (HEH!)
Birds......

They returned home. He had renewed hopes that the time away had improved the relationships with his family, but it felt like as soon as they returned home, as soon as they walked through the front door that the old resumed.

He returned to college for the last 2 weeks before Christmas break, having to work harder to catch up on what he'd missed.

Rob returned to Scarborough to visit the week between Christmas and New year, there relationship the same but different, he thought how it seemed like they were both on the same page. Not realising that the truth was she that she was trying to hide her growing feelings, feelings which hadn't faded like she'd hoped. That she was trying to find ways to deflect them, to find a way back to where they used to be. Back when she saw him only as her friend.

Her mental health also seemed to be back on an even keel, almost normal, not knowing that in part it was all an act, trying to 'fake it till ya make it'. Though he silently thought how normal is overrated and she would never be normal.

Imogen was laughing about how Gary, one of her surfer friends seemed to be taking an interest in her, and her and Clarissa chalking it up as points over the bimbos who usually followed his every move. As they talked Imogen hoped Gary could possibly be the distraction she needed, and also a way to prove that she had moved past her feelings for him. Though wondered if she could take that step.

Rob sat amused, especially hearing off his apparent nipple piercing, leading the conversation down avenues only they could joke about, a conversation which made Imogen blush.

"So…. Es nuestra casa major?" Imogen asked deflecting from the conversation about Gary.

"Well, the company sure is, but weather... not so much!" he laughed.

The Sunday they stood on the doorstep to say goodbye. Words weren't needed as Imogen nodded, reaching in for a hug. He thought how it was as if they both now accepted what their relationship was and how it was always going to be. A friendship, a connection that could never be broken.

"See ya! and keep writing to me!" Rob declared as he walked away, climbing on his bike, and riding away.

The New Year arrived, He reflected on how Imogen had seemed to move on, confirming that her feelings were just a reaction, a rebound, starved of affection and clinging on to the only person who'd ever showed her love.

He thought how the old saying went that if you love someone let them go and if they come back then you know it's real. He let her go, and fleetingly she never fought for more, it seemed as though she just shrugged her shoulders and accepted it. He thought maybe it was time for him to begin to search the field.

The new term also brought work placements, a time when he could really sink his teeth into the course, determined to prove himself. Feeling that maybe he could make a difference in some kids' life so that they didn't suffer like he had.

The first day of the first work placement soon arrived. Rob stood in the school reception waiting, trying not to let his nerves be visible. He looked around and down at the floor until his eyes fell upon his feet, one of his laces had become undone. He bent his knee at a slight angle before slowly bending further till one knee was on the floor, he fastened his lace before taking a grip of a chair arm to maintain balance.

His eye level lifted from the floor, getting ready to stand back up catching a glimpse of a pair of female legs walking towards him. He couldn't help but admire the long slender, almost perfect legs. His gaze lifted upwards to see who the legs belonged too, seeing a girl with long blonde hair walked in his direction. She sat a few seats away from the seat he was holding onto. He stood up, sitting down trying his best to evade her attention. he glanced over to her trying not to smile but unable to control his facial expression. She smiled back before looking away as though she was not sure how to react.

The time passed slowly as they waited. She was tall, fair and had a polite smile on her face.

"This way please!" a voice bellowed from the office door.

Rob stood up walking towards the old receptionist, before slowly realising the girl was also walking in the same direction. His hand rested on the door.

"After you" he spoke softly smiling as she walked past.

"Thanks" she replied.

He followed behind as they walked along the grey washed out corridor of the old school towards the staff room.

"Right! You two... Make yourselves comfortable and someone will be along in the next half hour to take you to where you're meant to be..." The receptionist said opening the staff room door with a fob.

The room was empty. Rob sat down picking up a magazine to try and distract himself. He watched as she reached into her bag, pulling out a novel, sitting crossed legged and started reading.

The door opened, he watched as she bookmarked her novel, placing it in her lap as she looked around nervously. He continued watching her until she caught his gaze. She smiled before glancing down to avert his gaze, tucking her golden hair behind her ear as though to cause a distraction, as her eyes lifted to see if he was still looking at her.

Rob was still looking at her, as though lost in her. She lifted her head tilting it slightly looking right into his eyes.

"Hi I'm Rachel", she said in her charming voice which was sweetened by her smile.

Her voice resonated in his ears. Her fingers with neatly manicured nails again tucked her hair behind her ears which had fallen back over her face.

"Hey! I'm Rob" he replied placing his hand out in front of him as to beckon a handshake. She took his hand shaking it smiling, her head bowed a little causing her hair to again fall.

As the day passed, he discovered she was also on placement, happy to discover he'd be spending more time with her over the coming weeks.

"You fancy going for some food to celebrate us surviving our first day?" he asked as they left the school later that day.

"Yeah! Why not!" she replied.

They sat at the small Italian along the road, in time for happy hour. The silence echoed.

"Hey, I am sorry. It's just I don't speak much. I've never been into conversation, I kind of prefer my books" she commented as they scanned through the menus.

He thought how why it was he seemed to be attracted to nerds, extremely attractive nerds that is!

"Hey, it's fine! I'll do all the talking" he laughed.

They talked, laughed, and got along so well. He discovered she was 17 which made his heart sink, though she didn't look 17, or act 17. She held herself in a way he'd only seen in mature women.

He enjoyed the week getting to know her.

The Thursday night, a few days before his 24th birthday. He received a letter. He opened it hoping for a card at least. His birthdays always passed with little acknowledgement. He unfolded the letter and began to read her words.

Happy Birthday! You may have noticed I've not sent you anything... the reason... well, the reason is because I am your present, OK, I'm not your only present, that would be pretty poor part on me.. but I'm also your courier! Yes! Don't go having a heart attack but I'm going to come back up to Newcastle!! Well I've got to do it sometime and what better reason than to give you the birthday you deserve!

He smiled. Picking up his phone.

Hey Girl! Got your letter, looking forward to unwrapping my gift. See ya Saturday, got loads to tell you so it saves me writing it down!

Saturday lunchtime he stood looking out of his window and staring at his phone. Wondering where she was, she should have arrived already.

His phone bleeped.

"Got caught out by the rain, have to go back, sorry x"

He sat on the bed deflated, wondering whether that was the truth or if she'd bottled it. His phone bleeped again, this time a picture of herself wet, next to her bike pulling a sad face.
As he stared at the picture, he could see she was writing another message.

Sorry! Love you. Have a great birthday and I'll hopefully see you soon?

Cold and wet, she headed back towards Scarborough, as he sat deflated.

He couldn't reply, he didn't want to reply, not wanting her to know how upset he was, how much of a disappointment his birthday had been, instead he scanned through his phone, scrolling down to Rachel.

He dialled, she answered.

"Hey! It's my birthday, and well I'm all alone, fancy going for a walk or food or something?" he asked.

She agreed, arranging to meet in Tynemouth. He walked down the stairs, picking up his jacket. His mother stopped him asking.

"Where are you going! I thought Imogen was coming? I've made lunch!"

He sighed.

"She couldn't make it, she got caught in the rain, so I'm off out to meet up with a girl from placement."

His mother grumbled in Spanish under her breath walking back into the kitchen. He knew she didn't approve and knew she would disapprove even more if he knew her age!
He had a good time with Rachel listening to her talk, watching her smile, her laugh. At first it felt uncomfortable. They sat together trying to find things to keep the conversation going, afraid of the pause. Watching her he could tell she was thinking so deeply before speaking. He just listened, not feeling ready to reveal himself to her. She would say something, and he would politely laugh, not talking about anything that really mattered. Though in a way he found that a refreshing break. His deepest secrets, his hidden pain, his problems all hidden out of sight, hidden by the pretence. He returned home as the rain began to

fall heavy, the storm which Imogen got caught in had finally reached Newcastle.

He sat in his room watching the rain fall heavy, the skies darkening, the wind howling rattling the tree outside. He turned on his radio to cover the sounds from outside and to break the silence within.

He picked up a pen and began to write.

Big thank you for trying to get up for my birthday, loved the picture!! Would have loved to have seen you soaked through in the flesh!... It reminds me of that wet t-shirt competition you entered! Miss Bike?? Whoop Whoop!!!!

He paused for a moment, before continuing...

Get, get, down, is on the radio, it reminds me of the other week. So I now, as well as the image of you in a wet t-shirt, with the silhouette of your bra, I now also have visions of you doing the splits and Abi having to help you back up! I was too busy laughing at the time to help!

I've met a girl called Rachel.... My mum is having a fit! Can you give Rachel a character reference for me? Mum will listen to you!

Please?? Will love you forever... wait I already will, I'm not doing too good at this bargaining stuff.... How about I let you win our next race???

He was disturbed by his mother shouting up the stairs, beckoning him down for dinner. He closed his notepad, planning to return to the letter when he returned. He turned off his radio and walked out of the room, slowly walking down the stairs.

When he returned, he forgot about the letter, his mind focussing on the next day, another hospital check-up. He had forgotten about it till his mother reminded him during dinner, scolding him for forgetting, reminding him that he should be acting his age, continuing with the usual conversation of when he was going to start working and contributing.

The next morning, he sat in the waiting room, the clock ticking slowly, the appointments over-run, realising he wouldn't make it to the school at all that day. His phone pinged.

Hey, you're not at school? You OK?

He hesitated, wondering what to write. He couldn't tell her he was stuck at hospital waiting for a routine check-up, he couldn't say how his life was a string of tests and appointments recording the failure of his failing body.

I'm just feeling a little under the weather and didn't want to pass any germs onto the kids.

He replied.

He scanned through his phone landing on Imogen, wanting to ring her, but couldn't. He'd told her to learn to stand on her own two feet and he thought how he needed to take his own advice.

He sat alone, he thought how maybe that was what he was destined for, to live alone, insignificant.

He returned home, the results weren't as bad as he was expecting, nothing had really changed, not worse, but not better. His mother quizzed him wanting to know every detail and scolding him for not asking specific questions.

"I'm not a kid anymore! But if you want to treat me like one why not come next time! Or write me a list of questions, that way you'll get your answers! Or maybe just ring the Dr if you're not happy!" he argued before storming up the stairs entering his bedroom and slamming the door.

He sat at his desk, the half-written letter peeking out from under a book.

He picked up his pen wanting to vent but instead he reigned in his feelings.

I went to the hospital for my routine check-up today. Rachel knows zilch about it, I don't think it's going to last between us, though don't tell her I said that if you meet her, I don't know why I think like that cause I do like her a lot, It's strange how the human mind works, especially yours... and mine.

And I'll be down in a couple of weeks, but I still think it is pretty unfair that you aint been coming up here, OK, you can't help the weather on my birthday but hey! Though if I'm honest I prefer getting away from here too, would I return if I'd escaped??

Chapter 34

The next few months past slowly, spring beginning to creep in. He found himself self-sabotaging his relationship with Rachel, making it over before it really began. He wondered if he would ever be able to have a relationship, or if he deserved it.

The arrival of spring also brought with it Imogen's birthday, a few days before he bought a card, writing inside.

Hey

Did you get that huge £99.99 bouquet of erotic, oops I mean exotic lillies from the lower valleys of Tibet??

No??... Dammn that pigeon! And your dad said it was a good carrier... Maybe when I told him to go to Scarborough, it went to Bambrough by mistake...

And yes, he is a HE because he didn't give me a kiss before leaving... and I saw its....... Maybe I've finally lost it and I shouldn't be talking to birds but that would result in celibacy...... or maybe not???

And just to say you maybe a year older but I can tell you are definitely more immature, in the best possible sense. Alas my work is done!

See you soon, birthday girl!

He rode down that weekend for birthday celebrations, any excuse for the gang to party. He felt like he'd been missed, and in part it had been like there was a black hole which only Scarborough could fill. Following that weekend, he began to spend more time back down at Scarborough, becoming disappointed when he realised Imogen would be moving in with Lorna over the summer.

He knew she wouldn't be returning home; it wasn't home anymore. He wasn't disappointed that she was staying but more so that the dynamic was changing. Clarissa was returning home for the summer break and the flat they had been living in was needed for holiday makers.

He sat at the priory daydreaming. He began remembering the last visit before she moved in with the girls a few weeks earlier. They spent the day racing around Oliver's Mount, and sitting on the grass verge overlooking the starting point like they had so many times before, where they would sit and put the world to rights, where they opened up.

She spoke to him about his fear to commit, at times sounding wise and together, yet he could still see the cracks, revealing that she wasn't as together as she tried to make everyone believe. Her letters revealed her true feelings as she struggled with the fear of failing her 2nd year and spending too much time over analysing her life and her mistakes.

She also sensed his anxiety at not being able to stay over the summer, as though his security blanket was being pulled from underneath him, the thought of not being able to just jump on his bike, rock up on her doorstep and be able to stay over whenever home became too much was frightening.

"Hey, I may be moving in with the girls but you're always welcome whether they like it or not! I'll sneak you in, or we can go camp on the mount, or I can use my charms on Gary and see if you can bunk at his... I'll never turn you away, you'll always have a place wherever I am." She spoke softly as he left the final time before she moved to the new house.

It wasn't long till the summer was on the horizon, with his course nearing an end, and Clarissa being gone, his visits became few and far between. He knew she was spending the time trying to find herself, to really make an effort to fix herself rather than just paper over the cracks. He knew she would call out if she needed him, but he knew this was one journey she had to take alone.

He also had to put himself first, to get through the endless reams of coursework if he was to pass. His term was slowly coming to an end, learning that he'd passed his classroom assistant course though wondered how, thinking he must have passed by the skin of his teeth.

He was thankful that he didn't have to endure yet another summer waiting for exam results. He had enjoyed the placements, finding somewhere he belonged, a purpose.

The last day with the class he'd been working with had a day trip over to South Shields, the morning filled with museum visits, but the afternoon spent down at the fair.

That evening he sat pondering what was next, having the sinking feeling of another ending, making him again think about where his life was heading. Was it time to get out in the real world?

He sat and began to write.

I finally finished all of my coursework! How you ask!

Well... enter qualified classroom assistant! Are you proud of me, well I know the answer, I know you're the only one who is! Oh, and yeah! I also passed my youth work certificate. God help the kids! Talking about God... the acorn gang were asking after you, what do I say??

I went to the fair today with the kids from school and got called a wimp for not wanting to go on the big rides, have I become boring and sensible without your wild influence?

Maybe this letter is a bit serious, I promise the next letter will be full of my insulting you, but I think I'm a better person because of you. More sensitive, I listen to people (well most people!), have a sense of humour... what I already had that, Ok... well I no longer snore, and no longer need the wotsits.. Too good to be true??

These past few months have been hard being away from you so much and the summer will be worse! The more time I spend away from you the more miss you but hey I guess that's only natural!

He thought how no-one seemed to care or acknowledge that he'd passed, though he never expected any different.

The next day, to celebrate he bought himself a new bike. A black TDM. He'd spent hours in the showroom indecisive, constantly changing his mind.

"I used to be indecisive. but now I'm not too sure!" he muttered to himself as he changed his mind for the fourth time.

Walking out of the showroom he beamed, like an excited child, looking back at the showroom, at the bike in the window he whispered,

"In 2 days, you'll be mine!" thinking of where his first ride would be.

As he climbed on Buzby, he leant forward, his hands resting on the fuel tank,

"Hey it's OK, you're not being replaced, you got me through some tough times and we've had some adventures" he whispered gently patting the bike, while looking around hoping no-one had noticed he was talking to a bike!

The two days dragged. Returning from a very long and fast ride on his new bike, his mother complained about another useless bike taking up space in the garage, and how was he going to pay for the upkeep, and how maybe he should stop being lazy and get a job. He shook his head as he walked through the house returning to his room.

Whenever he was sad or having a bad day his first instinct was to write to Imogen, a habit formed over those past years. he had been excited to tell her about his new bike but as usual his mother had ruined that. He sat down to write. Her words from that last visit still echoed in his mind, that he always had a place with her, the only one who ever accepted him for who he was.

He began to write.

Hey sweetness!

I think you're one of the sweetest girls I've ever met, you say such nice things, I know your always there for me, I'm glad we met.

You make me happy when skies are grey, please don't take my sunshine away!

Yes that was serious but I think it's still nice to let you know how I feel about you now and again.

Hope you are at least feeling ok. If not, write to me! Even if your last few letters haven't been a bundle of laughs, I don't mind if you need to write to someone who genuinely cares for you! You know I will always be here.

Anyway, enough of the soppy stuff!

You know the last time I stayed over before you moved in with the miserable pair. I remember waking in the middle of the night and saying to you 'what', because a faint whispering had woken me. What were you saying? Were you trying to drum into my subconsciousness to get a bigger bike?

You do talk in your sleep!

I can't believe you aren't aware of how you were making noises and talking about Kawasaki zzr's in your sleep. Well I've just bought myself a bigger bike.

I suppose you'll get to see my new bike when you next come up here! Heh, heh.. Ok, you're not laughing...

He couldn't help but laugh wondering if it would dare her to make the journey, though he knew he would give in first, he was needing an escape and now could get to Scarborough quicker.

A week later he returned home from shopping for his mother. He placed the shopping on the kitchen floor, as his mother began to urge him into the living room.

As he entered the room, he spotted Imogen sitting there waiting for him. The shock registering on his face. Before he could hide it, a small smile played on his lips.

Imogen stood up and walked towards him falling into his arms. She could feel his warmth and the comforting sound of his heartbeat. His hands wrapped around her back, drawing her in closer. He needed her as much as she needed him. He pulled his head back, wiping the tears from her eyes.

His mother brought in the tea, they chatted. Imogen looked frequently at Rob trying to take her cues from him, wanting to spend her time with him, but feeling the need to satisfy his mother who hadn't seen her for such a long time.

She wondered how long was the polite length of time to sit there listening, nodding, and trying to be courteous. When his mother looked down to her cup Imogen looked at Rob, raising her eyebrows and shrugging her shoulders, before returning to a feigned smile as his mother looked back up in her direction.

His mother asked attentively of her studies. Imogen talked about her course, of her dance. It felt freeing to have someone want to know, to pay a genuine interest. It was refreshing for her to have someone who was genuinely interested in her studies, in her life, her family weren't, but she was also aware of Rob's issues with his family, their lack of support for him, and she was determined to make the visit about him rather than her.

She had thought a lot over their relationship over those past few months realising how much he gave, and how little she gave back in comparison, he would move mountains for her when she struggled to fight through her fears, or fight through the rain, thinking back to his birthday. Nothing she could ever give or do would be enough.

The atmosphere was broken as his mother changed topic slightly. As always, the conversation steered to comparisons, to using the prior conversation to knock Rob down.

Delivering one of her off-hand comment as she began tidying away the cups.

"See Roberto, Imogen is making something of herself, when are you going to do something with your life, like your brothers, your sister...If you had went to university like Imogen, you could have also studied instead of staying here..."

Looking at Rob she could see how the flippant comments affected him. How they always did. She knew because like in her life flippant comments would break her and repeat in her mind for months after, chipping away destroying her from the inside.

Rob sat with the comment replaying over and over in his mind,

'Why hadn't he gone to Scarborough'

Those words cut like a knife, it hadn't been from a lack of wanting to, he self-sabotaged his future for his family out of loyalty and duty but got nothing back, now she was making out that it was his fault, making him wonder whether it had all been in his head, had he used the family as an excuse?

He no longer knew what was true anymore, but in that flippant sentence she had given permission for him to go, and he had a witness.

He looked over at Imogen seeing the growing look of distain on her face.

Imogen wondered why no-one else could see him for who he was. Why did success have to be measured on the qualifications you have, the job you get?

"Mama, leave him alone! He is perfect just as he is, and if he'd gone with me you'd be all alone, you should be grateful he stayed, he cares, he cares more than anyone I've ever met, isn't that what counts?" she spoke sternly standing up, standing between them.

His mother grumbled, a feigned attempt at agreement, as she took the dishes into the kitchen.

Imogen's hand gently touched his, looking at him giving a silent acknowledgment. He thought how no-one had ever stood up for him the way she had.

Imogen sighed following his mother into the kitchen.

"Mama, go sit down, we'll put the shopping away and do the dishes" Imogen spoke politely, turning slightly to disguise rolling her eyes.

His mother put down the tea-towel, as Rob joined her in the kitchen. As his mother walked out of the kitchen her words echoed.

"When are you two going to get engaged?"

Imogen shook her head, as she closed the door. She looked up at Rob. There was a moment of silence, a moment where no words were needed to be spoken, a quiet understanding, a look which spoke deeper. Imogen nodded smiling, before walking closer to him, stealing the tea towel from him, splashing him with water. What ensued was a fun playfight, which like many times before brought a serenity, an acceptance.

"Should we tell her she'll be waiting till I'm 30 or was it 40?!" Imogen joked as she splashed him one last time.

"Come on, we may as well get this sorted so we can escape!" Imogen continued.

They finished the dishes and put away the shopping before quietly heading up to his room, hoping to avoid another confrontation.

She sat on his bed in his small box room. The walls covered in drawings. On his bedside table sat a framed photo. Imogen and Rob sitting on Buzby and Kitt2 taken on Oliver's mount.

She looked at her image, the smile on both of their faces, the happiness evident.

They sat talking. He talked about passing his course but still lost about where he was heading, and his mother's comments didn't help.

He spoke of how at college he was always the oldest, and the older he got he found it harder to fit in with the young students.

"I doubt I could survive another year of college; I think it is definitely time to hang up the student card for good" he muttered

".... Maybe it is time for me to get a real job" he laughed.

The conversation swayed onto Imogen, Rob wanting to deflect away from his problems but also out of deep concern after reading her letters of late. She had promised herself that visit would be all about him, but she found it impossible not to let it all out, to reveal how much she had been struggling. She opened up on what had been happening those past few weeks, revealing where her mind was at, and for a few sweet hours she didn't have to hide behind a mask, not of happiness, not of coping, she could always be honest and get heart felt advice.

She talked about her revisiting her memories of her past and trying to come to terms with her life so far. Of how she had been trying to write but couldn't.

"You can write... I've got plenty of letters to prove it" he answered jokingly.

She playfully hit him with a nearby cushion.

"Silly! I meant I can't write anything else, writing to you comes naturally, but I've been trying to write my life thinking it might help me deal with all the crap, you know that essay thing my lecturer suggested that I told ya about, apparently it'll help me heal or something stupid….. Oh and

I had been trying to write a love story, but what do I know about love!" she replied.

He smirked winking trying not to laugh as he spoke.

"We both know you can write..." pausing mid-sentence he feigned a cough, knowing she could read between the lines.

He placed his clenched fist up to his mouth and spoke words through feigned coughs.

Cough, "Catsuit"

Cough "whip"

He tried not to laugh as he continued...

"…… You forget I've read your raunchy stuff!"

Raising her eyebrows, she answered.

"Not helping! Ok I can write about..." she paused pursing her lips.

"It's not like I've not had realms of experience..." she uttered sarcastically before pausing. Her tone dropping before trying to continue without allowing the images to replay in her mind, not wanting to re-open that door and risk causing her to break-down again.

"But not love, except you, but you don't count, cause it's not the type of love that will get girls gushing." She continued.

"What!? Are you saying I'm not a chick magnet?" he declared hitting her with the pillow.

"Your words, not mine!" She replied trying not to laugh.

She pursed her lips, before a smile crept across her face looking at him thinking that yet again, she was there for him, and even though he was having problems of his own, he always put her first.

That selfless heart she'd fallen in love with.

She fell silent as she looked at him. She paused for a moment as her mind deflected back to some of the thoughts over the past few months. Looking at him she pondered on all the thoughts she'd had about their relationship. She had been re-reading his letters, the letters which had gotten her through, bringing with it the realisation that without him she wouldn't be there. She leaned forward, her hands resting upon his, looking down, avoiding eye contact she began to speak.

"I know I've written my thoughts to you many times but sometimes the words have to be spoken... Thank you for everything. I'll never forget the moments you have laughed with me, cried with me, helped me. You are the friend who sees me for who I am. You believe in me when no-one else does, ever did, even in the face of any rumour, and even when I was impossible... I needed a guardian angel, and……" She took a deep breath before continuing.

"…instead I got you… And so, I thank God, the universe and every star above that our paths were woven together so intricately."

He pulled her in close.

"You know that you have a piece of my heart, and I will protect yours always, my dear sweet Imi." He kissed her forehead.

"Come on, enough of this soppiness and deep and meaningful's!.. Pint in the Bay???" he asked pulling her to her feet.

"Yeah, why not! Dad's there. I said we'd probably pop in"

"Yeah, he always buys me a pint when I pop in, usually a bribe for me to spill my guts about what you've been getting up to!" he replied.

Imogen stood open mouthed

"Traitor!" she declared loudly trying not to laugh as they walked down the stairs.

"Mum, I'm heading down the bay with Imi, to see her dad, back soon" He shouted, as they left the house, not waiting for a reply.

They walked arm in arm to the club to meet up with her father.

They entered the Bay, her father stood up, shaking hands with Rob, he nodded at Imogen, before walking to the bar to buy them their drinks.

As they sat down the rain began to fall heavily, the skies darkening. The night passed quickly; Imogen's father continued to buy their drinks. Outside the sky grew darker. Soon the bell at the bar began to chime, last orders. Imogen looked out of the window. It had stopped raining.

"Isn't it good that it's stopped cause we all know you're a lightweight who can't ride in the rain" Rob whispered nudging her.

"You're never going to let me live that down, are you?" Imogen asked cloyingly.

"Come on!" she beckoned as she finished her drink, taking his hand and pulling him to his feet.

"Hey Dad, I'll see ya back home, got to get kitt from Rob's" she shouted over to the bar where her father stood buying his final pint of the night.

They walked past him, heading for the exit.

"See ya round kidda" Her father spoke to Rob, shaking his hand.

Imogen and Rob left the bar, the cold wind howled around them. Imogen pulled her coat in close as Rob wrapped his arm around her.

They walked slowly back to his house to pick up her bike. Standing beside her bike they hugged.

She thanked him again for always being there, for putting up with her,

"You know... Whenever I reach for you, you're always there with your soft words. Sometimes its like I come to you like a child needing you to 'kiss' everything better. And you do, every time, you're endlessly patient, the patience of a saint to put up with this disaster! But, again Thank you for being you. And no matter what anyone says, including the old battle axe... Don't ever change, not for anyone."

She paused for a moment.

"I just hope you know I will always be there for you." She continued.

He held her in his arms.

"Well time for me to go. I guess I can't stand here all night" she spoke as she wiped a tear from her eye, their hands parting, before stepping back, turning and walking away towards her bike.

He followed, standing at the gate.

"Come down whenever you need" she spoke reassuringly as she turned the key in the ignition.

"You know... The next race day at the mount... The gold cup, well its 6 weeks away" he said smiling, giving a wink. He leant in kissing her softly on her cheek.

"6 weeks is a long time! I do hope you're coming down before then!" she replied as she placed her helmet on her head.

The rain was slick on the ground, so dark as to only be seen by reflected streetlamps, and the sky was a painting in a million shades of grey.

"Be careful, the roads are still wet" he spoke as she turned the sat on Kitt, turning the key, getting ready to kickstart.

She could hear the love in his voice. Imogen smiled replying,

"I know you taught me to ride but I'm not a novice anymore, I can handle a little surface water"

Rob leant in to give her one final hug.

"I know, but I still worry about you" he replied as she kickstarted her bike and revved her engine.

She waved to his mother who was staring out behind the curtain. She pulled out of the street and raced back home. The clouds had cleared, the moon shone brightly in the sky.

He watched her leave, he walked into the house and up to his room, where he sat thinking over the day, and smiling recalling when she stood up for him. He stared at the clock, wondering if she'd made it home OK. He sat on the bed dialling her number; the phone rang out going to answerphone.

"Hey Imi... it's Rob. I just wanted to make sure you got home safe. Sorry to bug you if you are already in bed. Just checking on you, see you soon. Goodnight."

A few minutes later his phone bleeped with a text telling him she'd arrived home safely.

Chapter 35

The weekend arrived, Friday evening he knew Imogen was starting her first shift as a barmaid at a local club, he looked at the clock 7.00pm. He had a feeling deep down that she would be scared, he could see her standing in Scarborough having a panic attack. She might be OK he thought to himself, but just in case he picked up his phone and sent a text.

You've got this! Go get'm! Ring you later x

Imogen looked at her phone, reading the message. She was stood outside the club taking deep breaths, just before the text arrived, she had whispered.

"I can't do this!" As though a silent prayer, and as always, he was there, as though psychic. She smiled as she placed her phone in her pocket and walked in.

Rob walked over to the bay, not wanting to spend another night alone in his room. He arrived at the Bay hoping Brian would be there, or Charlie but they weren't. He sat alone at the bar nursing his pint.

He sent a text to Charlie,

I'm in the bay if fancy joining.

But quickly came a reply .

Sorry mate, another time.

As last orders rang-out he ordered a final drink and sat watching as the barmaid frantically began cleaning, he stared at his phone waiting.He contemplated ringing, not knowing when the right time would be, wondering if she would be finished yet. He walked out of the door which faced the shore, hesitating in the doorway, still staring at his phone. He crossed the road looking over the bay watching the waves crash over the piers.

His phone rang.

"Hey! It's me, am walking home so thought I'd ring to say I survived, just!"

"Well, I've just been in the bay giving my weekly report... Only joking your dad wasn't there tonight... I was Billy-no-mates. " he replied with a touch of humour which ebbed away as the realisation of having no one set in.

They talked as she walked home; he began to also walk home. Hearing her voice and her caring tone helped but couldn't wash away his feelings of loneliness. Their conversation was broken as she reached her front door.

"Well, I'm at the front door, gotta be quiet 'cause the girls will be asleep and there'll be hell to pay if I wake them, LITERALLY!!" she stated as she stood by the front door, her hand resting on the handle, not wanting to end their conversation.

"Night, sweet dreams" he whispered down the phone as his hand rested on the handle of his gate.

"Night" she whispered before cancelling the call.

A few days passed, a letter arrived, he opened it reading her words.

Had a bad day... Some bimbo, called Jolene told me today that no guy wants a plain ordinary girl like me, and those that do only want me as a friend....

Well she is kinda right. Look at us! Suppose I could take Gary up on his offer? That would shut the self-obsessed bimbos up!

Oh.... And I have been conned! I only came up to Newcastle because you promised me a ride on your new bike...... Alas, Promises Promises!

He laughed realising that she never did get a ride, or even a look at his new bike. Folding the letter and placing it in his drawer with all of her other letters he resolved that if the weather was good the next day he'd ride down and surprise her.

The next morning, he woke up early, riding down, riding fast, full throttle hitting 100mph, feeling exhilarated. He arrived at her new house; the curtains closed. Standing outside he sent her a text.

Imogen was awoken by the sound of her phone. She wiped the sleep from her eyes, she'd been working the previous night. She looked at the clock, 9am.

She picked up her phone, a text from Rob. She opened the message, reading the words, having to read a second time for the meaning to sink in.

A promise made.... A promise kept; your chariot awaits dear princess!

She laughed as she fell out of bed.

Wondering whether she had received the message he decided to start the engine and give it a few revs.

The sweet sound of an engine revving filled the air. She ran to the door, opening it, stood in her oversized t-shirt, she looked up the alley catching a glimpse of Rob sat on his TDM at the top of the alleyway.

"What's this, lazy bones! I've been up for hours...." He shouted.

"Shhh!" she said looking around with her finger resting on her lips as a smile began to creep across her face, biting her bottom lip to disguise it. He sighed shrugging his shoulders before turning off the engine.

"2 minutes!" she continued, her dimples showing as she pursed her lips before again gently biting her bottom lip.

"I'm timing you!" He replied as she closed the door.

As he sat waiting Imogen threw on her clothes, quickly tying her hair back, grabbing her jacket and helmet she flew out of the flat.

The door closed behind her.

"Just over..." He sniggered as he started the engine.

"So, what time did you get up to get here?" She asked.

Looking at his watch he replied

"2 and a half hours ago...... It only took an hour on this beast...."

She shook her head, trying to disapprove, but couldn't resist that smile.

"One day you're going to kill yourself or someone else you know! Then who is going to keep me in line???" she asked trying to be stern though secretly wanting to know what it was like to ride that fast.

"Just get on and shut up!" he replied laughing.

"Yes Sir!" she replied with a salute.

They rode up to Oliver's mount, the track was clear and quiet.

"You ready?"

"Always!" she replied!

He opened the throttle, picking up speed. The acceleration was so fast that it was almost overwhelming. 100 mph in a little over 5 seconds. Sometimes his knee would be just skimming the ground as he took the bends, Imogen shadowed his every move like she had done so many times before, but never at those speeds.

They pulled up at the side of the starting markers, sitting on the grass verge.

"So, what's next for you? Or are you planning on becoming a pro biker, and me your roadie??" She asked distracting him as he was about to take a bite from the chocolate bar in his hands. In his hesitation she stole it from his grips.

"Hey! That's the thanks I get for riding down here to give you a ride!" he questioned.

"Fight you for it......" she grinned, holding it out of reach.

"What this time? You know whatever you say I will win, I always whip that sexy little ass of yours"

"Yeah, right, in your dreams sunshine!" she giggled.

Imogen snapped the chocolate in half, passing half back to him.

"So, what is next?" she asked again.

"I'm taking up art, maybe I can draw some real life, blonde, naked woman......"

"You never change" She replied sighing.

"Talking of Blonde bimbos...... Are you going to date that Gary?

And... The nipple piercing... is it the left or the right...?"

Imogen laughed, shaking her head.

Rob pulled out a piece of paper and a pen and began to draw as Imogen looked out watching the swallows circling the skies above.

"Finished" He proclaimed handing her the picture, a picture of Imogen.

"That's not me, she's beautiful......" Imogen stated, holding the picture in her hands.

"Hey stop that now!!......... He pulled her in close for a tight embrace, his chin rested on top of her head. His arms clenched her tightly.

He continued to speak as he held her.

"You aren't just pretty on the outside you have a beauty somewhere deep within. Stop this self-doubt, why do you choose to be silver over gold, a dull reflection over being a real star with light of your own. This world needs stars like you to guide the way, ones with hearts as pure as yours. That Jolene chick is not right about no-one wanting you for anything more than friendship! You were getting more than a few advances by men when we were last out at planet even if you didn't notice. You just need to open your eyes to love or it will pass you by. Not all guys are like Jacob, you could get someone perfect like me….. And when you think you've found someone who deserves you, they need to get my seal of approval" his words trailed off.

"…So, do you think I'd make a good artist?" He asked pulling back, his hand gently brushing against her cheek.

"Priceless, I'll treasure it forever" she replied.

"It will have pride of place next to your other drawing of me, maybe it'll be worth something someday…." She winked.

"Like any artist, my art will be worthless till I die, then it'll sell for millions, at least you won't have to wait forever to…."

Imogen interrupted him mid-sentence.

"Hey, I've told ya, your gonna live a long life, wife, kids, the works, even if I have to give you one of my kidneys, and not one from a tin from ASDA" she laughed nudging him.

Imogen stood up with her mischievous playful smile creeping across her face.

"Let's see what you really got old man" Imogen announced as an attempt to change the mood and distract him from those thoughts.

As she spoke, she ran down the grass verge to the start line where his bike, newly named 'the beast' sat. The black of the bike chassis was gleaming from the mid-morning sun rays as though to say, 'ride me'.

"Old? Cheeky mare" Rob answered as he caught up with her on the track, pushing her playfully.

Imogen danced along the track stopping at the start/finish line before spinning round looking back towards Rob. She pursed her lips quickly followed by biting her bottom lip as she removed her phone from her pocket. She stood on the line with one hand pointing up into the air, the other hand in front of her, holding her phone in the palm of her hand.

"What you doing now?" Rob asked, though he knew what she wanted. His cheeky grin began creeping across his face.

"I'm giving you your start and timing you.." she answered almost seductively..

Rob climbed on his bike edging it into one of the grid positions. He turned the key starting the engine, the sound filling the valley. He fastened his helmet before adjusting his position. Twisting the throttle, he sat waiting. Focused, ready...

"Ready!?" Imogen shouted over the sweet sound of the revving engine.

Rob nodded, knocking down his visor.

"3-2-1-go!" Imogen shouted.

Her hand dropped by her side as he sped past, the rush of wind excited her, almost as though removing every ounce of air from her lungs leaving her breathless. She spun round like a giddy child to see him reach Mere Hairpin, before disappearing out of sight.

Rob reached Mere Hairpin with the perfect balance of speed to negotiate the tight 180 bend. He leant over to his left creating a perfect lean angle, almost defying gravity as the bike took the corner with ease finding the perfect alignment of the apex as he began to exit, accelerating out of the bend. He straightened up, changing gear, increasing speed as he hit the steep incline up Barry's rise to the top of the mount. Reaching the top of Quarry Hill, he leant right for the next turn, keeping a tight line at the Esses. He had ridden that track so many times over the years on Buzby that he knew his breaking markers. That combined with an almost perfect measure of counter-steering allowed him to negotiate the track without losing speed.

He resisted looking down at his speedometer as he glided down the back straight, rounding past the mount cafe and monument to begin the final stretch. The sun gleamed on the road surface as he perfectly negotiated the road through Drury's and Mountside Hairpins, onto the bottom straight feeling as though he was flying as he negotiated Jeffries jump. Slowing slightly to manoeuvre through the chicanes of Farm Bends with ease. The concentration was visible on his face as he increased his speed into the final straight.

Imogen waited patiently watching the stopwatch on her phone. She could hear him before she saw him. As he came into view her finger eagerly hovered over the stop button, jumping like an excited child as he crossed the line pulling a catwalk wheelie as she pressed stop on the timer, looking down at the lap time smiling.

"Well how did I do?" Rob shouted as he slowed to a stop and looked back over his shoulder.

He turned off the engine, before dismounting and placing the bike on its side stand, walking back towards Imogen as she ran towards him.

"Best time ever!" she squealed.

"1.52.02" she continued throwing her arms around him.

"You know you'd have other riders eating your dust if you entered" she continued before composing herself, turning to walk back to the grass verge.

"Come on, let's go get some food…..." Rob suggested changing the subject, avoiding her statement, not wanting to allow himself to dream.

Imogen shrugged, protruding her bottom lip, and looking at him with her puppy-dog eyes.

"OK…Hop on.. One more lap then it's time for food… Deal?" he suggested as he picked up her helmet passing it to her, instinctively knowing her thoughts, as though he could read her mind.

"OK. Deal" she answered smiling as he picked up his bag.

They headed down to the seafront, eating fish and chips as they watched the boats in the harbour. The boats were scattered over the harbour like autumn leaves on a pond. The colours were beautiful, random. The cold sea air brought a freshness to the hot summer sun. The cry of the gulls wheeled overhead.

He watched one of those rare moments where she came alive, unafraid to dance on the sand, carefree as though life was perfect. He wished she could stay like that forever rather than her highs always being followed by a low.

It felt like a perfect day, a perfect memory to treasure forever.

His visit was short but sweet. Not wanting to be stuck in Scarborough with no plan of where to stay. The afternoon was rolling in. The darkness of the evening daring to encroach on the remaining light of the day.

"I guess it's almost time for you to head off" Imogen sighed as she stared across at the horizon, the sky adorned with pinks and oranges reflecting upon the sea.

"We've got time for at least one more lap around the Mount" Rob exclaimed draping his arm around her shoulder as she stared into space.

They rode up to the mount for one final lap. As they rode around the track, she thought how there was never anywhere in the world she would rather be than on the mount with Rob.

He dropped her back at the flat. The window curtains were twitching, the girls watching. Imogen dismounted removing her helmet. She stood, her arms gently swaying with so many thoughts running through her head, so many things she wanted to say but could never form the words, not wanting him to leave, not wanting to admit that her life was nothing when he wasn't there.

Rob dismounted removing his helmet, looking at her as though mirroring her thoughts wishing he never had to leave.

"Don't forget to find me somewhere to stay for the Gold Cup…. And go visit Clarissa in Leeds. Go have a brill time!" He spoke softly as he cupped her chin before leaning in, kissing her softly on her cheek before riding off.

A week passed, he was sat in the living room watching the local news, a young barmaid had been attacked. His thoughts quickly turned to Imogen, thinking about her walking home late on an evening.

He picked up his phone sending a text.

Hey just checking in. I heard on the news a barmaid up here was attacked walking home. I'm now worried about you getting back from work! And am going to be worrying every night now! Take kitt, or get a taxi, or have someone walk you home. It may sound selfish, but I can't lose you"

She replied hastily, though secretly liking that someone cared enough to worry.

This is Scarborough, not Newcastle! But I'll text ya every night if it'll help?

She began texting every night after a shift just to let him know she was safe.

It was in one of those texts she declared she was going to go on a date with Gary. Reading the text, he sat torn, not knowing how he felt about it. He refused to admit there was a hint of jealousy which occasionally slipped out in his letters, the letters which were becoming less due to the regular text updates.

Her letters were becoming darker, and a few appeared to be written while drunk. It tore him apart worrying about her, but he had to let her make her own mistakes and be there to catch her when she would fall.

She'd told him how following her visit she burned everything that connected her to Jacob, she'd dealt with that, but was beginning to realise that he wasn't the problem, she had so much more to deal with, things that only he knew. He wrote many letters that summer which he never sent.

Reading her most recent letter, a few days following the 'date' he could feel something wasn't quite right. He'd been spending the weeks volunteering at a summer school, he realised it had been almost a month since his last visit.

Fancy me coming down tomorrow?? Promise you a fast ride/high speed cop chase on my new bike!? No talking necessary!

He arrived that following morning, Imogen looked like a shell, broken. She smiled and climbed on the pillion seat, wrapping her arms around him, they rode for hours along the coastal routes, before returning back.

"Thanks" she smiled, before looking away,

"You still coming for Gold cup" she asked hesitantly, looking down, biting at her fingers.

"Would I not??" he replied.

See ya in a couple of weeks, and please write, you know I wish I could help you through whatever this is" he spoke filled with concern.

"I'll be OK, and you help me more than you'll ever know, I've just got to sort this shit out myself" she replied walking away, turning briefly, smiling.

He smiled back before revving the engine and pulling away.

A week later a large envelope arrived, inside a bound book and a letter. He unfolded the letter.

Hey, my writers block has ended. I finally finished that essay. It only took a couple of months, and the support of a couple of good mates, one in particular. I wrote you a poem, and a short story I've included them with this letter. Now, I could have written about bikes but that would be far too predictable, Horsepower.... Lol... enjoy.

He sat on his bed opening the book, he smiled as he read her words, the passion. He almost choked reading the story, becoming lost in the detail, at parts touching upon erotica, revealing that secret side that no-one else saw buried in her deepest fantasies.

At the end of the story she wrote...

I hope you enjoyed it. For so long I've fought against my deep thoughts, becoming confused, believing I was dirty, damaged, and all that, but I think I've finally turned a corner, able to separate the experiences which have tainted me, they no longer control me, and I think I'm just about learning to embrace life, and love, and all that.

Thank you for always being my knight in shining armour.

After reading the story his eyes fell upon an envelope hidden inside. A poem, titled Your world.

A tear fell from his eyes as he read her words. He picked up his pen and began writing back in response.

Can't wait to see you again my dear Imi. Have you sorted out where I'm staying??
The poem your world was brill but made me sad. You should definitely not stop writing you have a responsibility to exploit this and any other gifts you have to the fullest! I'm being serious!

He sat wondering what else to write, there was so much he wanted to say, but couldn't find the words, or could but couldn't dare to write them.

Chapter 36

The weekend of the Gold Cup arrived.

Rob Rode down late Friday afternoon, meeting up with Imogen at the biker's café on the North shore, allowing them sometime alone to talk, before going to Gary's flat.

They parked their bikes and walked along the shore together, hand in hand... The warmth of his hand against her cold hand was like bringing hope, like he always did.

"You will always be my guiding star Rob, thank you for everything" she spoke.

He could see something different in her, almost like seeing the Imogen he used to know, the confidence, the smile, the wild nature, hoping this time it would stay, that she wouldn't slip back again, that this time she'd done enough to truly heal.

"Anything for my princess" He answered with an exaggerated bow.

They sat watching the waves crash against the shore, he spoke lovingly.

"I know you've felt lost for so long, as if sailing on those unchartered seas. I know you've been calling for help in every way possible, I'm just happy to help you find your way."

"I think I'm finally finding my way, I kinda lost it a bit back then, I know I've been hard work, and I've not liked who I was at points... There is some stuff I have to tell you before we head off..." she spoke before pausing, before continuing, revealing the battles she had been fighting over those past months, telling him about her drinking, returning to self-harm, and then also confessing about her brief fling with Gary, and telling him of the disastrous date, though reassuring him that all was now OK. Rob listened, he was understanding, non-judgemental, as always, her best friend.

His arms were encircled around her.

"You know, only you could kind of have a break down, to fall apart, yet nobody notice... afraid to let the world see you're vulnerable. OK, I noticed but that's different, I'll always notice..." he laughed while also portraying a deep concern, and love.

"Yeah, well as long as we don't turn this into one of our competitions, I need you to always stay strong, no epic falls from grace, I doubt I have the strength!" she joked, though deep down she'd wanted to say, she loved him, she was thankful for all he done for her and how never in a billion years could she repay the debt, and she knew that if the shoe was ever on the other foot she would never be able to measure up. She didn't think anyone could measure up to him.

As the sun began to fade, they walked back to their bikes and rode up to Gary's flat.

The Saturday was full of racing, music, and beers. As they walked around the main field in the cool autumnal breeze, Imogen saw a poster advertising the Miss Bike competition prior to the first race of the next season. The first round to decide on the finalists were to be held the following morning prior to the final races.

Rob followed her eyes.

"You entering again?" he nudged.

"Entering what and what do you mean again?" Gary chimed in intrigued.

"The Miss Bike Comp! Our Imi entered last year, the wet t-shirt round was very educational" he replied trying not to laugh.

"She kinda wimped out after that round though, she's too much of a scaredy cat to try again aren't you?" he said nudging her.

Imogen continued to walk, shaking her head.

Rob and Gary conspired between them to persuade her to re-enter, talking quietly before Rob spoke out loud.

"So Gary, talking about cats... have you seen her in her catsuit? Or her whip?" he continued.

"Will you pack it in!" Imogen replied hitting Rob and pulling him along.

"I'll pack it in if you sign up! I'm sure Gary would love to hear some stories..." he replied trying not to laugh, his smile breaking out.

"Yeah, she is too much of a wimp" Gary interrupted as they neared the sign-up stall.

"Dare ya" Gary said nudging her.

Never one to back out from a challenge she decided to put her name down,

"Ok, you're on! And this year I'm planning on winning!" she replied filling in the entry form.

As she filled in her details, she thought how it could be another step into rebuilding herself.

She scanned over the heats wondering what she had got herself into!

That evening they found themselves in the Rock club. Rob had never been, but it was Gary's favourite haunt, and somewhere Imogen had been spending a lot of time at those past few months. As Imogen looked around, she thought about the state she was in the last time she as there, the state she got herself into, her mindset at the time, wondering whether she would ever be able to be normal without constantly slipping backwards. Her thoughts were disturbed by the sound of laughter, she turned looking in the direction of Rob and Gary, seeing them laughing and joking, playing off each other. She was struck with the sobering thought that finally it felt like everything was back to normal. She just hoped there would be no more potholes or pitfalls to de-rail her, or her friendships.

Rob looked over at Imogen with the sobering thought that the next day he had to return home. He always tried to push that fact to the back of his mind, to not allow it to dampen the good times, but sometimes he couldn't escape the reality. He sat back watching, catching glimpse of her laughing. He thought about how maybe one day he would look back and those reckless and crazy days and nights would be the 'Good old days', hoping that they would remain in his memory and not the days in-between.

At the end of the night they all returned back to Gary's flat. The conversations were interrupted only by jokes, often at the expense of one of their friends. And Imogen being a girl did not excuse her from their jokes. To them she was one of the lads.

The Sunday was spent back on the mount, all feeling a little hungover. Watching as Imogen sailed through the heats, standing cheering.

"Whoop Whoop" he shouted as he watched her up on the stage looking confident.

Consoling her when finishing in 2nd place, but reminding her that still guaranteed her a spot in the finals the following summer... The afternoon they watched the finals, before slipping away to spend some time alone before he had to return home.

They sat in her room, she pulled out a journal bursting with scraps of paper,

"Well this is basically my life" she declared as she turned the pages.

As they looked through the pages, she knew she couldn't undo all the hurt, or erase all the bad, would she want too? Because the bad just highlighted the good even more.

She knew she was who she was because of all of her experiences through life. But mostly she was who she was because of Rob's love and never-ending support. Now she finally knew who she was, she knew what she wanted in life, and vowed to never again slip back, allowing others, or her past to break her.

"It helped me write that stupid essay, though if I'm honest it did kinda help, but you know what doing this journal really shows? It shows you... I was blessed the day you walked into my life, and I will never forget what you did for me, I know I sound like a broken record, but no matter how many times I tell you, and thank you, I know it'll never be enough" she spoke as he flicked through the pages.

"Well that's enough about me" she stated as she stood up.

"Fancy a drink? Food? I'm getting a bit peckish.." She continued in the hope of changing the topic of conversation.

"Aye, why not, as long as it's not another pot noodle!" he declared as he stood up, following her into the living room.

Rob jumped onto the chair placing his legs up on the table and his hands behind his head, glancing over at Imogen as she continued into the kitchen,

"Let's see what we've got!" she uttered as she opened the fridge in search of something for them.

The girls returned home.

"Hey!" Rob waved from the settee, as Lorna and Cassandra entered. They looked in his direction, unimpressed.

"You do know he's not staying... You know we have a strict no boyfriend rule..." Lorna stated as Imogen stood making sandwiches.

"Hey, I'm the NOT boyfriend over here... Never have been, never will!!" Rob declared.

"Sorry we just have strict rules..." Cassandra replied before walking over to him

"Hi, I'm Cassandra" she smiled as she walked over towards him.

Imogen stood raising her eyebrows and scrunching her face thinking how she didn't mind him falling for anyone, as long as it wasn't one of them. She watched as they seemed to act perfect around him.

"So do you go to church?" Lorna asked sitting opposite him.

Imogen shook her head sighing wondering why that was always the first question, either that or 'are you a Christian'.

"Er, yeah I go to Imi's church, she got me going back when she was the lead singer of the worship group and youth outreach..."

he answered glancing over at Imogen watching the scowl across her face.

"What?" Cassandra answered confused.

"Yeah, well there's a lot you don't know about me, perfect example of don't judge a book..." Imogen interrupted looking at Rob, moving her head as though to hint at going back to her room.

Rob stood up taking a plate from Imogen.

"Nice to meet you properly..." he spoke as he followed Imogen towards her room.

"You know if you want another pen friend, I don't mind writing letters..." Cassandra shouted over as the door closed behind them.

"Really!? Did you have too?" Imogen asked as she sat cross-legged on the bed.

"You can't tell me you didn't get a teeny-weeny bit of satisfaction from that..."

"Ok I guess..." she answered.

They continued to talk for hours until dusk, the darkening skies signalling the end of the visit, a visit which was over too soon.

"Stay another night" Imogen urged not wanting him to leave, he didn't take much persuading.

"The girls??" Rob asked in reply.

"Stuff them!   Though fancy a beach night?"

"Yeah why not!" he replied.

They spent the evening on the beach by a small bonfire like they had so many times before.

They were ready to see in another new academic year, but this time, for Rob didn't include a return to education, instead deciding to step out into the real world, keen to begin working.

They spent the evening drinking and talking, until they fell asleep.

They awoke to the sun beginning to break through the clouds, turning the black into shades of blue amidst the whitish dove-grey of the clouds that rippled outwards embellishing the sky.

Chapter 37

As the new school year began, he managed to get a part-time job at the local primary school, mainly working in the woodwork department.

The Autumn was beginning to turn. One Monday morning early October he received a letter from Imogen. He placed it in his bag as he ran out the door planning to read it later in his break, but as the day progressed it slipped his mind. The day had started like any other, but as the morning progressed it was different. The teacher who usually ran the class fell ill; the responsibility then fell solely upon him. He could hear his mother's voice in his head making him doubt himself and his ability. He took in a deep breath as he entered the class.

The class knew him, and for a moment thought they could play on his softer side but taking a deep breath he showed a stronger sterner side. He pulled in their behaviour with a fair stance, combined with his style of humour which they could relate to, and aspire to even. Teaching with a passion of a lifelong teacher, like someone who'd been through full teacher training.

The day inspired him, making him consider whether he should go into teaching though knowing that would entail going to university. He returned home that evening, sitting at the dinner table with his parents, he spoke of that day, and broached the topic of becoming a teacher, but instead of praise the response focussed on how he wanted to return to being a student, commenting on how Isabella had just started university, the cost, how he would fund it. The endless comments and criticism destroyed the little remaining happiness from the day, eroding any good by chipping away at him piece by piece. He returned to his room and began to think about moving out, thinking that maybe having his own space would be better for his mental health, escaping the constant comments from his mother which chipped away, undermining any good which he felt.

He shelved the idea of teacher training determined to at the moment at least to continue working, continuing to inspire a love of learning in the next generation. Thinking maybe when he had his own place, and some experience behind him he could revisit it.

It was a day later that he found the letter that he'd placed in his bag, the letter from Imogen asking if he would like to attend the ball with her.

He sat at his desk to write a reply. He wanted to write about school, about his mother, but instead decided to save that for face to face, instead he decided to make light of the offer to go to the ball.

I shall go with you to the ball!

Oh, yes sorry, how are you?

Sorry for taking so long to respond, it is for 2 reasons...

1) I've only just picked myself up off the floor
2) I had to find a tuxedo.. I asked Arnie (True lies) I tried it but it's too tight around my........
   Ahem........ Chest, and a bit loose around my bum, yes, I do have one too....

Though it's got nothing on yours... sorry going off topic!

Thinking though, I could just pad it out with something... or someone? Would you fit? Only joking!

He sealed the envelope drawing a large YES on the back of the envelope ready to post the next day.

The weeks passed quickly; school half term arrived. He looked at his suit hanging on his wardrobe door. He contemplated how he was going to get the suit down without creasing it, also the corsage he'd bought for her.

Sitting at dinner his father asked him about his plans, and he revealed about the ball, and hinted at using the car, his hints went unnoticed. He waited till after dinner when he could get his father alone to ask.

"Hey Dad, any chance I can take the car this weekend, if you won't need it?" he asked.

His father agreed, though his mother quickly had reservations, though gradually he found a compromise, he was allowed to take it if he did the shopping before leaving. As he left the room, he shook his head in disbelief because it was always down to him to get the shopping, so what was different this time?

The autumn ball soon arrived. Rob stood at her front door, in his hands a small box with the corsage and a bouquet of flowers in his other hand hidden behind his back.

"For you dear Princess" he declared as she opened the door.

She smiled as she beckoned him in, pouring him a glass of wine before continuing to try and position her tiara.

He looked at her. Her dark blue dress mirrored her body, held by fine shoulder straps of which one kept sliding off her shoulder and onto her arm. He stood up walking towards her, his hand gently brushing against her arm easing the strap back in place.

"Here let me help" he insisted as she turned towards him.

Gently he scooped her hair behind her ear, before whispering,

"Let's straighten that crown" as he gently readjusted her tiara.

They stood in a moment, as though their thoughts were communicating. As though that simple act spoke volumes, symbolising so much more.

He reached for the small box, opening it, lifting out the corsage and placing it on her wrist.

He looked in her eyes and remembered why he had loved her since the first time he saw her.

She smiled and blushed dipping her head to avoid his gaze.

"You know we've got time before we need to be there if you want a catch up?" she asked as she looked around, as though trying to make sure she had everything she needed.

She looked at him as he was lost in thought. The way she looked at him showed that genuine care which he had become to rely on.

"Maybe tomorrow... Tonight, is for fun, dance, oh and alcohol!" he exclaimed picking up his glass as though to make a toast,

"Tonight, we live!" he exclaimed before downing the contents.

They arrived at the spa, seated at large round tables for a 3-course meal. Following the meal, the lights dimmed, the disco lights turned on, bubbles filled the air, they just danced and drank.

As the night progressed he found himself admiring her even more, she didn't look like the lost girl, or the biker chick, his partner in crime, instead she looked like a beautiful woman to whom he was feeling attracted too in a way he never had before. He thought about making a move, to say what he said a year ago was not true, but instead decided to wait till he was sober to know whether what he was feeling was genuine, or whether it was just the drink and the atmosphere. He also wondered if she still felt that way or if it had just been a reaction, she'd never gave any indication that she did. He was unaware that deep down she did still occasionally question her feelings, regretting always choosing Jacob over him, but had resigned herself to just being his friend because to be able to call him her friend was enough.

They celebrated the night as friends.

It was a magical evening, an evening of friendship, not just for them, but also a time for Imogen and the rest of the gang to celebrate the beginning of their final year before being thrust out into the open world.

As the evening began to end, they walked arm in arm out to the balcony the stars were shining brightly, the full moon lighting up the sea beneath them. Imogen thought back to that magical night on the beach following their exam results.

"Aim for the moon..." Imogen softly whispered

"...... and if you miss, you'll still be among the stars..." Rob continued.

Imogen smiled.

"That goes for you too, you know" she replied nudging him.

"The past couple of years have gone so fast, you know I've no idea what comes next, do I stay here, return home, if I can call it home cause it's not been home for so long." She spoke as she looked out over the harbour.

Inside she was also asking herself where they were heading, scared of losing him, her rock.

Rob's hand rested gently on her shoulder, as if reading her mind, he spoke softly and reassuringly, whispering gently.

"We will always be in each other's lives. I can guarantee it if you can, we've come this far, I think I've proven I'm here for the long-haul…."

Imogen rested her head on his chest, his arm encircled her. An answer wasn't needed.

He answered for her

"Of course, I Know you can. We have something very special. Something God knows all about, it's called unconditional love and friendship."

Imogen looked out at the night sky lost in thought.

They returned back inside. Rob ran over to Clarissa, Imogen walked slowly behind, stopping to scan the room, to watch the world unfold around her, as though wanting to freeze time for a moment, to capture it, a memory never to be forgotten. For once life was perfect.

Imogen watched her friends on the dancefloor. Rob, with his arm around Clarissa. As she looked, she thought how she would never forget the moments they laughed together, cried together. The moments he helped her. She would never regret or forget any of those memories. She would carry him with her forever. Wherever their paths would lead.

She walked back out onto the balcony. She thought back to their conversation the year earlier, and she believed she was finally there, she was happy alone, and had found a way to love herself.

She had reached a point where she didn't need to rush into the arms of anyone just to gain affection and love.

She contemplated how the next ball would be there graduation ball, she wondered if she would have a partner for that ball, would it be Rob, or would some lucky girl have snapped him up, or, looking back into the hall at the dancefloor, she wondered if he and Clarissa would stop dancing around each other and become a couple?

The night ended, the perfect evening, one which would stay in their memories forever.

As everyone headed home, they walked along the side of the spa as the moonlights splashed down its watery white-silver glow onto the sea below. They stood watching the waves crash against the sea wall recalling all of their wave dodging over the years.

"We've had some great times here in Scarborough, haven't we?" Rob asked.

"The best! And I know I wouldn't have survived without you, and it probably would have been boring without you!" she said nudging him,

"So, do you know what you're going to do after?" Rob asked as they stood huddled together in the cold autumn night air.

"I don't know yet, though I'm seriously considering staying here... Scarborough kinda feels like home" she replied looking up at him, wondering whether it would be too much to ask him to move down.

"Yeah it does feel like home doesn't it" he replied, feeling more compelled to move down, but feeling hesitant on suggesting it until he knew himself if he could make his dreams become reality.

"Hey, join us this New Year" Imogen suggested, nudging Rob as they began walking back towards the flat.

"You're on!" he replied.

They returned to the flat, everyone was still awake.

"Wine?" Clarissa asked as they entered the living room.

"Why not!" Rob replied taking hold of a glass passing it to Imogen before taking a glass for himself.

"Rob's joining us for New Year!" Imogen declared as they again toasted the night. Which caused an eruption of "cheers!".

The weekend ended, bringing with it a return to Newcastle with a fresh determination towards the future, the future he dreamed of, away from the negativity of home.

Soon the New Year was upon them. They stood in the bar which had become a regular haunt over the years.

As the clock ticked closer to midnight, they held crossed hands singing Auld Lang Syne, celebrating the dawning of the new year.

The beginning of a new chapter in their lives.

As they all stood together Imogen began reflecting, looking back, thinking how you can't start the next chapter of your life if you keep re-reading the last one. She reflected how she had made that move, ready to move on, excited for what was to come. Rob was looking around reflecting on how that New Year would be a new start. Starting that new year as he planned to continue, in Scarborough, where he was eventually planning on staying once he'd tied up loose ends determined to start putting himself first.

Imogen sneaked outside to watch the fireworks being set off at the castle.

She looked back into the bar at her friends, Rob, Clarissa, Simon, laughing. Without looking at her, their smiles still extended towards her.

She was surrounded by friends, real friends. Something she doubted she would ever have. And of those Rob was the greatest friend she could ever have asked for, a friend who saved her in every way a girl could be saved.

Looking out at the sky and as a shooting star crossed the sky over the south shore, she made one wish, a wish for him. But not just a wish but a prayer. A silent prayer caught on the wind.

"God... I know I've been a bit distant of late but Thank you for giving him to me. Help him find happiness out there...."

He walked out joining her on the balcony. His arms encircled her...

"What are you doing out here alone?"

She sighed. A sigh of excitement and of fear. Her sigh carried on the breeze, as if freeing her.

"Just reflecting, looking back, looking forward...... but whatever happens we have each other so I know we will both be fine"

The crowd joined them outside, with wine glasses in hand, Clarissa passed a glass to Imogen.

"To us!" there toast echoed out as the glasses clinked together.

The party continued through the night. One perfect night, one perfect moment in time.

Chapter 38

The winter soon turned to spring, as Rob concentrated on his job, gaining more hours, gaining experience. He began thinking ahead, wondering what if he moved to Scarborough, moved in with Imogen, maybe start at the university.

He kept thinking back to the ball wondering if they could become something more, but he always found an excuse to not broach the topic, then changing his mind again returning to his previous stance of how they could only ever be friends.

He began thinking of relationships, analysing himself, deciding to stop the self-sabotage, and using his illness as an excuse, to take his own advice, and possibly be open to love, he just wasn't sure whether that could be with Imogen, or with someone else. Trying to decipher his feelings wondering if anything could grow from such a friendship, or whether that ship had well and truly sailed.

He knew he had to know for sure, he wasn't going to mess her about. He thought how in every other way they were in sync but when it came to whether to take their friendship to the next level they were never at the same place at the same time, maybe they were never meant too? He questioned himself over and over. He contented himself with the believe that if they were meant to be, they would find a way in time, at the right time, and if not what they had was enough.

Their letters continued to bring each other support yet continuing the light-heartedness which broke through.

He could see she still at times doubted herself, reading her most recent letter panicking over finals, and trying to please everyone else. He would ask what she wanted and instead she would list what everyone else wanted.

"Stop thinking about what everyone else wants, what do you want" he found himself repeatedly asking.

He sat and began to write.

Hey,
Brace yourself to be insulted again and again. Who said life was fair eh?

Nah, I'll save those for my next letter, I think I still need to polish some of my insults, so instead here's a soppy letter to make you sick instead!

Well I do aim to please!

He continued to write, to build her up, while throwing in the odd insult and silly drawing. As he ended the letter he pondered, his pen in his mouth, he again began to write.

But seriously You'll do anything to make someone else happy, but you don't know how to be happy yourself.

A few weeks later, one sunny Saturday morning he received a text, his heart dropped.

I've met someone.... Will tell you more when I see you!

He knew one day it would happen, he was a fool to think it wouldn't, and part of him had wanted her to find someone, he'd pushed her so many times to find love. Maybe it'll just be a fling? Maybe it's just what she needs, a bit of fun to get through the next few months.

He sent a reply back.

Stay safe, and remember you deserve the world nothing less

He just wished he was the one capable of giving her the world.

It was a couple of days later when she rang him, he could hear something different in her voice, as she talked about this guy called Marcus, she was falling in love, his heart sank.

Their letters and calls dropped away to a minimum as she became lost in her new love, at times he felt forgotten, and knowing her past began to be dubious of their relationship, urging her to slow down, worried that she fell to hard, too fast.

She was caught up in a whirlwind of emotion, at times it felt like she had forgotten about him. He thought how for so many years they had been each other's world, but now everything was changing, she was in love, at times he felt surplus to requirements.

While searching for a birthday card for his mother, his eyes fell on a card with Eeyore, the words missing you. He smiled remembering the day he won Eeyore for her, and every visit seeing it upon her bed, a reminder of their love.

He bought the card, and returning home began to write.

Things change and I get sad, but the times we've had of which I'm glad...
Miss you lots!

He sat reflecting on how they were due to visit Newcastle that following week. He wondered; would he like him? Part of him hoped he wouldn't, it would be easier to despise him then, like he did Jacob. Though in the next breath he hoped that this man who she'd fallen for could give her all she deserved, and that they could maybe become mates.

"Just as long as he deserves you!" he whispered as his finger brushed against the picture of them together.

The day came, the day they were visiting. They had planned to meet in the bay.

Rob was sitting at a booth near the window, his hands nursing a bottle of beer, His hair was even neater than usual, and he was smartly dressed, deciding to make an effort.

Rob's gaze turned away from the window, looking up from his phone, he spotted Imogen. As she walked in, she was beaming in a way he'd not seen before. He tried to put on a brave face as he stood up. Rob smiled like a long-lost brother. His hand brushed against her arm, in an almost uncomfortable embrace, wondering how much contact is too much. Trying to negotiate a new normal.

"Hey, Imi. How are you?" He asked as he kissed her cheek and leant in for a hug. Marcus watched, taking a deep breath.

Rob glanced over at him, trying to read him, wanting to analyse his reaction as though to make sure he wasn't another Jacob.

He knew Imogen, and he knew how far she'd come but he also knew how easy it was to fall, to feel like she didn't deserve the best, but rather defaulting to someone like Jacob.

Imogen could read him like a book but was determined to show him, prove to him that this was different, Marcus was different, she was OK, though understanding why, expecting nothing less..

She had fallen hard and fast, but still had that small part of her mind which kept her in check, and she knew she would also have Rob. Love is blind, she'd been blind before. In part, she brought Marcus to meet Rob for that reason.

Imogen smiled, stepping in accepting his embrace.

"I'm good thanks, this is Marcus" she replied. Looking at Marcus she drew away from the hug.

Trying to hide his jealousy Marcus reached out his hand. Rob reciprocated shaking his hand warmly and firmly with the perfect squeeze making eye contact but was not yet ready to trust him. Imogen sat down opposite Rob, pulling her skirt down as the hot sticky leather seat made contact with her bare skin. Marcus sat next to her, his arm wrapping around her.

Imogen had told herself that if it came to it Rob would always come first, would always win. Any man who wanted to win her heart had to accept their friendship to be worthy, though was finding it hard, wondering if she could see that through, if it were to come to that. She had fallen in love, she thought she had loved before, but this was different, she thought, before questioning herself

"Is it just passion and lust entwined?" she asked herself while remembering those past couple of weeks.

Rob watched the affection between them, finding it hard to trust a man who seemed so perfect. Rob had watched Imogen be hurt before; he was determined not to let that happen again.

Marcus walked to the bar to order drinks, glancing over his shoulder watching the 2 friends catch up.

Imogen moved closer to Rob as they talked, Imogen apologising for being so distant those past few weeks, urging him to tell her what had been happening, asking about work, and his plans. He couldn't tell her how his plans had now all fallen apart as he'd been thinking of moving down to Scarborough or telling her that is father had been becoming frail, fearing losing him. Instead he put on a brave face and made out everything was perfect.

He looked over at Marcus who was watching them. Marcus watched thinking how they had history, this man knew her deeper than anyone, and that he knew things about her that she wasn't ready to trust him with.

Returning to the table, Marcus bravely struggled through the ensuing small talk. Imogen sat uncomfortably, worrying whether they would get along. Friends like Rob didn't come along too often, they'd been through too much to ever throw it away.

Imogen left the men alone briefly, going to the ladies for a few moments alone to compose herself, and to give them time alone. She stood staring at her reflection, tightly gripping the sink, bowing her head she whispered under her breath.

"God, please make them get along" stopping suddenly as another woman entered. She took a deep breath and looked up, looking at her reflection.

"Right!" she declared, her hands dropping, taking one last glance before heading to the bar to buy the next round.

Another pint of lager for Marcus and Rob, and an archers and lemonade for herself.

While Imogen was away Rob spoke sternly.

"Imogen is special, but I guess you know that… But behind that confident girl is a fragile heart. I can see she is falling in love with you, my question is… do you deserve her love? I've got to say I will be watching!"

Marcus hesitated, looking across the room, watching Imogen walk towards the bar, watching as she stood waiting. He took a deep breath before replying.

"You can trust me mate…. I'm kinda falling for that girl and will not hurt her or let anyone else hurt her, she is something else isn't she! No girl has made me feel the way she has…..."

He hesitated, taking a drink wondering whether to let his thoughts become words, which would then make them real. He continued,

"You know…. I've heard people… lads say that they'd die for some chick, and I always thought it was cliché, but God, I would do anything for that girl… and well yep…" he stopped short of verbalising his feelings for her.

Rob smiled understanding where he was coming from.

Marcus lifted his pint glass to his mouth, taking a gulp of the remaining lager. As he gulped it back a little of the golden liquid drizzled from one side of his weathered lips. As he wiped it away, he looked over at Imogen smiling.

"…..but don't go repeating that!" He laughed.

The atmosphere had lifted as the men were united by their need to protect her.

Imogen returned to the table.

"What are you two being so secretive about?" she asked as Marcus pulled her down onto his lap.

"Just secret men's business" Marcus replied a sly smile escaping.

The rest of the afternoon passed with Rob slowly beginning to believe he could get used to this new normal, he was beginning to like this guy.

6pm, Rob left, giving Imogen a warm embrace asking her not to leave it so long next time. The men shook hands. Imogen felt relief that the two men in her life were getting along.

Rob left the bar intending to head home, but instead continued walking along the coast. His emotions in overdrive. She was happy, she was with someone who loved her, he was no longer dubious after seeing them together, and he seemed an alright guy, maybe they could become friends in time? But still it felt like his heart was breaking.

He reached the Gibralter rock and climbed over the railings, scaling the side of the castle. Sitting down on the grass verge overlooking the waves crashing below. He wrestled with his thoughts; she had never been his. Had he made a mistake pushing Imogen's advances away?

Though watching Imogen and Marcus together he knew he didn't love her in that way, he saw the spark, the magic, the sexual tension which was evident between them, he knew he could never have given her that, they never had that attraction but still in that moment he felt jealous, and angry for letting her slip through his fingers, before wondering if it wasn't that he was jealous of Marcus for gaining her love, but instead being envious of what they seemed to have, jealous that he didn't have that with someone.

That he wanted someone, someone to love him wholeheartedly, to be someone's number one.

"Will I ever find a love like that?" he asked himself as he continued to look over the sea below.

It also felt as though he had nothing else to live for. He had begun to hope, to dream, to plan, moving to Scarborough, flat sharing building the life that he let slip through his finger's years earlier.

He thought about his father, his health was failing, becoming frail, thinking what if he dies? Knowing he'd be even more inclined to stay to look after his mother. He then began to feel guilty for having such selfish thoughts wondering what type of son he was for thinking that way.

He'd never felt so alone in the world than he did that night, he felt too tired to fight on. He thought how easy it would be to edge forward and just fall.

His phone pinged.

Hey! Amigo!

Seems you guys were getting along?? Going to show Marcus the bright lights of Whitley! But hey, always remember you're my BFF, soulmates and all that... love ya, see you soon x"

It was as if there was still some cosmic connection between them, whenever he was low, it was as if she knew, and vice versa. Her text was enough to pull him back from the edge, but not enough to escape the darkness.

Those following weeks he threw himself into days and nights of drinking and partying. Again, beginning to find solace in the bottom of an empty bottle. He'd always fought so hard to not return there but time and time again he found he couldn't stop himself. Over those years when he began to slip, she gave him the reason to stop, to never let it go too far. Her need for him and his support had given him purpose, a reason to fight back. Now it felt as though there was nothing left I his life worth living for.

The weeks dragged on has he began to spiral downwards not directly because of Imogen and Marcus, but because of how that in part seemed to shatter his plans, feeling trapped and alone, feeling lost and hopeless, and not having her to fall upon, not wanting to shatter her bubble.

Chapter 39

He woke up from another night of partying, another hangover trying to remember what had happened the night before, the sun shining through the window.

The letterbox made its distinct sound. He ran down eagerly hoping for a letter from Imogen, it had felt like an eternity since he last received a letter. Flicking through the post, a mix of bills and junk mail, there was no sweet envelope filled with love.

He couldn't help think about all the times they spent together, thinking how summers would never feel the same, reflecting on how things used to be, how they could have been, wondering if all the promises they made had now turned to dust.

Returning to his room he picked up his note pad and pen and began to write...

Hello stranger

I think you're stranger than most, but that is why I love you. Wait, should I be saying that now? Maybe I should stop writing soppy love letters to you now. How's life?

Busy since you hardly write anymore.

I do miss you, well I miss having someone to laugh at hmmm, I mean with...... I guess it's understandable. Is he the Jealous type?

He seemed an ok guy when we met, he passes, he has my approval. From what I could see he really has fallen for you. But remember I'm always here. Your moving into stranger territory.

P.S.
I do hope you are ok, and everything is ok and everything works out ok, for the people you love the most..... OK?

Two days past and the letterbox was again graced by the sweet envelope, the elegant handwriting...

My dear Rob

I'm so sorry for neglecting you lately. Jealous? I didn't think so, but something happened and now I'm scared he is as controlling as Jacob, or maybe I'm overthinking? Maybe I'm seeing problems that aren't there, I don't know anymore.... I love him more than I can put into words. I thought I loved Jacob, but this is something on a different level.

Maybe it's partly lust, or well that is how it started. Can you fall so hard so fast? But I can't have another Jacob. And whatever happens I will always need you in my life. Wherever the winds take me.

He picked up his paper and began writing...

My dear Imi

He wanted to write, that she should forget him, that maybe then their friendship would return to what it was before Marcus, but he wasn't that selfish or possessive, feeling guilty for allowing those thoughts to enter.

Images of her smiling face, and replaying images in his mind, seeing the love between them, which was evident just being in their company, and remembering Marcus' words that night. He thought that after Jacob she needed happiness, and he wasn't Jacob. He continued to write

Follow your heart. He didn't seem to be anything like Jacob. But he does seem to be a little over-protective/jealous? Want me to come down and sort him out?

You need to decide is he worth fighting for? How much does he know about you??? Maybe open up, let him in.

But remain true to who you are. If you need a shoulder to cry give me a shout and you know I'll

come running, well, I mean on my bike... I wouldn't run all that way for anyone, not even you.... I think it would kill me, though... I guess if there was ever anyone I would die for, it would be you my dear.....

Always Rob x

A couple of days later his phone pinged... A message from Imogen

Hey received your letter, I do need your shoulder, but more than that I need a long fast ride on the back of your bike. Miss you. Imi x

Rob looked at the sky, the sun was shining, he needed a ride. He hopped on and as if by auto pilot he began heading south to Scarborough.

The distinct sound of a motorbike engine revving could be heard from her room where she sat in contemplation. She walked to the front door.

"Your chariot awaits!" Rob spoke eloquently with a flamboyant bow.

She jumped aboard, holding on tightly, her head resting upon his back, watching the world in a blur passing by. It felt like time had rewound, back to when she could just 'be', they could just 'be'.

Her thoughts tumbling as they rode, thinking over the pitfalls which had begun to shake her relationship with Marcus, thinking how she knew life was never perfect, and like the perfect ride life had to have its bumps, that sometimes difficult roads lead to beautiful destinations, she began thinking, could she give him one more chance?

Rob rode along the country roads, pulling into a lay-by, alongside a small brook. Removing her helmet, the sun shone across her face. Shining upon her, as if to fill a darkened soul. The light shone upon her with an ease that the world craves to grasp, but never seems to capture.

She didn't ask how he was, oblivious to the turmoil that he'd been living through.

He knew from years of experience that she got lost in her own problems which could come across as selfish and self-obsessed but he also knew that if she there was a problem she'd drop her problems to try and be there and secretly liked that he could for one day return to being the rock, the knight in shining armour, and being back in Scarborough it was as if everything that dragged him down was left on the road in, but he knew he'd end up picking it back up on the ride home.

They sat together by the brook in silence.

There was no need for words, she just needed to exist in his presence, surrounded by his love. She closed her eyes to the world and its troubles. A brief smile stretched across her face as his arm encircled her. Imogen began to speak, spilling out her heart, her conflicted feelings, trying to make sense of emotions.

How she was afraid, and second guessing every feeling, every emotion.

She told him how he followed her one day, and how she reacted. She also told him how while in Newcastle he saw her reality, telling him how a group of youths decided to try and attack her, but Marcus had scared them away.

Her thoughts verbalised flitted back and forth, defending his actions, that maybe the attack had caused him to become overprotective.

Her thoughts bounced asking, was he jealous or over-protective? How could he love her if he didn't truly know her? Would he love her if he knew all the ugliness? And asking... Was she ready to jump, or step back and walk away?

Rob allowed her to talk, remaining silent listening attentively like he had so many times before.

A shadow from a cloud passed overhead as if to for-warn of a storm to come.

Rob stood up, his arm outstretched,

"Time to get you home… Want to beat that storm! It's not like I can be stranded in Scarborough. It's not like the girls would let me stay"

He took her hand guiding her to her feet. He stood in front of her, his hand gently caressed her cheek, instinctively guiding her hair behind her ear, like he had done so many times before. His smile infectious, causing a smile to creep across her face. He placed her helmet upon her head, before climbing on his bike, revving the engine.

"Come on slow coach, hop on!"

They returned to the flat. Before leaving he held her hands delicately.

"Us men make mistakes; you know I've made plenty. And hey, after that attack before spring harvest I wanted to follow you everywhere, to keep you save, I think us men sometimes have a hero complex, maybe he does more than most since he does it as a job. What is worse? A man who wants to protect you and wrap you up in cotton wool, or someone who runs and leaves you to die... Maybe you need to try and reach a middle ground? If you genuinely love him go for it. Maybe write him a letter?"

He kissed her softly upon her cheek like he had so many times before, before leaving, returning home.

As Imogen sat trying to formulate her feelings, she began to feel overcome with guilt. Thinking how many weeks she was lost in Marcus's arms, forgetting Rob, not keeping in touch, yet as soon as she hit a stumbling block he came running. She didn't know how to say sorry, to show him he was still important in her life, not just for selfish reasons, but she couldn't find the words, or a way to show him, then again became lost in her relationship, thinking, it was ok, Rob was bound to know, and thought if anything was wrong he'd reach out, not realising that the reality was different to her beliefs, that his world was crashing down around.

Rob continued to drink and party, as though going full circle. He couldn't understand his feelings, it wasn't really that he'd lost Imogen, she was never his to begin with, but instead had lost the life he'd dreamt of, the life that twice he let slip through his hands. He looked at his life, coming to the conclusion that he was nothing, he was a failure, the only place he felt like someone was in Scarborough, and with Imogen, now he was back to being a 'nobody'.

He found it easy to hide it from Imogen, he didn't want her to see him like that, and he knew she was immersed in her newfound romance to notice.

His father had also began becoming frailer. His health had become fluctuant, good days, and bad days, though the bad were beginning to outweigh the good. His mother was frantically worrying. Wondering whether to go to the hospital or to stay home and hope he would improve.

He'd spent the morning walking reflecting having received the news via text that Imogen and Marcus were engaged. He wondered was that all he was worth... A text?

It all seemed so fast. He spent the afternoon drinking in the bay alone. He'd hoped maybe Brian would have been there, or Charlie, anyone to stop him feeling so alone.

He returned home slightly intoxicated, to his mother frantically pacing the floor.

"Where have you been?" his mother demanded.

"I've just been down the bay, that's all" he replied knowing that would just add fuel to the fire.

"I need to get your father to the hospital, and as usual you were out drinking!" she replied her temper rising.

"I'll drive you" he said without hesitation, without thinking, reaching for the car keys by the door.

He'd heard his mother's disappointment and cold-hearted replies many times but this time the argument grew from nowhere into a fury like never before.

"No! You've been drinking! That is all we need!" she replied grabbing the keys from his hand, the jagged key cutting through his skin.

Words flew from her mouth. Words that he knew she'd thought many times and had at times insinuated but had never really verbalised, never saying out loud until then.

"You are a useless boy! I'm ashamed of what you have become, look at you!" she screamed as she reached for the phone dialling for an ambulance.

Rob stood in shock. He'd always knew she was disappointed in him, and there was no way those words could be taken back.

He stood in the doorway, his hand on the door frame to steady himself, knowing without it he would have fallen to the floor.

Slowly he began to step backwards, as his mother turned walking towards the living room while talking on the phone, he kept stepping back almost stumbling, till he was stood in the porch. He looked at his mother, before turning and walking out of the house, down the street, aimlessly walking, not even sure of where and why. Till he reached the quarry. He found himself scrambling through the wood, the leaves scrunching under foot. He watched as the sun was dropping low in the sky reflecting in the lake, and shadows forming. He stood in the silence, alone. He fell to his knees in the long grass crying.

"I am not enough, I'm useless!" he shouted as he sat rocking back and forth, mumbling to himself, tugging at his hair, wanting to do something, anything to cause pain to distract from the pain inside.

"God! Why? Why is you keep punishing me?" he screamed, though doubting he was listening, doubting whether he was real.

He looked at his cut hand, at the blood, wishing he had something to cut deeper with. His heart began beating loudly like a heavy drum only he could hear.

He stared at his phone, wanting to ring her, like she did when she needed him, but he couldn't bring himself too, he didn't want to disturb her happiness, the day that she got engaged shouldn't become overshadowed by his problems, and he doubted whether she would come running to save him like he did. He wasn't willing to take the chance of one more let down.

Instead he scrolled through Facebook looking for a distraction, a party, somewhere he could drink himself into distraction, to disappear.

He found a house party in Whitley. He left the quarry walking aimlessly towards the town, stopping at the off license on the way to buy a bottle of vodka. He drank as he walked, finishing the bottle as he reached the street, allowing the bottle to fall out of his hand, smashing to the floor.

He stood looking at the broken glass, before walking on.

Chapter 40

He approached the house as loud music reverberated from inside the house party.

He entered, putting on a mask that everything was great, the fun guy everyone knew, though what he portrayed was far from how he really felt. He continued to drink, just wanting to forget.

He felt like a hypocrite, so many times scolding Imogen for going down that path, yet in that moment it was the only path visible to him.

He picked up two shot glasses filling them before downing them determined to get mortal, not caring.

Raquel watched from the far end of the table. He was to be her next conquest. She closed her hand around her glass as she walked up to him. She decided she wanted him, and she always got what she wanted...one way or another. Her flirtatious nature was evident as she approached him. She walked up to him, not looking where she was going, or that was the part she was playing, it was all a part of her plan. Bumping into him, causing his drink to be spilled on to her hair and jacket. She looked up, looking straight into his eyes.

"Oh my. I am so sorry I'm such a clutz, I wasn't looking where I was going" she claimed, as Rob reached for some tissues from a nearby table. Placing her drink on the table she slowly began removing her top, throwing it toward the window.

"I was a bit overdressed anyways" she exclaimed as she stood in a short crop top styled bra which accentuated her breasts.

He downed two more shots before settling to slowly nurse a fourth as he watched her blatantly attempt to flirt.

At first, he wasn't interested but her confidence was intoxicating, and he thought how she seemed quite hot, and fun. The more he drank the more he began to think why not?

With a slur to her words while intending to sound seductive, she asked.

"Aren't you going to get me a drink?"

She was playing a game; one she knew she could win without trying too hard. He shook his head in an attempt to clear his thoughts.

"You know I'm not one to take no for an answer" she continued leaning in till her flesh touched his body.

"And when I want something, I always get what I want" she continued taking his shot glass from his hand before downing it and slamming the glass on the table beside him, her other hand sliding under his damp t-shirt.

"Come on" she whispered seductively picking up a full bottle of vodka and leading him through the room and up the stairs.

"Nothing wrong with a bit of casual sex, and a bit of fun" he thought as she guided him to the bedroom. He wanted to fill that empty hole inside.

He awoke the next morning in a strange bed, his head was throbbing. He rubbed his eyes before reaching for his jeans on the floor, his phone in the pocket. He reached for his phone, checking the time, ignoring the message notifications. It was 6:00 am. As he put the phone down, it all came back to him.

He sat up with regrets, shaking his head in disbelief. It wasn't him, sleeping with random girls, and especially not girls like that, but then that was maybe why in his drunken state he did go with a girl like her, wanting to for once not be him.

He returned home, the atmosphere could be cut with a knife, his father had been admitted into hospital, he wanted to visit but his mother refused, he died the following day. It felt like his whole world had fallen apart and was filled with regret that he wasn't there and angry at his mother's part in that.

He wanted to speak to Imogen, he needed to do it in person and needed to get away, before doing or saying something he would regret.

The ride down he regularly took his eye off the road, and at times leaving it till the last moment to take a corner, he didn't care if he died, and dying on his bike would be a fitting end he thought as he continued to take risks, but something stopped him from going that far.

He arrived in Scarborough falling into Imogen's arms, the tears streaming, telling her about his fathers' death, his mother's words and the way she kept him from seeing him.

"I never got to say goodbye, she stole that from me" he sobbed in her arms.

"Why didn't you ring me?" she asked as she held him as he talked of how hard he'd been finding things lately, though not disclosing what had happened the night before, feeling too ashamed to share that mistake, hoping it would disappear, and could be forgotten.

"You've got your life with Marcus now" he replied.

"Hey, listen to me…. It's always been us against the world, and in a way always will be, yeah things have changed a bit but Marcus knows how much you mean to me, and I maybe a crap friend sometimes, but I'm always here, and you're always welcome here, you're family and always will be"

"Stay tonight, go back tomorrow, you need to be there, you need the closure, and if you want, I'll be there with you at the funeral, I'm sure your mum will be on best behaviour if I'm there!"

"Are you going to ride up 'cause you know what happened last time you made a promise to come up" he joked trying to lighten the mood.

"You're never going to let me live that down, are you?" she asked nudging him.

"Nothing would stop me, if I had to ride through gale force winds and hurricanes, I'd be there, cause you've always been there for me, what sort off friend would I be otherwise?" she replied though filled with guilt that she hadn't been half of the friend he had.

They spent the day together talking, the evening Marcus joined them as they sat on the beach besides a small bonfire like they had so many times before, but now 3 instead of 2.

He watched the affection between them still wondering if he would ever get that sort of love, though still not believing he deserved it. They tried to not make him feel like a third wheel but no matter how hard they tried he still felt that way.

He returned home the following day, before leaving Imogen urged him to reach out when he needed, no exceptions.

"I maybe crap at replying to your letters these days but still write, or ring me…" she urged as he put on his helmet.

"Ok, I promise" he replied as he revved his engine.

"Be careful, I still need you" she urged as he dropped the bike into gear and pulled away.

Back home he watched as the family rallied round, taking charge of the preparations, as he felt pushed aside. His brother was returning, the prodigal son, the perfect son welcomed back with open arms, yet the one who stayed pushed aside.

To get away he walked into Tynemouth sitting in Collingwood pub, sat in the corner with pint, he began writing.

Well the prodigal son is returning tomorrow; guess we'll finally get to meet his new lassie.... I wonder how many adventures she's had. heh, heh!!

Me, well I'm still in the way, still the disappointment... funeral on Monday, though I'll ring you in a few to tell you just in case this letter goes by snail mail.

As he placed the letter in his pocket and pulled his phone out, he could hear people around him talking, he was sure they were talking about him, but then he thought he was becoming paranoid. He stood up, finishing his pint, picking up his jacket.

"Hey, here you struck it lucky with the town whore" He heard someone shout as he walked back through the bar. He glanced over at some lad that he didn't recognise, holding up his glass as though to toast him.

The following few days the gossips began, he was another notch on her list, he discovered she had 3 children to 3 different men. But still he believed it would all die down, someone else would become topic of conversation, as long as he never had to see her again.

A week later the day of the funeral arrived.

Rob stood in his room staring at his reflection, standing in a dark jacket and trousers, thinking how the last time he wore a suit, he also wore a colourful bow-tie, though that wasn't a suit he was wearing that day but a fancy tux, going all out, on what was one of the happiest days of his life, which was in stark contrast to that day, which would be the worst. He stood waiting, waiting to leave in a black funeral car.

He made his way downstairs, surrounded by people he'd never met, and some he barely knew, everyone bringing their condolences to his mother, his brother, his sister, some forgetting about him, others giving a feigned condolence to him.

He looked around wondering would she turn up? The sky was dark, it had rained heavily for days.

"Well it's just me myself and I" he muttered under his breath as he walked out, following the rest of the family.

Outside, stood beside a silver/blue Z3 stood Imogen, Marcus remained sat in the driver's seat.

Imogen walked up to his mother to give her condolences, handing over a wreath, before walking up to Rob.

"I said I'd get here come hell or high water. We'll follow behind, Marcus is going to drop me off and then go meet up with my dad, I think he has some sucking up to do, don't you.." she winked, before continuing.

"I'm here for you" she continued taking his hand, leaning in for a hug.

They arrived at the small chapel in the middle of the cemetery, waiting as another funeral procession was leaving. It felt like a conveyor belt.

"Was this all a life amounts too?" he thought as they waited to go in.

They stood at the front, before sitting on the small wooden seats, Imogen sat a few rows back. He glanced over wishing she could be beside him, he needed her, but tradition stated who sat where, and she wasn't his girl, so she had no place being there, well that's what he was told. He watched as everyone bowed their heads as the music began. He thought how maybe it was to show respect, though it felt forced, as part of the pantomime of funeral etiquette. As he looked up the aisle seeing the coffin being carried down, he thought maybe people bowed their heads because they were too afraid to look at what was coming. He wondered would there be this turn out at his own funeral. Would it be empty? He thought about his grave, how it would become overgrown and forgotten, he would be forgotten.

The coffin wobbled as they carried it to the front and gently placed it down.

The chapel fell silent.

He watched his mother as she wiped tears onto her sleeve and rested on her brother's shoulder. He sat through the service, as though just going through the motion, holding back all of his feelings. As the service ended the mourners left through the exit door, as he stood outside, he could see another set of mourners waiting. He walked over to Imogen, standing in front of her, struggling to hold back the grief any longer.

When the words would not come, the tears did. Tears flow steadily, silently down his face, feeling bruised inside, numbness, emptiness, at having to say goodbye, though really unwilling to acknowledge the finality of his father's death, the only one who seemed to genuinely care.

They went to the wake. Imogen sat holding his hand feeling unable to know what to do, what to say. She tried to give him what he needed even though she had no idea what that was. She tried to show empathy, but as she'd never lost anyone, she truly loved she had no comparison. She'd been to funerals, some family funerals, but never a tear fallen, it was never anyone she couldn't live without, never anyone whose parting would change her life forever.

She thought of people in her life. She thought how there was no-one, apart from Rob, she could never imagine a world without him in it, or Marcus... Thinking how the more time they spent together the more she thought she wouldn't be able to live without him either. She tried to imagine those feelings in order to understand, but felt like she couldn't, feeling like she was failing him, that she'd again failed as a friend.

"You wanna get out of here?" she asked as he stared into space, staring at everyone talking, sharing memories, while he sat apart from them all.

"Come on" she urged pulling him to his feet.

"I think you've done your bit, now you need to put you first" she urged as he stood, he looked over at his mother.

"OK, let's get out of here" he replied.

They walked down to Tynemouth, the rain had ceased, creating a rainbow. They sat on the gravel beach near the boat house, lighting a small bonfire.

The fire crackled as they stared up at the rainbow. They sat together, quietly for a few hours till the sun began to set in the distance. As the darkness filled the sky, he stared up at the stars that were filling the sky, Marcus arrived with a few cans, sitting down beside them, opening a can and passing it to Rob, before repeating and passing one to Imogen, before opening a third. They sat quietly drinking.

Chapter 41

The following weeks went slowly, the atmosphere at home improved slightly, or returning to what it was before. With everyone gone it was only him who remained, as always. He thought how in reality his mother had no choice but to be pleasant, as he was all that was left.

The grief came and went in waves, some days felt normal, but then he would feel guilt at forgetting, other days he couldn't escape his father's memory, imagining standing beside him as they tinkered with the car engine, or with Buzby.

He decided he was going to make an effort, to make him proud, he was the only one who had faith in him so maybe sorting his life out was a way of honouring him? He thought about getting his own place, to following his dreams, whether that was in Newcastle or moving down to Scarborough to be nearer Imogen and Marcus, wherever he ended up he needed his own independence. His father's death also got him thinking of his own mortality, wondering how long his kidneys would hold out.

Six weeks after that party, that one-night stand, he realised he was never going to be able to escape it. Raquel was pregnant. She claimed the baby was his, from what he'd heard the baby could have been anyone's, but the thought of being a father brought some light back into his life, he just wished it had been with anyone else, and also was afraid to build his hopes up just in case.

It wasn't long till the mind games began.

He was the father; he wasn't the father... She wanted him to be part of the child's life, switching to the decision he was getting no contact unless he paid her...

He dreaded telling his mother, another failure on his part, a child out of wedlock...

He wondered how could he tell Imogen? She was wrapped up in preparations for graduation and the upcoming wedding. He didn't even know if he was the father, there was probably a long list of possible fathers he thought.

He decided he would wait till after the wedding to tell her what had happened, and the fact that he could be a father, that would be the only good to come out of such a horrible event which he had tried to erase.

He was determined to be the guy Imogen saw through her rose-tinted glasses.

A letter arrived.

Hey mate..
How do...
The wedding..... Now I would have you as my maid of honour though can't quite imagine you in a dress. So would you mind being our usher.... Big responsibility, you get to boss everyone around.....

He sat reading her letter, filled with the usual chitchat, as though she just let her thoughts tumble onto the page. He'd heard her say how his letters had gotten her through those past years, but her letters had also gotten him through. Finishing reading the letter he sat down to reply.

Hi.

Yes I would love to be your usher as long as the contract doesn't actually involve me being your servant and doing everything you command, wait... hasn't that been my role all these years??? Though I think that role of being your servant come slave should now be passed to Marcus.. Does he know what he's getting himself into I wonder!? Has he had the 'pleasure' of seeing your leather catsuit and whip??

OK... I promise to behave! I can hear you laugh...

Well best get this letter in the post and head to work!

The week's past slowly. He found working, a distraction to his life, and the constant games by Raquel, and as predicted his mother was far from pleased, though the thought of becoming a grandmother eased her disappointment and temper.

Raquel was able to put on the perfect act when she met his mother, as though making him out to be a liar. He wondered why he expected any less, his mother had never believed him, she always took anyone else's side but his.

He sat frustrated. The wedding only a couple of weeks away. He wanted to tell Imogen about Raquel, to vent, to have someone on his side, but he didn't want to spoil anything for her, deciding to wait till after the wedding. In reality he was more worried about seeing the possible disappointment in her face than his mothers, his mother was always disappointed, but Imogen saw him differently, he was afraid of falling from the pedestal he'd been placed upon.

He began writing.

Long-time no write, less time no see.

Hey Marcus see ya on the 18th for your stag do...

Imogen... See you soon... I have my suit sorted, and alas I won't be bringing a guest, I'm thinking of taking a vow of celibacy from now on me thinks...

He thought his chances of finding someone was low enough before, but now who would want him with a child and tied forever to someone like Raquel. He thought how if this was what she was like now, he couldn't imagine the sort of games she would play once the child was born, though at least then he'd know for certain whether he was a father or just a toy for her to play with.

The week before the wedding soon arrived.

Wednesday evening. He was standing in the Bay with a drink in his hand, a low alcohol lager, having made the decision to try and stay sober, as much as possible as alcohol had gotten him into his latest mess.

He stood chatting to Charlie.

"I don't see that lasting long, seen it before" Charlie laughed as he watched Rob take a drink, his face scrunching up as the liquid hit his taste buds.

"It just takes some getting used too, if I am going to be a dad I'll need to be as fit as I can be, this body is shit enough to begin with" he replied trying to take another drink.

Brian walked past, heading home,

"See ya Saturday kidda! The big day".. he spoke cheerfully, patting Rob's shoulder as he walked by.

"Yep, see ya then Bri" Rob replied.

"So, it's the big day this weekend?" Charlie asked.

"Yeah, it is"

"You don't sound too infused" Charlie quizzed.

"It'll be a good day…. It's just I'd been her go too for so many years, always us against the world. The most important person in her life. Now I'm second, again… and it kinda sucks big time, though I'm happy for her…. Really… and Marcus is an alright guy but still… and now I've got the headache of Raquel, life aint going as I planned…." He hesitated for a moment, taking a gulp of his pint before continuing.

"Though there's always the stag do!" he laughed.

"God help him if you're in charge, and when have you ever had a plan mate?" Charlie asked.

"I'm not in charge, there's a bunch of firemen on that already, I'm apparently supposed to be there to make sure her fiancé survives, and gets to the wedding in one piece… It's not like I can rock up at the hen party, I just don't know where I fit anymore... and yeah, me having a plan... guess you're right there!" he laughed in reply.

"I thought she knew you... putting you in charge of behaving... I'd love to see that one" Charlie laughed.

"Yeah, but whatever Imi requests, I do.. She still has me wrapped around her little fingers"

He spent the rest of the evening reminiscing and laughing over their exploits over the years and enjoying the company of a friend.

The following day he rode down to Scarborough, ready for the stag that evening, and wedding a few days later. Hoping to be able to have a few days without having to think about the problems back home.

Chapter 42

The day of wedding arrived. Rob stood in the lobby of the hotel.

He sent a text to Imogen.

"Hey imi, are you decent? I'm downstairs"

Rob stood there waiting.

He watched Imogen walk towards him looking beautiful, he'd thought that back at the ball she looked stunning and could never improve on that perfection, but she looked even more beautiful. The love shown in her eyes made her look radiant.

"I'm off to get ready with your future husband but wanted to see you first…. I know your dad is giving you away, but it's kind of like I'm also giving you away…."

He reached forward taking hold of her hands. A single tear sat upon his eyelid.

"Stop it, you'll make me cry and ruin my make-up!" she spoke sternly trying not to smile.

Looking into those deep brown eyes she thought how it should have been him walking her down the aisle or by her side with Clarissa.

"Now go make sure my fiancé is at the church waiting!"

He leant in, giving her a hug, followed by a delicate kiss on her cheek.

"Yes, my lady" He retreated with an overstated eloquent bow. He walked back to the adjacent hotel where they had stayed the previous night, returning to their room where Marcus was impatiently pacing the floor. He entered the room; the suits were hanging on the wardrobe door. As he entered Marcus was pouring himself a stiff glass of vodka, he looked up acknowledging Rob,

"Where did you disappear too?" Marcus asked as he entered.

"Went to check on your future bride and get some fresh air" he replied.

"Want one?" Marcus asked, holding his glass up, his hand shaking...

Rob paused before answering. He'd been trying to remain sober lately, too many days and nights drinking in silence, hoping that the answers to his life could be found at the bottom of the glass and then the bottom of the bottle and the next. He was beginning to realise the drink was never the problem, but rather the use of the drink, he'd had that conversation many times with Imogen, especially when she began using drink to escape her problems, he just found he was never good at following his own advice.

He looked up at Marcus,

"Hey, why not" he answered.

It was a celebration, it would be rude not to, he thought as Marcus poured the drinks. He thought how he'd used the same reckoning for the stag do 2 nights earlier.

"Thanks for being here mate, means a lot. I know you've always been Imi's friend, but I hope that we can become good friends... I can imagine it wouldn't have been easy since me and Imogen got together, and I'm sorry if I've been greedy and kept her all to myself... I do know you guys have a pretty unique friendship..." Marcus spoke sincerely, his nerves showing through.

"Hey, it's OK, and yeah it's been strange not seeing her as much as I'm used to, but you both have been there through some pretty crap months so thanks" he replied holding his glass forward.

"To friendship" Rob spoke as Marcus lifted his glass, the glasses clinked together in a toast.

Rob took a sip looking at Marcus, he could see the nervousness in his body language, the sincerity.

He was beginning to accept that he wasn't Imogen's first anymore, but he was content being her second to someone like Marcus...

His thoughts were interrupted by Marcus

"What if she has second thoughts? Doesn't turn up?..."

"Hey, don't be nervous... As I said.....I've just seen your bride to be, she'll be there, and she's instructed me to make sure you get there!"

Their conversation was broken by the arrival of the best man, and a few other firemen piling in through the hotel room door. After the initial raucous they poured themselves drinks and began getting ready.

Rob stood quietly getting ready. Taking his time slowly buttoning each button on his shirt, he watched the others, joking, filling the room with banter. Marcus, every now and then would try to bring him into the fold, but he still was always on the outside.

He thought back to the stag night a few nights earlier, the usual questions of...

'What do you do?'

He wondered why that was nearly always the first question when meeting someone, why is a person's life defined by what job they do?

He remembered standing there trying to think of a response, thoughts tumbling through his mind.

He stood there, taking a drink of his pint knowing he couldn't say he was unemployed, that his teaching assistant contract had come to an end, or he hadn't been in the best headspace to work, and how in a way he'd defaulted to what his mother saw in him, he was just a bum, a layabout, finally living up to her expectations. He skirted round the question saying he was a youth worker, currently between projects, hoping they wouldn't see through the cracks in his story, he wasn't really lying just being economical with the truth.

As he looked around watching them, they all seemed so confident. He thought how there was once a time he thought he knew everything, was confident, though giving a small laugh he realised he was trying to create a persona which had never really existed. He could fool people, and at times looked confident, and could pull it off but he knew it was just as fake back then as it was there and then. It had just got harder to keep up the pretence.

He thought how the second question which was always asked after, 'what do you do', was always geared towards family and relationships, and like clockwork, that question was asked.

He shrugged it off, not wanting to answer. It wasn't like he could say he may have gotten some girl pregnant who already has a trail of kids from different fathers, or that the only girl he'd ever thought about settling down with one day was marrying their friend.

He remembered how Marcus interrupted the interrogation.

"Leave the poor guy alone! It's not an interrogation, I thought we were here to get drunk and celebrate my last night of freedom" *Marcus interrupted placing his arm on Rob's shoulder.*

"Come on, didn't you say you were buying me my first drink" *he continued guiding Rob towards the bar.*

"Cheers" *he toasted as they stood in silent contemplation.*
The night improved and his skill at organising drinking games came in handy, but although they tried to include him there was a brotherhood amongst firemen, and he wasn't one of them, he also barely knew Marcus, not really. They visited a few bars, but then it was on to a nightclub to dance the night away with cocktails and tequila slammers, ending the night at the casino. Not getting back to the flat until 4 am the following morning.

He thought how they needed that day before the wedding to recover, the majority of the day a blur before taking their belongings to the hotel.

"Hey mate, stop daydreaming... We've got a wedding to get too" Marcus said placing his hand on Robs shoulder disturbing his thoughts.

He followed as they walked out of the hotel room, down the corridor to the reception area.

He caught a glimpse of himself, his reflection in the window.

"Pretty hot!" he thought, the tuxedo brought something out of him, and it made him think back to the last time he wore a tux, the prom.

In the tuxedo it felt like a mask hiding who he really was, instead it demonstrated a self-respecting pride and confidence that had been wishing to surface for so long. He had a job to do, and although it wasn't much, he was determined to do it to the best of his ability because she'd asked him, and all he wanted was for her wedding to be perfect.

"Maybe I'll find a bird" he muttered under his breath before laughing knowing how that phrase got him into trouble so many times in the past.

He laughed to himself remembering how sometimes he deliberately wrote about finding a bird or referring to some girl as a bird to bate a reaction knowing he would get thumped in return. It was as though part of a fun ritual, finding ways to wind her up till she took the bait.

They got to the church, Rob dived straight into his role of usher, walking around making sure everyone took their seats, and that everyone knew what was happening. The sound of conversations were drowned by the music of the organist. He walked up and down his hands sweating as he looked round to check everything was ready. As he looked at the congregation, he noticed that the groom's side was filled with fellow firefighters in their formal dress.

Once everyone was seated, he waited at the back of the church watching the door. He looked down the aisle at Marcus standing in silence. His hands joined together placed in front of him as though to stop himself fidgeting, standing in the silence, looking around, nervously.

Rob glanced at his watch, 1.05pm. He looked back up scanning the church. He watched the best man placed his hand upon Marcus' shoulder reassuringly.

He looked back towards the door spotting Imogen in the doorway. Their eyes met.

He winked, smiling at her. He gazed upon her in awe, he had never seen her look so beautiful. She looked stunning; the dress was her in every way. He glanced forward. Marcus caught his eye. Rob nodded as though to give an indication that all was OK before slowly walking down the aisle to take his place next to the best man.

"She's here" Rob whispered. Marcus breathed a sigh of relief. He took a few steps back, taking his seat on the front pew, ready.

The music began to play. Marcus looked up the aisle anxiously waiting for his bride to appear.

"Please stand for the bride..." The minister proclaimed.

The little flower girls appeared dressed in little white dresses with a blue sash, as they walked slowly, they threw flower petals down the aisle ahead of the bride. Once they reached the front Imogen appeared at the back of the church. Rob had already seen her, he looked at Marcus to see his reaction as she came into view.

Reaching the alter, she stood next to Marcus. Rob watched as Brian let go of her hand, stepping back, standing in silence waiting for the wedding to begin.

"You may now take your seats" the minister instructed as he looked at the couple. The church fell silent, so much so you could hear a pin drop. The best man took his seat next to Rob as the service began.

"Dearly beloved we have gathered here to join Imogen and Marcus in holy matrimony......"

Rob sat listening, while also thinking, again his thought returning to whether that would one day be him, something which felt further and further away.

"Who gives this woman to this man?" The minister proclaimed in a loud confident voice.

In a quiet shaky voice Brian replied,

"I.... do." Before stepping back.

He watched as Imogen looked over at her father. He followed her eyes. He could see Brian on the other side, the Brides side. For a moment he thought how shouldn't he have been on that side? He looked at Brian and as he looked, it looked like he had tears in his eyes. He was stood pursing his lips, trying to look away, not wanting anyone to see him overcome with emotion.

Rob thought how he knew that her father was not one to normally show emotion, watching him, a tear also formed in the corner of his eye, understanding the emotions her father was feeling for in a way he felt that way too, he was giving her away to another, she was no longer his responsibility, a position which in a way had given him purpose, a reason.

Imogen glanced across at Rob, he caught her gaze, smiling he nodded, as though to acknowledge his thoughts, his position in her life. She looked back at Marcus, and the wedding truly began.

The wedding was magical, like a fairy-tale, perfect vows, with a little humour thrown in as Marcus replied "why I" but due to nerves ended up sounding like a Geordie slang term, wye-eye... causing many of the congregation to laugh, including Imogen, she looked over at Rob, that little laugh he'd witnessed so many times.

The minister cleared his throat then began, the declarations, beginning with Marcus.

"Do you Marcus Delaney take Imogen-Kelsie Herrington to be your lawfully wedded WIFE…in the Covenant of marriage…."

"I do." Marcus declared staring lovingly into his brides eyes.

The declaration was then repeated towards Imogen. Rob watched as she pursed her lips, her voice shaky as she replied.

"I do…"

He listened as they recited their own vows to compliment the official vows that they had taken. He watched the look of pure love and adoration in Marcus' eyes as he took her hand.

Again, Rob's thoughts turned to himself, wondering if he would ever get married? What would his wedding be like? Could he cope with his family being there, with the fake pretence. Would he find someone who he loved the way Marcus loved Imogen? And more importantly would anyone love him the same way in return.

He wished that if there was such a woman for him, she'd find him sooner rather than later.

"Can we have the rings" the minister spoke looking over in his direction, Rob looked at the best man standing beside him.

Marcus was also looking over at his best man, waiting. Rob laughed as he watched the best man, giving a look of shock, pretending to have misplaced the rings, frantically searching his pockets. Rob could tell it was an act, and something he would have thought of doing if anyone ever valued him enough to be their best man. Seeing the fear in Marcus' eyes, the best man relented, smiling, producing the box which held the rings. After the exchange of rings, the priest announced,

"You may now kiss the bride."

He stood outside the Church. The ground was mottled with dry and wet patches. In parts it was as though the ground was kissed by the rain, glistening in the sun which was shining creating a rainbow. When they entered the church, the sun had been shining. He stood watching as the guests spilled out into the carpark. He watched Marcus' Grandmother throwing confetti, watching Imogen smiling and laughing lost in the moment, lost in the day. He stood against the railings with his hand skinning across disturbing the raindrops which rested delicately upon the metal. He thought how the autumn was always bittersweet, as he began recalling the memories, the times when he had felt blessed to always have Scarborough. The days and the memories he would never forget. He thought how in those moments he had no idea they would become the good old days. He wondered if you always look back and think the past was better than it was, always looking back rather than living in the moment, living for now. Although he knew it was in part true, he knew his memories were true, they were days where he truly lived. He thought about the days in between, the days back home and the many times he took the wrong fork in the road. Back when he stayed behind, not being able to find the courage to leave and being held back by blind loyalty. Wishing he didn't invest so much in what other people thought, being able to feel comfortable in himself. Wishing he hadn't reached for the bottle so many times especially that night with Raquel. He let his mind wonder thinking of all the changes that were coming. His thoughts were disturbed by Imogen shouting over across the carpark.

"Oy! Rob! Get your ass over here for photos!"

He glanced over at her, seeing the magical sparkle in her eyes caused a smile to play upon his face. Smiling he walked back across the carpark towards them.

After the general photos outside of the church they moved on to the town hall for more photos of the couple and the wedding party. He watched from the gate watching as they stood on the grass with the south shore as the backdrop capturing those perfect moments to treasure forever. The photographer began organising those waiting, taking photos of the family and wedding party. Slowly he began walking away back towards the hotel not feeling that he deserved to be there Feeling surplus to requirements. Slowly he walked back to the hotel.

After the obligatory photos there was to be a wedding reception back at the hotel. He walked down the red carpet which had been put down while they were away. He scanned the empty function room before walking to the bar standing waiting. As he sat drinking his pint Brian crept in by the side door joining him at the bar.

"Bit posh for me like but we betta take our seats kidda" Brian spoke as he took his pint from the bar, his other hand resting upon Rob's shoulder as though to guide him away.

"Thought you'd still be at the photos?" Rob asked as they walked towards their seats. The seating plan had him sat next to her father which put him at ease.

"Aye, av dun mee bit.. Now they are doin them again with Karen's fella in my place" Brian replied taking his seat.

Rob took his seat looking at Brian who didn't appear to show that he was phased by it, but he wondered if like him he also felt out of place and redundant. To have another man step into his shoes, wondering if maybe that would one day be him.

As guests continued to enter, he scanned the room. The room began to buzz with excited chatter broken by the entrance of the happy couple. He watched as the couple entered. The room fell silent followed by an applause which spread across the room as they took their seats. Watching them, it was as though they weren't interested in anyone around them, as though it was just them.

After a few moments, the best man rose from his chair followed by the sound of his teaspoon rapping on the side of his wineglass as though to signal everyone to silence for the speeches.

As the speeches were delivered, ending in a few very short words from Brian, he thought how he would have given a good speech, if he'd been asked, but that was not part of his duties. Usher just felt like an empty title, and after all they'd been through, he thought he'd be more. He felt like kicking himself for such selfish thoughts.

The hours dragged following the reception before the beginning of the evening party. He arrived dateless but assumed Clarissa would be there. She was, but was not alone, bringing with her, her new boyfriend. He took a seat next to Brian.

The evening began with the first dance, Rob watched them, looking at her so happy, thinking how that was all he'd ever wished for. Following came the Father-Daughter dance. Imogen walked over taking her father's hand, trying unsuccessfully to pull him to his feet.

"Ya na I divvent dance!" her father stated sternly, though seeing the disappointment in her face he looked over at Rob.

"Hey kidda, dance with her in my place" he continued.

Imogen sighed, glancing over at Rob. He put down his pint looking back at her, shrugging his shoulders as though to say it's up to you, though there was nothing he wanted more in that moment.

Imogen walked around the table taking Rob's hand,

"May I have this dance?" she asked.

As they danced, she looked around the room.

"Any nice birds you got your eye on?" she asked trying not to laugh.

"Birds eh? I thought you hated that derogatory term" he replied.

"Yeah I made you think that, well I had to keep you towing the line, someone had to whip you into shape, but nah, not really, never bothered me as much as you think... I just played you! I knew the more I reacted the more you'd do it and it gave me a reason to beat you up! We're quite a pair me and you, though now we're supposed to be all grown up... But now look at me married, who'd have thought hey?" she wiped her eye, then playfully punched his shoulder to disguise her emotions.

"Just wish could find you somebody" she whispered as the song finished, standing in his embrace.

"Hey can I have my wife back mate" Marcus interrupted in a playful tone.

"You do know anyone else and I'd be jealous" he continued jokingly as he reached out his hand, to which Rob responded. His hand clasped Marcus' open hand which quickly followed with both men moving closer, into an embrace. Imogen stood beside them placing her hands around them.

"Sorry to break up this bro-fest but can I have my husband back?" She asked cheekily as they stepped apart.

"Come on, you owe us a drink!" She continued walking towards the bar, looking back to check they were following.

The rest of the evening the happy couple were too loved up to really notice anyone.

The evening slowly ended as Imogen and Marcus disappeared. Rob sat at the bar reflecting over the day.

The couple had a few days away for their honeymoon, Rob stayed in Scarborough, looking after the flat, an excuse to not go home, not wanting to return to Newcastle to deal with Raquel. He needed to escape her, even if just for a while, though even in Scarborough he found that impossible.

His phone began to be filled with messages from Raquel. Again, the same being repeated, like a broken record... One moment he was the father, the next he wasn't. She would ring and start shouting abuse if he failed to answer.

When Imogen and Marcus returned, Rob returned home to Newcastle.

Chapter 43

A few days after returning he sat in his room, reading over the texts which filled his phone. He thought how many times he'd decided he was going to tell Imogen but always found an excuse.

Before leaving Scarborough to return home they had went on a bike ride up to the mount where he had decided that he was going to confess all, but the words wouldn't form. he knew he couldn't do it with words.

He sat holding his pen, trying to work out what to write

Should I be writing love letters to a married woman, maybe we should rethink this writing malarky, or maybe not...

The wedding was perfect, and you guys looked so happy, I wonder if I will ever find that ... I doubt it!

He paused for a moment before nodding, and continuing...

I'm kind of writing cause I have something to tell you and I don't think you'll be happy, I couldn't tell you to your face, not bearing to see the disappointment. I gave you such a hard time for almost falling into

Gary's arms, then I do the same, I guess I've always been a do as I say not as I do kinda guy, just look at my riding!! Well anyway back to the point cause I bet your talking out loud telling me to get on with it... Well with Dad dying, you getting engaged, me losing my job and all that I kind of found myself on the dark side, I broke our deal and didn't contact you to pull me back cause you were so happy. So I ended up having a one night thing with some lass... The type of girl that makes a hobby out of it and well... She's pregnant with my child... Well she says is mine, then changes her mind.... A lot of mind games and all that. So maybe I'm gonna be a Dad!! Do you think I'll make a good parent? Between us we've got a lot of 'not what to do' experience!

You know before you got with Marcus, I was thinking of moving down to Scarborough, but then thought 3's a crowd. Although now we've found this new thing, I guess if I am this kid's Dad, I'll want to stay up here to be near... and maybe a baby might help attract the single ladies??? Yep always trying to find a positive!

He knew he was fooling her and himself with that last comment, slowly giving up hope of that going to happen. He thought how before Raquel he believed it was near impossible with his health issues and his messed-up mind, but now with her forever stuck in his life he doubted anyone would be willing to take on that mess.

A few days past, days staring at his phone knowing she would have received his letter, wondering if she was going to ring him or whether he'd receive a letter. When he got no reply, he began wondering if that was the end of their friendship. He could imagine the disappointment in her eyes.

The dam burst open, the sobs were tearing his body apart, feeling out of control, trembling. He couldn't even hold his hands up without failing as it began to feel like his body was paralysed. He'd tried so long to remain strong, to keep it together, trying to be strong for far too long but he wasn't strong enough to keep it up. He felt like a failure, he was a failure, or so believed. He believed he had managed to keep up the pretence back in Scarborough, but back home it wasn't as easy. He had thought that he could try and rebuild his life but as usual back in that room alone everything felt too much, too difficult, too impossible.

The never-ending ceaseless mind games, the loss of his father, and the constant echoing feeling of failure which was justified by the comments of those around him, were too much to bear. The only good thing giving him the strength to hold on seemed to be slipping through his fingers.

If it was the end, it ended on a high, he thought as he flicked through photos on his phone, photos up on the mount, their smiles speaking volumes, and photos from the wedding, of him with Imogen, and photos of the 3 of them together, he began laughing while looking at photos of him and Marcus. The memories were all he had left, clinging onto them as though they were the only thing keeping him holding on. He'd had hopes and dreams of them becoming good mates, but maybe that was also shattered, just like his life was shattered into too many pieces to try and fix.

He thought how she'd got her life back on track just as his fell apart, maybe it was meant to be that way so that they could be each other's rock when needed, thinking how that was the way it had always been but if that was so, where was she now? He began becoming overcome by selfish thoughts, thinking how whenever anyone needed him, whenever Imogen needed him, he was always there, but where were his friends now? It was beginning to feel like no-one cared about the hell he was going through, or had been going through., He had hidden the true extent of his feelings but he had thought how with the depth of their relationship she should have seen past his walls, that real friends should be able to see through the façade.

He began feeling guilty for feeling that way, knowing he could have opened up to her in Scarborough, that he was expecting too much for her to read his mind. He wondered whether he was he in part keeping her at arm's length? He knew he was in a way pushing her away, just like he was pushing everyone who cared away. He just wished she knew how overwhelming he felt his life was, thinking how sometimes all he needed was a hug, for someone to fight back against his wall, for him to mean so much that someone was willing to put in the hard work, instead of acceptance, apathy or just the cold shoulder, the being ignored because it is too difficult to understand. Thinking how just that knowing someone cared that much, that support, was worth more than words could ever say.

His mother entered his room. He could see the look of disgust as her eyes scanned the dark dirty room filled with dirty dishes which hadn't made it back downstairs, and an array of empty bottles. He could see the disappointment in her eyes, the belief that he was living up to her expectations. Her facial expressions indicated that it was not a peaceful discussion, reciting her list of complaints about him.

Though in the midst of her longwinded rant, glimpses of concern shone through, reiterating how she was worried he was sleeping too much, not taking proper care of himself, that he didn't socialise, and that he didn't go to see any of his friends, but as quickly as it appeared again it vanished as her tone returned to one of disgust and disappointment.

"... and bring down all of these dishes! This room is disgusting!" she uttered as she walked out closing the door behind her.

The sobs which he temporarily managed to rein in whilst she was there continued till the point he was almost choking upon his own tears, leaving him wondering whether it was possible to drown in your own tears.

Those days he barely left his bed preferring sleep, where the dreamworld was so much better than reality.

It felt like he was dying inside, he didn't really feel anything, almost void of emotion, or maybe already dead, but his body just going through the motions like a zombie.

Death is forever, like constantly sleeping but without waking up, it sounded peaceful and at times felt a better option than what was going on in his head. Maybe it would be better than this place? He thought.

His thoughts were broken by a message, a picture of a scan, a baby, a real baby, the image making the whole thing seem a lot more real.

A voice echoed in his head, a stern voice, as though replying to his earlier thought, replying NO!

Deep down he knew he couldn't give up, especially if there was going to be a child who needed him.

Chapter 44

His thoughts were broken by the revving of a bike, listening he recognised that sweet sound. He thought how others may not be able to differentiate but to him it was as though every bike had its own voice. If he wasn't mistaken it was the sound of Kitt.

He began to think his mind was creating things that weren't there, his mind had played tricks on him too many times lately for him to build his hopes up, just for his hopes to be shattered.

His phone pinged.

Hey! Lazybones! Curtains closed? You can't be still asleep on such a beautiful day.

He opened his curtains, the light flooding into his darkened room, the light causing him to wince as they adjusted to the light.

He looked down seeing Imogen sitting upon Kitt looking up at his room. She caught a glimpse of the curtain moving before seeing him looking down from his window. She smiled waving beckoning him to come to her.

He quickly got dressed leaving his room, heading downstairs, and outside.

"You know the rugged unshaved scruffy look doesn't really work on you!" Imogen joked as he walked nearer.

"I'm here to kidnap you... Honest I'm on strict instructions, and I'm not letting you be responsible for my failure... but first how's about a ride to somewhere for a proper catch-up" she continued...

"Oh and in case it hasn't click that was an instruction, not a question... I'll just wait here, go on... Shoo! Go get ready, and I mean properly!" she instructed with a sternness in her voice which said don't mess with me.

Imogen waited, looking around at the place that once was home, remembering when that house portrayed love. Reminiscing of the day they painted the fence and sitting on the grass which was now overgrown. Visualising Levi jumping craving attention. Remembering what was once a family home which now felt like a hollow shell.

Rob opened the garage door, Imogen climbed off Kitt and walked up the path peering in.

"So, WE going on the beast? Or giving Kitt some company on Buzby?"

Imogen stepped further in observing how the garage looking empty. Her eyes scanned the room.

"Where's the beast?" Imogen asked as her eyes looked over the car and Buzby resting against the wall.

"Mamma made me get rid, to help cover costs, am not working, not really contributing, and hey, baby on the way, responsibilities and all that"

"Couldn't part with Buzby so the TDM had to go, and wouldn't get much for this old bike anyway"

"Hey, you'll hurt her feelings!" she declared while patting the fuel tank.

"It's pretty rotten, you shouldn't have had too…" her words trailed off as her hand gently rested upon his arm.

"Well let's get out for a race along the coast" she declared as Rob knocked the bike from its stand, wheeling it out down the path.

"First task is to re-fuel these two.." Imogen stated as she turned the key in the ignition. Looking at Rob she continued.

"And I'm paying… Been given an advance on my fee to deliver you!" she joked as she dropped the kickstart, lifting slightly from her seat to kick down with enough force to cause the bike to begin to purr.

She watched as Rob pushed down on the kickstart, with Buzby returning a grumble in return.

"Now either riding a bike without a kickstart has made you lazy, or Buzby is telling you she's in a huff! You know I don't think she liked being replaced by a bigger better model, I know I sure wouldn't!" she continued laughing before leaning in as though to talk to his bike.

"Buzby, please be good. I know he can be a pain in the arse, but we could both do with you being on your best behaviour today!" she continued while gently patting the fuel tank, before returning her hand to the throttle giving a twist to allow the sweet revs reverberate through the air.

Rob stood, leaning slightly giving another push down, to which the bike began to purr.

"See! She just needed a bit of love, like any woman!" Imogen winked biting her bottom lip before placing her helmet on her head, fastening her straps.

"Morrisons first!" Imogen declared as she pulled off, slowing at the end of the street to give way she glanced back in her rear mirror to check he was still behind her before pulling out at speed.

"You're getting old slow coach!" Imogen declared as Rob pulled up alongside her at the fuel pump.

"In your dreams!" Rob declared as Imogen began filling the tanks.

"To the hill?" Imogen asked having been thinking back to those early days, that first ride, when life felt so carefree.

"OK, and you'll be eating my dust!" Rob declared.

Imogen watched that smile return bringing with it something which had seemed lost for so long. Rob thought how that was the first time he'd smiled or been happy for many weeks. Though he knew one ride wasn't going to fix his life, but rather it was a welcome short distraction.

They sat upon the hill observing the same horizon as though time hadn't passed.

"I know I should have been here sooner, I'm a shit friend, but I had some audition I had to do, not that it's an excuse" Imogen spoke out as she watched the branches of the distant tree move in the breeze.

Rob sat in silence, not knowing what to say, not being able to find the words to verbalise his thoughts, his feelings, or the past weeks where the days had merged into each other, not wanting to admit out loud how far he'd fallen, afraid to reach out, to admit that he wasn't the man he had wanted to be, to be the man she saw, not wanting to break that illusion but on the same page wanting to be close to her, to let her in, as he knew he couldn't do it on his own.

"So what is the name of my now number 1 enemy? Do you think I can use her as target practice... I fancy brushing off the dust on my archery skills"

"Her name is Raquel.. And I remember I've seen your target skills..." he answered.

"With a name like that... Well.... It's kinda like the 'Karen' thing..." She paused as the penny dropped to what he was implying in the back end of his comment.

"Hey! What you saying! I'm not that bad if I recall" she continued while punching him in the arm playfully.

"I think you're recalling your dreams just like your dreams of thinking you're faster than me" He replied getting amusement from his roasting of her, watching her react in response.

She saw for a moment his face light up but too soon it faded, breaking her heart.

"I wish you could see yourself through my eyes, I forget you can't see through my mind…...." Imogen spoke through the silence.

"I got your letter and could read between the lines. And even before it I could tell things weren't quite right with you, but I selfishly got lost in my own happy ending to really ask questions, I'm sorry, but I'm here now, and forever will be... no judgements here... Though...." She paused wanting to lighten the conversation.

"....Thought we weren't going to turn our breakdowns into a competition.... but you win hands down!" She proclaimed, trying to disguise her deep concern.

"You'll make an awesome dad! World's greatest dad…. You're already world's greatest friend.

"And I know…. You'll find someone who will bring a calm to your crazy… I kinda made a deal with God and I'm sure he'll honour it. We're kinda back on track, well almost, not quite back to acorn days but hey!" She paused, realising that again she was diverting the conversation in her direction, being all about her.

"But….You need to get out of here, whether that be in Scarborough or somewhere here, just find a place and make it home, to make a life, maybe not exactly the life you had planned but I know God has plans for you, and can make diamonds from even the roughest of stones"

Listening to her words it was like having the young Imogen back, the girl who believed God would, and could fix anything, did she have enough faith for the both of them.

"Look, come back with me for a few days, 'cause I'll not live it down if I return without you… Then come down as much as you need, but just don't shut me out, your surrounded by people who love you, but I know you always believe your alone, I've been there… And no matter how many levels of hell you descend down, you know I'll follow, the dark holds nothing to us when we're united."

"Let's walk…" she declared reaching out her hand, wanting to break his silence, or more so to break the relentless sound of her own voice.

She wondered what was going through his mind, wondering if she was breaking through, or whether the walls were too thick and deep, and her too weak and useless to really make an impact.

"You know, no matter how many times we've been here, we've never really explored what lies beyond." She continued.

She took his hand and began trying to pull him too his feet but failing. She let go of his hand staring at him with those puppy dog eyes that he was never able to resist. He soon relented, standing up.

"OK, come on then" he replied offering his hand. She took hold of his hand and began walking. Walking down the far side of the hill towards the small patch of woodland. As they walked it was almost as though she was skipping. He smiled thinking how it was hard for her infectious nature not to rub off on him.

"You know I still remember the first time you brought me here... like it was yesterday, yet also feels like a lifetime ago.." she uttered as she looked back at the hill, hoping that reminiscing would engage him in conversation.

"Yeah I guess back then we never really realised the importance of those days, realize how precious those college days that we spent together were. Those days spent together, that first meeting. The rides and celebrations....friendship....Oh, and those English classes..." his words trailed off as a small smile began to show.

"Yeah, those classes when you tried everything to distract me, oh and stealing my pens!" she laughed nudging him.

They continued to walk a little further stumbling upon a small brook. The scent of damp moss and lichens filled the air. Imogen tossed a stick, watching it slowly being carried away. She sighed having so much she wanted to say but had been struggling to find the words, she also didn't want to overload him with verbal diarrhoea in which her true thoughts and feelings would go unrecognised. Pursing her lips and taking a deep breath she began speaking, not knowing where her words would take her, hoping God would take over and deliver the words he needed, the words she wanted him to hear.

"Look, just ask me for help, just ask…. And I promise that when you do, I'll be there, I'll try and move heaven and earth, just like I know you would, and have. To ask for help is not a failure, but a chance of a gift; like the gift you gave me, cause to be asked is trust…. It is one way to truly show love, words never do enough, never enough to repay the debt, let me repay that debt. So, when I give to you, it is with love and gratitude. What else are we here for other than to help each other, save each other… sharing our love in our actions" she uttered.

She paused watching as Rob picked up a stick.

"Pooh sticks?" he suggested giving no indication as to whether her words were getting through.

"OK" Imogen replied picking up a stick.

"Ready? 1…. 2….. 3…." He spoke before tossing his stick into the water with her stick following in quick procession.

They walked watching the sticks flow downstream, watching the path of water which manoeuvred around rocks and cascaded in its haste, and admiring the abundance of wildflowers that were glimmering along its banks.

Imogen decided to try and continue to talk…

"I'm nowhere near wise, but I'm just reiterating what a wise person once told me, that wise person needs to swallow their own words… You watched me put up with so many who were bad for me, people getting a kick out of cheap stunts that boosted their egos at the expense of my own. Allowing other's thoughts and opinions to have more value than my own, you showed me. You taught me not to give in to them, not to feed them. Good people feel good when they lift others up, poisonous people feel good when they put others down. Good people get addicted to doing good. Poisonous people get addicted to causing the hurt. I wish I'd stood up for myself sooner, had listened to you sooner, and above all, I wish you'd came into my life earlier, but when you are being so emotionally drained by others it's harder to do than it is to say. I believed things would change, or more so that I deserved everything which was thrown my way, but with you, and with the passage of time, it was my attitude and belief that changed, or more that you helped me to change.. Now you have to do the same, to gain the space to re-grow back into being the person I have always been proud off, a person who brings others emotional support, the selfless, amazing, loving hero who saved a broken girl. Unlike me you can't cut off all these people completely, your mother, your family, and obviously you'll always in a way be connected to………." Imogen coughed not wanting to speak her name but also not wanting to speak the word she wanted to say in replacement.

"But you can limit how much control you allow them to have, and can stop them from derailing your destiny…"

"Oh and looks like I win!" she declared as her stick reached the small waterfall first.

"Come on, we best get back to the bikes, we've got a long bike ride ahead of us, and if you haven't figured it out yet, no is not an option" She continued pulling him back in the direction which they'd come.

They returned back to Rob's flat for him to pack a bag, though he continued to try and protest believing that the offer was just empty platitudes, that he would be in the way, thinking how they should be in the midst of the honeymoon period.

The break was just what he needed, time to have fun without thinking of his responsibilities, his failures. Giving time to think and reflect and when Marcus was at work it provided ample time for him and Imogen to talk, to thrash out everything which threatened to consume and destroy him.

A few days past, he knew he had to head home at some point. The penultimate day before leaving was mild, the warmth of the day carrying through to dusk... They all spent the evening on the beach, as the sun began to set, the light faded away till even the

shadows were swallowed by the encroaching darkness. The sky became a sea of black the stars and the moon shone brighter in the sky, as if to remind him that even in the darkness there was light. They sat beside a small bonfire which delivered warmth as the cold night air began to sweep in off the sea.

"I love this song! I wanna dance!" Imogen declared as she stood up and began to dance barefooted upon the sand.

Imogen reached out her hand fluttering her eyes, her bottom lip protruding giving a look which neither man could turn down.

"Dance with me!" she continued aimed at Marcus but as he shook his head her gaze diverted to Rob.

Rob passed his bottle to Marcus before standing up, taking Imogen's hand. They danced so close, filled with alcohol induced adrenalin, but he knew that there was an understanding and an acceptance between him and Marcus.

Marcus watched laughing, knowing that if she had been dancing that close to any other man he would have been struggling to hold back, to contain his jealousy, but with Rob there was an understanding and through that a friendship was growing.

They'd had a few spats over those few months as the new dynamic found its clear ground, spats which mainly consisted around some of their crazy rides and daredevil stunts. Though Marcus knew there was no way that Imogen could be reined in, she was wild, a wildflower, an adrenaline junkie, and that was always part of the attraction.

Feeling dizzy Imogen fell onto Marcus' lap, his arms catching her, as she began kissing him with a passion.

Rob sat back down, turning away as though to try an avoid seeing the very public displays of passion which had become a regular sight. He knew they tried their best to not make him feel like a third wheel but sometimes that wasn't possible, and in part he wouldn't have wanted them to put on an act just to accommodate him. But sometimes it reminded him that he wasn't deserving of that kind of relationship, that kind of love which is all encompassing.

Imogen broke away from the passionate embrace and fell onto the sand between the two men, her arms reaching around them resting on their shoulders.

Rob opened another bottle.

"I think she is getting a bit drunk..." Rob laughed with a bottle in his outstretched hand, inviting Marcus to take it.

"Becoming a lightweight" Marcus replied.

"Hey!" Imogen interrupted.

"What like you?" Rob laughed in reply winking at Imogen.

Marcus let out a small laugh as Imogen began to fall back pulling both men backwards until they were all lying looking at the stars.

"The 3 of us will always be together!" She exclaimed, before beginning to drift off, broken by moments of clarity.

The night soon ended, and with it dawned the day to return home.

Her words over those couple of days, and also the love and compassion that was shown provided plenty of food for thought, plenty to think over as he tried to rediscover his path in life.

As they stood outside the flat, Imogen swung her arms, as though to disguise her worry wishing she could trade places, or

for him to be able to stay forever, never needing to go back, to stay in their perfect world.

"So…..You're gonna try this time right?" She asked as he leant in for a final hug.

"Yeah, and I'll see you soon, and I'll write, and phone and all that" he promised.

"Well, you better!" she declared as she wiped a stray tear from her eye as Marcus walked down towards them holding out his hand for a handshake, firmly gripping Rob's hand before pulling him in for a manly embrace.

"Look after yourself mate….. and remember you're always welcome here" he commented as their hands parted and instead placed his arm around Imogen drawing her in close.

As he pulled out of Scarborough he stopped, sitting musing over the past few days.

"Who am I?" he thought as he stared at his distorted reflection staring back from the road sign.

Nodding he reflected on how he was just a man, a human, a guy who'd made mistakes, had fallen, was far from perfect and never would be, but that was OK, and he shouldn't ever feel guilty for not being perfect or living up to others unreachable expectations, he had people who loved him, who had his back no matter how dark things got or how far he'd fallen. Thinking how he'd been feeling lost and confused, becoming too lost in the detail in the so-called failures, but none of that helped.

Climbing back on Buzby, turning the key he took a deep breath, again repeating the question...

"Who am I?"

Nodding he mulled over where the true answer to the question lay, knowing that the only way to know was found in the hearts of those who truly loved him no matter what, and those he wanted to share his life with.

"I have a heart full of love to give, and I'm loved, and I guess I've looked death in the eye!" he spoke out loud as he kicked the kickstart to head home to begin a fresh.

Chapter 45

The following months were hard, and he had a few slips backwards, but every road has potholes he frequently told himself.

He returned to Scarborough many times, whenever he just needed a shoulder or a pick me up, or just a good old drink with mates. He found himself a flat back home, moving but not moving too far still remaining there for his mother, although still wasn't always appreciated, but slowly a new way of being became formed, his mother softened which brought peace.

He decided to try and work on relationships, but knowing when to retreat, and when to give up, something which he would never normally do, his selfless heart constantly becoming black and blue.

He battled with his faith from being angry at God declaring he didn't believe, and feeling as though God had let him down, asking why he never got the life he wanted. He never asked for much in comparison to others, then thinking how maybe God had been in the storm with him bringing him closer, guiding him, saving him.

He wondered how he was always happy being the one to save another and how maybe God brought good out of even his worst moments, showing him that reaching out and accepting help from friends is not a failure.

Isabella was in her 2nd year of university and had been trying to reach out, feeling alone and also feeling empty and lost from the death of her father, he thought how she didn't really have anyone, and thought back to Imogen's early years, thinking maybe he could also be help to her, and at the same time find a way to rebuild their broken sibling relationship, he also thought that it was only a few short months till his child would be born, so the last few months before needing to step up, to somehow become a responsible adult, to which Imogen laughed when he spoke that out loud.

He sat in his new flat, sitting on the balcony looking out over the river below with Imogen on loudspeaker.

"I'm going to go visit Isabella on Friday, if ya fancy joining? She's having some housewarming party..." he asked not wanting to go alone.

"Sorry, am working" she replied, the disappointment evident in her voice.

Rob felt dejected.

The silence was broken by Marcus shouting over,

"I'm in mate, am sure we lads can get up to some mischief.... While the cats away the mice shall play", he continued laughing, Rob could hear Imogen hitting Marcus, in the same playful way she used to hit him for coming up with those types of comments.

"So, you've had the pleasure of the catsuit?" Rob asked through his laughter.

"And you! pack it, or I'll come up and give that ass a good whipping too!" she shouted in playful banter.

"Is that a threat or a promise?" he replied.

Imogen sighed,

"God! I've had it with you two, give a girl a break" she uttered before walking away to the bedroom to get ready, leaving the door slightly ajar to continue to hear the conversation.

"You're on Mate!" Rob replied.

"Come here first, then we can drive over..." Marcus suggested.

"Well, I guess I'll get to HIT..." Imogen interrupted, coughing mid-sentence whilst picking up her phone

Clearing her throat, she continued,

".....I mean SEE you tomorrow.... Gotta rush, see ya later" she continued before hanging up the call.

He rode down to Scarborough the next day, leaving Buzby in the company of Kitt before climbing into Marcus' car, heading across the country to Manchester. They talked on the car journey down.

"So what's this job our Imi's got?" Rob asked.

"She's dancing at the Grande... it's OK but she's really pushing herself a bit too much, then she's still got the bar gig... It's almost like a full-time job babysitting her, making sure she's eaten etc, she never seems to take a break, always on full pelt.

"Yeah mate, she's always been like that, and I had that responsibility for many years, kinda glad someone else took over" Rob joked.

"So, anyway, enough of her for the next two days, this is purely lads time!" Marcus declared as he turned up the music and opened the roof of the convertible at the push of a button.

They arrived at Isabella's block of flats. The sky was beginning to darken as the late afternoon began to set in. They walked towards the entrance, becoming face to face with the concierge. In a way it felt like a posh prison, though they couldn't work out whether he was there to keep people out or to keep the students in!

After gaining permission to enter they walked up the cold concrete stairs. The music could be heard as they neared the 15th floor. They continued up another 2 flights of stairs arriving at the 17th floor.

The flat was small, and compact yet managed to fit in more people than they thought possible. The living room was overtaken by a DJ set, the DJ stood against the wall with headphones covering one ear, as though listening to the next track, getting ready to mix, as though being in some expensive club. The entire living room and adjoining kitchen was dark. The thick black curtains were closed to keep out the remaining light of the day. A mix of red, green, and blue flashes scattered across the room from the spotlights. Everyone who walked through the door was given a "Starter drink"

As Rob and Marcus downed the contents of the glass, neither wanted to ask what it contained! They continued through the living room a bouncy castle was being erected in the adjacent room, the dining room, which answered the question to why the dining table and chairs were in the corridor outside.

"God, these lot are crazier than the students in Scarborough!" Rob declared as they looked at each other, before picking up another drink from the table near the kitchen, slowly edging forward through the mesh of people as the music pounded.

Rob threw himself on the bouncy castle, landing amongst fresh-eyed students, to which Marcus imitated causing people to fly into the air.

Someone began shooting water balloons through the room and out the windows using a slingshot causing water stains to fall down the wallpaper.

"She's gonna have a lot of clearing up to do!" Rob declared as he watched the students becoming crazier.

"Not our problem is it? What's the saying not my monkeys, not my circus or something" Marcus replied laughing as he stumbled up from the bouncy castle and began walking over to the nearby table.

"She's not your responsibility, we're just here to have fun and get smashed" Marcus reiterated while munching on a sausage roll before grabbing a couple of drinks from the table, walking back towards the castle passing one to Rob before jumping back upon him.

As the night progressed the bouncy castle became sticky from spilled drinks, and they became more intoxicated as the night progressed.

Rob began tossing wotsits in the air trying to catch them in his mouth as they fell. Missing his mouth, he picked up two of the wotsits from the bouncy castle before sticking them in his nostrils.

"Y'no… I once told Imi that I slept with cheesy wotsits up my nose!" he laughed as they continued to bounce beginning to feel motion sickness.

"Thought tonight was an Imi free zone, and I think you're probably certifiably crazy" Marcus laughed.

"I thought you'd know that by now and it was just a slip" Rob answered placing his phone back in his pocket before bouncing and landing upon Marcus for a playfight to ensue.

As midnight passed people gradually began to leave, though the party continued into the early hours. As the hours past the music began to fade, becoming a level accustomed to background music.

Rob and Marcus fell asleep on the castle. Rob was awoken in the early hours by two male students landing on top of them and by the early morning sun streaming through the curtains.

"It's going down, I'm yelling timber!" Rob heard Isabella yelling. Rob began nudging at Marcus who was still asleep, slouching next to him almost upon his chest with his mouth slightly open as though catching flies. The occasional snort escaping into the air.

"God, he's almost as bad a sleeper as Imogen!" he laughed as he continued to try and awake his friend.

"You better move!" Isabella continued as the air was slowly being removed with the fan being turned off. The castle began to collapse, falling upon them almost suffocating them.

They lay almost on top of each other clambering out from under the thick orange fabric.

"Hey maybe we should keep this one in the vault" Marcus laughed as he found his way to his feet.

Rob began trying to help with the cleaning with the flat looking as though a tornado had ripped through it.

"Leave it mate!" Marcus stated trying to guide Rob through the flat.

"Thanks for coming bro!" Isabella shouted, running over for a hug as they hovered near the door.

"No probs sis... Been a bit of a wild party and by my standards that is definitely saying something!" he declared.

"Learned a bit in Ibiza you know!" she answered as though it was a competition, to prove she wasn't as perfect and prim and proper as their mother had people believe, an act she was very good at portraying.

"I think I need a burger or something before even thinking about driving!" Marcus declared as they stood by his car, feeling nauseous. As though ready to vomit as the fresh air hit.

As the morning began to pass leading into the afternoon they drove back east, back home to Scarborough. By the time they returned home Imogen had left for work. They sat upon the settee to relax for few moments.

Marcus awoke to Imogen hitting them with an inflatable banana.

"What time is it?" Marcus asked rubbing his eyes.

"Erm, about 11.30pm" Imogen stated as Marcus pulled her down onto his lap, causing her to continue to fall till her head was almost in Rob's lap.

"What!?" Rob woke with a startled expression.

Imogen laughed as she rolled over landing on the floor with a thump.

Well I'm gathering you two had fun? Good to see you's got back in one piece..." she spoke trying to remain serious, while wanting to laugh.

"Well I guess you're staying?" Imogen asked as she stood up, trying to hide her jealousy of being left out wishing she had been with them.

"So, I've heard about this dance gig, do I get to watch?" Rob asked.

Scrunching her face, she answered.

"Well, If I'm right, Marcus is pulling a night shift tomorrow, so stay over another night, come watch then we'll hit the clubs after… not fair that you boys get to have all the fun!" she answered as she began walking to her room.

"Night Boys!" Imogen declared, with a mischievous look upon her face as she closed the door.

"Erm... I think that's my cue..." Marcus laughed as he climbed off the settee, to follow.

"Night mate!" he continued as he opened the door following her into the bedroom.

Rob rolled his shoulders before laying back, trying to get comfortable, before closing his eyes and returning to sleep.

Chapter 46

He returned home with the next few months feeling like a rollercoaster, the due date creeping upon him.

April quickly arrived.

He was absent from the birth, finding out by text message that he had a daughter. He had spent months not wanting to completely believe in case he was to find out it was all fake, that he wasn't the father, he thought how soon he'd know for sure through a paternity test, but as soon as he looked upon that beautiful little face he knew she was his, and that the test was just for physical validation.

That evening after holding her for the first time, 2 days old, he sat staring at her image, remembering how those tiny fingers curled around his little finger, and remembering watching her looking through those brand new eyes at what must be such a strange world. He thought how her eyes were more brilliant than he could have dreamed they would be, and seeing those eyes gazing back at his filled him with awe in a way like never before.

He remembered feeling too scared to pick her up, to hold her, scared of breaking her. Remembering that first moment with his little girl in his hands.

He mulled over how he'd never felt love like the love he felt as he held his daughter for the first time, vowing to be the father she deserved and to shower her with love, protect her.

Holding her in his arms he promised her the world and intended to do everything in his power to show her she was wanted and loved, that it would be worth having to tolerate Raquel as the girl in his arms deserved the world.

The sound of her cry resonated in his head, remembering hearing that first cry, which maybe to everyone else was annoying but to him was one of the most beautiful sounds he'd ever heard, so overwhelming it brought him to tears, happy tears for the new person that he made, and he was already filling up with love for her.

His mother began playing the doting Grandmother, and for a while it brought them closer as she began helping with childcare on the days which he was allowed to have her. Raquel continued to play the perfect mother in front of her, bringing manipulation to a new level.

He decorated and furnished a room for Katrina, though began to wonder when if ever he would be able to have her sleep over. Raquel claimed it was because Katrina was too young to be separated from her, that she needed a routine, his mother always agreed, scolding him for complaining. Refusing to listen to him, not believing when Rob repeatedly stated that Raquel was regularly going out, leaving the children with childminders to hit the clubs, and maybe looking for her next baby daddy...

He was repeatedly scolded for uttering such accusations. It felt as though his mother always took her side.

Katrina was 4 months before Raquel allowed Rob to have her overnight. She was going away for a girls weekend in Spain, so dropped Katrina on him with little notice, not that he minded, living for the quality time with his little girl who was growing too fast, and he had been worried that he'd miss out on all the milestones.

That first weekend felt like heaven as her bright blue-green eyes found his and she laughed the sweetest little laugh, as only a baby can laugh. A sweet sound unblemished by the hurts of life, her little face glowing, filling his world with smiles, and seeing her eyes light up whenever she saw him, daddy's little girl, he hoped that would never change. Spending that first night sitting on the floor beside her cot soothing her with lullaby's and gently stroking her soft blonde hair, not wanting to leave the room, not wanting to leave her alone, not wanting to miss a moment, staying there till he couldn't hold his eyes open any longer, falling asleep beside her.

When Raquel returned, he began getting access most weekends, though still Raquel played games, cancelling whenever she felt necessary, usually in response to him not falling to her every whim.

As those early months past, finding someone to share his life with had fallen to the way-side, occasionally creeping in when seeing couples with their babies, wishing that he'd had someone to share those moments with, at time imagining himself with a woman who he loved, and she loved him in return. Their child being the visual representation of such perfection.

The Autumn arrived, soon Halloween and Bonfire night were upon him. The first Christmas as a father was on the horizon Katrina was approaching 7 months. He'd barely gone out since Katrina had been born, and also very rarely going down to Scarborough, not wanting to be so far away from his girl, only going down for day trips, but rarely staying over with the exception of when Imogen ended up in hospital. It was a few days after bonfire night when he received the call from Marcus. He could hear in his voice the concern and worry. As usual he didn't think twice, hopping on his bike, heading down to Scarborough.

"I'm OK, I promise, I'll be out in no time" she insisted as she watched Marcus and Rob fussing over her. She'd never liked being made a fuss over and hated being ill, not wanting to become like her mother, feeding off the attention that people gave till she began creating bouts of illness, to the point of faking cancer.

Rob watched Imogen wanting to take away the pain. He'd watched her many times over the years masking the pain, over-compensating with painkillers, trying to pretend there was nothing wrong, and fobbing it off as IBS.

A couple of days later she was home, with again the Drs declining to investigate, just dealing with the problem at hand. An apparent blockage which once past she bounced back, again throwing herself back into work He knew he couldn't say anything as he was exactly the same, and she wasn't his responsibility anymore. He stepped back knowing she was Marcus' responsibility now.

Chapter 47

December

The Friday before Christmas. Imogen and Marcus had returned earlier that day to visit her father. What was planned as a flying visit culminating in them staying overnight to spend the black eye Friday with Rob. They ventured out to the bars in Whitley Bay on what was a mild evening. Charlie joined them in the Fire station pub. A few other friends had promised to join later in the evening. Gradually they began working their way down from the fire station slowly working their way down towards South Parade,

As the night progressed everyone began to fall away, Imogen and Marcus heading back to her Father's around 10pm, as Imogen was beginning to struggle.

"I'm staying on mate" Rob replied as Marcus asked what he was doing.

Imogen had urged them both to continue without her, to put her in a taxi, that she'd be fine, not wanting to leave Rob alone. They both declined her request with Marcus insisting that he leave with her.

"I'll be fine, am bound to bump into others at some point, am not ready to head home yet, the night is still young" Rob continued.

Waving them off in a taxi he sauntered down the street. He stood outside of Havannah, the bar was bustling inside and out. He entered and began walking through the club towards the bar. He stood alone in the club scanning the crowd. In the corner stood a redhead with another girl with shocking blue hair. His eyes continued to search for faces he recognised. Against the wall near the bar stood a blonde chatting with a brunette. As the blonde turned, she caught his eye, and in that moment, it was as though his world fell apart, as though somehow, she had bewitched him.

Ordering a drink, he continued to watch her. He stopped moving, stopped breathing, it felt as though the air had been knocked out of him. Entranced by this beauty who had put a spell on him.

Had she even noticed him? He thought

"Gorgeous" he whispered under his breath as he watched her.

Her curves were shouting his name. She had a smile worth dying for, and even across the darkened club he could see her eyes sparkling though from the distance he couldn't tell if her eyes were brown or blue. He knew he had to go nearer; it was as though she was drawing him towards her.

Her laugh was like magic and he was awe-struck by the way she tossed her hair over her shoulder as she listened attentively. He was amazed at how open and outgoing she was. Her resounding confidence overflowing. There was only one way the night was ending, and that was them leaving together. Every glance at her was making him more anxious to know her, to talk to her. He slowly began walking in her direction trying to build up the courage to make his move. The crowds disturbed his line of sight. He moved, trying to find her again but she had disappeared; his heart sank.

He'd remembered laughing at Imogen as she tried to describe her feelings that first moment that she met Marcus, but until that moment he thought Love at first site was just a fairy-tale.

He walked to the bar, buying another drink. He could think of nothing else but her. It was as if she had bewitched his very soul.

He knew he had to find her. He necked back his drink and began searching the bar, pushing himself through the crowds with no avail. She was gone.

He left the club, entering every bar down towards parade, in hope of finding her again. The hours past. He was almost ready to give up, losing all hope. Standing at the bar, in Hairy Lemon's, holding a pint, he caught a glimpse of her on the dance floor. He couldn't hide the smile which crept across his face when he knew he'd found her.

He looked over at her, trying to build up the courage to go and talk to her. She turned catching his eye, she smiled an innocent smile as if silently giving him permission.

He walked up to her, his hands sweating, the chemistry was undeniable. A girl had never made him feel that way before, and doubt would ever again, this was a once in a lifetime chance that he was not going to let slip through his hands.

 He spun her round, lifting her off her feet.

"You're the girl for me, I've been searching for you all night" He spoke before kissing her, taking her breath away.

Goosebumps lined his skin, not the kind that comes from the cold, but the kind that only comes when nothing else matters except the 'right here, right now'. In that moment it felt like the world had slowed to an almost stop, the rest of his world becoming an unimportant blur.

"You know you have the most amazing smile and the kindest eyes" He spoke as he took a short step back until his eyes again locked on hers, the pale blue into deep emerald.

His right hand raised up to her cheekbone before tucking her golden wisps behind her ear, slowly moving in closer. Close enough for her to feel his body through her clothes. He stood waiting, contemplating his next move, wondering if it would be too much to kiss her again. They stood as though frozen in time, he leant in further hovering for a moment. She inhaled deeply, as his lips came closer and closer to hers. His lips delicately brushed against hers. Their breaths mingled. His arms encircled her as they kissed. Feeling the caress of her lips upon his were softer than he could ever have imagined, filled with swirls of emotion he savoured each moment.

Breaking away she stepped back smiling a sweet yet slightly seductive smile which had him entranced. Slowly she turned

walking away towards the door, leaving him stood speechless unable to move as though glued to the spot.

"Well, you coming?" she spoke casually as she turned looking in his direction.

Startled, he downed his pint grabbing his jacket before hastily following her like a lost puppy who had fallen head over heels in love.

They walked down towards the promenade looking out across the shore. They spent the rest of the night and into the following morning together talking. He didn't want to see her go, worried that once she was gone, he never saw her again.

As the hours past the streets became empty. As the sky began to become light from the rising sun. Dawn was breaking disturbing the darkness of the night. They began walking up into town until they stumbled upon a café which was open for business. They walked in through the white framed glass door which looked as though it was ready to fall from its hinges. They sat at a table with him still holding onto her hand, not wanting to let go. The café provided a soft dim light from the old lightbulbs which were slowly becoming enveloped by the light from outside.

They sat drinking coffee and sharing a cooked breakfast. He didn't want to leave, to be parted from her. She scribbled her number on a napkin. Ring me... she said as she exited the café.

The rest of the morning was a daze as he returned home and collapsed on to his bed trying to make sense of the night before.

That night marked a new beginning, not that he knew it. Before that night, before Frankie he thought he knew what his life was supposed to be, who he was, but after meeting her, well, there was just after...

Chapter 48

That first Christmas he managed to spend a few short hours with Katrina but spent the remainder alone in his small flat, his mind still focussed on that girl…. Frankie.

He spent days since that meeting in Whitley bay holding her number in his hand as he contemplated ringing her, though not wanting to destroy that perfect night.

Boxing Day, he headed down to Scarborough. Marcus was working. Imogen had persuaded Rob to come to spend the days between Christmas and New Year with them…. With her.

He didn't really need much persuasion. Not wanting to be spending those days alone, the days which are like a dark void.

They sat huddled together overlooking the shore, watching the waves crash against the sea wall below. The night sky reflecting in the sea. She looked down at her watch, 4am. Marcus was due to join them for breakfast at 5am.

They had spent the night clubbing in their old haunts as though trying to recreate those wild nights.

An hour earlier they had left the club, staggering, walking arm in arm, back towards her flat. They stopped to take a break, a break which turned into longer as they sat upon an old wooden bench on the cliff top reminiscing about their 'good old days'.

The bench where they were sat had witnessed so many memories. Imogen felt like her whole world was changing, that September she'd began a masters at York, while also continuing to dance at the Grande, which gave explanation to Rob on why she was struggling so much recently, seeming constantly tired, and maybe explaining the reason she ended up in hospital.

That January she was beginning a stint in a touring production of Rent, and Marcus had been offered a promotion at a few different locations but all further south, and they'd made the decision to try moving down to the outskirts of London, as there would be more opportunities for her. She admitted how facing London was going to be a challenge in itself, with the risk of again unleashing painful memories, though she promised she would be OK, that she would reach out, find help if it became too much.

She explained how they would be in Scarborough for 4 more months, or in reality Marcus would be, before the final move, the final goodbye.

She removed her high heels, rubbing her aching feet. Rob began massaging her feet like he had so many times in the past. A smile crept across her face as the memories filled her mind.

They were caught in that moment between being drunk and sober. Caught in a haze yet also seeing everything clearly. She stared into those eyes, the words stumbled from her, trying to put her thoughts into words.

"I'm gonna miss you, you know…. I hate to leave you all alone. We all need someone. We're all looking, even if you say you don't need or want anyone. You can't let your fears stop you taking that step. Please promise me you won't close yourself off to love… You need someone to love you, you deserve someone to love you…"

His gaze dropped away from her for a moment, as a cheeky grin crept across his face.

"Funny you should say that… There's something I've been meaning to tell you…"

He talked of that night out, after they had gone home, he spoke of the woman who had captured his heart. Imogen sat in silence listening, watching, noticing how his eyes lit up, as he spoke of her.

He spoke with a glow she'd never seen before, as he told her how he'd always thought what she described was impossible, dismissing and not believing her the many times she talked of how she fell in love with Marcus..

She had told him he would find love, that the right woman for him was out there, but he had never believed her, until now.

As he spoke, she resisted uttering the words.

"I told you so!" though he knew she was speaking those words in her head.

Imogen smiled knowing her prayers had been answered.

She had always wished he would find love, she had begged God to give him happiness, to give him someone who could give him the world, because if anyone deserved it, he did. But in a small way her heart sank, she couldn't explain her feelings. It wasn't that she was jealous, she loved Marcus. She loved Marcus in a way she had never believed was possible.

But now it was real.

She knew that with the move on top of that her world was changing. She was unsure whether she could survive in a world where Rob wasn't there, he'd been her safety net for so long. The thought of losing that filled her with fear, wondering what if she fell again. Marcus knew of many of her issues but for most it was as if they were glossed over as though to make them not as bad. Words like rape never being uttered instead replaced or ignored completely, but Rob had been there, he knew every detail from her life, her childhood down to the smallest detail. The ugly details that no-one else knew. He'd lived through a large part of her journey with her as she tried to work through her life, trying to negotiate through the damage. With him saving her more times than she could remember.

She didn't know if she was ready to lose that.

"… and… So, what happened next?? Did you ring her??" She asked inquisitively, distracting herself from her thoughts.

He looked away shrugging. "Nah, not yet anyways…. Doubt she'd even remember me"

Imogen pushed him. hitting him across the shoulder with her strappy shoe.

"You big idiot!" What am I going to do with you?"

"Ow, that hurt, you bully!" he protested.

"Well I need to knock some sense into you. Ring her! You big goof!" she replied.

"You know... You could ask her out for New Years Eve? Maybe it could be some sort of omen or something, you never know it could be the start of something…"

"You with your romance and fairy-tales! But yep I might..." he replied sounding confident yet inside was unsure whether he could. Wondering whether he could allow him to believe that the connection from that night could become more, though there was nothing he wanted more.

"Hey! None of this 'might' stuff… Go find your happy ending!" she replied before pausing.

After taking a pause and a deep breath she continued speaking. As the words fell from her mouth, she in part wished she could take them back, saying too much, revealing too much...

"I just hope that she knows what she's got, they don't make many like you. She's a lucky woman! If she loves you even half as much as I do, then you've found the one, but hopefully she'll love you even more... You deserve to be loved by someone who can love you the way you deserve to be loved "

What followed was a silence as the sun slowly began to rise upon the horizon.

The sky above was still dark as the sun began to appear in the distance. Beginning as a delicate line of brilliant orange and yellow, pouring out from the sun creating a line upon the horizon beneath the dark neon blue ocean of the night.

Slowly the sun began to rise ascending into the sky. The darkness was slowly being replaced by a breath-taking display of radiant colours. Bright streaks of red, pink, and orange slowly overcoming the dark blue and purple of the night sky. Silvery wisps of clouds scattered across the depths of the sky, highlighted by the pinks and golds expanding along the horizon.

They had watched so many sunrises over the years but this one felt different, as if to symbolise not just a new day,
but a new beginning, a new life, a new start, but with that also an ending.

She thought how that sunrise was one of the most beautiful sunrises she had ever seen, maybe because it was the last that they would see together.

She looked down, trying to conceal the single tear which escaped her eye, falling down her cheek, wiping it away, hoping that he hadn't noticed. His hand cupped her chin, gently lifting her bowed head. Their eyes made contact.

"We made a promise, to always be in each other's lives. I don't intend to break that promise, even if life is taking us down different paths, we will find a new way. You'll always be my little Imi."

His words pulled on her heart.

She wondered how their relationship would now work, where she would fit in his heart. It felt like the end, almost like a goodbye, and in a way it was. That moment was bittersweet for she knew that even if it didn't work out with that girl, she had to let him go.

She knew it could never be the same. That nothing is ever meant to stay the same. Their relationship had changed when she married Marcus, yet they found a new way, but now with the move so far away, and with him falling in love she knew that life was pulling them apart.

Like many times before, she vowed to always love him, to value their friendship, but this time part of her knew things would never be the same.

He had been there for her, saved her in so many ways, she wanted him to be happy. She knew that if she remained a big part of his life, he would never be able to let go. Always their waiting to save her from herself. Always the hero she had found him to be. His selfless heart was bigger than anyone she'd ever known but she knew even his heart wasn't big enough to be shared.

She thought how this woman he had fallen in love with deserved to have all of him. He deserved a life which didn't involve constantly rescuing her and she didn't need rescued or saved anymore because he had completed that mission. He had healed her, fixed her, showed her what love was, and opened her heart to the possibility of finding and accepting love.

"We've sure had quite a journey together you and me, a few bumps along the way but I sure loved the ride... You know I was always stubborn, but you broke down my walls. Along the way I don't really think I realised what I had, and I apologise if I ever took your love for granted. You know I've loved you always and always will. You watched me grow from a fresh-eyed girl into a woman, and a married responsible woman at that..." she watched him laughing.

"Hey, I'm trying to be serous here and pour my heart out..."

"Yeah but you said you're responsible.... Sorry... continue....." he answered laughing before trying to restrain himself.

"Well, I know for sure that the woman I am today is due to you, would I even be on this earth if it hadn't been for you... I'll always cherish the friendship we have and take it with me wherever I go... you know when we met you said you liked fixing things, well I think you done a good job on fixing this wreck of a girl I don't know if I can ever be truly fixed, or ever be perfect, though who is??? But because of you I'm no longer broken"

"Shut it soppy pants, you're talking like this is the end, like we're never going to see each other again, you don't get rid of me that easy, I stick around like a bad smell..."

They agreed to always remain in each other's lives, though deep down she knew that what they had was changing.

They remained there as the sun provided a warmth, her head nuzzled in his chest, not wanting that moment to end. He continued to tell her how she would forever be his best friend no matter where life took them.

She spoke of how she had promised him all those years ago that one day he would be God father to her children. She laughed as she explained how that included teaching them to ride when they became old enough.

"I'd say the same, but I doubt mother of the year would ever let me, or you take Katrina on a bike! And, now being an old, wise parent, and having seen the scrapes you've gotten yourself into I doubt I'd want her to become anything like you!" He stated as though to gain a reaction...

"I am so offended that you see me as such a bad influence! You really are getting old, is that a grey hair?" she joked in response as her hand reached towards his head.

His hand reached out to intercept, she looked up at him with her wrist in his hand, as though frozen.

The tears began to creep down her face as she continued to wonder how she could manage to survive without him being so close by, losing her safety net. He stroked her cheek as he had so many times before brushing her hair behind her ear. His lips tenderly brushed her cheek, as they had so many times before.

He leant back; their eyes met. They became lost in the moment as she felt herself drawn to him like a magnet.

They hovered with their lip's inches apart, their breaths mingling.

She thought how there was once a time, long past where deep down she had longed for that moment, but time and circumstance always got in the way. But that was worlds away, now it wasn't what she wanted. She loved Marcus more than she ever thought she could love someone, knowing that Marcus was the only man she ever wanted to kiss for the rest of her life, and she knew Rob didn't want it either.

Her thoughts scattered through her head. Maybe he was just trying to self-sabotage his future happiness? She wasn't going to go there, not even as a parting goodbye. Knowing that taking that step would have tainted a relationship which was deeper than any other, a sacred friendship. She knew going there would also destroy the perfect world she'd created and had longed for, wondering if like him her default returned to self-sabotage. In the back of her mind her fears lingered. They would occasionally come to the forefront of her thoughts causing her to wonder how long Marcus would love her, and how long it would be till the bubble burst and he realised the ugliness deep within her.

Rob, in that moment was replaying their lives, the security of being needed, also filled with fear, yet at the same time filled with excitement. Daring himself to have the ability to allow himself to dream, to want, to hope. To dare to put himself out there, to dare to believe he deserved such love.

Their foreheads touched as if they were both on the same page.

Marcus arrived; his hands rested upon their shoulders.

"Come on, I don't know about you two, but I'm starved!" he stated as Rob and Imogen pulled apart.

"Yep, come on, I'm in!" Rob replied, standing up.

Imogen took one final look over the horizon then turned looking at Rob and Marcus laughing and joking, knowing how blessed she was to have someone like Marcus to love, and to have his love in return, but above all to have such a friend who saved her life, knowing that without him her life would most likely have ended a long time ago.

Rob looked over in her direction.

"You joining us or what?"

"Yep!" she replied smiling.

As she stood up, she pondered on how no matter where their paths took them on from that moment, she knew that what he did for her and what he gave her would stay with her forever.

EVERY STORY HAS AN END....

BUT AS IN LIFE..

EVERY END IS A NEW BEGINNING..

This is not the end…
It is not even the beginning of the end
but is perhaps….

….the end of the beginning…

About the Author

Alexia Lockhart is a wife and a mother who is also a romantic with a love of reading and writing romance and poetry. Her writings were always kept hidden, a bit like a personal diary.

Only 2 people saw her writings, her best friend who inspired this book, and encouraged her to never give up writing, and her husband who is her strength.

This book which is the first part of a spin-off book was written as a prequel to the Wildflower Series, which written to honour her best friend, an incredibly special man, an angel. This book has hopefully continued to do the same.

A man who sadly passed before seeing his story.

Other books by this author

In time you will learn more about the two characters Imogen and Marcus. Learning their back stories and what makes them who they are. Some books are still being written, check-out the website for more information.

Nobody's Hero. Part 2. A Time for Love.

Continue to follow Rob's story written in real-time following him beyond the Wildflower years.
At the end of Part 1 he met Frankie.
Does he find his happy ending? Is love enough?

Becoming Wildflower.

The first book in the Wildflower Series. We meet Imogen at the end of her second year at university as she begins to struggle with life. She is encouraged to look back over her life, looking at what made her the young women she was, and those who influenced her Life. In this book we are first introduced to Rob, the friend who saved her. There is a lot of cross-over between this book and nobody's Hero Part 1 as we see their friendship through her eyes.

Wildflower - Becoming His.

The second book in the series. In the book Imogen meets Marcus. The book is an erotic romance. There is an edited version, though still has some erotic content.

Wildflower Belonging.

The third book in the Wildflower series.
Is there ever such a thing as a fairy-tale happily ever after??

We follow Imogen and Marcus as they navigate through married life. As they encounter troubles including chronic illness, depression, PTSD, abuse, and loss.

Difficult roads often lead to beautiful destinations but only if you work at it and never give up. Can they find a way to support each other, and be each other's rock?

Wildflower Captured
The fourth book in the series which goes deeper into one part of book 3, another erotic romance which just compliments book 3

Connect with Alexia Lockhart

I really appreciate you reading my book! Here are my social media coordinates:

Find my page on Facebook:
https://www.facebook.com/Imogenkelsie/

Follow me on Twitter:
@imogen_kelsie

Follow me on Instagram
@imogen_kelsiewildflowerseries

Visit my website:
https://www.imogenkelsie-thewildflowerseries.co.uk/